BECOMING MRS. ABBOTT

KIERSTEN MODGLIN

BECOMING MRS. ABBOTT is a work of fiction. Names, characters, places, images, and incidents are products of the author's imagination or are used fictitiously and are not to be construed as real. Any resemblance to actual events, locales, organizations, or persons—living or dead—is entirely coincidental and not intended by the author. The scanning, uploading, and distribution of this book without permission is a theft of the author's intellectual property. No part of this publication may be used, shared, or reproduced in any manner whatsoever without written permission except in the case of brief quotations embedded in critical articles and reviews. If you would like permission to use material from the book for any use other than in a review, please visit:
kierstenmodglinauthor.com/contact
Thank you for your support of the author's rights.

Cover Design by Kiersten Modglin
Copy Editing by Three Owls Editing
Proofreading by My Brother's Editor
Formatting by Kiersten Modglin
Copyright © 2016 by Kiersten Modglin.
All rights reserved.

First Print and Electronic Edition: 2016
kierstenmodglinauthor.com

To anyone who has ever been told they can't or they won't; to everyone who told me I could and I would.

PRAISE FOR BECOMING MRS. ABBOTT

"If this is Modglin's debut, remember her name, people. You will see it again--on the New York Times Best Seller's List. If anyone is meant to be a crime fiction writer, it's Kiersten Modglin."

TWISTED B*TCHES BOOK BLOG

"Every character contributed to the web. I honestly didn't know who was telling the truth, and I frantically turned pages to find out what happens next."

LUKE SWANSON, AUTHOR OF THE TEN

"Kiersten Modglin had me on the edge of my seat with every emotion pouring out of me as I read this book."

BOOKS AND COFFEE BLOG

CHAPTER ONE

CAIDE

April 1994

Caide Abbott walked into Carlton's Bar for one reason and one reason only: it was a mere block from his dorm which meant he could get pass-out drunk and still find his way home. He sat at his usual spot near the end of the bar and, without even having to ask, Rupert slid him an ice-cold beer. "Thanks," he mumbled, tipping his beer toward the bartender before taking a sip. Carlton's was a dive bar that most hadn't heard of, and those who had claimed it looked too shady to enter. It was a gathering ground for biker crowds, middle-aged men who lied to their wives about working late, and teenagers who proudly sported their fake IDs. Caide had stumbled upon the bar one night and graciously slipped into the mellow atmosphere unlike any he'd experienced before. This was his crowd. They knew him here. They liked him here. Caide never had to worry about how he looked, or what he said here. The crowd at Carlton's let Caide fade into the background, taking much needed breathers from his tedious college schedule.

He was on his fifth beer when he hazily laid eyes on her. She was sipping a cosmopolitan at the opposite end of the bar, laughing with a gaggle of girlfriends. Caide tossed back another gulp of beer, taking her in. Her coal black hair hung loosely past her shoulders and she kept tossing it back and forth as she talked. In all his years coming to Carlton's he'd never seen anyone like her there. Actually, he couldn't remember seeing many girls there. Ever.

She took another sip of her drink when she noticed him staring. A bit of red liquid splashed onto her lip and she licked it off. She smiled flirtatiously at him. There was something familiar about her—something welcoming.

"Hi," he silently mouthed across the noisy bar.

"Hi," she mouthed back, turning to laugh with her friends. Caide had finished his beer and was working on the next when she finally approached him. "So were you going to come introduce yourself or just keep staring from across the bar?"

"Well, I guess we'll never know now, will we?" he teased, touching her hair. "Can I buy you another drink?"

"You'd better before this one wears off." She smiled. He liked her smile.

"I'm Caide."

"Nice to meet you, Caide."

"Do you have a name?"

She nodded slowly. "Elise. I'm Elise."

"Okay, Elise." He laughed as the bartender sat another cosmopolitan down for her.

"Wow. You're good. I don't think you even ordered that." She took the last sip of her drink and traded it in.

"They don't let my drinks get empty here. You're with me now, so I guess yours won't either."

She tipped her head down, staring up at him from behind

long eyelashes and said, "Do you want to move this somewhere a little less noisy?"

Like my bed? "Sure. Follow me." He led the way to a booth in the back. She surprised him by sliding in on the side where he sat down. She was really close to him now; he could smell the perfume on her neck and the alcohol on her breath. "So what brings you to Carlton's? I don't think I've ever seen you here before."

"My friend Stacia got dumped this week. We're here being anti-guy."

He snorted. "I think you're sort of messing that plan up."

"Probably." She bit her bottom lip. "Are you worth it?"

"I guess we'll find out, won't we?" The cheesy flirting filtered by the alcohol-induced haze had Caide leaning into her. *God, she smells so good. I'll bet she tastes good.* His lips grazed hers. His palm found her thigh, running his fingers along the hem of her red dress.

"So do you go to school here?" she asked, her face inches from his.

"Yeah, I'm a business major. You?"

"Of course you are." She rolled her eyes playfully. "I go to school in Raleigh. We just wanted to get out of town for the night."

Caide nodded. "Well, I for one, am glad you did." She ran her hand up his leg, his pants growing tighter by the minute.

"Girl, are you coming or what?" An irritated voice rang out from behind her. Caide peered around her head to see the group of girls that had surrounded her by the bar now standing beside their booth.

"Yeah, this place is boring. I want to dance," squealed the short blonde who was swaying in her spot.

"Girls, I'm sorry," she said, looking back and forth between them apologetically. "Can I just catch up with you all later? I kind of want to hang out here for a while."

"Are you sure?" A quiet one in the back spoke up, looking genuinely concerned for her friend. Her gaze caught Caide's hand rubbing the hem of her red dress and he bashfully pulled it away.

"I'm sure. I'll be fine, I promise. I'll call you guys if I need anything." The group sighed in unison, making their way out of the bar without trying to hide their frustration.

"Be safe," she yelled after them, turning back to Caide with an embarrassed look on her face. "I'm sorry about them."

"No need to be sorry. I'm sorry they couldn't see how awesome this place is," Caide teased.

She looked around the room doubtfully before taking the last sip of her drink and standing. "Right. I'm going to get another. Do you want one?"

He still had half of his beer left and the room was already spinning, but he smirked at her with a quick nod. "Sure." He watched her stumble up to the bar and order their drinks.

As she made her way back to the table she set the drinks down and fell into the booth, knocking the table and splashing half of her drink onto her dress. "*Shit*," she said, rubbing her hand over the spill. He grabbed a napkin, innocently sticking his hand up her dress, underneath the spill and attempting to soak it up. When he realized where his hand was, his face turned red. He looked up at her coyly, waiting to see her response. Without hesitation, she lunged at him, wrapping her arms around his neck and running her fingers through his hair. She tasted of cigarette smoke and alcohol, but it had never been more enticing. He ran his hands over her curves through the thin fabric of her dress, his heart pounding in his chest.

"Do you want to get out of here?" she asked, perched on his lap, her lips grazing his ear. Without responding, he stood, grabbing her hand, and slapping two hundred-dollar bills in Rupert's palm as they ran past him on the way out the door.

God, I love this bar.

THERE WAS a phone ringing somewhere in the distance. *Oh, for the love of God, make it stop.* Caide rolled over, placing a pillow over his head. He was drifting off to sleep when it came again. He rolled back over, cursing under his breath and trying to read the clock on the nightstand. Four fifteen a.m. With sleep still fogging his brain, he looked around the room.

Where am I? It was then that he noticed the beauty lying next to him, her dark hair hanging over her face. The events of the past night came back to him in a blur. He looked around the hotel room, not even able to recall checking in. He ran his finger across the soft skin on her back. She stirred slightly, not waking. Then came the phone ringing again.

He rolled out of bed, grabbing his boxers off the lamp beside the TV. He tiptoed to the opposite side of the room where his pants lay, and pulled his cell phone out of his back pocket. Why in the world had his parents insisted that he carry this thing with him? What could people possibly need a phone with them all the time for? He flipped open the bottom and put the speaker to his ear.

"Hello?"

"Caide?" Her voice hit him like a ton of bricks. *Rachael.* Why hadn't Rachael crossed his mind even once that night? Sure, he had planned to break up with her months ago, but after her dad passed away, Caide just couldn't find it in his heart to hurt her again. He looked to the bed, guilt filling him. He'd break up with her today. He owed her the truth.

She deserved better than this, and he couldn't keep it up any longer.

"Hello? Caide?" Her voice rang through the line again.

"Rachael?" He walked to the bathroom, switching on the vent and praying not to wake his partner.

"Can you hear me?"

"Yes, I can hear you. I'm sorry, Rach. I'm still half asleep. Is everything okay?" She was silent on the other line, but he could hear sharp breaths. *She's crying.* "Rachael? What's the matter?" She'd had a rough few months, since her father's death, but Rachael wasn't dramatic, if she was calling him in the middle of the night he knew it couldn't be good. "Rachael? Please talk to me. Did something happen?"

More sobs. "Caide, I'm—I'm so sorry. I'm pregnant."

He heard the words but couldn't comprehend them. He sank to the ground with his back pressed against the door. He was silent, running it through his head.

"Did you hear me?"

"Yes. I heard you. How could this have happened? We were so careful. I don't understand. Are you sure?"

"I'm late. I'm really late."

"That doesn't always mean anything, right?"

"I took a test, too, this morning. It was positive."

"Okay. Okay, so you're sure then, I guess."

She began crying again. "Caide, what did we do? Oh God. How can this be possible? We were so careful." Her cries turned into loud, obnoxious sobs. "This can't be happening."

He sat there, his head resting against the door—thoughts racing, stomach churning. He knew what had to be done, and he hated himself for it.

"Marry me," he said finally. It wasn't a question. It was what would be done.

She sniffed a few times on the other line before her response was heard—a quiet, "Okay."

"Okay. Meet me for breakfast at eight thirty at Renaldo's. We'll figure it all out."

"Okay."

"I'll see you then."

"Caide?" she asked, her voice so quiet he wasn't sure he'd heard it at first.

"Yeah?"

"Um, thanks," she said. It was an awkward end to a terrible conversation, though he couldn't help but smile.

"You're welcome. I'll see you." He hung up the phone, it's battery already starting to die. He lay down on the bathroom floor, pressing his cheek onto the cool tile. He stayed there for what could have only been minutes but seemed like hours, trying to make sense of the world he'd once known. No tears came, just a lump in his throat the size of Alaska. Finally, he sat up. His mind was made up. He turned off the vent, crawling out of the bathroom and collecting his clothes quietly.

Throwing his shirt over his head he made his way toward the door. Before opening it, he cast one last look at the woman lying on the bed. She slept peacefully, unaware of the tragedies going on in the world around her. There was something captivating about this stranger, something he couldn't quite put his finger on.

An idea struck him. He walked back over to the bed and stood over her. He touched a strand of her hair lightly, moving it out of her eyes and sighed. "I love you," he whispered, then closed his eyes, feeling a cool tear escape. He turned and walked back to the door, trying to push the thought from his mind. He couldn't explain it, really. Not even to himself. He'd just wanted to see how it felt—how it would feel every day for the rest of his life: saying those three words to a woman he was sure he'd never truly feel them for.

CHAPTER TWO

RACHAEL

May 2000

Rachael was roused from sleep by the sound of laughter just beyond her bedroom door. She yawned, stretching out on her bed and rubbing her eyes sleepily.

"One, two..." She heard the tiny voices whispering as they grew closer. She shut her eyes just in time for the door to spring open. "Three." She opened her eyes from a fake sleep to see her children grinning at her with their toothy grins. Brinley's blonde curls bounced playfully as she hopped up onto the bed. Rachael reached across, pulling Davis up.

"Good morning, you two."

"Happy Aminaversary!" Davis shouted. She couldn't help but smile at how well his speech was developing. Before she could respond, she smelled breakfast headed her way.

"What do I smell?" she asked, teasing her children.

"We cooked you breakfast, Mommy." Brinley smiled, turning to face the door. It creaked open slightly, allowing room for Caide to squeeze in.

"Good morning, sweetheart. Happy Anniversary." He set the tray down on her lap and kissed her forehead.

"Happy Anniversary to you, too." She smiled up at him, kissing him firmly on the lips. She took a sip of her orange juice and a bite of a biscuit before frowning at her children. "Well, you don't expect me to eat all of this, do you? Dig in."

Davis clapped his hands as both children began to devour the breakfast. Caide sat down on his side of the bed, wrapping his arm around her.

"There's plenty more in the kitchen," he whispered in her ear.

"Thank you, you didn't have to." She snuggled her head onto her husband's chest.

"So what are we going to do today?" Brinley asked, a smear of purple jam on her cheek.

"Well, for starters, you are going to take a bath," Rachael rubbed the jam off of her daughter's face and licked her finger, "before we have to eat *you* for breakfast, and then I was thinking we could go to the park."

"Yeah!" Her children squealed in agreement.

"Go get ready for your baths then." She patted their bottoms lovingly as they hopped off the bed and raced toward the door.

She watched them disappear down the hallway before turning toward Caide and kissing him playfully. "And as for *you*, I figure we'll wear them out with the park and then when they have nap time, we can play."

He kissed her back, his lips firm. "Actually, it may have to wait until tonight."

She pulled back. "What? It's Saturday."

"Rach, you know we've all been having to work more than usual. We've been swamped lately."

"You mean you didn't already tell them you wouldn't be in today? Caide, it's our anniversary. I already asked one of the girls to cover my class today, and told Corie we don't need her to watch Davis."

"I'm sorry, Rachael. You didn't tell me that," he insisted, standing up from the bed.

"It's our anniversary. I shouldn't have to tell you," she said, though her husband was no longer looking at her.

"I don't want to fight with you. You look beautiful this morning. I love you." He kissed her head again, not meeting her eye. "I'll try to come home early."

"I'm not fighting," she mumbled, but he was already gone. She sighed, reaching for her phone on the night stand and dialing Corie's number. She answered after the third ring.

"Hello?"

"Corie?"

"Hey, Mrs. A, what's up?"

"Well, it turns out, I will need you to watch Davis today after all, if you're still available?"

"Yeah, sure. Is everything okay?"

"Everything's fine. I just have to go into work unexpectedly. It'll only be for a few hours." She chewed the skin around her thumbnail nervously as she spoke.

"That's fine. I'll be there in an hour."

"Thanks, Corie. You're a life saver."

CHAPTER THREE

CAIDE

It was after five when a knock on his office door alerted Caide to the time. Chester Mason popped his head through the door way. "Good Lord, Caide. What on earth are you still doing here?"

Caide glanced at his watch and rubbed his temple. "I guess I just lost track of time. I'm still trying to get ahold of the last witness for the Templeton case."

"Well, you go on home. That'll be here Monday. We're headed out for the night."

"Have a good night," Caide said, nodding and closing the file in front of him.

Mason walked out the door, waving a hand over his shoulder. A few moments later, another knock sounded on his door.

"Come in." The door slid open and there was an overwhelming scent of vanilla perfume suddenly filling the air.

"Blaire? What are you still doing here?" he asked before he saw her.

Mason and Meachum's secretary walked into his office, her blonde hair piled high into a bun. "Meachum wanted me to give you these copies before I went home for the day." She handed him a stack of papers.

"Thanks." He flipped through them.

"Files for the Silverman case, and the last three are from the Ackles' pre-trial. I tried to keep them separated but they've had me running all day. That was the last thing on my To Do list."

"Okay, thanks. Looks like we're set then. It's getting late and you look as exhausted as I feel. You about ready to head on home?"

Blaire touched her hair defensively. "You saying I look bad, Caide Abbott?"

"You never look bad, Blaire," he said honestly, placing the stack of papers on his desk.

"You'd better say that." She tossed him a playful wink as she headed for the door. "Hey, do you want to go grab drinks after this? I mean, if you're getting ready to head out too."

He glanced at his watch again. "No. I can't tonight. Rachael's expecting me home. I should've been home hours ago but I have a few more phone calls to make. You go on though, don't wait for me. I'll lock up."

"Rain check?" she asked, batting her eyelashes.

He sighed, already dialing a number. "Yeah, rain check."

IT WAS JUST after ten when Caide finally walked into his dark house. It was silent—not even a TV going. He tiptoed across the living room, walking into the kitchen to grab something to eat. The table was made, set for one. She'd made his favorite pasta and garlic bread. She'd even bought an expensive bottle of wine. He walked over, sticking his finger into the cold pasta and trying a taste. There were two drawings, one from each of his children, and a new watch laying beside his plate.

Great, I'll have three helpings of your world famous guilt, Mrs. Abbott.

The light in the kitchen flipped on suddenly and he turned around. His wife stood behind him, an icy look on her face.

"It's probably cold. We ate hours ago."

"Thanks. I'll warm up some leftovers."

She shook her head firmly. "There are none."

"*Okay then*, I'll find something else to eat." He walked to the refrigerator, plate in hand.

"I bought you a watch. Apparently yours is broken."

He whirled around. "All right, here we go. I'm sorry I'm late."

"Why don't you just record yourself saying that? You could replay it every time we have this fight and save yourself a lot of effort." She crossed her arms over her chest, her lips puckered.

"I'm not fighting. I had to work to provide for this family. Sometimes that means I'm going to be late, and that's a sacrifice we just have to make."

"That's a sacrifice *we* make, Caide. Your children. Your wife. We sacrifice life without you."

He scowled. "Oh, don't be dramatic. I come home every night."

"Yeah, sure. After we're in bed. After they're asleep. This has to stop, Caide. Our kids need to see more of you."

"I've told you, once work slows down I'll be home more. It's just busy right now. Mason and Meachum is booming and I can't slow down. They need me."

"We need you too," she insisted, narrowing her eyes at him.

"More than you need money? Or this house? Or this

food?" He slammed the plate into the sink, watching it smash into pieces.

"Don't do that. Don't come home in a bad mood." She moved to clean up the mess but he stopped her, using his arm as a barricade between her and the sink.

"I'll clean it up. Can I—please can I just eat in peace?"

She stepped back, her expression unreadable. He grabbed a bowl from the cabinet and filled it with salad, walking to the table for his wine glass.

"Fine." She twirled around, headed back down the hall. "Happy Anniversary."

CHAPTER FOUR

BRINLEY

Mommy has a bowl of cereal made for me and I eat it very fast because I am ready to go to the park. Mommy is getting Davis dressed, who looks funny because he is so sleepy.

"Daddy, are you going to the park too?" I ask because I want to know. He brings his coffee cup over and sits beside me.

"Of course I am, Peanut. Just like I said I would."

Sometimes Daddy calls me 'peanut' even though it's not my name. He kisses the top of my head. I am all done with my cereal, Bubba is dressed, and Daddy takes the last drink of his coffee so we can go.

We walk to the car and I see a big puddle beside my door, which is funny because we are inside the garage and plus it hasn't rained in a long time. Mommy and Daddy are too busy talking to see and I am excited because I loves to jump in puddles. If no one sees me jump I will not get into trouble.

I walk up to the big puddle and count: *one, two, three, jump!* It is so fun to jump but I am sad because now there are brown spots on my socks from the puddle. I will definitely be in trouble if Mommy sees. Mommy helps Davis into his carseat on their side but Daddy doesn't have to help me because I am a big girl. I climb into my booster seat—it's a carseat for big girls—and snap the buckle. Davis is yawning because he is sleepy and he has a piece of cereal in his hair, which is funny.

I tell him, "Bubby, we are going to the park." He smiles at me because he loves the park too. The car smells funny today, and kind of makes my head feel dizzy. Mommy and Daddy are talking a lot and it is rude to interrupt so I cannot ask if they smell it too.

"Moo-sic," Bubby says because he wants Mommy to turn on the radio. She turns it up and we sing along. I look out the window, waiting to see the park. Instead, I just see trees, which are boring. I notice mom and dad have stopped talking so I decide I will ask if they smell the funny smell. Also, the water on my sock is starting to burn me a little bit.

When I look at Mommy I laugh because she looks like she has eaten something hot. Her eyes are as big as basketballs and her mouth is wide open. Daddy is grabbing the wheel with Mommy and he keeps saying, "Pump the brakes, Rachael. Pump them. Pump. Don't panic. Pump."

My mom's name is Rachael, but I just call her Mommy. I don't know what he is talking about but I notice we are starting to drive sideways and off the road and we are going fast, like the rides at the fair. This is not the way to the park. We should stay on the road to go to the park, even *I* know that and I'm a little girl.

"Why aren't we going to the park?" I yell, even though my daddy is talking and I know it's rude.

"*Park! Park! Park!*" Davis screams.

Mom and Dad ignore me, which is rude. Now, I will be

rude. I chant loudly with Davis. My dad turns to me. He is crying like he is sad.

"Stop," he yells and I feel sad too. I want to tell him I'm sorry, I do, but then I am turned sideways, and then I'm upside down and I hear a loud bang and then my mommy screams and my bubby cries and then it all goes black.

CHAPTER FIVE

RACHAEL

"It looks like your brake lines were cut on something. From the amount of fluid lost, I'd say it had been leaking for a while. Honestly, Rachael, you all are lucky to be alive."

Rachael kissed her daughter's head again, sitting in the waiting room of the ER. "Thank you, Emmett. Please let me know once it's fixed." She hung up the phone, looking around anxiously for Caide. It was nearly midnight and Davis was the last to be released. She picked her daughter up, sitting her in her lap, and squeezing her cheeks between her palms. "I love you so much, kiddo. I don't know what I would've done if I'd lost you."

"You'd find me." Brinley smiled at her. The hall doors swung open and Caide walked through, carrying Davis who was smiling proudly, clad in a bright blue leg cast.

"My baby," Rachael cried, rushing toward them and reaching for Davis who immediately started crying. "What did the doctor say?"

"He doesn't have a concussion, just a hairline fracture in his femur and three stitches here." He pointed to the gauze bandage above his eyebrow. "He'll be pretty sore for a while, but all in all he's fine. We're all fine." He pulled Rachael into his side, hugging her tightly.

"What did your doctor say?"

"No sleep for the next twelve hours for me." She touched just above her ear where they'd shaved her head for stitches. "He said it's a minor concussion. They got the swelling to go down, but he just wants to be on the safe side."

"And this?" He ran his finger across the bandage that ran down her neck and onto her chest.

"Oh, it's just a cut from my seat belt. It wasn't even deep enough for stitches. I just have to keep it covered for a while." He looked worried, staring at the stitches on her temple. "Brinley got a clean bill of health though, not even a scratch."

Caide picked Brinley up and kissed her hand. "I love you, peanut."

"I love you too, Daddy." She wrapped her arms around his neck. He glanced at Rachael.

"So, have you heard from Emmett? Any news on the car?"

"Yeah, I did. It's pretty bad. He says it's fixable, but just barely."

"Did he say what caused it?"

"The brake line was leaking. He said it had been for a while. It could've been a lot worse. If we'd gone on the interstate, or if we'd been on a busier road..."

"We didn't. We're fine. We're safe." He kissed her forehead. "We're lucky actually." He ran his arm around her waist and pulled her closer to him as they walked to the waiting cab.

Rachael knew he was right. They were lucky to be alive, lucky to have such minor injuries, but Rachael couldn't deny the nagging feeling in the pit of her stomach, the feeling telling her that they weren't lucky. They weren't lucky at all.

CHAPTER SIX

CAIDE

"Come in." It was Caide's first day back at the office since the accident and he was staring at a mound of paperwork. His door opened and he immediately smelled the familiar vanilla perfume.

"Good morning, Blaire. How are you?" She shut the door, sitting down on the corner of his desk.

"I'm okay, but what about you? How are you feeling? I've missed you so much."

"I'm okay, just a bit of a sore shoulder. I didn't get it too bad. It was Davis who got hurt the worst."

Blaire smiled and inched closer to him. "Aren't you going to say you missed me too?"

"Blaire," he said testily.

"Caide." She smiled, touching the hem of her skirt.

"I've told you I can't." He looked away from her, staring at the stack of papers in front of him.

"Yes, but I've told you what Rachael doesn't know—"

"*Would* hurt her," he said firmly. "You should go. I've got a lot to catch up on." He stood up, walking to his door.

"You're just going to keep lying to yourself, then? What

about all the dinners and drinks? You were married then." She paused, waiting for him to respond. When he didn't, she went on. "I see the way you look at me, Caide. If you truly didn't want me, if you truly didn't want *us*, I'd back off. I'm not stupid and I'm not desperate, but if you're in a marriage because of loyalty rather than love, you deserve better. You deserve to be happy." She was dangerously close to him.

He opened his door. "You should go."

She smiled at him painfully before leaving his office. He shut the door quickly and heaved a sigh of relief. He hadn't made it back to his desk yet when there was another rap at his door.

"Yes?" he called as the door opened.

"Caide?" Mr. Mason nodded politely to him. "I hadn't had a chance to say hello this morning. How is everyone? Back in working order?"

Caide laughed. "I don't know if you could ever call us 'in working order', but we're all much better, thank you. We appreciate you giving me the time off for us all to recover."

"Of course. Though, I'm afraid we've let the place crumble while you were away. I tell you, Caide, I don't know what we'd do without you. Your dad sure didn't know what he was doing letting us snatch you up." He chuckled.

"Thank you, sir."

"Have you talked to Malcolm lately?"

Hearing his father's name burned Caide like a sunburn. "I make it a habit not to."

Mason's cheeks went red and he looked down. "Right. Well, I came to tell you that since you've been gone we rescheduled our meeting with Mr. Mock."

"I'm sure he was delighted about that," he said under his breath.

"Well, he understands that we need you at our meetings.

However, we had to reschedule for tonight. Please tell me you can make it?"

Caide didn't have to think about it. "Yes, sir. What time?"

He let out a sigh of relief. "Bart and I will leave early to get the table. I'll need you and Blaire to come right after work. Just ride together so there won't be a delay."

"Blaire?"

Mason looked confused. "Well I'm sure you know we'll need her there. We'll need someone who knows what our schedules look like and you've got enough on your plate without having to worry about scheduling future appointments."

"I don't mind. It's no trouble."

"Nonsense, Caide. Blaire has already agreed." He paused, spying the look on Caide's face. "Unless that's a problem?"

"No, of course not. I just prefer bringing Brian." Caide tried to wipe the look of frustration off his face.

"Brian is busy tonight, or we would. His wife has a doctor's appointment that he can't miss. Just make sure the two of you are on time tonight—you know how Mock is—I want to make sure he gets the right impression. Especially after we had to reschedule."

"Of course, sir. We will be there."

"Great. Okay, well, I'll let you get back to work."

Caide nodded as Mason shut the door. He walked to his window and peeked through the blinds into the lobby. Once Mason was well out of earshot, he rushed to Brian's desk.

"Thanks for calling Mason and Meachum Law Office, this is Brian speaking. How may I help you? Yes, sir. Okay. Yes, sir. Right, I understand. I apologize for that. Of course. I can have him call you back before the end of the day today. Yes, sir. I'll make sure of it. I apologize again. Yes, sir. Thank you." He hung up the phone, looking embarrassed.

"Everything okay?" Caide asked.

"That was Mr. Woolard again. I told him you'd call him earlier but he said you never did."

He slapped a palm to his forehead. "Oh. Brian, I'm sorry. It completely slipped my mind. I'll call him back before I do anything else."

Brian nodded. "That's all right, sir. No problem. You've got a lot on your mind right now. I understand."

"Thanks. Listen, I need you to do me a favor."

Brian stood up from his desk. "Anything. What can I do for you?"

"I need you to go with me to this dinner tonight with Mason and Meachum."

Brian's expression sank. "Sir, I can't. I've missed the last two appointments. Gwen will kill me if I miss this. We're supposed to find out what we're having today. Short of the actual birth, I don't think there's another appointment I *can't miss* as much as I can't miss this one."

Caide pressed his lips together with a nod, mentally cursing the bad timing of it all.

Brian sighed. "Well, if it's important, maybe I can see if she'll reschedule. Or maybe I could ask her mom to go with her. Or maybe I can just be late. What time do you think the dinner would be over?"

Caide held up his hand in protest. "No, don't be ridiculous. Of course not, go be with your wife. And congratulations, by the way. I didn't even know she was expecting."

Brian looked confused. "Sir, you sent us a gift congratulating us when we found out. Four months ago?"

Caide nodded, reminding himself to thank Rachael for always being one step ahead of him. She never missed a beat.

"Right, sorry. Of course I did. The accident has me all messed up. Congratulations again."

Brian nodded, visibly relaxing. "Thank you, sir."

Caide forced a smile and walked back to his office, defeated. *Well, damn.*

"HAVE A GOOD NIGHT, RANDY," Caide called to the janitor who was busy cleaning the windows. He walked out the door to find Blaire already waiting by his car.

"You're driving," she said simply. He opened his door, climbing in before unlocking her side. She stared straight ahead, obviously not letting go of the day's events.

"Blaire, look, I don't know what to say to you. You're great, you know that. Some guy will be lucky to have you—some very, very *single* guy. We have to work together and I don't want some big awkward cloud hanging over our heads, Mason and Meachum are bound to notice."

"Oh, *come on*, Caide. We both know they don't notice anything. We've worked together for three years. You've led me on for three years. Do you even know how that feels? All the dinners and the drinks and the late night phone calls? All the times I've stayed late just to talk to you when you and Rachael were having problems? It wasn't just business; it's never been just business between us. You can't keep pretending. I see how you act when your wife is around—how you look at her. I just feel sorry for you, Caide. I can't imagine how exhausting it must be to pretend to be so in love all the time. It could be better than that; it *should* be better. You just, you make me feel like a child, like this is all one-sided, but it's not. You can't believe that it is."

"Blaire, yes, okay? I've led you on. Of course I have. God, you're beautiful and ambitious and fun, and Rachael and I have gone through several rough patches. The embarrassing truth is, I've used you to get through them. I know it's wrong. I know you deserve better. I just…I can't give you what you want. I know I've made you feel like maybe someday I could, but that was wrong of me. I'm not a good guy. I'm not good for you. I have two kids to think about and a wife who, despite our problems, has never been anything but good to me. Everything I do affects them. I just can't do this. I'm sorry. I am. I wish I could make this easier."

Blaire was silent for a second, looking out the window. "You hide behind your family because you're scared of what will happen if you admit the truth. You're scared of what will happen if your perfect little world shatters. But, Caide, the world isn't perfect and at the end of the day, it doesn't matter how people see you or what anyone thinks—it only matters how you feel about yourself. Whether or not you are happy. So, just tell me you're happy and I'll back off."

"My happiness has never been what matters here," he said, watching Blaire's hands shake in anger.

"You aren't a bad guy, Caide." She looked toward the window attempting to hide her tears. "You're trying to do the right thing and I know that. I just wish the right thing didn't have to hurt so badly."

Caide felt a lump in his throat as they pulled up to the parking meter. "Can we just do this dinner tonight? Just get through it civilly and then we'll talk some more on the way home?"

Blaire nodded, pulling down her mirror to adjust her makeup. Caide, unsure of what to do, politely opened his door and waited outside for her to collect herself. Once she was finished, they walked into the restaurant together with perfect smiles on their faces. Like every other day of his life, everything relied on pretending nothing was wrong.

CHAPTER SEVEN

BLAIRE

Blaire and Caide walked toward the car, waving politely to Mr. Mock. Mason gave them a discreet thumbs-up. They climbed into Caide's car in silence, the smiles disappearing from their faces like a weight being lifted. Blaire was unsure of what to say or how to approach the subject again. Caide Abbott was unlike anything she'd ever experienced. She'd never been the smartest or the richest, but Blaire had always known she was the prettiest. She wasn't necessarily conceited, it was just a truth she'd grown to live with. Being pretty had made her independent. She'd known from a young age that if she ever wanted to make it out of her small town she'd have to work her butt off to get a scholarship and that's exactly what she'd done. She'd put herself through college and gotten a degree that would land her a job with power—one that would make the world listen to her. Finally, she'd be in a position to make people see her as more than just a pretty face.

When the time had come, she'd found herself on the doorstep of Mason and Meachum Law Office. It was the biggest karmic joke ever that she'd worked so hard only to

BECOMING MRS. ABBOTT

settle for being a secretary. Three years later and still she stayed. She'd stayed for Caide. And despite what everyone said, despite the pitiful looks she received from the all-knowing eyes at the office, she was sure Caide had been falling for her too. Maybe he wasn't now, she couldn't be sure, but at one point he was. Because of that, he'd made her love him. He was the first man whose eyes didn't go directly to her chest when he spoke to her. He treated her with respect, and that was something Blaire had never been given before.

Suddenly the car stopped, interrupting Blaire's thoughts. She stared at her front door. "My car is at work." He stared straight ahead, gripping the steering wheel with both hands. Blaire grabbed his arm. "Dude, my car is at work." He turned to look at her and her heart fluttered. They stared at each other, unmoving and silent for what seemed like a lifetime. Then, despite everything he'd been saying all night, despite every feeling he'd denied, he was kissing her. He kissed her like it was the last time he'd ever kiss anyone, like she was oxygen and he couldn't catch his breath. He kissed her like she was his lifeline, the only thing keeping him from dying. He kissed her deeper than she'd ever been kissed. He kissed her like he loved her. And then, just as quickly as it had begun, it was over.

"You should go," he said, rubbing his knuckle over his lips.

Tears filled her eyes. "Caide, please. You can't keep doing this to me," she whined. Before she knew what was happening, they were kissing again. His hands filled her hair, his thumbs caressing her cheeks. The kiss was sweeter this time, her tears rubbing onto his skin. They kissed for what could've been hours, maybe even years. Blaire's heart raced and her skin blazed. They gripped each other tightly, gasping for air but not wanting to stop.

"I love you," came his breathless whisper. She'd heard it,

but she couldn't believe her ears. He was still kissing her, his hands through her hair.

She pulled back, though it broke her heart to do so. "What?"

The realization of what he'd said resonated on his face. He was silent, his mouth hanging open.

"Caide? What did you say?" Blaire recognized the lack of emotion in his eyes then; it resurfaced, like it never left. The light switch had flipped inside of him.

"You should go."

"Caide?" She begged him to repeat himself, grabbing his arm tightly. He shrugged her off.

"Damn it, Blaire. Go." She jumped back at his harsh words.

"We crossed a line tonight." His voice was barely a whisper. He wiped every trace of her off of his lips. "We crossed a line tonight, Blaire. It can never happen again. I need you to understand me. *Never*. Now go."

She blinked, trying to clear her head as she reached for the door handle, unable to speak. She exited the car with her head held high, never looking back. She resisted the urge to wipe away his kiss, though her lips were still burning and red. When she reached her door, she opened and shut it quickly, barricading herself behind it. She watched through the blinds as he drove away, praying he'd stop, praying he'd run up her doorstep and demand to see her—to apologize, to explain everything, maybe even to kiss her again. As his taillights faded down the dark street, she let out a breath through shaking lips, feeling the all-too-familiar tears flood her eyes. She walked to her bedroom and sank into her bed, still fully dressed. Then, like so many nights before, she allowed herself to drift to sleep crying over Caide Abbott.

CHAPTER EIGHT

CAIDE

Caide drove to the office the next morning unsure of what to expect. As he pulled up, he noticed several people standing around a tow truck as they attempted to tow Blaire's car.

Damn. He'd forgotten all about leaving her without a car.

"What do you think you're doing?" he demanded, hurrying toward the tattooed man whose sleeveless shirt introduced him as 'Smittie'. "That's an employee's car. You have no right to tow it."

The man turned to him, holding a clipboard. He smelled of cigarettes and diesel fuel. "Who are you?"

Caide huffed. "I'm Caide Abbott, the executive assistant here at Mason and Meachum. Now, that is an employee's car you are towing. She has every right to park here."

"Listen buddy, all I know is I got a call to come pick up a car with four flat tires. I don't see any others around here, do you?"

"Flat tires?" He looked down, finally noticing that the car's tires were, in fact, flat. Just then, Blaire burst out of the door, looking distraught.

"Caide?"

"Blaire? What happened?"

Blaire shook her head. "Someone slashed my tires last night."

"Did you call the cops?"

"I did. They filed a report but there are no witnesses and we only have cameras on the inside so they'll be of no help. They didn't seem optimistic that they'd find anything. It was probably just some kids acting out."

"I'm so sorry. I can't believe it. We've never had any trouble here before."

"I know it. Meachum's talking about installing security cameras outside now." She shivered.

"Listen," he said pulling her out of earshot of the tow truck driver, "about last night—"

She held up a hand to stop him. "Don't. Just don't. I don't want to hear it. Let's just forget about it, okay?"

"You're sure? I just wanted to say—"

"I just can't hear it today, Caide. Not with everything else going on. Just forget it, please." He nodded, following her into the building, and telling himself there was nothing he'd like more than to be able to forget it.

CHAPTER NINE

RACHAEL

Rachael heard the doorbell ring from the kitchen. She stood, setting Davis in her seat. "Don't move, okay? Keep my seat warm. I'll be right back."

Davis nodded, watching intently as his sister tried to put the Little Mermaid puzzle together again. Rachael walked to the door, wondering who to expect. As she got to the door, a smile filled her face.

"*Audrey?*" she cried, pulling the door open and lugging her best friend into a hug. "Oh my gosh! I can't believe it's you. I've missed you. It's been way too long."

"I know, Rach. I've missed you too. So much. I'm sorry I haven't called in a while. John and I have just been so busy." She shrugged half-heartedly, shutting the door behind her.

"Wait? John? So John's still in the picture? The last time I talked to you, you were both ready for a divorce."

"Gosh, has it been that long?" she asked, dropping her purse to the floor. "Yeah, we're still together. He asked me to go to therapy. You know, after I lost the baby, I just sort of lost touch with everything. It was a last resort, but our therapist is amazing. You'd love her. I swear she's a miracle worker. We're a lot better now. Actually, I have some big news."

"What?" Rachael asked, her gaze wandering to Audrey's flat tummy.

"No." She rubbed her stomach. "Not that. We're, um, we're moving back home."

"What?"

"We put a down payment on a house yesterday. It's over on Hillsboro. It's so adorable, Rach, you're going to love it."

"That's amazing, Audrey. I'm so glad to have you home, the kids will be too. We've missed you so much." She pulled her into another hug. "I'm glad to hear you and John are doing better. He's good for you. I've always thought that."

Audrey smiled. "Thanks, Rach. So, tell me about you guys. What's been going on?"

"Oh, you know La Rue, nothing new ever happens. Although, you did miss a bit of drama last week. We had a car wreck."

"A wreck? Oh my, Rachael. What happened? Was anyone hurt?" She reached for her friend's hand, looking her over.

"Not seriously, no. Just a few scrapes and bruises. Poor Davis got the worst of it."

Audrey's eyes went wide. "Davis? Oh, Rachael. I haven't even met him yet. Has it really been two years since I last saw you? Can I meet him?"

"Of course." Rachael couldn't believe how quickly the time had passed. She led her into the kitchen. "Brin, I've got a surprise for you."

Her daughter's eyes immediately lit up as she jumped from her chair into Audrey's waiting arms. *"Aunt Audrey!"*

"Oh, Brin Brin, I've missed you so very much. Look how big you've gotten. I can barely hold you up anymore." Audrey held the girl out from her chest so she could get a good look at her. Brinley smiled, hugging her neck. "And who is this handsome fellow?" Audrey playfully rubbed Davis' hair. He ducked behind the back of his chair, hiding his face without a response. Rachael bent down next to him.

"Davis, darling, this is your aunt Audrey. Can you say 'hello'?"

Davis looked from his mother to Audrey and back a few times. "*Hew-woh*," he mumbled under his breath finally.

"You know, the last time I saw you," Audrey told him, "you were just a tiny little baby inside your mommy's tummy. You didn't even have a name yet."

"He didn't have a name?" Brinley asked, astonished.

Audrey nodded, matching their enthusiasm. "That's right. But I think your mommy and daddy picked out the best name of all. In fact, can I have it?"

"No," Davis cried, shaking his head feverishly.

"Please? I want it. I'll be Davis from now on," she teased.

"No! I Davis." He laughed.

Audrey held out her arms for him and he leaned into them cautiously. "Oh, fine. You're Davis. I can't believe I'm just meeting you, little guy. I love you so much." She kissed his cheek. "So, do you guys want help with this puzzle? Who is that? Ariel?" Audrey pulled up a chair, holding Davis in her lap.

Rachael smiled. Before she could sit down, she heard the phone ringing. "Will you watch them for a second?"

Audrey nodded, already invested in the puzzle. Rachael ran to the living room and lifted the phone to her ear.

"Hello?"

"Rach, it's me."

"Hey, Caide, is everything okay?"

"Yes, everything's fine. I just wanted to let you know I'm—"

"Let me guess: you're going to be late again?"

He paused, heaving a sigh. "Mason's client is about to

walk, we just have to put together a closing argument. He's a big client, babe. We can't afford to lose this one."

"You were out late last night too. We miss you. Brinley's been asking about you. Please just come home tonight, just one night."

"I don't have a choice," he said, his voice low.

"You know, I thought after the accident things would be different. I thought maybe you'd change. Guess I was just kidding myself, huh?"

"Look, I'm in with Mason now. I promise I'll try to finish up early. I'll see you tonight."

"*This evening*, Caide."

"Right. See you then."

"Okay, be careful." There was silence on the other end of the line. Rachael stared at the phone and heard the dial tone start up, letting her know the call was over. "I love you too," she whispered to a man who'd long since quit listening.

CHAPTER TEN

CAIDE

Caide hung up the phone, looking around his empty office. His desk was piled high with paperwork but he couldn't keep Blaire out of his mind long enough to focus and get anything done. She hadn't stopped in to see him all day, which had Caide worried. He knew she was hurt, and she had every right to be, but she'd never stayed mad at him for so long before. He knew he had no right to be upset with her, but he was. For the past seven years Blaire had been there for him even when he'd pushed her away. When he and Rachael had nearly split up before she became pregnant with Davis, it was Blaire he'd run to. When he'd heard there were going to be complications with the pregnancy, it was Blaire who'd listened to his worst fears. When he was stressed over work, Blaire had made it all better. He'd never meant to fall for her, but after years of never admitting to himself how he felt, last night had made it clear. It had never hurt so much to be ignored.

He'd watched his door like a hawk, waiting to see the knob turn, to smell her vanilla perfume, but it hadn't happened. If he wanted to see her, it was clear he'd have to make the first move. Until he talked to her, until he cleared the air, the pile of work on his desk wasn't going to be touched. He walked out of his office with determination only to find that she was leaving Mr. Mason's office, his hand on her back.

"Well, just make sure you collaborate with Caide about any potential candidates and let me know when you have a decision. I know you'll make the right choice; you two make a great team." He shook his head. "It's a shame. It won't ever be the same around here."

Blaire nodded politely and walked to her desk where Caide was waiting.

"Candidate for what?"

"Excuse me?" she asked defiantly.

"What candidates? What was he talking about?"

She grimaced, looking down and beginning to type something on her computer. "The candidates for Mason and Meachum's new secretary."

"What? They need two?" He furrowed his brow at her.

"They need one. I put in my notice."

The words hit him hard. He waited for her to smile, to say she was kidding, but she didn't. Instead she continued to type, avoiding his eye contact. "You did what?"

"I'm leaving the company."

"Why?" he demanded, leaning down closer so no one could eavesdrop. "Not because of last night?"

She looked up from the computer screen, her eyes full of pain. "You don't get to ask me that, Caide. You don't get to ask me why and you don't get to care."

"Of course I care. How can you say that? You can't just leave because you're mad at me. It's not fair. You'll regret it if you leave like this."

She frowned at him, shaking her head and whispering heatedly, "I am not leaving because of you, first of all, so screw you. I'm leaving for me. This is the first thing I've done for myself in so long I can't even remember, so no, I'm not going to regret it. Thanks for caring."

"Blaire, please—"

"I'm busy, Caide. *You should go.*" She threw his own words back at him like knives, each word piercing his heart.

"Fine." He walked away slowly, allowing time for her to call him back—maybe even follow him to his office.

She didn't.

IT WAS after seven and Caide still hadn't been able to focus on his work.

How dare she just leave?

If he wasn't home soon Rachael would go crazy. He grabbed his files and locked them in a drawer, sighing. He opened his office door to find Bart Meachum standing in his doorway—hand in the air— prepared to knock.

Meachum laughed. "Caide, I was just coming to ask where the party was."

"Sir?"

"It seems the entire office stayed late tonight. I was just wondering if I'd missed something."

Caide stepped out of his office to glance around and saw Blaire and Brian both working busily at their desks. He smiled at Meachum. "I guess you're right. No one gave me the memo either."

Meachum patted him on the shoulder. "Go home, Caide. Get some rest. We'll see you in the morning."

Caide agreed, watching as his boss left the office. As the door shut behind him, Caide found himself walking toward Brian's desk. "Big day today?" he asked.

"Yes, sir," Brian said, still jotting something down on a

sheet of paper before looking up. "It's been hectic. I'm just about finished for the night. I just didn't want to leave anything unfinished, especially after I bailed on you last night with dinner."

"Don't worry about that. We all have lives outside of this place; though sometimes I think we forget it. Don't give it another thought, okay? Go home whenever you're ready. This will all be here tomorrow."

Brian let out a relieved sigh. "Can I be honest?"

"Sure."

His shoulders slumped. "I overheard Mr. Mason and Blaire talking about interviewing for a new secretary. I've been worried all day. I didn't know we had any open positions, so I kind of assumed—"

"That we were firing you?" Caide laughed. "Brian, no. We wouldn't want to lose you, trust me. You're the best assistant I've ever had. The decision to ever let you go would ultimately be mine, so rest assured that as long as you want a job here, it's yours."

Caide saw the weight lift from the man's shoulders instantly. With that being said, Brian began to stack up his paperwork, filing it in a drawer. "Thank you, sir. I'm going to head on out then, if you're sure there's nothing else you need tonight?"

"I'm positive. We'll see you in the morning." As he left, Caide made his way to Blaire's desk. Realizing that they were the only two left in the building gave him a certain thrill.

"What are you still doing here?" he asked, tapping his knuckles on her desk.

Without responding she handed him a list containing seven names. Caide looked it over. "And this is?"

"That," she began, finally looking up at him, "is a list of potential candidates to replace me. I emailed you each of their resumes. Mason wants us to pick five to interview by

BECOMING MRS. ABBOTT

the end of next week. I like them all, so I need you to look over them and narrow it down for me. Number three is particularly interesting, she has an awesome resume—nearly eighteen years of experience."

"You want me to narrow the list down?"

"Yes."

He tossed the paper into the trash can. "Done."

"Caide." She pursed her lips.

"No one, no matter how much experience they have, *no one* will replace you. You know that."

"Caide." She grabbed the list from the trash and handed it back to him.

"You're really going to do this?"

"Do what?"

"You're going to leave?"

"Yes, I really am."

"Where will you go?"

"Somewhere. Anywhere." She stood from her desk, walking around to face him. "Caide, do you know I have a master's degree? I graduated with honors. I worked my ass off in college to be able to make a name for myself, but here I am: fetching coffee and answering phones. It's crap. It's crap and you know the worst part? I have no one to blame but myself."

"What do you want? A raise? A better title? Whatever it is —just name it, I'll make sure that it's yours."

"You're not listening to me. Don't you think they've offered me all of those things? You don't have to advocate for me, Caide. You don't see the work I put in for this place. I've put my whole life on hold for this company and it's gotten me nowhere because all I think about is you."

"Just tell me what to do. Anything. We can't lose you."

"There's nothing for you to do. Just find someone to replace me so we can all just move on."

"Is this about last night? Because I said I'm sorry—"

"It's not about last night. Last night I finally got what I've been wishing for all these years. You finally admitted that this isn't all in my head, that you actually feel the same way I do. When you kissed me, I thought I'd feel so happy, so in love, *so loved*." She paused, her eyes searching his. "Instead I felt dirty. I've dreamed of that moment, Caide. Last night I finally realized that what I've spent the last three years of my life hoping for...it wasn't actually what I wanted at all. I'm better than that. I deserve more than some secret kiss in a dark car. I deserve someone who will be happy to kiss me, someone who will want to love me back. I just deserve better and I can't get that as long as I stay here."

"It's not like I mean to hurt you, you know that I care about you. I just can't hurt my wife either. I can't leave her."

"You don't want to leave her. Or maybe you don't know what you want—either way I'm leaving. Just please have me a list by the end of the day tomorrow." She patted his chest and turned to walk away, grabbing her purse from the edge of her desk. Caide lunged at her, not sure of what had come over himself. She turned to him—he was sure she was about to object—but before she had the chance, he pressed his lips to hers. He felt his heart pounding, his pulse immediately responding to their kiss.

She pulled away, looking confused. "Caide, I can't..." She tried to step back, though he could already see her eyes giving in. He grabbed her arms, pulling her to him again.

"Please. Please just give me a chance to figure this all out."

"I've given you chances."

"Just a little while longer."

"Say it then."

"Say what?"

"Tell me how you feel about me."

He paused, his conscience was heavy with guilt, knowing

another line was about to be crossed. He squeezed the bridge of his nose between his thumb and forefinger. "I love you, okay? I do love you. Maybe I've loved you all this time."

And just like that, she was his. She threw her arms around his neck, her eyes rife with tears. He ignored the feeling of her tears hitting his cheeks as their passion grew. He allowed his hands to travel and she didn't stop him. He rubbed her shoulders, slowly easing her blazer off. Her breathing quickened and he pulled back. "Should I stop?"

She kept her eyes closed, as if she were savoring the moment. "No."

Caide didn't ask twice. He lifted her up, sitting her on her desk. His hands explored her, stopping at her skirt's hem line. He wanted her. All of his pent up passions had been building for too long. His shaking hands found their way to her blouse, fumbling as they undid each button. His heart pounded, making it hard to focus, and he couldn't catch his breath.

He'd never known passion like this. His hands found her hair again and he gently laid her down across the desk. His lips never left hers and her tears never stopped falling as they both crossed a line they'd sworn to themselves they'd never cross.

CHAPTER ELEVEN

BLAIRE

It was during this, during the passion and the heat of their sex that she'd heard it.

First, she wasn't sure about it, they were making so much noise she'd just dismissed it. The second time, she'd prayed to a God she wasn't sure she believed in that she'd made it up. She'd prayed harder than she ever had, shut her eyes, and allowed him to continue. The third time, however, she'd known they had to stop. She'd heard them. She was sure of it. *Footsteps.* They weren't alone in the office.

She tensed up, pulling away from him. He stopped, panting.

"What are you—"

"Shhh." She silenced him, holding her finger up. "Did you hear that?"

"Hear what?" he asked, looking around.

"I heard something."

"What do you mean? We're the only ones here."

She pushed him back, adjusting her skirt. "I heard someone upstairs." They stood quietly for a while. Blaire walked to the door, checking the parking lot. "There are no cars out there, except yours."

He zipped his pants, his eyes wide. "Are you sure you aren't just being paranoid?"

"I know what I heard."

"Do you think they heard us?"

Blaire shrugged, afraid to make any noise. "We should leave," Caide whispered. Blaire nodded, feeling uneasy. She sat at her desk, readjusting and gathering her things.

"Come on. I'll take you home." Caide held his hand out to her.

"No," she said hurriedly, "we can't leave at the same time. If someone is here, I don't want them to see us leaving together."

"No one would suspect anything. I'm not comfortable leaving you alone."

"I'll be fine. Honest. I'm sure it's nothing. It's probably just Randy or one of the other cleaning ladies. I just need to collect myself. I'm calling a cab now."

"Are you sure?"

Blaire sensed relief in his voice. "I'm positive. I'll be fine."

Caide pulled his keys from his pocket, kissing her cheek. "I'll see you tomorrow."

"We can't do this, you know," she said, causing him to turn back as he walked away. "I won't help you cheat on her. Tonight shouldn't have happened, not like this. You have to choose and if you won't choose, I'll choose for you."

He walked back to her; this time his kiss landed on her lips. "I choose you. But, it's not that easy. You have to let me tell her gently."

She kissed him back. "Promise me?"

He nodded. "Are you sure you don't want me to wait?"

"Go," she assured him, picking up the phone. "I'll be fine."

CHAPTER TWELVE

CAIDE

Caide's heart was pounding as he pulled into his cul-de-sac. His mind raced with thoughts of Blaire—and then thoughts of Rachael. How could he ever tell her what he'd done?

He'd never been able to admit to Rachael when he'd messed up. Everything about her was just too perfect. She never made mistakes like he did. He loved his wife, he truly did; she was the mother of his children and she'd been there for him when no one else had. But, the truth was, they didn't laugh together anymore. They didn't enjoy each other's company like they should.

Caide had known for a while that it was going nowhere, but he had the children to think about and Rachael was just so *fragile*. Since day one, he'd tried his best to do right by her. On the day she announced her pregnancy, he'd sworn he'd never be 'that guy.' He'd do whatever he had to in order to protect his family. His own parents had never been great role models, and he'd vowed to make sure his children never felt that way. Of course, it hadn't been that easy.

Caide had a lump in his throat thinking of what the next

few days would be like. He pulled into his driveway, half expecting Rachael to jump out and attack him, confront him, and accuse him of doing exactly what he had been. None of which happened.

Instead, he tiptoed unscathed into the house. He crept down the hallway, spying Davis in his crib asleep. Across the hall in Brinley's room, his wife lay in their daughter's bed, the two sleeping peacefully. Rachael stirred as the light hit her. He shut the door quickly, careful not to wake her. He walked to the bathroom, knowing he should shower. He turned on the water, stripping out of his clothes and climbing in. He stood still, letting the hot water scald his skin before grabbing a wash cloth and tirelessly scrubbing off every bit of evidence from the night.

CHAPTER THIRTEEN

BLAIRE

Blaire knew the look of a woman who'd been cheated on. She'd seen her mother wear it so many times it was burned into her skull. She knew the way their eyes glazed over. She could remember how their expression went blank, empty from pain, and weighed down by the emotional weight of the worst thing a man could do to a woman—the worst way they could hurt them. She'd seen how deep, how dark the pain could get. Tonight, she'd become an accomplice to that pain. She'd turned into the woman she'd sworn to never become. Blaire hated herself for what she'd done. The guilt ate away at her heart.

That was why she agreed to go into the bathroom.

"Come with me," she'd been told.

Why not? Blaire thought. *There's nothing you can say to me that will be worse than what I'm saying to myself. Nothing could hurt worse than this.*

She was wrong. Upon entering the restroom, Blaire was confronted with the worst pain she'd ever felt. She tumbled to the floor, her head pounding. Her vision blurred, coated by blood. She couldn't see her attacker. The blows came—so hard and so fast that she lost count of how many there'd been. She laid on the cold floor, feeling her blood flow around her, warming her quickly cooling body. Her thoughts jumbled—she swore she could see them on the floor mixed into her blood: letters, words, memories mixing with the crimson dye. Things that used to mean something. Blaire tried to find anything comforting to think of—a song or a story she'd loved as a child. She tried to remember where she was, what was happening; she tried to remember her name. Finally, when all else failed, Blaire Underwood fell asleep—a dreamless sleep, from which she knew she'd never wake.

CHAPTER FOURTEEN

RACHAEL

Rachael busied herself in the kitchen, cooking breakfast for her sleepy little family. It was after six when Caide finally woke up and joined her.

"What are you doing up so early?" he asked, fixing himself a cup of coffee.

She rushed past him on her way to the pantry. "I didn't sleep very well. Brinley's class is having Parent's Day today and we're supposed to bring a snack. I thought I'd make cupcakes. Besides that, apparently if I want to see my husband, I'm going to have to start waking up with him."

Caide yawned, ignoring her comment. "Smells great. Why didn't you tell me it was Parent's Day?"

She froze, a hand on her hip. "Would it have mattered?"

"Of course it would have. Unless you don't want me there."

"Of course we want you there, I just assumed you'd have some unavoidable meeting."

Caide took a sip of the hot coffee, leaning against the counter. "How about I call in today? I could go with you to

Parent's Day and then we could take them to the park afterwards."

Rachael stared at him. "Are you sure?"

"Of course."

"Caide, do not make me go in there and get those babies all excited just to break their hearts when you change your mind."

Caide took a bite of his toast. "Go tell them. I can miss." Rachael rushed toward him, kissing his cheek. He cupped her cheek and pulled her to him, kissing her mouth slowly. "I love you." His eyes had a hint of sadness she hadn't noticed before.

"I love you too. I'm going to go wake the kids. They'll be so excited." Rachael went to Davis' room first, sitting down on the side of his bed. She leaned over and kissed both of his cheeks. "Davis." She took his hand and kissed his fingertips. "*Daaavis.*"

He began to stir, rubbing his eyes with tiny fists. Rachael leaned down and rubbed her nose on his. This was her favorite part of every day: waking her children up. It came before the chaos had set in, before she could be stressed out. Just the few quiet moments she shared with her children each morning. She loved it. Rachael had been born to be a mother. Even with as much as she loved her dance studio, being a mom was the best, most exciting career Rachael could've ever imagined.

"*No*," Davis cried.

She smiled, pulling his hands from his eyes. "I made your favorite breakfast and I've got a big surprise for you."

He opened one eye. "What?"

"Daddy says we're going to the park," Brinley announced, racing into the room, wide awake and with Caide trailing behind her, a smug grin on his face.

"I texted Mason," he told Rachael. "Now, who's going to beat me to the kitchen?"

"Me!" their children yelled simultaneously.

Rachael smiled, picking Davis up and racing to the kitchen.

"I won," Brinley teased.

"I think it was a tie," Rachael said. Davis smiled, wrapping his arms around his mother.

"I love you Mommy."

"I love you too, sweetheart. I love you so much."

CHAPTER FIFTEEN

CAIDE

Caide followed Brinley over to her desk. "This is where I sit every day, Daddy. See my name? B-R-I-N-L-E-Y. Brinley."

He bent down, hugging his daughter. "How did I get so lucky to have a daughter who's this smart?"

She giggled. Her teacher, a kind looking woman in her early fifties, began addressing the parents from the front of the classroom.

"Welcome everyone and thank you all for attending Parent's Day. Your children are so excited that you could make it today. I'd like this day to be a chance for each of you to see where your children spend most of their day. Feel free to mingle and meet the other parents. We have plenty of refreshments. The children have all worked hard decorating the classroom with their best work and I know they can't wait to show you everything. I'll be available to answer any questions or discuss any concerns you have, but I think the kids can take it from here. Oh, and I'd just like to say, it is such a pleasure to teach each of your children. They are all such great little people and I've truly grown to love each one of them this year."

With that the children began to lead their parents around the room. Brinley grabbed her parents' hands, pulling them toward a giant bulletin board in the back of the room.

"See that one?" She pointed to a drawing. "That one's mine. It's our family."

As Caide started to tell her how great the drawing was, he felt his phone begin to vibrate. Rachael looked at him.

"Turn that off," she said through gritted teeth.

"Sorry." He reached in his pocket, hitting the button to silence it. As he began looking at the next piece of art Brinley pointed out, he felt it vibrating again. This time he pulled it out of his pocket, checking the caller ID. He looked apologetically toward Rachael. It was a number he didn't recognize. He silenced it once again, shoving it back into his pocket. "Sorry, Brin. That's a great picture though and look how well you wrote your name at the bottom."

Brinley smiled. "Thank you, Daddy. Mommy, everyone is eating all of the cupcakes we brought. Can I have some too?"

"Of course you can, sweetheart. Just one though. Could you bring an extra over here for your brother?"

Brinley nodded, skipping off toward the snack table. Rachael sat Davis down in the chair, handing him a book.

"Who is calling you?" Rachael asked, keeping her eyes on Brinley.

"I don't recognize the number. Probably a client or someone with the wrong number. They can call Mason if it's important."

As he said the words, his phone rang again. This time the caller ID read: **Bart Meachum**. "Honey, I've got to take this. It won't take long I swear." Rachael looked away, disappointment radiating on her face. Caide hurried out of the classroom, pressing the button to answer the call. "Hello?"

BECOMING MRS. ABBOTT

"Caide? Where are you?"

"Didn't Mason tell you I wouldn't be there today? There's a parents day thing at my daughter's school. They asked us to attend."

"You should get down here as quickly as you can." His voice sounded strange.

"Everything okay, Meach? Rachael will kill me if I leave right now. What's going on?"

"I'm not sure what I'm allowed to tell you. We just need you at the office right away."

They know. Caide sighed. "Okay. Give me a few minutes."

"Thanks." Caide hung up his phone angrily. He walked back into the classroom, his head hung low. He couldn't take the look on Rachael's face.

"We have to go," he told her, keeping his voice low.

"What are you talking about? Don't do this. Caide, please don't do this to your daughter." Caide watched as Brinley stood laughing with a group of her friends. "I don't have any choice, I swear. I tried to get out of it. There's some sort of emergency at the office."

"What kind of emergency?"

"I'm not sure, but they wouldn't ask if it wasn't serious."

"Or maybe they're just mad that you missed a few days because of the accident."

"That's not it and you know it. Mason and Meachum have been nothing but good to us. After my parents disowned me, we would've been out on our own, if it hadn't been for them. They risked their friendship with my dad to make sure I had a job and we weren't going hungry. I know it's important. I'll go there, fix the problem and be home within an hour, I swear."

She pressed her lips together, refusing to look at him. "You know what, Caide? You go. Take a cab. I'm staying with our daughter because I promised her I would and because she has been talking about this day for weeks. You can meet us at the park afterwards."

"Okay." He kissed Davis' head, turning to walk out the door.

"Caide?" she called.

"Yeah?" He turned to see his wife's cheeks flushed from anger.

"If you don't show up, if you break your daughter's heart...I'm not sure where that will leave us. I'm done letting you hurt her."

CHAPTER SIXTEEN

RACHAEL

Brinley stared at her mother through the rearview mirror. "Why did Daddy have to leave? He always has to leave. He didn't even get to see my cubby."

Rachael adjusted the mirror, unable to look at her daughter. "Remember honey, Daddy has a very important job that pays for our house and our food and our toys, right?"

"Yes ma'am."

"So sometimes he has to leave even though he'd rather be with you all the time."

"But he promised he'd take me to the park."

"I know, Brin, but Mommy's taking you to the park instead. Daddy promised he'd try really hard to meet us here."

"Okay."

Rachael could hear the pout in her daughter's voice. "Now, don't give me that pouty face. We're still going to have fun, right? Mommy's just as fun as Daddy."

"But you're always here. We always play with you." Rachael's heart hurt for her daughter.

She pulled into the parking lot. "Well you'll just have to

have fun with me anyway." She stepped out of the car, unbuckling Davis. Brinley climbed out, racing for the swing set. Rachael carried Davis to the swing beside her, maneuvering his cast into the leg hole.

"Who wants me to push them?"

"Me! I do!"

"Me too!"

Rachael pushed their backs gently, watching their heads fly back in laughter.

"Higher!" Brinley called, her curls blowing in the wind. Rachael pushed, laughing as her children did, enjoying the moment so much that nothing else mattered. Growing up without a mother, Rachael had promised herself that her children would never know what that was like. She couldn't understand how Caide could miss moments like this— moments where the kids were happy and carefree and able to just be children in a world in such a hurry to make them grow up. It broke her heart for her children to miss their father so, but even more, it broke her heart for Caide who she was sure would one day be filled the regrets of an absentee parent.

CHAPTER SEVENTEEN

CAIDE

Caide pulled up to work an hour later—finding a cab at this time of day was next to impossible. As soon as he pulled into the parking lot his skin lined with goose bumps. There was an ambulance and a parking lot full of cop cars, lights flashing.

"What the hell?" He paid the driver as he hopped out of the cab, walking apprehensively toward the entrance. Before he could reach the door an officer stopped him.

"Whoa, buddy. You can't go in there. This is a closed crime scene."

"I work here," Caide objected. "What's happening?"

"What's your name?" The cop eyed him suspiciously.

"Caide. I'm Caide Abbott."

The cop took a step back and spoke into his shoulder. "Chief, we've got a Caide Abbott out here. Claims he works here."

The response was instant. "Send him in." The cop stepped back, pulling the door open for Caide and allowing him to pass through. As he did, all eyes were on him. Mason and

Meachum could be seen in their offices, talking with police officers.

A brawny officer with a gray mustache approached Caide. "You Caide Abbott?"

"Yes sir. What happened here?"

"That's what we'd like to know. Come with me." The man led Caide to his office, which Caide noticed had been raided. "Sit." Caide did as he was told. Two additional officers followed them into his small office and shut the door.

"Do you know Blaire Underwood?" the first officer, the one Caide assumed must be the chief, asked.

"Oh my god, did something happen to Blaire?"

"Answer the question." The man's face was unreadable.

"Yes. Yes, of course I do."

"What is the nature of your relationship?"

"We work together." Caide swallowed.

"That's it?"

"What do you mean? Can you please tell me what's going on? Is Blaire all right?"

"Actually, she's not. Blaire Underwood was brutally murdered last night and, by all accounts, you were the last to see her alive."

Caide's heart plummeted; he felt bile fill his throat. His forehead was immediately drenched in a cold sweat. "M-murdered? What? What—no. That's not possible. Wait, you think I did it?"

"That's exactly what we think."

"But I wouldn't. She was my friend. I have no reason to want to hurt her. How could you think that?"

"Sources tell us the two of you were hostile toward each other yesterday. We were also informed that Miss Underwood put in her resignation. So you tell me why a young woman who has worked at a job for," he paused, looking at his paperwork, "three years would suddenly quit her job

BECOMING MRS. ABBOTT

with no explanation. What would make her do that, Caide?"

"I—" Caide couldn't breathe. "I don't know why. I begged her to stay."

"You don't know why, huh? Well, here's what we know. We know that you sent your assistant home, which conveniently left you two the only ones in the building last night. We know you wanted to be alone with her; what we don't know is why."

"I didn't tell Brian to go home, I just—"

"You didn't? You didn't tell him and I quote," he read from the notepad again, "'Go home. This'll be here tomorrow.'"

"Well, yes, but that's out of context—"

"Now, either you're the world's coolest boss, or you wanted to be alone with our victim. And speaking of things that will be here in the morning, you weren't. You conveniently called in this morning. So tell us, Caide, tell us this is all some huge coincidence because, by my count, right now you're looking mighty guilty."

Caide sighed, unsure of where to begin. "Okay, yes. I told him to go home. He's my assistant and his wife's pregnant and he's been working very hard to impress me. Blaire doesn't work for me. I couldn't tell her to go home like I could Brian. Only like Mason or Meachum could've. And besides that, I have no motive. She's been a great friend to me. I can't believe she's gone." He put his face into his hands. "Oh, and I called in because my daughter had a parent's day at her school today. You can check into that if you'd like."

"Oh, we will." The officer jotted down a note. "See, we checked into your work history. According to your bosses, you never miss work. Never. So, what? There were no parent's days until now?"

"I assume there have been some, yes," Caide said quietly, his throat dry.

"It's convenient, then, that you chose to go to this particular one, isn't it?"

Caide frowned. What else could he do but tell the truth? As much of the truth as he could. "I owed it to my daughter to go. I've been a pretty bad father lately. I've been working too much. My family and I were recently involved in a pretty bad car accident and it's put a lot more pressure on me to be more present. That's why this particular parent's day was so important. We may not have lived to see it. There's no other reason. I'm trying to be better. The only thing I'm guilty of is being a bad father." Caide felt a lump in his throat as he admitted one of his darkest fears.

"Well, you'd better hope that's true because we've gotten ahold of the security tapes from last night and since our examiners say the murder took place here, this should be a pretty open and shut case."

Caide knew then that he was going to be sick. "She was...you didn't tell me...it happened here?"

"It did. In that bathroom, right across the hall. Your friend was beaten to death. What kind of a sick bastard could do that?" He smirked, obviously getting a kick out of torturing Caide.

With that, Caide grabbed his trash can, hurling up the contents of his stomach. When he was finished, the officer sat back in his chair looking smug. "So you sure you don't have anything you need to tell me?"

"She was my girlfriend, okay? That's what you'll see on the tape. We were in love. That's what you're going to see. That's all you'll see. Whoever did this, it wasn't me, but I hope they burn." Cool tears burned his eyes as the reality of what he was being told finally hit him. Blaire was dead. Gone. Really, truly gone.

How could this have happened? He should've stayed with her. He should've never left her alone, especially after she'd heard the noise upstairs. What kind of a person just leaves someone alone after something like—that's when it hit him: the noise.

"Wait, someone else was here last night," he said quickly, leaning forward in his seat. "Right before we left, Blaire swore she heard someone upstairs."

The officer seemed genuinely interested in that information, his face growing serious. "You didn't think to call the police? Or at least check to be sure of who it was?"

"We were scared. Not of being hurt. We worried that maybe they'd heard us. We didn't want our affair to get back to my wife. We just wanted to get out of here. Her car was in the shop. That's the only reason she stayed later than me—to call a cab. If I'd known she was in danger, I would've stayed. Of course I would've stayed. Or I would've gotten her out of here. These things don't…they don't happen here. I thought we were safe."

"If you're telling the truth, the tape will tell. If you're lying, if you came back in this building last night, if you did this to that poor girl, you'd better not leave town. We'll have cops patrolling your neighborhood, you can count on that. I want no funny business. We'll be in touch."

Caide nodded, swallowing hard. The cops left his office one by one. Caide knew the case against him was solid. The tape may be his only saving grace, but using it in court would mean ruining his marriage, if not his life. He leaned over the trash can again, emptying the remaining contents of his stomach into the bin until there was nothing left in him, until the emptiness in his stomach matched the emptiness he felt in his heart.

CHAPTER EIGHTEEN

RACHAEL

Rachael checked her watch. It was nearly seven and Caide still hadn't showed up. She sighed. The sun was setting. She had no choice but to pack the kids up and head home.

"All right guys, it's time to get home and eat supper."

"But, Mom, Dad said he'd be here soon," Brinley insisted.

"I know baby, but I told you Daddy may not be able to make it."

"But if we leave and he does come, he'll be sad that we didn't wait for him."

"Daddy will know where to find us, I promise."

Brinley held onto the chain of her swing. "No. I'm not leaving. I want to wait for Daddy."

"Brinley, Daddy isn't coming. It's getting dark. I'm going to call him and tell him to meet us at home, okay?"

Brinley looked at her in disbelief. "I don't want to make Daddy sad."

"You could never make him sad. He loves you."

"Will he get to eat supper with us, then?"

She chewed on her lip, trying not to let the familiar tears

form in her eyes as she stared at her daughter's heartbroken expression. "I think he will. It's getting late. He may be on his way home now."

Brinley let go of the swing begrudgingly, her knees caked with dirt and her hair frizzy from the wind. Rachael hoisted Davis out of the sandbox he'd been playing in, dusting the sand off of him. "So you'll go with me, then?"

"Okay, I'll go. If Daddy comes here do you promise you'll tell him I wanted to wait?"

"He won't come here, Brin."

"Just promise," the girl argued, one hand on her hip.

"I promise."

"Good. 'Cause if he's sad I'm going to be really mad." "Okay, darling."

"I mean *really* mad, Momma."

Rachael sighed. "Okay, Brin, if he comes you can be mad, but he's not coming. I'll call and tell him not to."

Brinley began walking to the car, a dismayed look on her face. "Fine."

CHAPTER NINETEEN

CAIDE

Caide snuck into the house just before midnight. He'd had the cab driver drive around La Rue for the past few hours, dreading the turmoil he'd face at home. He felt as though his world were collapsing around him, as he knew it would soon enough. When he'd left the office, no one would look at him. He couldn't ignore the hushed voices that grew quiet when he entered the room. He wanted to scream for himself, cry for Blaire, kill whoever had done this, and, most of all, avoid Rachael until this had all blown over. He knew it would be impossible. Even once the charges were dropped, Rachael would hear how. For all he knew she'd probably already heard.

Tomorrow, he'd have to tell her everything before she could hear it from someone else. Tonight, he just wanted to sleep.

He walked to the kitchen, hanging his jacket over the chair and placing his shoes neatly under the table. When he made his way back to the living room, he spied the pillow and blanket Rachael had laid out for him—a sign of the argument that was to come.

He fell asleep as soon as his head hit the pillow—still fully dressed—and dreamed of a world without death and heartache. He dreamed of a world that, just a few hours ago, hadn't seemed so out of reach.

CHAPTER TWENTY

RACHAEL

Rachael woke up the next morning alone. She walked to the living room to find her husband sleeping peacefully, still fully dressed from the night before. Infuriated, she ripped the blanket off of him and flipped on the light. Caide stirred, covering his face, still blissfully half asleep.

"What the—" He yawned sleepily, looking around as if trying to figure out where he was.

"Late night?" Rachael asked, her words filled with venom. A look of realization filled his face.

"Look, Rach—"

She held her hand up. "Save it. Save whatever little speech or excuse you have planned, just don't waste your breath. How dare you? How *dare* you?" She paced the living room, trying to maintain her fury. "You let that little girl down last night again. Now, me, I'm used to your disappointments and Davis is too young to understand what a letdown his father is, but your daughter looks up to you. You're her hero, Caide, and you just *keep* breaking her heart. We waited for you yesterday. At the park. We waited until seven and when it was finally time for us to come home I basically had to drag her away. Do you know why? Not because she wanted to play longer, not because she didn't want to take her bath or go to bed, not for any normal reason that a child should want to stay at the park. No, your daughter wanted to wait for you—she would've waited all night if I'd let her—because she was scared, no, she was *terrified* that you would actually do what you promised her and show up and she wouldn't be there. Do you hear me, Caide? Your five year old daughter was terrified to let you down, when all you do is let her down every single day."

She stopped talking, tears welling up her eyes. She waited for him to comfort her; he didn't. She waited for him to apologize or explain; he didn't. Instead, he was silent. "Aren't you going to say anything? Aren't you going to do *anything* besides sit there with that dumb, blank expression on your face you've worn for the past six years? Your indifference toward this family makes me sick. I'm sick of it, Caide."

She wasn't sure what had come over her, the anger swelling in her chest like a balloon. "You *will* go wake that little girl up and you *will* take her to school. You will stay and eat lunch with her and you will pick her up and spend the afternoon with her. You will or so help me, Caide, tonight when you get home we will be so far gone—" She stopped, her gaze trailing out the window. *What is going on?*

"Caide, why are there a half-dozen police cars pulling down our road?"

Suddenly out of his trance, Caide shot up from the couch, looking out the window. He turned back to face Rachael, his expression frantic. He held her shoulders firmly. "*Listen to me*. This is bad, Rach. Blaire Underwood was murdered yesterday. Well, the night before. That's why Meachum called me. That's why I never came to the park. I'm a suspect. They're coming for me."

Rachael blinked her eyes quickly, trying to make sense of what he'd said. "What? What do you mean? Why would they think you had anything—?"

He interrupted her, speaking quickly. "We don't have time for me to explain and we sure as hell don't have time for you to fall apart so don't start crying. You're terrible in crisis, Rach, but you can't be right now. You have to hold yourself together, do you hear me?"

He shook her. "You can't fall apart today. The kids are going to need you. I didn't do it, okay? You have to believe me, I didn't do it. No matter what you hear, I need you to remember that. Remember that I never meant to hurt you. They have no case against me, so I just need you to be strong until they have to let me go. Now, please go. Keep the kids in their rooms. I don't want any of you to see this."

Rachael stood there, afraid if she took a breath she'd fall apart. Maybe if she was still long enough, she'd wake up from this awful dream. He pushed her backward just as there came on knock on their door. *"Damn it, Rachael, go."*

She turned around, sure her legs would give out as she ran, and hurried to her children, desperate for them to comfort her as much as she would have to comfort them.

CHAPTER TWENTY-ONE

CAIDE

Caide heard the knocks on the door in slow motion. He heard 'Police! Open up!' as if he were underwater. His whole world slowed as he walked toward the door. There were a handful of cops standing on his porch. "Can I help you?"

"Are you Caide Abbott?" asked a young man with red hair and freckles. His expression was somber.

"I am, but I told the other officers everything I know yesterday."

Another officer spoke up. "Mr. Abbott, is your wife home?"

Caide was taken aback. "My wife? What do you want with my wife? If it's about the tape, it's a private matter and I'd like to—"

The man spoke again, interrupting Caide and holding out a piece of paper. "We have a warrant for the arrest of Rachael Abbott for the murder of Blaire Underwood. This gives us permission to search your home." He handed it to Caide and with that they entered the house, shoving past him. Their words hit Caide like a ton of bricks, his knees buckling underneath him. He didn't follow them as they searched the house for Rachael. Instead, he listened silently to the helpless cries of his children and wife—screaming for him, screaming for help. The police led Rachael into the living room in handcuffs. Brinley clung to her legs with all of her strength.

Rachael was in hysterics as the officer continued to read her rights. "Caide," she cried when she saw him. "Caide, what is going on?"

Caide couldn't look at her, his head feeling fuzzy. Brinley ran to him, slapping his chest over and over. *"Stop them! Daddy, don't let them take Mommy! Stop them! Please!"*

He pulled her into his arms, letting her cry and scream into his chest. She eventually gave up, though tears continued to hit him through his shirt. He kissed her head and rocked her back and forth, still unable to look at his wife as they escorted her out the door.

He wasn't sure how long he sat there, his daughter crying in his arms, him unable to make sense of anything. All he could do was sit, listening to her cry, listening to his son scream out for him from his bed. When reality finally set in, he walked to Davis' room and carried him to the living room. Neither of his children spoke to him. He changed Davis and sat them at the table. He reached up into the pantry and pulled down a breakfast bar for each of them.

"Mommy says sugar isn't good for us on school days," Brinley whispered quietly, picking at her bar.

Caide knew he was doing a terrible job at being a comforting father. His children needed him; they needed him to be strong like he'd told Rachael to be. The thing was, he'd accepted his fate. He knew that he may be arrested, may even go to court. He'd known it was coming and had been prepared for it. He could've never prepared for this though. He wasn't good without Rachael. She took care of things. She ran the household. The thought of life without her terrified him. He stood from the table, leaving his children confused, traumatized, and alone.

"Your mom isn't here. Eat." He walked down the hallway, dialing the only person he could count on right now. She answered on the second ring.

"Mr. A? What's up?"

"Corie, is there any way you can get here?"

"Of course," she answered without hesitation. "When?"

He sighed. "Five minutes ago?"

CAIDE PULLED up to his office, still dressed in what he'd worn the day before. He rushed into Mason's office, all eyes on him. "We need to talk."

Mason sat back in his seat. "Look, Caide. We were all questioned by the police. You have to understand. No one said anything to intentionally paint you in a bad light, I hope you understand that. None of us believe that you are capable of this atrocity. Of course, as soon as this all blows over, your job will be right here."

"Rachael was arrested this morning. Not me, Rachael. My wife, who makes me take spiders outside to let them go, was arrested for *murder* today. I don't care who said what to the police. I need your help."

Mason nodded. "Caide, I'm sorry. I can't imagine what could make them believe Rachael is involved in something like this. Anything you need, we're here for you."

"That's why I'm here. I need you to represent her. You know her as well as you know me. You know she isn't capable of this. You two are the best lawyers on the East Coast, I can't imagine anyone else saving my wife. I need you to fix this."

Mason's face grew troubled. He sat up straight to his

desk, examining his hands. "Surely you must understand why I can't do that. Look, Caide, we know Rachael didn't do this. I need you to know that." He stared at Caide, the wrinkles around his mouth more prominent as he pressed his lips together. "But if we represent this case, if we defend the person charged with murdering an employee, the press will go crazy. It could destroy this firm."

"This will destroy her life," Caide yelled, slamming his fist on the desk.

Mason stood. "Out of respect for Blaire's family, we have decided not to take place in this trial—on either side. It's a sticky situation all around, Caide. I'm sorry. I am. I'd do anything I could for you, you know that, but this is a conflict of interest that we just can't be a part of."

Caide placed his head in his hands. He'd expected this answer, deep down he'd known this would be the case, but he also knew his wife hadn't done anything wrong. She couldn't have. She physically wasn't capable of this. He turned, suddenly feeling as though he couldn't breathe. He had to get out of the office, had to go see Rachael. Mason didn't try to stop him as he raced out the door. He was used to this type of behavior from angry spouses, as was Caide. Caide, however, was usually on the opposite side of the desk.

CHAPTER TWENTY-TWO

RACHAEL

Rachael pressed her forehead to the cool window in the back of the car. She felt nauseous. She'd never even run a stop sign before and now she was being accused of murder. The car smelled of vomit and urine, and the leather squeaked whenever she moved.

She wanted to tell them that there must be some mistake, that they had the wrong girl. She wanted to make them understand that she couldn't possibly have killed anyone. She needed them to listen to her, to believe her, but instead she sat quietly, letting her head hit the window with every bump they hit.

She sat silently because she couldn't think of a single thing to say that would make sense. So many questions swam through her mind. As they drove past her studio she wondered if Caide would remember to call off practice, she wondered what reason he'd give. She didn't have time to be angry with her husband, though she was sure she should be. Instead, she worried. She worried about whether or not the kids would get to preschool and daycare, whether he'd remember that Davis preferred Cheerios over Lucky

Charms, and whether he'd remember to pick up groceries. She worried about whether he'd even make it home to feed his children and put them to bed. Her head was full of worry as they pulled into the station. The officers parked the squad car and escorted her into the building. Several strangers looked at her with disgust. An officer sat her on a bench and handcuffed her there before walking away. Rachael sat for several hours, her stomach growling, before someone finally approached her.

"Come with me," said the young cop, unhooking her from the bench and leading her to a room she recognized immediately. "Stand by the wall and hold this. I'm going to take your mug shot."

Rachael felt tears rush to her eyes once more. This was real. Somehow, it was only then hitting her. From that moment on, she'd have a mugshot floating around on the internet. What would parents think? Would they pull their kids from her class? She quickly brushed the tears away, walking to do as she was told. Once the pictures were taken, the cop grabbed her arm once more. She led Rachael into a room with no doors, only several stalls with benches.

"Open up." She held out a long Q-Tip. Rachael opened her mouth, trying not to gag as the officer swiped her cheek. She held out another one, wiping in between each of Rachael's fingers. "Empty your pockets into this bag, then change into these." She stepped back, making no attempt to give Rachael any privacy and laid an orange jumpsuit on the bench. Rachael emptied her pockets, pulling out a wadded up tissue from wiping Davis' nose the night before, and a pony tail holder. She placed them into the plastic bag and began undressing. Her hands shook as she took each item of clothing off, trying to maintain what little dignity she had left. She was standing in only her bra and panties when the cop laughed. "All of it off."

She removed the rest of her clothing, covering herself with one hand and reaching for the orange jumpsuit. The officer pushed it back with her foot, shaking her head. "Squat down and cough." Rachael's face flushed from embarrassment. "Look, if you don't do it, I'll have to search you. This is a lot easier on us both." Rachael nodded, still trying to cover herself. She bent her knees, grabbing onto the wall to keep from falling down. She coughed. "Again." She coughed again, her face burning from humiliation. The cop handed her the jumpsuit and she anxiously threw it on. She handed her clothing over to be shoved into another bag. The officer led Rachael to a cell and shut the door behind her.

The cell was tiny, less than half the size of the ones Rachael had seen on TV. There was a toilet in the corner with no means of privacy in place and a small bed with sheets that smelled of body odor and mildew even from where Rachael stood. Rachael sat on the floor next to a puddle of something wet. She drew pictures in the dirt on the floor, allowing her mind to travel to places far away from the four walls surrounding her.

CHAPTER TWENTY-THREE

CAIDE

Caide sat in the office of Mason and Meachum's biggest competitor. His legs shook from anticipation. A secretary with red hair and a warm smile approached him. "Mr. Hampton will see you now."

Caide stood, wiping the sweat from his hands onto his pants. He followed her through three ordinary looking conference rooms into Mr. Hampton's office.

"Mr. Hampton, this is Caide Abbott." Argus Hampton looked up from his desk. His face was stern, his eyes distant and cold. The thick, dark hair he boasted in his commercials was salt and pepper now, thinning a bit at the top. He stood, shaking Caide's hand firmly.

"Mr. Abbott, it's nice to meet you." He waved his secretary on and gestured for Caide to have a seat. "What can I help you with today?"

"First of all, I think you should know that I work for Mason and Meachum Law Office. You may have heard about the employee we lost yesterday." Hampton neither confirmed nor denied that he'd heard, so Caide continued. "They brought me in for questioning. I answered their questions honestly, but they still believed I had something to do with Blaire's murder. This morning every cop in town shows up at my door. I assumed they were there for me. Instead, they arrested my wife. I don't know why or what they have on her but she's being held in the county jail and they won't let me see her. My bosses won't represent her because it would be a conflict of interest. I know how successful you are. You're our biggest competition and I know the types of cases you win. We need the best that there is and that's you. Rachael didn't do this. I know my wife. She couldn't do this," Caide said again, turning the phrase around in his mind, forcing himself to believe it.

Hampton nodded, showing no emotion. "You're saying they arrested her on the spot? They didn't bring her in for questioning first?"

Caide shook his head. Hampton's expression told Caide how bad it was. "I'll tell you what, let me run down to the station and see her. I'll try to get her out on bail and find out what it is they've got on her." Caide nodded his head, relief washing over him. "Leave your number with my secretary, and my check. My retainer fee is ten thousand and I'm worth it. I'll call you as soon as I have news."

Caide stood to leave. "Thank you so much. I'll pay you whatever it takes for you to focus on this case. I need my wife back."

Hampton nodded. "I'll do what I can."

CHAPTER TWENTY-FOUR

RACHAEL

Brady Clemmons, the man in the cell next to Rachael, had stolen his girlfriend's car and ran her over with it. Rachael leaned against the cool metal bars of her cell, listening to him talk. He told her how he'd been in the army for eight years and how he'd grown up in southern Georgia. He told her about walking to the grocery store in the mornings with his grandma when he was young and how his pet German Shepard had passed away from cancer.

Rachael listened to his voice as it traveled through time. She heard it crack as he spoke of his best friend's last hours in the war and the laughter in his voice as he talked about the night he graduated from high school. He told the stories well and it was easy for her to forget what he'd done.

Suddenly, a buzzer sounded in the hallway and Rachael heard the door open. She looked up to see a man walking toward her. He was stern-looking, his graying black hair was neatly combed, and his suit fit his muscled frame well. There was something about his presence though, that made the room fall silent. He commanded respect.

He approached Rachael right away, turning angrily to the

officer following him. "Is there somewhere I can speak to my client? Alone?"

The officer pointed to a door off of the hallway and opened Rachael's cell. The man led her into the room, shutting the door behind them. He sat down at a table in the center of the room, avoiding Rachael's confused stare.

"Sit," he said firmly.

"I don't understand."

"Put your butt in this chair."

Rachael sat obediently, though her expression showed annoyance. "I know what 'sit' means. I meant I don't understand why you're here. I didn't ask for a lawyer."

"Your husband hired me. You can waive council if you'd like, but it'd be a mistake." He flipped through his paperwork. "My name is Argus Hampton. Your husband's bosses kindly refused to represent you, so he sought me. Wise choice. I'm going to do everything I can to help you. I just have a few rules we need to go over first: number one, do not tell me that you're guilty. I don't want to know. It's not going to change the way I represent you. Two, don't lie to me. Those rules almost always contradict each other. Be sure you don't break either. I'm not going to ask you anything that isn't pertinent to your case. If I ask you and you lie to me, you will be the one to suffer, not me. I can't tell anyone anything you don't want me to, so be honest. I need you to trust me and tell me what I need to know—*only* what I need to know. You will do exactly what I say. When we go to court, we will practice your testimony and you will stick with what we practice. No surprises. If you stray from the path I lay out for you, you will deal with the aftermath. Any questions?"

A million. She shook her head no.

"Good. Now, I have a few." He tapped a pen on the desk, staring at his notepad. "How did you know the victim?"

"She worked with my husband." She placed her hands on

the desk, folding and unfolding them nervously. She couldn't seem to sit still.

"How was your marriage?"

"Fine."

He raised his eyebrows. "If you're going to start breaking my rules already, I'll just go ahead and leave."

Rachael grabbed his arm instinctively as he stood to exit. "No. I'm sorry. Don't leave. My marriage is—"

"I don't have time for niceties Mrs—"

"My marriage is falling apart," she cried. "I love my husband. I do. But he puts so much focus on work and I focus on our kids. We're like business partners more than anything."

"How long had you known about the affair? Was it his first?"

She sucked in a breath. *The affair.* "Excuse me?"

"The affair between your husband and the victim. How long had you known?"

So this is what it feels like when your world comes crashing down. "I—I didn't."

He looked up at her. "You didn't? You didn't what?"

Rachael cleared her throat. "I didn't know my husband was having an affair."

"I asked you not to lie to me," he said. Rachael closed her eyes, trying to keep her tears at bay. She was silent, trying to think back. Could it be true? Caide and Blaire? "You know, you play the hurt wife card pretty well. We can use that in court for sure."

Rachael brushed away a tear. "I'm telling you I didn't know. I didn't know he was having an affair. You told me not to tell you I'm guilty because you already assume I am. You've accused me of lying to you twice in the five minutes since we've met. How can I trust you if you don't extend me the same courtesy? I didn't do this. I didn't kill her, for the record, and I didn't know my husband was having an affair until just now. I'm trying to hold it together but my life is falling apart all around me and I'd just appreciate it if you could at least pretend to be a little sensitive."

"We don't have time for sensitive. They're pushing your case to court quickly. That's not normal, which means they must have something good against you. Look, I know I said I don't want you to admit guilt and I'm going to try to find something, anything, to save you because I'm damn good at my job. But the affair matters because, if all else fails, we're going to have to look at a crime of passion charge. A few years and then good behavior could lead to parole. I'm going to do what I can for you, whatever I can, but you can quit playing innocent and save us a lot of time."

"I'm telling you I didn't do this. They can't have proof. They're bluffing."

"They aren't bluffing, okay? Not about this. Your arraignment is being scheduled for next week. You will stay here until then. Look, whatever they have on you, it was enough to lock you up without even an interrogation. From what I've gathered, you stand a decent chance at getting a temporary insanity plea. You are a first time offender, you've got an impeccably clean record, and your husband, whom you love more than anything, the man you share a home with, the father of your two children, was having an affair. People will sympathize with you. We'll say you were distraught, you snapped. I'll train you on what to say."

"You're going to train me to plead guilty to a murder I didn't commit?"

"If it comes to that, yes. I'm still getting up to speed on your case and looking for anything to get the charges dropped altogether. Usually that means pointing the finger at someone else. So, I'm looking for viable suspects. But, I'm just preparing you for the worst, in case that doesn't work.

I'm telling you that's the only way to get a crime of passion verdict. You were out of your mind with jealousy and you're sorry."

She slapped the table firmly. "Mr. Hampton, with all due respect, I won't confess. If that's your legal advice, if you can't figure out what truly happened, I'd be better off representing myself. I won't admit to something I'm not guilty of."

"If you won't do as I say, you will go to prison for a long time. This is my legal advice. That is what will help you. If you don't want my help, I'm done here."

Rachael stood up, her arms crossed. "Take me back to my cell. Tell my husband I want someone else. Anyone else."

"Trust me, no one else will take this case. It's too much of a risk. You'll get stuck with a public defender who's too overworked and underpaid to remember which case he's working on. I want to help you, Mrs. Abbott. I'm doing everything I can."

"Anything short of believing in me is not what I need."

"Fine."

"Fine." She huffed, walking to the door. She didn't speak to him as the officer walked her back to her cell.

Hampton watched her as he shut the door. "Take care of yourself, kid."

She stared back at him, hatred burning through her. She refused to look away until he was out of the hallway. Once he was gone she sank into the wall, the cold concrete scraping her skin the whole way down.

CHAPTER TWENTY-FIVE

CAIDE

ONE WEEK LATER

"Thanks again, Corie, I hope they weren't too much trouble."

"They were fine, Mr. A. Although they kept asking about Rachael. Have you heard anything?"

"Not yet. I should hear from her lawyer today. It's…it's going to be okay." He said it more to reassure himself than her. He didn't want to admit he'd driven to the courthouse today, expecting her to walk out before the day was over.

Corie nodded, walking toward the door. She stopped. "Oh, Mr. A?"

"Yeah?" Caide looked up at her.

"You should know that your children missed you today, too. It wasn't just Rachael they asked about. They really miss you some days." She paused. "Oh and, today at nap, Davis had some nightmares. If you give him some milk and sit with him, he's usually okay. If you sing to him, he'll fall right to sleep. He'll always ask for a story, but that just keeps him awake longer. I have class the rest of the week, but if you need me to take them to school or daycare, just let me know."

"Thanks, Corie." Caide shut the door behind her gently. He thought about turning on the TV but was worried he'd see something about the case that would make it all worse. Instead, he walked to the front porch, looking up at the stars. The peace of the moment allowed the day's events to flood his mind. He felt cool tears brim his eyes, not honestly sure who he was crying for.

Interrupting his thoughts, he heard his phone ringing from the living room. His immediate thought was that Rachael would answer it. On the second ring, he realized she wasn't coming and bolted inside. He grabbed the phone from the table. It was Hampton.

"Mr. Hampton, what did you find out? Did you see her?"

There was silence on the other line for a brief second while he heard Hampton take a breath. "I did see her. I'm afraid I don't have good news. The judge refused bail and her trial is set for six months from now."

"What? *Six months?*" Caide gasped, rubbing his head in frustration. "She has to stay in jail all that time?"

"The judge is trying to prove a point with her. He doesn't want to look soft."

"What do they have on her?"

"I'm meeting with the prosecutor and judge tomorrow to go over all the evidence. Whatever it is, her record's perfect, Caide. For them to hold her without bail, well I'm just not sure what I can do."

"I just don't understand what I'm missing."

"I think you should know, I advised her to take a plea bargain, one for a crime of passion. I think she'd have a real chance at getting a low sentence."

Caide paused before answering. "You think she's guilty?"

"I don't know everything yet. She's insisting that she's

innocent. But I'm telling you that by the looks of it: a quick arrest, no bond, and a speedy court date, it sounds like they've got quite a lot to convict her. In my professional opinion, pleading out may be her only option."

"Find out what they have on her. Find out what they have before I'll agree with you. I hear what you're saying. I know what this looks like, but I just need to know what they've got."

Hampton agreed. "Okay. I'll call you tomorrow once I've heard their case."

Caide hung up the phone, his heart feeling heavy. Could the woman he married have killed the woman he loved?

CHAPTER TWENTY-SIX

HAMPTON

Argus Hampton walked into Judge Daniel Crafton's chambers and grimaced at the prosecutor. Jeanna Avery was a very powerful attorney with a winning record that lawyers everywhere envied. Her blonde hair was tucked behind her ears neatly with pins and her suit had been pressed. She turned to him, nodding. "Hampton."

"Avery. Good morning, Judge Crafton."

"Morning, Hampton, take a seat. We have a lot to go over and I have to be out of here by ten." Hampton sat down, trying to read the look on Avery's face. "So, we're meeting to go over evidence on the trial of," he looked down at a file on his desk, "The State vs. Rachael Abbott. Charges against her being?"

"Murder one," Avery answered.

"Right. We have a bit of evidence to go over. Avery, whenever you're ready."

"On May twelfth at nine eighteen a.m. a nine-one-one call was received from the Law Office of Mason and Meachum, located at 118 North Raymond Street. Mr. Chester Mason reported that an employee of his was found dead on the bathroom floor of his office. Upon further investigation it was found that Blaire Underwood, a secretary for the law office, had been brutally beaten over the head and murdered. The medical examiner confirmed that the crime scene was where the murder had taken place. Her autopsy showed blunt force trauma to the parietal, occipital, and left temporal lobe, causing severe bleeding and swelling of the brain. The fatal hit was determined to be to the parietal lobe. Miss Underwood was dead within an hour."

She paused, glancing over her notes. "The murder weapon was a triangle shaped object, with one point being deeper than the rest, later determined to be the metal soap dispenser which contained fragments of the victim's hair, scalp, and blood. We also found blood not belonging to the victim on the soap dispenser. The owners of the law firm reported that they had left that evening around seven, leaving only three associates in the building: the victim, Caide Abbott, and Abbott's assistant, Brian Sparks. Mr. Abbott had missed work the day of the investigation so his assistant was interrogated. He revealed that Mr. Abbott had allowed him to leave shortly after seven, leaving only the victim and Mr. Abbott in the building. Shortly after the officers were able to locate and interrogate Mr. Abbott, he revealed that he and the victim had been in a relationship. According to the coroner, the death occurred at approximately eight thirty p.m."

Avery checked her notes once more. "We requested copies of the security footage from the office that night. After examining the security tapes," she paused for dramatic effect before continuing, "we discovered that Caide Abbott had in fact left the office at seven forty-five p.m., just as he said, with the victim very much alive. We also discovered that they had not, in fact, been alone in the office like they had thought. The security cameras are not in place in the back of the building, which is how we believe Ms. Abbott must have arrived, however, the tapes do show her watching her husband and the victim having intercourse. After her husband left, she approached the victim, led her into the bathroom, and left fifteen minutes later. The victim never left the bathroom. Upon her arrest, Rachael Abbott provided a DNA sample. We are still waiting to get those results back."

Hampton swallowed, rubbing his jaw. "Oh. Is that all?"

Avery smiled. "That's all."

He collected himself quickly. "You think that warrants first degree murder? C'mon. People are going to pity her. There will be women in the jury, wives who've been cheated on. Tell me you'll consider a plea bargain."

"Sympathy or not, it was a good thirty minutes before we see Ms. Abbott approach the victim, after she'd seen them in action. That's premeditation, even more so if we can prove that's why she went there in the first place." She thought for a moment. "I'd consider a plea for ten years plus probation."

"For a crime of passion? You've lost your mind. Try three years."

"This isn't up for negotiation, Hampton. Ten years and probation or no deal. Our case is solid." She sat back in her chair, looking smug.

He thought for a moment. "Fine. Let me talk to my client."

"Don't leave me hanging on this, Hampton. If I don't hear by the end of the week, the deal is off."

"I'll call you," he said to Avery. "It was good to see you, Judge Crafton."

"You too, Hampton. Take care." The judge waved farewell as Hampton exited his chambers and headed to his car. He climbed in, cursing aloud and slamming a fist into the steering wheel. He could kiss his latest winning streak goodbye.

CHAPTER TWENTY-SEVEN

RACHAEL

Rachael heard a knocking sound somewhere in the distance. *Bang. Bang. Bang.* She opened her eyes and rubbed sleep from them. A young police officer was beating on her cell door.

"Wake up," he said, apparently annoyed. "You have a visitor."

Rachael sat up, praying for just a second that it might be Caide bringing good news. Instead, she found herself looking into a face she'd hoped to never see again.

She walked to the cell door. "We have nothing left to discuss."

He stared into her eyes. "I met with the judge and prosecutor today. You're going to want to hear what I have to say."

Rachael backed up, allowing her door to be opened. She ignored the twinge of pain as his hands took hold of her wrists in the same place they always did. She was sure she'd have a permanent bruise there when she finally made it out. She allowed him to shove her down the hallway into the room where she'd met Hampton before.

"So what did you find out?" she asked as they entered the room.

Hampton paused, pulling out a chair and waiting for her to take a seat. "After reviewing the evidence against you, I have to stick with my original suggestion. A plea bargain is going to be your best bet. They've offered us ten years. I'd hoped for less, but it's certainly better than a life sentence. I think it's a fair deal."

Rachael's anger welled in her. "Didn't I tell you no? Didn't I tell you I won't plead guilty to a crime I didn't commit? I won't do it. I want you to fight for me. Even if you don't actually believe me, I'd like you to pretend you do."

"Rachael, with the evidence they have, you won't walk on this."

"What evidence? What could they possibly have on me? I'm innocent."

"They have you on tape," he blurted out.

"What?" She took a breath, clutching her chest.

"They have you on tape taking the victim into the room where she was murdered and then leaving alone. They likely have your DNA on the murder weapon. If this case goes to trial, you will go to prison for a whole lot longer. So, I'm telling you, I'm begging you, take the plea. It is your only chance."

She stared at him indignantly. "Then they're lying."

"God, woman, they're not lying. Why would they do that?"

"I don't know. Maybe it's a fake tape. Those exist, right?"

"Rachael." He looked at her seriously. "I know this is scary, okay? I don't, for one second, believe you planned this. I know that ten years seems like a long time but, with good behavior, we may even be able to lessen the sentence. I want to help you but you have to let me."

"In ten years, my daughter will be fifteen and my son will

be twelve. I'll have missed their whole life. How can that ever be okay?"

She sobbed aloud, standing up and walking to a corner of the room. She sank to the ground dramatically, pulling her knees into her chest. Hampton let her cry alone for a few minutes before walking over and touching her back.

"It's going to be okay. I know it doesn't seem like it right now, trust me I do, but it will be."

She looked up to him, unable to express how hopeless she felt. He sat down beside her. She noticed his eyes—they'd once seemed so cold, but the deep brown irises held a kindness she'd never noticed. "How can you possibly know it'll be okay? My life, my marriage, it's all over."

A pained look filled Hampton's face, and he let out a sigh. "It's not, trust me. It gets better."

"You couldn't possibly know that."

"I mean, I didn't get arrested for murder, no. But my wife cheated on me too. I, at least, know how that feels." He huffed. She looked at him, her eyes wide. "The pain goes away after a while. Prison isn't ideal, I know, but I promise you I'll work on getting your sentence lessened."

"What happened?" she asked.

"Nothing. It's no big deal. I just wanted you to know I've been there. Hell, most people have been there."

She wiped a tear. "Is it crazy to still love him?"

"No, it's not."

"Do you still love her?"

"No. But that took a long time."

"Tell me what happened. Please. It'll make me feel better."

"Hearing about my pain will make you feel better?" He laughed.

"Misery loves company," she said bitterly.

"Fine, but then you have to make a decision about the plea. I have to let them know soon."

"Deal."

He sighed. "Diedra and I were married young. I was only seventeen at the time. We were good together, but she wanted a family more than anything and I wanted to focus on school and my career. We fought about that."

He stared at the wall, avoiding her eye contact. "We started fighting too much. One day, she told me if I wouldn't give her a family, she'd leave me. I still remember that look in her eyes: wild, ravaged. It told me she was serious. So, I gave in. We tried for two years with no luck. Finally, one day she comes to me and tells me she's pregnant. It was so out of the blue. We were in the car and she just blurted it out. It was the best feeling. I didn't realize until that moment how much I wanted to be a dad."

Rachael's mind drifted with his story. He seemed to have forgotten where he was and who he was talking to. She rested her head on the wall behind them.

"When she was about eight months along, I got sick. I couldn't keep anything down and I lost a bunch of weight. I went to the doctor and they ran all of their tests. I found out I had testicular cancer. Apparently, it had been there for a while, and the hormone imbalance that helped to cause it had also caused me to be sterile. The doctor told me I'd never be able to have kids; that I'd *never been* able to have kids."

He stared at his hands, squeezing his fists together. "Of course I told him something must be wrong with his tests. I scheduled my surgery for the cancer and I went on my way. That night on our way home, I told my wife what he'd said and she said, 'This is our miracle, then. God has given us a miracle baby.' She cried the whole way home, I thought she was just happy."

"What do you mean?" she asked, when he didn't say anything else for a moment.

"The night the baby was born, she went into labor while

we were eating dinner. I remember suddenly feeling like I'd stepped in a puddle. It soaked through my socks and shoes. I rushed her to the hospital, and she had a quick delivery with no complications. The best luck we could've hoped for. When it was over, the doctor came to get me. I'll never forget that look on his face. Confusion, fear, even pity.

I thought my wife was dead. I thought I'd never see her again. When he said he'd take me to see the baby, I followed him. He took me to a room with a giant glass window where I could look at all the infants. I tried to look for my black hair or Deidra's round nose. When I was about to give up, I spotted my name: Hampton. It was a small bed in the far left corner." He pointed, as if she could see it. "In it was the most beautiful African American baby I'd ever seen—but it wasn't our baby. 'There must be some mistake' I told him. He just showed me to my wife's room without a word. I ran to her, sure she'd tell me it was a mistake or some cruel joke. Instead, I found her sobbing. I walked to her bed, gathering her in my arms and rocking her while she cried. For two days, I sat by her side, watching her nurse and care for a baby that wasn't mine. The day we were released from the hospital, I told her I needed an explanation. She handed me the baby while she packed. She'd always liked to stay busy when she was giving bad news. She told me how she'd met a man at the library. His name was Thomas Beckett. He was going to school to be a teacher and my Deidra had always loved reading. They had met at the library every day for months while I was in school. I'd been in school, busting my ass to make a better life for us, and she went off and got herself a boyfriend."

Rachael watched him carefully, anger still on his face after all this time. He continued. "After nearly a year of them seeing each other, he got accepted into a study abroad program and left. About a month later, she found out she was pregnant. So, instead of telling me the baby may not be mine, she just prayed it would be. Instead of preparing me, she let me find out the hard way. The day I told her about my cancer, she'd been crying because I'd confirmed her fears. She called Beckett that night after I'd gone to bed and told him about the baby. He told her he wasn't in a position to help her raise a child. She was a coward and a cheater, but no matter how mad I was at her, I'd fallen in love with that beautiful baby. I knew that my decision of whether or not to leave would decide his whole future. I remember his little fingers were so tiny, he used to wrap them around mine." He held his hand out as if he were touching his son's hands. "So I stayed. I raised him with her for two years. We named him Sawyer. He was the sweetest child, so happy and smart. One day I came home from work and they were just gone. She left a note on our bed, it said: Thomas came back. He wants to meet his son and make up for lost time. Thank you for all you've done for us.' That was it. No apology. Just three sentences. She took my son from me without so much as an 'I'm sorry.'" He scoffed.

Rachael spoke up. "That must've been horrible."

He blinked, looking her way. Suddenly, he seemed to realize how much he'd just revealed to a stranger. He cleared his throat. "It was. I've never told anyone that story and I don't like to talk about it. I just thought, maybe, it would help you to know you aren't alone. As far as I can tell, the only difference in our situations is that Thomas is alive and Blaire isn't. Between you and me, the only reason that is, is that I've never met the man. If he'd been at my house that day, there's a very real chance I'd be sitting right where you are."

Rachael pulled his arm off her shoulder, taken aback by his harsh words. "I need you to fight for me."

"What?"

"I've made my decision. I won't take the plea. I need you to fight this case. The tape is fake. It has to be."

"We'll lose."

"If we lose, we lose doing what I asked of you and I'll just have to be okay with that. I just can't plead guilty and know we didn't try. Please."

"Okay. I'll try. I'll investigate the tape. I'll do everything I can to help you, but just know that it's not what I think is best."

She nodded. "I know."

"You will likely go to prison for a long time."

"Then, so be it." With that, she stood, walking to the door and waiting to be released. Hampton opened the door and the guard led her back to her cell. She stepped in with all of the bravery she could muster.

"Take care of yourself," he said.

She nodded, refusing to speak. She'd said time and time again that she was innocent, but he refused to believe her. It stung and she couldn't help but feel anger toward him. Rachael could see in his eyes that he wanted to trust her. She just had to figure out how to make that happen.

CHAPTER TWENTY-EIGHT

RACHAEL

SIX MONTHS LATER

Despite the wait, the day of the trial arrived too soon. Rachael had been pacing back and forth in her cell for hours, much to the dismay of Brady, who kept waking up and yelling at her to keep it down. Every inch of her skin tingled with anxiety.

Officers had been walking past her cell all morning, their menacing smiles searing her. Rachael couldn't help but hope that maybe, just maybe, this time tomorrow she'd be in her own home again.

She watched the clock meticulously, waiting for the small hand to reach eleven. Soon, someone would come to collect her. They'd walk through the doors, pull her from her cell, and lead her to the room where her fate would be decided. She hadn't heard from her family in the entire six months she'd been in jail. She missed her children. She longed to hold and hug them again. She knew they must miss her as well. Still pacing, she rubbed her hands together attempting to dry the sweat from her palms. As the clock struck eleven she walked to the door of her cell, grasping the bars and waiting. After ten minutes had passed, she watched as the door finally creaked open and a group of officers walked through. The oldest one carried a pair of handcuffs. He stopped at her cell.

"Rachael Abbott?" She nodded. "It's time for your trial. Turn around and put your hands behind your back."

Rachael turned around, placing her hands behind her, and hoping he wouldn't notice how much she was shaking. She heard him slide her cell door open. He slapped the cuffs on her, squeezing them too tight. He pulled her through the cell doors and allowed her to look back at what had become her home. She prayed she'd never set foot in a cell again.

CHAPTER TWENTY-NINE

CAIDE

Caide sat in the courtroom just behind Hampton. His hands shook as the room began to fill. He reached up and tapped Hampton's shoulder.

"Hey. You never called me back. I've been trying to reach you. Did you find out anything new?"

Hampton stared at Caide, a grim look on his face. "Your wife is a stubborn woman."

The sinking feeling in Caide's stomach grew even worse. To his right, he heard someone let out a sob. He turned to see an older woman, probably in her late forties, with her brown hair stacked high around her head. Her eyes, even from across the room, were red and swollen. She glanced at him and Caide knew her immediately. He'd stared into those brown eyes so many times before, though they had been in a younger body. Blaire's mother looked away without any recognition, sobbing into her tissue.

Suddenly, the doors opened on the side of the courtroom and everyone fell silent. Caide watched Rachael walk into the room. She looked so small in the giant orange jumpsuit. She scanned the crowd. *She's looking for me*, he thought, but instead her gaze found Hampton. She was led to the bench where he sat. He watched Hampton pat her shoulder softly, giving her a small smile.

Don't you smile at my wife. Jealousy welled up in his stomach. Rachael hadn't even looked his way. The past six months had gone by in a blur, but until this moment, it hadn't occurred to him how much he'd missed his wife. Aside from missing her housework and cooking, he truly missed her presence. He wanted so badly to reach out and touch her, or even just to hear her voice, but instead he sat still, patiently waiting for her to look back.

As the judge entered, Caide was pleased to see a familiar face. Judge Crafton had worked several cases that Caide had been on before. He was a fair man. After being seated, the judge nodded to the defense table. "In the case of The State vs. Rachael Abbott, murder in the first degree, how does the defendant plead?"

Hampton looked to Rachael. She stood up, looking the judge in the eye. "Not guilty, Your Honor."

Caide watched Hampton visibly sigh. The judge pushed down his glasses to give a look of concern. "Very well. Counselors, you may begin."

Caide recognized the prosecutor as Jeanna Avery, a short, plump lady with blonde hair curled just below her chin.

She approached the jury, pressing her maroon suit firmly to her thighs. "Ladies and gentleman of the jury, I am Jeanna Avery, attorney for the prosecution. On May eleventh of this year, Blaire Underwood, a beloved daughter and friend, came to work just like any other day. What she didn't know was that she would never come home again. Today, you're going to hear from Blaire's coworkers, who will tell you how she was always willing to help out, how she was kind and loving to everyone, and how she may have trusted the wrong person. You'll hear from her best friend who will tell you how Blaire was focused and career driven until she met a man and fell in love and suddenly lost her way. The only problem," she wagged her finger in the air, "this man wasn't available to Blaire. You will hear from the owner of a local auto repair shop who will tell you how on the day of Blaire's murder, her tires were slashed: was it an innocent prank or prelude to a violent crime? You'll hear from detectives who have DNA evidence pointing to Mrs. Abbott being at the scene of the crime. You'll also see a tape that shows the defendant with the victim just minutes before the murder. All of this will help you see, without a shadow of a doubt, that Blaire Underwood's murder was not an act of self-defense or a crime of passion in the heat of a moment. It was nothing less than the merciless, premeditated act of a heartless woman." She stared at the jury, walking proudly back to her seat.

Hampton stood up slowly, walking to the front of the room. He began, the jury staring at him in awe. "The prosecutor is going to try and convince you that my client is a hardened criminal, deserving of punishment to the full extent of the law. I, however, would rather have you know the truth. I am going to lay out the facts for you—the facts that we know and the questions left unanswered. You see, for prosecutors everything is black and white, good or bad, right or wrong. Everything is simple. But we all know life doesn't work that way, right? It isn't always yes or no, this or that. As a defense attorney, we work with a lot of gray. We deal with the *in between*—the fine line, if you will. We are realistic. We believe in people. I believe in my client. I believe that people have bad days, and bad moments, and bad lives. I believe that at their worst, people can make decisions that will haunt them forever. All I ask is that you listen to what we have to say, listen to my witnesses, think about my questions, trust what we can prove, and question what we can't. If you do that…maybe, just maybe, you'll leave here today seeing a little more of the gray."

The jury nodded to themselves as Hampton took his seat again and Avery stood. "For our first witness, we'd like to call Miss Allie Olson to the stand." A young woman who had been sitting beside Blaire's mother stood up. She had long brown hair and walked slowly, wiping her eyes as she went. As she approached the witness stand she was sworn in and then allowed to take a seat. Avery walked toward her quickly.

"Hello, Allie. Can you tell us how you knew the victim… Miss Underwood?" She opened her mouth to speak, sniffling again. Before any words could come out, she covered her mouth, openly sobbing. Avery grabbed a box of tissues, handing them to the witness. She wiped her eyes, remaining silent for what seemed like an eternity.

Finally, she spoke. "Blaire was my best friend."

"How often did you see Blaire?"

"Once or twice a week. We used to be together a lot more, but she got busy with her work and I met my fiancé. We drifted apart." She began sobbing again.

"What do you mean she got busy with her work?" Avery asked, speaking over her sobs.

"Blaire was brilliant. Headstrong and stubborn, but driven. She was the type of girl who would obsess over a perfect GPA. She worked so hard to graduate at the top of our class, so when she took a job as a secretary, I assumed it was temporary. I figured she'd eventually put her degree to use. Instead, she stayed." She laughed through her tears. "Actually, she loved it. I'd never seen her so happy. The longer she was there, the more she worked: longer hours, weekends, whatever. She never complained."

"Do you think she put her career before her social life?"

She nodded. "I was her best friend, but I guess that isn't saying much because I was also her *only* friend. She never had any time to date or to go out with anyone. She was too focused on school and then work to ever make any new friends. She was so focused that it sometimes made it hard for others to get close to her. I think she wanted it that way. Until she met him."

"Who do you mean?" Avery coaxed. Caide groaned to himself as the witness pointed across the courtroom to where he was sitting. Avery's eyes lit up. "Let the record show that the witness has identified Caide Abbott, the defendant's husband. Allie, do you know how they met?"

"They worked together." Allie dabbed her eyes, her crying quieted for the moment.

"You said she made it hard for others to get close to her until she met him. Did Blaire tell you they were friends, Allie?"

"Yes. At first it was just a work thing, but then she told me they started hanging out outside of work."

"What did they do?"

"He took her to dinner. They went out for drinks."

"So, they went on dates?"

Allie shook her head. "She never used that word. He's married. Blaire's from a broken home. She never wanted a relationship with a broken man. It tore her apart how easily she fell for him."

"She fell in love with him, yet they weren't together?"

"She wanted to be. He said he didn't, but he kept taking her out. It never made any sense to me. Or to Blaire, for that matter, but she didn't want it to stop."

"How long did this go on?"

"For about three years, on and off. Some weeks I wouldn't hear about him at all, and some weeks he was all she talked about."

"At what point did they become involved romantically?"

"I'm not sure. Blaire wasn't proud of it. She kept the relationship pretty secretive. She told me about two years ago that he was going to leave his wife."

Caide shot up out of his seat. "She's lying."

Hampton lunged for him quickly, his eyes wide.

"Mr. Abbott, I don't allow outbursts in my courtroom. If you want your chance to be heard, by all means, step up to the witness stand. Otherwise, one more outburst and I will have you thrown out of this court quicker than you can stand," the judge bellowed.

Caide bowed his head. "I'm sorry, Your Honor. It won't happen again."

Hampton whispered, "What are you thinking?"

"She's lying. Put me on the stand."

"You know I can't do that. Avery would tear you to shreds."

"But she's lying."

"Counselor," the judge warned. Hampton turned away from Caide, ending the conversation. The attention fell back to the witness.

"I'm so sorry about that, Allie. Apparently *neither* of the Abbotts can control their emotions. Did Blaire tell you when she was going to leave her job?"

"She called me the morning that she was going to quit, the day she died. She had left her car at work and needed a ride. On the way there she told me she was quitting. She said she had to leave town."

"Did she tell you why?" Avery's brow raised in feigned concern.

"She just said she couldn't do it anymore. She couldn't keep letting him break her heart. I didn't blame her."

"Did you ever see your best friend again?"

"No." She was silent for a moment, dabbing her eyes again. "She called me that night. She asked if I could come pick her up from work."

"Did you?"

"No." Her voice grew shaky. "I told her I would, but before we got off the phone she said never mind. She said she had to do something and she'd call me back if she still needed a ride later. She never called back."

"Allie, I know how hard this must be on you. Could you tell us how Blaire sounded when she called you? Was she sad? Scared?"

She nodded, chewing on her bottom lip nervously. "She sounded upset, I guess, shaken up, but more than anything she sounded happy. She sounded really, really happy."

Avery patted Allie's hand. "No more questions, Your Honor."

CHAPTER THIRTY

HAMPTON

Hampton stood up, walking toward the witness stand and adjusting his red tie. "Allie, you stated that Blaire was your best friend, yet she suddenly started ditching you for her career and Mr. Abbott, correct?"

"She wasn't *ditching* me. She was busy. That didn't make her any less my best friend."

"But how did that make you feel? You must've been angry that she wanted to see you less."

She cocked her head to the side. "I was happy that she was happy. I have a fiancé and a life, too. I didn't just sit around waiting to see her."

"How did you feel about her relationship with Mr. Abbott?"

"Objection, Your Honor. This witness is not on trial. Where are we going with this?" Avery asked.

The judge looked to Hampton, eyebrows raised. "Withdrawn," Hampton said with a sigh. "You said the victim told you the defendant's husband was planning to leave her?"

"Yes."

"Did he?"

"*Objection*! Your Honor, my witness is not an expert on the Abbott's life."

Hampton raised a hand. "I'll rephrase. Did Blaire ever tell you that Caide Abbott had left his wife?"

"No," she admitted.

"Did you ever see them together?"

"No."

"Did you ever hear him say he *would* leave his wife?"

"No."

"Did she ever show you any proof that they were anything more than coworkers?"

"No, but—"

"You said she was heartbroken over him, correct?" he demanded, raising his voice.

"She loved him. She was devastated they couldn't be together officially."

"Had you ever met Mr. Abbott before this trial?"

"No."

"You'd never seen their relationship first hand?"

"Asked and answered, Your Honor," Avery called.

"Move on, Hampton," the judge agreed.

Hampton leaned against the witness stand. "Since you never saw the relationship, or any proof of it yourself, isn't it possible, Miss Olson, that Blaire exaggerated a bit? Would you say it's possible that the whole thing could be attributed back to wishful thinking?"

The witness shook her head. "She wouldn't lie."

Hampton held his hands out in a shrug. "She said he was leaving his wife two years ago and yet their marriage is still legal and binding today. Are you willing to swear under oath that you know Blaire and Caide Abbott were having an affair?"

She paused. "I only know what Blaire told me."

"Yes or no, Miss Olson?"

"No."

"Thank you. No further questions." Hampton walked back to his seat, adrenaline pulsing. He heard the witness step down from the stand and Avery begin to speak.

"For our next witness, I'd like to call Brian Sparks to the stand." Hampton heard cautious footsteps. He turned slightly to see a young man with pale skin and bushy black hair walking toward Avery apprehensively. As he was allowed to sit, Avery approached him. "Brian, as I understand it, you knew the victim quite well, is that correct?"

He cleared his throat, leaning into the microphone. "Yes. We worked together for nearly three years. I started just after her. Blaire was great."

"Tell me, when did you notice that the relationship with Mr. Abbott and Blaire was less than professional?"

He twisted in his seat nervously. "I didn't. I mean, they were friendly. No more than anyone else." He shot a look of apology toward where Caide was sitting. "Our workplace is complicated. Our bosses are great, they run the show. Blaire and Mr. Abbott were behind the curtain. They were a great team and they kept the place going. They had to work together a lot more than the rest of us. Dinners, early mornings, late nights. Of course we all had suspicions, but they were never founded. They were very professional."

"What can you tell us about the night Blaire was murdered?"

"Well, earlier that day, Blaire had put in her notice. She told me right after she did it. She asked me if I have any friends who were qualified to take her place. She really didn't say why she was leaving, just that there were things she wanted to do that she couldn't do here, which I understood. We all stayed late that night. Mr. Abbott had missed a bit of work after his car accident, so he was catching up. Blaire was looking at resumes, and I was running a few last-minute errands. We're all pretty guilty of late nights."

"Who was the first to go home?"

"I was. I left around seven thirty. Mr. Abbott and Blaire were still working."

"What made you leave when you did?"

"Mr. Abbott told me I could go home and finish tomorrow. My wife is pregnant, so he encouraged me to go home to her."

"That was sweet of him. Did he frequently send you home before your work was finished?"

He ran a hand through his hair nervously. "He's a great boss. He's never made a big deal out of my schedule as long as I get everything done on time."

"That's not what I asked."

"He was just trying to be nice," he said, his voice squeaking a bit.

"Yes or no."

He hung his head down. "No."

"So he wanted you to leave that evening?"

"Objection, Your Honor. She's leading. The witness can't speak to Mr. Abbott's intentions."

"Sustained. Watch it, Avery."

"In your opinion, did he seem to want you to leave?"

"No. He just seemed stressed. He was behind in his work, he hadn't left his office all day. In my personal opinion, he was being nice because he knew I had already stayed more than two hours over the time I'm scheduled to leave."

"Were there any cars in the parking lot when you left?"

"Mr. Abbott's. Blaire's was in the shop that day."

"To your knowledge, was there anyone in the building besides the two of them?"

"Not to my knowledge."

"Could someone have been there? Hiding?"

"Our office is pretty open. The private offices stay locked, so I don't think anyone could've hidden in there without a key and there was no one in the lobby."

"There was nowhere else to hide? Nowhere at all?"

He paused. "Not unless they hid upstairs, I guess."

"What's upstairs?"

"It used to be used for more office space, when a real estate company owned our building. When Mr. Mason and Mr. Meachum bought it out, they knocked down the walls and made it into a space for meetings and office parties. We rarely use it."

"Who knows about the upstairs portion of the office?"

"Only employees."

"And all of the employees were out of the office or downstairs, right?"

"As far as I know. I mean, I didn't check."

"So, as far as you know, the only people who know about upstairs and could've been hiding there were employees?"

"Yes."

"Except you just said you used the upstairs for meetings and office parties?"

"Yes. Okay, so I guess a few of our major clients may have known or anyone who's catered our parties."

"What about family members who attended office parties?"

"Well, yes."

Avery leaned in as if she were hearing juicy gossip. "Brian, had Mrs. Abbott ever attended an office party upstairs?"

He swallowed loudly into the mic. "Every Christmas."

"So Rachael Abbott could have, in fact, been hiding upstairs without anyone knowing?"

"She could have, I guess."

Avery smiled. "No further questions."

Hampton watched the witness visibly relax as Avery took her seat. He stood, walking toward the stand.

"Brian, had you met Mrs. Abbott before today?"

"Yes."

"What do you think of her? What's she like?"

"Objection. My witness is not here to character witness for the defendant."

"I just want to know his opinion of her, Your Honor. He's welcome to tell me her bad personality traits, if he chooses," Hampton argued.

The judge shook his head. "Overruled. The witness may answer."

"Rachael's great. She's always been very kind to everyone at the office."

"Thank you. Do you know if the Abbotts live near your office?"

"Everything in La Rue is pretty close. I believe they live about a half hour from the office if traffic isn't too bad."

"How long of a walk would that be?"

"I'm not sure."

"If you had to guess."

"I don't know. Maybe two hours?"

"So, since you didn't see Mrs. Abbott's car in the parking lot or surrounding areas, we're going to assume that, if we believe as the prosecutor would like us to, Mrs. Abbott walked to and from the office without anyone noticing she was missing?"

"I guess so."

"Thank you. No further questions."

CHAPTER THIRTY-ONE

RACHAEL

Dr. Alex Page was a medical examiner for the county. He spoke with a passion for his work that reminded Rachael of women in yogurt commercials. His thick brown hair and perfect smile helped the room to hang on his every word.

"So you examined our victim, is that correct, Dr. Page?" Avery asked.

"It is. The body was brought to me on the evening of May twelfth. I found the victim to be perfectly healthy before the murder, she had four severe blows to her skull. Two in the parietal, one in the occipital, and one to the left temporal lobe. The fatal hit was determined to be to the parietal lobe, though any of the blows would've proven fatal by morning."

"And what did you determine about how she died from the autopsy?"

"Well, from the pattern of her injuries, it appears she was struck from behind first. She was turning back to face her attacker as the injuries continued. The placement of the injuries also tell us the attacker was shorter than the victim. The victim was five-foot-six and she had been wearing heels, so add an inch or two. The attacker, by my calculations, must have been five-foot-four or five-foot-five at the very most. The force of the blows were extreme. The attacker used much more force than necessary to just knock out the victim."

"And what does that tell you?"

"When our bodies are scared or angry, our adrenal glands produce adrenaline. Adrenaline allows us to be quicker or stronger than we usually are. The fact that that much force was exerted on the victim tells us one of three things: the attacker was a male, the attacker was scared and acting in self-defense, or," he paused before continuing, "the attacker was angry."

"And were you able to determine which one fits our attacker?"

"Well, obviously there is no way to know for sure, but I was able to narrow it down. First, I believe I can rule out the idea that our attacker was male because, as I stated, the attacker was shorter than our victim. I don't know many men who are five-foot-four, though it's not impossible. There was also no evidence of rape, which is inconsistent with most male-on-female cases. I would also rule out self-defense. I don't believe our attacker was scared. For one thing, the attack started from behind, our victim facing away from the attacker, most likely caught off guard. Also, the attacker did not stop after the fatal blow occurred. From the angle of the last few injuries, it appears our victim had already fallen but was still being attacked. In most self-defense cases, the attacker would have hit until the assailant was down and then ran away, whereas a vengeful attacker would have hit until their anger subsided, which seems to be the case here."

"So you're saying?"

"In my professional opinion, with what evidence I have now, I believe our attacker was angry."

"Doctor, is there any way to know whether or not our victim knew her murderer?"

"Short of actually being there, there's no way to know for sure. However, we didn't find any defensive wounds on our victim. No scratches, no bruising, no hair between her fingers, or skin under her nails. It doesn't appear that there was a struggle, which does make me believe that our victim did, in fact, know her attacker and, therefore, was not expecting the attack."

"Dr. Page, you said you found no hair or skin cells on our victim, yet you did find DNA not belonging to our victim at the crime scene, isn't that right?"

"It is. Upon investigation of the crime scene, we found blood on the murder weapon that was not a match to our victim. It appeared as though the murderer may have cut his or her hand on the weapon during the attack."

"And were you able to find a match for that DNA?"

"The blood came back as a positive match for the defendant, Mrs. Abbott."

"Thank you. No further questions."

Hampton looked over at Rachael, who was visibly shaken. Her pale skin and purple lips made her look more ghost than human, and he was sure she was going to be sick. Hampton pulled the waste bin from beside him, placing it next to Rachael's feet. He patted her hand, standing up and facing the witness stand.

"Dr. Page, can you explain the pattern of the blows to the victims head again?"

"Objection. Your Honor, asked and answered again. If Mr. Hampton is not paying attention that is not the court's problem."

"I have a point, Your Honor."

"Answer the question, Doctor."

"As I said, the first blow occurred at the occipital lobe—"

"Can you show us where that is?"

The doctor sighed, turning in his seat to point to a spot on his skull just above his neck. "The first blow was here. They moved in a clockwise position around her skull hitting here, here, and here." He pointed around his head, stopping finally just above his left ear.

"And you said that pattern indicated what?"

"It indicates that the victim was attacked from behind. She was turning back to face the murderer as she was attacked."

Hampton paused, pretending to think. "That's what I thought you said. However, my question then becomes, if the victim was attacked from behind, why did the prosecution just use your testimony that the victim must have known the attacker because there were no defensive wounds? If the victim was, in fact, attacked from behind as you have now stated twice on record, would there be defensive wounds?"

"Not necessarily. The victim did turn around, though."

"Yes, as she was being beaten to death." He placed a hand on his hip in shock. "Are you saying she wouldn't have put her hands up, or tried to defend herself if it had been someone she knew attacking her? That she would've only protected herself from a stranger?"

"No. Obviously not."

"Then your testimony is, to be frank, useless, isn't that right?"

"I was only giving my opinion."

"Also, you stated that my client's DNA was found on the murder weapon. I'm assuming you found her fingerprints as well?" Hampton asked.

"No. We did not find any fingerprints that could be positively matched to Mrs. Abbott."

"Why do you think that is?"

"Most likely she was wearing gloves."

"So it is your opinion that my client wore gloves to attack Miss Underwood from behind, but the metal soap dispenser she used during the attack was able to cut through her gloves and into her hand, causing her to bleed enough that it would be found by your team. You didn't, however, find any fingerprints from my client, presumably because she wore gloves, correct?"

"Yes."

"How many prints did you find on the murder weapon?"

"We found twelve distinct pairs."

"Okay. How were you able to determine that there was more than one person's blood at the crime scene?"

"The crime lab found two separate types of blood. Our victim was O negative. The murderer was A positive. We ran the results against both Mr. and Mrs. Abbott as well as several different control subjects, Mrs. Abbott matches eleven out of thirteen of the markers for the DNA."

"Eleven out of thirteen? That doesn't seem very certain."

"Quite the opposite, those are very good odds. Cases have been proven for nine out of thirteen, some even less. It means there are only about one thousand other people in the entire world who could've committed this crime."

"And yet those people aren't on trial."

"There is an eighty-five percent chance that Mrs. Abbott is our murderer, based solely on the DNA evidence alone. Those are great numbers."

"So you say. What I'm hearing is that there is a fifteen percent chance we could send an innocent woman to prison. Babies are born every day simply because condoms have a fifteen percent failure rate."

"It is impossible to have a one hundred percent match.

We had a very small sample to work with; my team and I are very happy with the results we received."

"You're perfectly happy with eighty-five percent? Let's say, for a second, I bake a batch of cookies. I give you a cookie and I tell you that if you eat it there is an eighty-five percent chance you won't be poisoned, would you eat it?"

The doctor scoffed. "That's ridiculous."

"I'm simply putting things into perspective. There's an eighty-five percent chance, Doctor, that you'll eat this cookie and go on the rest of your day, perfectly healthy and with your sweet tooth satisfied. Are you going to eat the cookie or aren't you?"

"No. I wouldn't risk my life over eighty-five percent."

Hampton grimaced, walking back toward his desk. "No, just my client's life. No further questions, Your Honor."

CHAPTER THIRTY-TWO

CAIDE

Just as Hampton took his seat, Rachael grabbed the waste bin below her feet and began emptying her stomach into it. The courtroom erupted with people jumping up, shouting, and gagging. Caide leaped to her side, reaching for her hair. A bailiff rushed forward, restraining him.

"I just want to hold her hair back. She's my wife." He struggled to reach her. Hampton stepped in front of Caide, grabbing Rachael's hair as she sat up. He handed her a tissue and a glass of water, continuing to hold her hair.

"Can we get a recess, Your Honor?"

"Very well. We'll reconvene in thirty minutes. Everyone clear out and get some air. Bailiffs, take the jury back to the deliberation room and escort Mrs. Abbott back to her holding cell."

The bailiff finally let go of Caide, taking hold of Rachael's arm. Hampton threw Caide a stern look.

"Calm down," he said as he walked past, following closely behind Rachael.

Caide couldn't help but notice Hampton touching the

small of Rachael's back as they disappeared through the courtroom door. He felt as though he were going to be sick himself.

CHAPTER THIRTY-THREE

RACHAEL

The bailiffs led Rachael into a cell larger than her usual one. She felt lightheaded and her legs wouldn't stop shaking. There were hands on her back, leading her, but she couldn't tell whose hands they were.

She heard someone talking, a voice, mumbling under their breath. Everything sounded so distant. She sat in a corner, pressing herself into the solid wall, listening to the shallowness of her own breathing.

Her hands were cold as ice. She tucked them under her legs, trying to warm them. She watched the shape of a person walk her way but she couldn't make her eyes focus on who it was. She saw two gray pant legs in front of her. The legs were talking. Why couldn't she understand them? She only saw fuzziness, only gray. She held her stomach, terrified she was going to be sick again.

CHAPTER THIRTY-FOUR

HAMPTON

Hampton walked down the dimly lit hallway to where Rachael was being held. At the end of the hall were two guards. They stepped aside, allowing Hampton to pass through. He looked around the cell, expecting Rachael to be sitting at the small table in the center of the room. Instead, it took him a few moments to locate her sitting in the far corner, knees to chest, staring blankly into space.

"Rachael," he called softly, trying not to spook her. She didn't look his way, didn't acknowledge his presence at all as he walked toward her. She didn't seem to notice she was crying, tears cascading down her cheeks. He inched toward her, afraid to move too quickly.

"Rachael," he said again once he was standing in front of her. He bent down, wiping her tear-stained cheeks with his sleeve. She didn't look up at him. He'd planned to come talk to her, make her see reason. He'd hoped that seeing all the evidence the prosecution had would make her understand that he was only trying to help her. He had planned to try, once again, to convince her that a deal was the only thing going to save her. Seeing her silent tears fall, however, made him think twice about saying anything.

Instead, he slid down the wall beside her, watching her hands shake as she cried. She leaned her head onto his shoulder, acknowledging his presence for the first time. He slid his arm around her shoulders, pulling her into him. He knew legal advice was not what she needed right now. This, this moment right here, was all she had needed since he'd met her, and he was finally ready to let her have it. He let her cry and cry some more, sobbing openly for everything she'd already lost.

CHAPTER THIRTY-FIVE

RACHAEL

The legs had moved. They were standing in front of her, but now she felt them beside her. He wasn't talking. Or maybe he was. She couldn't be sure. Rachael had never felt so lost and alone as she did in that moment. Her stomach was churning again, ready to blow at any moment, and her hands would not stop shaking. She leaned her head over onto something soft and warm. The smell of fresh linen and a soft smelling cologne eased her stomach. His scruffy cheek scratched her forehead, but she didn't mind. For the first time in weeks, Rachael felt safe. She watched him shift his hands, her eyes starting to find their focus once more, onto hers. Her fingers found the warmth they'd been craving. She cried, her tears coming from a place she could not explain, emptying her soul of an endless pain.

She tried to find her voice, to tell him thank you, but it was hidden deeper in her chest than she could reach. Instead, they sat softly, him gently rocking her back and forth, and her pretending she was anywhere but here.

CHAPTER THIRTY-SIX

CAIDE

Caide walked the halls of the courthouse, looking for one person. She had to be there somewhere. Suddenly, the doors to a hallway he'd yet to check opened and he saw her emerge.

"Avery," he called, running toward her.

She crossed her arms, smiling. "Caide Abbott. You're the last person I'd expect to come looking for me."

"I need a favor."

"And why would I do you any favors?"

"I need you to put me on the stand."

She stared at him for a second, her expression stoic. "You know I can't do that."

"You can. I'm requesting it."

The smile left her face. "You have to know that's a suicide mission. I mean, I want to win this case as much as the next person, but to win like this—it hardly seems fair. What could you possibly have to gain?"

"She didn't do this, Jeanna. I have to do what I can to help my wife. They won't even let me talk to her. This is all I know to do."

"Abbott, look. I can't imagine what this must be like for you, but you aren't thinking clearly. I hardly think of you as a friend, but I'm not completely heartless. Being a witness for me, it's only going to hurt your wife's case. I won't help you. I won't go easy on you. I came to win."

"Hampton won't put me on the stand."

She nodded, her eyes wide, brow raised. "For good reason. There are laws in place for a purpose."

"Look, I know what I'm doing. It's got to be you. I'm not asking you to do me any favors. I'm not asking you to go easy on me. I know what I'm getting myself into better than anyone. Please. Just put me on the stand."

She was silent, staring at him haphazardly. "I'll talk to the judge. I'm not making any promises. You'd better know what you're doing, Caide."

"I do."

"I won't go easy on you."

"I know."

"I'm going to make you look really, really bad."

"I know that too."

"I'm going to use everything you say and everything in my power to make sure that your wife goes to prison for a long, long time."

"And I'm going to use everything in my power to make sure she doesn't."

Avery nodded as Caide turned to walk back toward the courtroom. She was tough. He knew a lot about her from Mason and Meachum. She'd had three rough marriages and lost her son a few years ago. Caide had seen her be ruthless and he knew today would be no different. He knew she thought he'd just given her the golden ticket to win this case, but he was planning to use that every bit to his own advantage.

CHAPTER THIRTY-SEVEN

JUDGE CRAFTON

"You want to do *what*?" Daniel Crafton was a reasonable man. In his eight years as a judge, he'd seen a lot of crazy things in his courtroom, but never had he been asked what he was being asked now. "Avery, you've got to be joking. You know the laws."

"The law says that the husband and wife can choose to waive it. Caide Abbott has requested this. He knows what he's doing, Your Honor."

"Of course he doesn't. If he did, he wouldn't ask. What does he have that makes him think this is a good idea?"

"He wants to help his wife. He's usually one of us, Daniel. But today is different, today he's a hurting husband on the opposite end of the bench. Today, he's just like any of them. He thinks he can help."

"You think he can't?" He leaned forward in his chair.

"Hampton won't put him on the stand. Whatever he's planning to say, I'm not worried about it hurting my case. I don't believe he's thinking straight." She crossed her arms.

"I wouldn't be." He rubbed his temple, taking his glasses off his nose.

"Look, I agree it's probably a bad idea. I didn't like it at first either, but if this is what it takes to lock up a guilty woman, then so be it. I have to try. A woman is dead, Daniel. He was having an affair with that woman; maybe he was in love with her, I don't know. I can't imagine this from his point of view, but it's time for him to decide who he's loyal to and if I can use that to my advantage, then I'd like the chance to do that. I just want justice to be served, through whatever means necessary."

"Fine, but you're going to tell the defense, not me. Where is Hampton?"

"I haven't seen him since you called recess. I can check with his client?"

"No, send a bailiff. You stay here and come up with a damn good reason why this is a good idea. If there's one thing I don't need, it's to be on Argus Hampton's bad side."

CHAPTER THIRTY-EIGHT

BAILIFF ISAAC LAWSON

"Bailiff Lawson," came Avery's voice through the empty hallway. "Go get Hampton quickly please. Tell him the judge needs to see him immediately."

Lawson nodded. "Yes, ma'am." He took one last sip of his Dr Pepper before throwing it out. He walked through the hall of holding cells, all full of people waiting for their trials. Even working around criminals daily, they still made Isaac nervous. Finally, he reached the cell where Mrs. Abbott was being held. He stuck his key into the door and pulled it open.

He laid eyes on Mr. Hampton along the wall, Rachael Abbott's head resting on his shoulder. Unmoving, they sat side by side, both of their eyes closed. They looked so comfortable, it was easy to forget they were sitting in a jail cell, rather than on a cozy back porch somewhere.

As Isaac took a careful step toward them, Hampton's eyes shot open. "Sir?"

A look of realization filled Hampton's face. He lifted Rachael's head off of his shoulder, leaning her onto the wall he'd been pressed up against. Standing up quickly, he brushed himself off and cleared his throat. "What is it?"

"Avery is in with the judge. She's asking for you—says it's urgent."

His face grew serious, the embarrassment fading. "Did she say what it was about?"

"They don't keep me in the loop, sir."

"Right, of course. Thanks. I'll head that way. Hey, listen, could I get you to stay with my client?" he asked, turning around as he got to the door.

Isaac swallowed, looking at the defendant, whose eyes were now open, staring dreamily into space.

"For God's sakes, kid, she's not going to kill you." He lowered his voice. "She's had a rough day. She just needs someone to stay with her." He moved the chair out from the table. "Just, here, sit in this chair and watch her. Please."

Isaac sat down, keeping his chair a safe distance from the defendant. He'd been working at the courthouse for only about a year now so he was mostly thrown on small cases: petty theft, a few drug charges, even a kidnapping once. He'd never been in the same room with a killer before. He wasn't *scared*, he told himself, just cautious. He still had a lot to live for.

Hampton rolled his eyes and darted from the room. She didn't move, not a single muscle. It was as if she thought if she was still enough, unnoticed enough, she might disappear forever. Isaac could swear he never even saw her blink. Was she even breathing?

After a few moments had passed, his heart rate slowed down. There was something about her that made him feel at ease, made him almost feel sorry for her. But she was a killer. He couldn't allow himself to feel sorry for a killer.

As if she'd heard his thoughts, her eyes turned to meet his. They say eyes are the windows into the soul. Isaac had seen many convicts in his line of work and he made a point to remember their eyes. They almost all had the same look, especially on their court date: empty, cold, cruel.

Rachael Abbott was one of the others—the different ones—the ones Isaac hated the most. It was them with their puppy dog eyes, their fake tears, and their faces with glimmers of hope that made him sick. It was this small group of convicts that made his job so hard. It was hard to hate someone, hard to convict someone, hard to hope for their downfall when they looked so...completely…innocent.

CHAPTER THIRTY-NINE

HAMPTON

Hampton walked to the judge's chambers with dread filling his stomach. He pushed the door open and was immediately met by Avery's smug grin.

"What's this about?"

"I've added a last minute update to my witness list, Hampton. I just wanted to let you prepare."

"Who?" he demanded.

Avery smiled, folding her arms across her chest. "Caide Abbott."

"My client's husband?" He looked to the judge. "You've got to be kidding me. You're allowing this?"

"Mr. Abbott has requested it," Avery answered for him.

"There are laws against this. You can't be serious."

"Those laws are to prevent trouble in the marital home, Hampton. I think we're way past that, don't you?" Avery asked.

"Judge?" Hampton begged.

"Hampton, the husband has requested it. I don't know why, but we're all just going to have to let this play out. Avery, you so much as step over the line once and I'll pull him from the stand. Hampton, you can use this to your advantage too. He wants to defend his wife, so let him. I don't like this one bit, for the record, but I'll admit I'm a bit curious as to what the husband has up his sleeve."

"Thanks." Hampton grabbed the door handle, anger boiling inside him. Caide Abbott was going to ruin his wife's only chance at freedom and Hampton had no idea why.

"Oh, and Hampton?" the judge called before he was completely out the door.

"Yeah?" He stopped.

"Prepare your client," he said, an apology in his eyes. "This won't be easy on her."

"None of this is," Hampton called over his shoulder, storming out the door.

CHAPTER FORTY

CAIDE

Caide's heart pounded. He tried to get a good look at Rachael, attempting to read her face but she wouldn't look his way.

Avery stood, looking out across the courtroom. "For our next witness, the prosecution would like to call Caide Abbott to the stand."

Gasps rang out throughout the courtroom. Rachael looked down, refusing to meet Caide's worried eyes. Whispers followed him as he approached the witness stand, and they were only silenced as Avery began her questioning.

"Mr. Abbott, could you tell us the nature of the relationship between the defendant and yourself?"

"I'm her husband," he replied, looking the jury in the eyes.

"And you've asked to serve as a witness today of your own accord, is that correct?"

"Yes."

"You weren't paid or coerced in any way?"

"No. It was my idea."

"Thank you. Now, can you tell the jury what your relationship was with the victim?"

A lump formed in Caide's throat. He'd known it was coming, but that didn't make it any easier. "We worked together."

"You are under oath, Mr. Abbott, just a reminder."

"She was in love with me." He sighed. "There isn't an answer to this question. We were close because we worked together. We had feelings for each other, feelings that shouldn't have happened. They were a mistake. We weren't actively together, she wasn't my girlfriend, and we weren't having an affair. She was a friend."

"Did you sleep together?"

"Yes. Once." He kept his eyes on Avery.

"On the night of her murder?"

"Yes."

"It was also pointed out earlier that you frequently took her out to dinner. Is that correct?"

"For work, yes."

"How many times?"

"Over the course of three years? I don't know."

"More than twenty?"

"Yes. Usually about once a week, so three or four times a month."

"Did your wife know about these dinner dates?"

"Again, not dates, but yes she did."

"And did these dinners include alcohol?"

He looked down at his hands in his lap, his face on fire. "Occasionally, yes."

"Were you ever alone with Miss Underwood for the dinners?" She leaned onto the witness stand as if they were old pals.

"Of course, a few times. I also ate alone with Brian, Mason, and Meachum on several occasions each. We work at a law firm that requires a lot of long hours and late nights. There is no difference in the dinners I had with Blaire versus the dinners I had with my other coworkers."

"Tell us, Caide, did you have sex with your other coworkers?"

A few of the jurors chuckled. Caide threw them a menacing glare. "No."

"There's your difference, then. So, walk us through the day Miss Underwood was murdered."

"Blaire was already at work when I got there. Her car had been left there because we had a dinner and she rode with me—at the request of our bosses. When I got there, her tires had all been slashed and the tow truck was there picking up her car."

"Let me stop you for a second, you took Miss Underwood to dinner?"

"Yes. With our bosses and a client."

"Why didn't you bring her to get her car afterwards?" "I just didn't. We were out late; we were both tired. I just took her home without thinking about it."

"Miss Underwood didn't ask you to take her to get her car?"

He paused, trying to word his story correctly. "It was a stressful night. We'd been in a fight. I didn't think about her not having the car until the next morning."

"Did you go into the house with her that night?"

"No."

"Anyone who can attest to that? A roommate? Maybe a neighbor?"

"No. I don't think so. It was late."

"Did you have sex with her that night?"

"No."

"Did you have intimate relations of any kind?"

His lips were tight as he answered, trying not to think of that night. "We kissed. It was a mistake."

Avery nodded. "So, you kissed her, you were fighting and then you dropped her off with no car. Was she upset?"

"Of course she was."

"Upset enough to call your wife? Tell her what had happened? Upset enough to set you up, to allow your wife to catch you two in the act?"

"God, no. Blaire wouldn't do that. She was mad, sure, but she still cared about me."

"So, when you got home that night, did you see your wife?"

"She was asleep."

Avery nodded. "Okay. Now, back to the day of the murder, Miss Underwood's tires were coincidently slashed, just after you'd had a fight with your mistress, what next?"

"We didn't see each other much that day at all. At some point during the day, she put in her notice. I didn't know she was planning to until it was already done. She never even told me why. I'd missed a few days of work after my car accident so I stayed at the office to work late. When I got ready to leave, Blaire and Brian were still there. I sent Brian home, as you know, because he had been working late. I was planning to head out myself. Before I left though, I admit, I wanted to talk to Blaire. I wanted to know why she was leaving, to make sure it wasn't because of me. Instead, I made a mistake." He looked at Rachael for the first time, his eyes pleading with her to forgive him. "I made a horrible mistake."

"You had sex."

"Yes." It wasn't a question but he answered anyway.

"Did you call your wife to let her know you'd be late?"

"Yes, I did."

"Did you tell her why?"

He looked down. Avery was getting way too much enjoyment out of this. "I told her I was working late."

"So you had sex with Miss Underwood. What next?"

"It was over as soon as it started. Blaire kept hearing a noise. She thought someone was upstairs."

"What kind of noise?" Avery asked, walking back to check her notes.

"I never heard it. I thought maybe it was just a janitor. We never checked to see; we were too embarrassed."

"So what did you do?" she asked, staring back up at him.

"I left. I went home. I mean, I offered to wait but she was upset and I freaked out. She said she'd call a cab and I could go, so I did."

"How gentlemanly of you. So, when you arrived at your home, was your wife there?"

"Yes. She was asleep."

"So you went straight to bed?"

"Yes. Well, no. I took a shower first."

"Are you a light sleeper, Mr. Abbott?"

"I don't know. Sort of."

"What I'm asking, Mr. Abbott, is: if your wife were to get out of bed in the middle of the night to, say, I don't know, commit a murder—would it have woken you up?"

"Yes. It would have. I always wake up when she gets up in the night to use the bathroom or if the kids have a nightmare."

"So you can be absolutely certain then, under oath, that your wife never left your bed that night?"

Caide started to nod, but stopped, thinking back to that night. "She never came to bed."

"You just said—"

"I said she was asleep, yes, but she was asleep in my daughter's bed. She never came to ours."

The jury looked at each other in shock but Avery didn't miss a beat. "Did that strike you as odd, Mr. Abbott?"

"My daughter is five. Rachael usually makes it back to our

bed once Brinley falls asleep, but occasionally she doesn't. I didn't think anything of it."

"Was she still in your daughter's bed when you woke up the next morning?"

He thought for a moment. "No. She'd woken up before me. She was fixing breakfast when I woke up."

"And what was her mood like?"

"She was happy, I guess. She was fixing breakfast for everyone."

"Did your wife ever give you any indication that she'd known about your affair?"

"It wasn't an affair, but no."

"Would she have told you?"

"Of course she would have. Rachael is smart. If she'd even had a hint that this was going on, there's no way she would've stayed. The morning she was arrested, we were having a fight about me letting my kids down. She was ready to leave me over that. There's no way she would've stayed if she'd known about Blaire. My wife is a strong person. She is a good person. She's the best person I know." He looked at Rachael, searching her blank expression. "That's how I know she couldn't have done this. She's amazing. She never pays our bills even a day late, she donates to homeless shelters and food pantries, she never forgets a birthday or an anniversary, and she's *always* there for me. She is a good person. A good person did not kill Blaire. My wife did not kill Blaire." Rachael smiled at him, briefly, but he'd seen it.

"Mr. Abbott." Avery stepped up to block his view of his wife. "I know you don't want to believe your wife is capable of this, but the fact is that *someone* killed Blaire Underwood. Whoever that someone is, they had access to the office keys, just like you; they had a reason to want Miss Underwood out of the way, just like you; and they were at the office that night with her alone, just like you. It seems to me that someone knew you were with Miss Underwood alone that night, they knew you'd be the last to see her and they'd made sure all of your coworkers were there to attest to that. They also knew your semen would be inside of the victim. They knew you'd been fighting with Miss Underwood. They knew once news of the affair was released, you'd have a motive. Adding all of this up, it almost seems like someone was trying to frame you for murder, Mr. Abbott. Someone who was angry at you, angry enough to kill and let you go down for it."

Caide swallowed hard, watching Rachael out of the corner of his eye. He looked to the jury who looked as shocked as he felt.

"So, you tell me, is there anyone in your life that would have more reason than your wife to want Miss Underwood out of the picture?"

Caide was silent. He'd made a horrible mistake taking the stand, it was written all over Hampton's dismayed face.

"Mr. Abbott?"

"No," he said quickly, not willing to meet anyone's eye any longer.

"Thank you." She turned to Hampton, her heels clicking as she strutted across the room. "He's all yours."

Hampton stood up, making no effort to hide his frustration with Caide. "Mr. Abbott, on the night of Blaire's murder, did you see your wife's car at the law office?"

"No."

"Did you notice it parked close?"

"No."

"Was it at home when you arrived?"

"Yes. It was parked in the garage," Caide said, trying to keep up with the rapid-fire line of questioning Hampton was throwing at him.

"Your wife was also at home?"

"Yes, asleep in my daughter's room." *As I said earlier.*

"Is your daughter a light sleeper?"

"She's five. Of course she is."

"Was your wife dressed for bed when you arrived home?"

"I don't remember. I'm sure she was."

"Wouldn't it have struck you as odd if she'd been dressed in ordinary clothes while in bed?"

"Of course."

"So you believe you would've noticed that?" Hampton stared at the jury, the judge, and the audience. His eyes didn't land on Caide once.

"Yes."

"Okay. So, according to the prosecution's theory...one of two things happened: One, your wife either walked, hid her car very well, or took a cab and was somehow at the office hiding, watching you with your girlfriend. She then waited until you left, murdered Miss Underwood, left your office, either drove, rode, or walked home, changed into her pajamas, and climbed into bed with your daughter without waking her, just in time for you to arrive home and find her, even though you were both traveling the same distance and you had an obvious head start on her." He shook his head. "The other scenario still involves your wife mysteriously arriving to your office in time to watch you without anyone seeing her, she then would've had to beat you home, change into her pajamas, wait until you fell asleep, hope that Miss Underwood was still at the office, drive back, commit the murder, then sneak *back* home in time to cook you breakfast. All the while, never waking you or your daughter up, never being seen by anyone, and since you mentioned her car being in the garage, somehow moving it in and out without alerting anyone she was leaving. Tell me, Mr. Abbott, short of your wife *literally* being able to time travel, do either of those scenarios seem plausible to you?"

"No. They seem crazy."

Finally, Hampton looked his way, a smirk on his face. "How long have you known your wife?"

"Six years. We celebrated our sixth anniversary in May."

"Are you a good husband?"

The question caught him off guard, causing him to open and close his mouth twice before answering. "What kind of a question is that?"

"One that our jury needs answered."

"I love my wife."

"That's not the question."

His face burned from the scrutiny and he wondered if Hampton could hear his heart pounding in his chest. "Look, I work a lot. Rachael hates it. The job that I work requires longer hours than I'd like, but I love my job. I haven't been fair to my wife, no, but I've never physically hurt her. I make sure we have the money to pay our bills and keep our family healthy. I'm a provider. I've always been. I'm not a romantic husband. I wasn't raised to be loving or nurturing. I'm not a present husband. Apparently, I'm not a faithful husband, so I guess you'd probably say no, I'm not a good husband. I do love my wife, though, and I've tried my best."

"No further questions, Your Honor." As he turned, Caide saw a hateful glare in Hampton's eyes. Caide sensed that he'd enjoyed seeing Caide humbled much more than he expected.

CHAPTER FORTY-ONE

RACHAEL

Rachael stared at her folded hands on the table, listening to Avery's heels clicking across the floor. Her head reeled from Caide's testimony.

"Mr. Smith, have you ever seen this woman before?" Avery held up a picture of Blaire, twirling it around so everyone could see her pretty smile leap from the page.

"Yeah, uh, she called my guy Rudy. Said her tires had been slashed. I went out to pick up her car at some law office."

"And when you got to the law office, what did you see?"

"Her." He pointed to the picture. "She was by her car. All of her tires was flat, had been for a while I think."

"Did you see that man?" She pointed across the court room to Caide. Mr. Smith scratched his head and squinted toward Caide.

"Yeah, he was there. He came running at me, too, like some lunatic, said 'Put that car down!' That's what he says to me. I told him, I said, 'I was called here to pick it up, buddy.' He was real mad at me, that's for sure. Like I was stealing his car or something."

"How did Mr. Abbott act toward Miss Underwood?" Avery asked, pointing to the picture again.

"Well, he was real nice to her, *real* protective. Kept watching me with her car. I thought maybe he was her boyfriend or something."

"You did?"

He nodded, wiggling his eyebrows. "Yeah, it sure seemed like it. You don't get that upset over a coworker, you know what I mean?"

"So you were a complete stranger, and yet you picked up on their relationship?"

He squinted his eyes, and Rachael assumed he must've been trying to look wiser. "They just seemed real close."

"Funny, then, that Mr. Abbott doesn't think his wife noticed." She raised her eyebrows at the jury. "No further questions."

Hampton stood from his seat briefly. "I have no questions for the witness, Your Honor."

"Very well. You may step down, Mr. Smith."

Mr. Smith climbed down from the witness stand, looking like a dog awaiting a treat. Avery stood from her seat, glancing at Rachael with unforgiving eyes. "The prosecution calls Detective Stan Wallace to the stand."

As she said it, a sharply dressed man in the back of the room rose from his seat, not looking directly at anyone. At the same time, a woman walked to a room hidden behind the judge's bench and rolled out a television on a cart.

"Mr. Wallace, can you tell me if this is a picture of the crime scene?" Avery asked, holding up a picture to a visibly disturbed jury and then to the stone-faced witness.

"It is."

"When did you arrive on the scene?"

"We received a call just after ten that morning and arrived just before eleven."

BECOMING MRS. ABBOTT

"Why wasn't a call made until ten? Surely a law office opens earlier than that."

"The staff at the law office is primarily male, excluding the victim, of course. No one entered the restroom where the body was discovered until a client stumbled upon it accidentally."

"And everything was left untouched until you arrived at the scene?"

"Well, it is a law office. They are very familiar with crime scene protocol."

"Who did you question first?"

"First, we spoke with a Mr. Chester Mason and a Mr. Bart Meachum, co-owners of the law office, followed by the client who found the body, a Mrs.," he looked at his notes and read, "Agnes Wimbledon. We then spoke to Brian Sparks, Mr. Abbott's assistant, and finally, Mr. Abbott himself."

"Did you question any of the janitors? It was earlier brought up that they may have been working upstairs during Mr. Abbott's rendezvous with the victim."

"We weren't able to speak with them that day, however, we have questioned them since. They were both off duty the night of the murder and both had solid alibis."

"What did you notice when you arrived at the crime scene?"

"The blood. There was a lot of blood, consistent to that of a head injury, but nothing ever prepares you for that. We noticed she was dressed and showed no signs of rape. We found the murder weapon, a metal soap dispenser with traces of blood on it, had been placed back on the sink where it had come from. The coroner determined that the victim had been dead about fifteen hours, which put the time of death at approximately eight fifteen the night before. All stories were consistent in stating that Mr. Abbott was the last to see the victim. He claimed to have left her alone and alive at around seven thirty. He, of course, became our prime suspect. We questioned him. He seemed suspicious, for sure, but news of the affair could have been the cause. We had no real evidence against him, so we requested copies of the security tapes. The owners were very cooperative with our efforts. We found pre-ejaculate inside of the victim, which was later determined to belong to Mr. Abbott."

"Now, you mention the security tapes. We have a copy of those here, is that right?" Avery asked, pointing to the television.

"Yes," he confirmed.

"At this point, Your Honor, we'd like to present exhibit seven for the court's viewing—security footage from The Law Office of Mason and Meachum the night of May eleventh."

She stepped back so the screen could be seen, pressing play with ease on her remote. Rachael could only see the side of the screen closest to her, but that was enough to tell her what was happening. She watched as her perfect little husband, her good husband, her husband who'd *'done his best'* screwed his secretary for the world to see. Rachael's blood boiled, she felt rage in the pit of her stomach unlike anything she'd ever felt before. She wanted to look away, but couldn't pull her gaze from the screen. Her eyes burned with tears, but she couldn't allow herself to cry. She tightened her jaw, her vision clouding with hatred. She hated her husband in that moment, more than she'd ever hated anything or anyone. She hated him with every fiber of her being, every ounce of her soul. She sat, the embarrassment of the situation written on her face, and pretended like it didn't bother her.

She felt Hampton's eyes on her, rather than on the tape, and wanted nothing more than to lash out. But she couldn't. She had to control herself.

"Your Honor," he called out, his eyes still locked on Rachael. "Is this necessary? Can't we just skip to the actual evidence? There's no reason to put my client through this torture."

"What's the matter, Hampton? Your client can't *control her temper*?" Avery asked, dragging the last three words out to prove her point.

"Actually, I think, considering the circumstances, my client is doing an exceptional job controlling her temper. It's inhumane to expect her to watch this. Please, Your Honor."

They both turned to the judge, who nodded. "I agree with Hampton, Avery. Have some decency. Skip to the end."

"Your Honor, I think it's important for the jury to see—"

"The jury has seen more than enough, Avery. As have I. Skip ahead or I will ask you to turn it off and dismiss your evidence altogether."

"Yes, Your Honor." Avery paused the movie on a not-so-flattering shot of Caide. There were chuckles heard throughout the crowd. She began fast forwarding, much to the amusement of the jury. A scream of rage built up in her chest. No one looked empathetic. Not a single person looked as though they realized they were watching someone's marriage being torn to shreds instead of a Saturday morning cartoon.

Avery paused the tape, tapping the screen. "Ah. Here you can see Mr. Abbott leaving the building. Notice the time, seven forty-five, just as he said. Miss Underwood watches him leave and then immediately grabs her phone. We see her dialing. Phone records along with Miss Olson's statement prove that's who she called. Now, we will see, watch the left corner closely…" She paused, watching as Blaire chatted happily on the phone. Rachael saw something shift in the far corner. "Up until this point, we couldn't tell that this shape was actually a person. As the tape goes on, you see the defendant moving toward the staircase and then walking down the stairs to approach the victim."

The jury gasped. Rachael looked up and saw a faint figure walking down the stairs. The blonde hair became increasingly clear the closer to the camera she became. As the figure moved closer, it became obvious to everyone, including Rachael, that she was staring at herself.

It's a crazy feeling, seeing yourself in a place you don't remember being. Like looking at photos of yourself from childhood, you know it's you, but you don't remember it. You can't think back to that day and remember how the ice cream cone tasted or how the water felt coming at you from the water hose. You can't remember exactly what your great grandma smelled like that day, or how that wrapping paper felt under your fingers. With baby pictures, you expect not to remember. You just smile kindly at someone else's memory, and then turn the page. This was different, though. Rachael watched herself walk across the screen. There were no words to explain how utterly confused and hopeless she felt.

"As you can see, the defendant stands in front of Miss Underwood. She remains calm, almost emotionless. Miss Underwood hangs up the phone. As this video doesn't have audio, and the film isn't clear enough to read lips, we can only guess that Mrs. Abbott must've said something to coax Miss Underwood into the bathroom with her. After a few moments...*yes*, there they go. Mrs. Abbott leads the victim into the bathroom, which as we know is where the body was later found. I'll fast forward just a bit because they were in the restroom together for around seven minutes." She stopped the video just as the bathroom door crept open. "And here you'll see Mrs. Abbott leaving the scene of the crime. Alone."

CHAPTER FORTY-TWO

HAMPTON

Hampton watched Rachael turn green right before his eyes. Her hands left sweat prints on the table when she moved them, which she couldn't seem to stop doing. He'd been sure she was going to pass out more than once.

Finally, he stood. He'd prepared himself for this moment, but he knew there was no true way to prepare to have someone mop the floor with your case.

"Detective Wallace, did you have any specialists look at the tape?"

"My team of forensic analysts, yes."

"I see. Now, maybe it's just me but these tapes certainly seem a lot more clear than the tapes shown on the news. Why is that?"

"Well, it's been enhanced, obviously."

"How do you mean?"

"We've enhanced it through a government-approved software."

"So, you've changed it?"

"No. Nothing was changed. It was put through a filter to remove the excess grain and enhance the quality."

"You just removed a bit of grain?"

"We were also able to pull bits of the video together, all through an approved software. It's sort of like a puzzle. It fixed the pixels to make them more clear."

"So, it guesses at what each pixel is supposed to look like?"

"I wouldn't call it a guess, no. More like an educated estimation. A very, *very* time tested, educated estimation."

"Right. Now, this educated, government approved *guess*... it shows my client leading Miss Underwood into the bathroom, correct?"

"Yes."

"Not pushing?"

"No."

"Not chasing?"

"No."

"In fact, my client is the one being followed, is that correct?"

The detective locked his jaw, obviously frustrated. "Yes, we can only assume Mrs. Abbott coerced—"

"You know what they say about assuming, don't you?" Hampton asked with a wink. "You also see my client leaving alone, right?"

"Yes."

"As I recall, earlier, it was pointed out that my client's fingerprints were not found on the murder weapon, correct?"

"No, they were not."

"In fact, it's my understanding that my client's fingerprints were nowhere to be found in the entire building, is that also correct?"

"Yes, but on the tape, you can see she isn't seen touching anything."

"But...she would've had to touch the murder weapon,

unless we're going to assume that along with being a time traveler my client is also telekinetic?"

The detective all but rolled his eyes at him. "She most likely wore gloves or wiped off her prints."

"Most likely." Hampton wagged a finger in the air. "See, here we go with the assumptions again. You say she may have wiped off her prints?"

"Yes."

"Yet she didn't manage to wipe off any of the other twelve sets of prints?"

"Apparently not."

"And she forgot to clean up her own blood or, better yet, get rid of the murder weapon altogether? She also seemed to have a blatant disregard for the security cameras, which I'm told are housed upstairs. If my client had been hiding up there, she would've seen the camera screens and known exactly where not to go. Now, let's go with the gloves theory again. It seems plausible, I guess." He walked to Avery's desk and grabbed the remote, rewinding the tape. "We see here my client enters the restroom. Tell me, Detective, is my client wearing gloves?"

He stared at the screen for a moment before answering. "No, she's not."

Hampton nodded, fast forwarding the tape. "And here she's seen leaving. Is she wearing gloves here?"

"No, but she could've taken them off."

"Did you find any gloves in that bathroom?"

"No, we did not."

"My problem with your theory is simple. In this video, my client isn't making any effort at all to hide her identity. Why would she put gloves on and take them off before and after the murder? Would she have had that kind of time? And let's just say she did—she took them off. If she didn't hide them at the crime scene, where are they? She's hardly dressed to conceal anything. So where did these gloves go?"

"I can't answer that."

"I see. Well, Mrs. Abbott." He turned to face Rachael, giving her a wink. "It looks like we've just added disappearing acts to your list of magical powers."

CHAPTER FORTY-THREE

CAIDE

Caide had to admit it: Hampton was impressive. For a case that had been declared open-and-shut, he had singlehandedly managed to drill holes in each of the prosecution's standpoints. The problem, however, was that he didn't have much of a defense. No solid alibi, DNA and video evidence standing against them, and a clear motive—Caide knew this was going to be a long shot. If Hampton managed to somehow pull this off, it would be nothing short of a miracle.

"As our first witness, the defense would like to call Audrey Hagen to the stand."

Caide's head jerked back, skimming the crowd for a familiar face. Before he knew it, there she was. Her icy blue eyes met his for only a moment, but he caught the flicker of anger in them. Caide hadn't seen Audrey in so long, though her visits used to be a common occurrence around their house. Up until two years ago, anywhere Rachael had gone, Audrey would follow, and vice versa. She wore her thick, black hair loosely around her shoulders, her stare unwaveringly solid as she was being sworn in. Her gaze didn't falter as Hampton approached her.

"Mrs. Hagen, you are a friend of the defendant, is that correct?"

"Rachael is my best friend." She flashed a reassuring smile across the courtroom to where Rachael sat, her Southern accent rearing its head already.

"Where did you meet?"

"Oh, she's been my best friend as far back as I can remember. We were in kindergarten together. Our dads worked together even before that."

"I see. Audrey, what can you tell us about your best friend?"

"Rachael is great. She's one of those people that you meet and you just latch to. She's so genuine about everything. She's that person who asks how you are and actually wants to know. She has always focused more on everyone else than herself, even to a fault. She's completely selfless; I've never met anyone like her. She volunteers every chance she gets. She'd literally give you the shirt off her back if it came down to it. Rachael tutored all throughout high school and college. She even skipped Junior Prom to tutor this freshman who was flunking algebra. I don't think she even thought twice about it. That's just who she is, you know?"

Hampton nodded, urging her to go on. "When we were in college, I was out every night: drinking, partying, whatever. I'd come home drunk as can be and Rachael never judged me. She never had a harsh word to say about me. She'd just be there. She'd clean me up and help me to bed. Some nights she'd stay up with me all night, just to keep me from choking on my vomit. Then, the morning would come and she'd have Tylenol and orange juice waiting for me, and she'd help me study for whatever I'd be too drunk to pass later that day anyway. I still remember the day she told me about this guy who'd asked her to tutor him in his psychology class. Apparently he'd offered to pay her four hundred dollars a session if she could help him pass the semester."

She paused, nodding slowly. "Rachael could've used the money. Instead, she made him volunteer at a local hospital with her—every Saturday afternoon for the whole semester. Knowing Caide, I'm sure he hated the idea at first, but Rachael grows on you. She has a way of making everything seem okay."

She stared at the mic, seemingly lost in her thoughts. After a moment, she looked up, moving a piece of hair out of her eyes. "Anyway, a few months later she stopped tutoring as much, and a few months after that she stopped altogether. Her nights were pretty much all taken over with Caide Abbott." She rolled her eyes playfully. "All Caide, all the time. They fell in love. For the first time in my life, I watched my best friend do something that was entirely just for her benefit. When her dad passed away our senior year, Caide was there for her. You should have seen them back then, they were so damn happy together. I think she brought out the best in him, and maybe he brought out a little bit of selfishness in her, which was exactly what she needed at the time. I think they needed each other. I've never been a big believer in fate, but I swear it was like the universe knew Rachael would need him that year. He loved her in a way I couldn't, and I'll always be grateful for that. He saved her that year. He was the only thing keeping her above water." She glanced at Caide, a small, sad smile on her face.

"But the thing is, Rachael needed Caide. She needed him to be a good husband and a good father. She's the kind of person who puts everything she has into the relationships and the people she loves. She gives and gives and gives, and if you have someone like Caide, who takes rather than gives back, eventually I think she had nothing left to give. Rachael was born to be a mother and a wife. She was made for it. She didn't deserve to end up this way. I'm not saying anyone deserves to be cheated on, but that girl right there?" She looked at Rachael. "She's one of the good ones. She didn't deserve this."

Hampton opened his mouth to speak, but Audrey wasn't done. "But you know the very best thing about Rachael? She takes the high road. She forgives and forgets. I've never seen the girl hold a grudge. If she had known about the affair, she would've forgiven him. She may not have stayed, but she would've forgiven him. She probably would've forgiven Blaire too. That's who my best friend is." She looked at the jury. "Look, I know you guys have to look at the facts, and, as far as the murder goes, I can't tell you much. I can tell you anything you want to know about Rachael Abbott, though. The biggest thing you need to know, is that she didn't do this. She's better than any of this. She deserves better."

As she said her last sentence, her eyes met Caide's one final time, and he saw only regret looking his way.

CHAPTER FORTY-FOUR

HAMPTON

Hampton smiled as Dr. Seth Carrigan took the stand. "Dr. Carrigan, can you tell our jury how you came to be acquainted with the defendant?"

"Sure." He shifted nervously in his chair. "I am a neurosurgeon at Hanover Baptist Hospital. I was the attending on duty on the day the Abbotts were involved in a serious car accident. Rachael Abbott was brought in to see me after a fellow doctor noticed her pupils were not responsive to light."

"And what can you tell us about Mrs. Abbott's condition when she came into your care?"

"Rachael had suffered a mild head injury and a few minor injuries. She was, however, responsive and alert by the time she arrived into my care. Her MRI showed some swelling in her left temporal lobe, a cerebral edema, which we were able to reduce with a drug called Mannitol and proper ventilation. Mrs. Abbott was released twelve hours later, once we were sure the swelling had gone down, with instructions not to sleep for an additional twelve hours."

"Twelve hours doesn't seem very long to hold her for such a severe head injury, is that typical?"

"It can be. I refused to release Mrs. Abbott until the swelling was completely down. She was closely monitored until that happened. Once the swelling had gone down, I felt comfortable abiding by the patient's wishes and releasing her. At the time of her release, all vitals were stable and had been for at least six hours prior."

"So you're saying the patient asked to be released?"

"Yes. She was a scared mother, unsure of whether her children were okay and her own problems were the last thing on her mind." His statement came out as more of a complaint than anything, so Hampton was surprised when he smiled dotingly at Rachael. "I'd expect no less from a mother. So, when I could find no other reason to hold her—"

"Are you saying you wanted to hold her?"

"It would have been ideal, yes. It is the best practice to hold head injuries, even minor ones, for at least twenty-four hours."

"Why is that, Doctor?"

"Head injuries are complicated—even unpredictable. The best defense we have is observation."

"What are some common side effects to head injuries?"

The doctor sighed. "Well, it depends on the severity of the case, obviously. Some of the common side effects are nausea, vomiting, dizziness, blurred vision, memory loss, slurred speech, drowsiness, headaches, sensitivity to light, irritability, loss of consciousness, blackouts, depression, seizures—the most serious being death. Of course, there are dozens more. Some people experience several, some none. We never know what to expect. I did tell Mrs. Abbott the risks and that if she were to experience any she needed to come straight back."

"I see. I heard you mention blackouts. Can you explain that to us?" Hampton asked, glancing at the jury.

"Sure. Several hundreds of head injury patients report blackouts each year, slots of time they can't remember. Some end up places without remembering how they got there. The best way I know to describe it is…you know how sometimes you are driving home from work and you pull into your driveway and suddenly realize you don't remember any part of your drive home? It's comparable to that, but worse. Patients have reported blacking out for hours, even days."

"It sounds a lot like sleep walking."

"Yes, it's almost exactly like sleepwalking. When blacking out, the person is no more in control of their actions than a sleepwalker. Sleep is the closest thing we know of to a coma. Studies have shown, during these blackouts the patients would be in a coma-like state, unaware and unable to control or recall his or her actions."

"Is there any way to prove a blackout has occurred?"

"Unfortunately, no. There is also no way to *disprove* an occurrence. Science just isn't there yet. We have yet to discover exactly what causes blackouts. Similar to seizures though, we are able to predict them merely seconds before they occur. Unfortunately, once a blackout is believed to have occurred, there is no way to truly know."

"Could an injury like the defendant sustained, in your opinion, cause symptoms such as a blackout?"

"She had substantial swelling in her brain for nearly two hours, and slight swelling for almost four. Although her swelling was gone before we released her, the brain is a mysterious thing—even to those who study it. In my opinion, and that's all this is, a patient with head injuries similar to Mrs. Abbott's had a possibility of suffering from any of the symptoms I listed previously, including blackouts."

CHAPTER FORTY-FIVE

CARRIGAN

Hampton's eyes relayed a distinct message to Carrigan: he'd done well.

"No further questions, Your Honor," he said, stepping away from the witness stand.

Carrigan spied the corners of Hampton's mouth trying not to smile and it made him practically giddy. Okay, being around Hampton made him giddy regardless, but so what? Carrigan had always been happy to help him out on cases when he could, and he genuinely liked the guy. He'd been happy to know his expertise could prove useful once again.

The lawyer to his left stood up, her stone cold eyes glaring at Carrigan as if she could read his thoughts.

"Dr. Carrigan, you've said it's possible that Mrs. Abbott experienced these so-called *blackouts*." She made air-quotations as if he'd been suggesting Rachael might have been under a witch's spell. "Do you have any statistics or research to back that up?"

"As I said earlier, there is no specific rhyme or reason to head injuries, but I did provide Hampton with several studies dealing with patients who have claimed to experience black-

BECOMING MRS. ABBOTT

outs, as well as findings from the vital check method that I described. It's all just theory at this point, but it is a widely accepted anomaly in the medical world. Each case is just incredibly different."

"So, basically, we should just take your word for it? Or better yet—her word for it?" She gestured toward Rachael.

"No, of course not. Any medical professional will tell you exactly what I'm telling you. There's no way to know, no way to predict, and no way to prevent the side effects of a head injury. Hampton will be happy to provide you with the studies we have found. It's a very real thing."

"I see. So, you released your patient without being sure she was going to be all right? 'Against your medical advice' is what they call it, I believe?"

"Yes, that's correct—against medical advisement."

"I'm assuming she was required to sign a medical release before checking out, is that also correct?"

"I was not the doctor who had her sign it, but yes. That is hospital policy."

"Why?"

"Well, we have patients sign them in situations like Mrs. Abbott's, basically releasing the hospital from any fault or malpractice suits due to the patient leaving without allowing us to follow through completely with their care. They sign stating that they agree that the hospital staff has informed them of our intent to care for and treat their injuries and given them a list of any possible adverse effects that may result from them waiving our care."

She wrinkled her nose. "So basically Rachael Abbott signed a waiver stating that she was aware of *every possible* outcome from refusing care? She assumed all responsibilities for everything she might or might not do because of her untreated ailment?"

"Yes."

"And were blackouts listed as a possible side effect?"

"Yes, of course."

"You're sure?"

"Positive. I went over the list with her myself."

"So if, by chance, Rachael had left the hospital, had a seizure on her drive home, and hit someone, she assumed liability for that?"

"Objection, Your Honor!" Hampton shouted. "My witness is not a lawyer and, therefore, not capable of answering a question of that magnitude. That is a question best directed at the hospital's legal department, and seeing as how that is not, in fact, the situation at hand, we should move onto something more relevant."

"Your Honor, this is *completely* relevant. If Mrs. Abbott has assumed responsibility, by signing that waiver, for a situation like that, how can Hampton hope to use this as a defense in a situation like this? The defendant accepted responsibility for whatever her actions may be. Rachael Abbott knew something like this could happen and she signed that paper and left the hospital that night anyway."

"I have to agree with Hampton, Avery. I see what you're saying, but it's not the situation at hand. Strike that question from the record and do not answer, Doctor."

Carrigan swallowed hard, his palms sweaty. Avery sighed, poorly attempting to hide her disdain. "Doctor, you've told us that Mrs. Abbott knew the risks of leaving the hospital before her twenty-four hours of observation were up, right?"

"Yes."

"You said twenty-four hours specifically. Not until she was better or until she was stable, but twenty-four hours. Why is that?"

"Well, typically we prefer to hold patients overnight, our goal being twenty-four hours of observation. Particularly with head injuries. During that time, we monitor our patients for any signs of duress. Obviously, if there are complications, their stay could be extended. Typically, stability for twenty-four hours is a great indication that they're going to be just fine."

Avery touched her hand to her chin, feigning deep thinking. "So, most symptoms show up within twenty-four hours?"

"Typically, yes. The first twenty-four hours are critical. If the symptoms don't present themselves within that time, even in a small degree, chances of them occurring drastically decrease."

"Twenty-four hours, huh? So I'm guessing that after thirty-six hours, chances drop again?"

"Of course. They drop continually."

"They'd drop even lower after forty-eight hours then?"

"Yes."

"And again after seventy-two hours?"

"Correct."

"Then, tell me Dr. Carrigan, how likely are symptoms to appear after approximately…one hundred and twenty hours?" She shrugged her shoulders as if she were just throwing a random number out, but Carrigan spotted something primal in her eyes that had him using every bit of his mental math skills to try and quickly figure out how long that would be. Long enough to be in the clear, most likely.

"Doctor?"

"Very slim. I won't say impossible, because in my line of work we've seen it all, but I'd go so far as to say I don't believe I've ever seen it before."

"According to the paperwork Hampton provided the court with, you treated Mrs. Abbott on May sixth. Miss Underwood was murdered on May eleventh. Forgive me, my math skills aren't what they once were, but that leaves five days between the accident and the murder. One hundred and twenty hours, give or take a few. Would you still say, given that time frame, that it's likely our defendant was suffering from a symptom due to her accident?"

Carrigan met Avery's cold glare. "You know, I've been a doctor for fourteen years, plus eight years of medical school, and five years of residency. After you do something for so long, you start to think you've seen all there is to see." Her eyes narrowed at him as he spoke. "I once had a patient come into the ER with acute abdominal pain in the left side of her pelvis. She had had a hysterectomy six years before that so we ruled out cysts on her ovaries and began exploring other options. When we did an ultrasound on the area, do you know what we saw?"

"Tell me."

"An ovary. An ovary so covered in cysts, it was ready to rupture. Her pathology report showed that her ovaries had been removed, but I guess they left some cells behind by mistake. Maybe two cells, maybe twelve. We saved that woman's life."

"Well, bravo—"

"Have you ever heard of a phantom limb?"

"No, I can't say I have." She crossed her arms.

"It's when amputee patients experience sensation, particularly pain, in a limb or limbs that no longer exist. That's actually quite common."

"What's your point, Doctor Carrigan?"

"My point is, Mrs. Avery, no matter the odds—everything is possible. Every single day we see things that are literally impossible: patients with no chance miraculously recover, seemingly healthy people are given two weeks to live, hearts keep beating, comas end. So I can't tell you that Mrs. Abbott had blackouts, but I can't tell you she didn't either. There's no way any of us could possibly know."

Avery pressed her lips together. "One last question. You

told us Mrs. Abbott had to be sedated because she was so worried about her children."

"Yes, that's true." It wasn't a question, but he answered anyway.

"In all the time you were treating her, did Mrs. Abbott ever show concern about her husband?"

Carrigan thought back to that day, caught off guard by the question, but he knew the answer immediately. He swallowed. "No. She did not."

"Thank you." Avery offered him a stiff smile, walking away from the stand. Hampton, however, wasn't smiling. Instead, he was staring at Rachael, who was thrusting her head into the trashcan, filling it once again.

CHAPTER FORTY-SIX

RACHAEL

Hampton's arms led Rachael through the hallway toward her cell. She could no longer see through her tear-filled eyes. He rubbed her shoulders, helping her to sit in the chair.

"Can I get a tissue in here?" he yelled over his shoulder to no one in particular.

Rachael heard the compassion in his voice, compassion she hadn't noticed before. She couldn't help feeling grateful for all he'd done for her. Without Hampton, she felt as though she might just slip off into nothingness, and at this point she couldn't help feeling like even that would be better than where she was.

Hampton took a paper towel from an officer and kneeled down so he was eye level with her. He wiped her chin, gently pushing her hair back from her face. His gentleness only made Rachael cry harder.

"Don't cry. Talk to me."

Rachael sat back, trying to recall the last time she'd even heard her own voice. Had it really been days? "I need to know. Do you believe I could've killed that girl? Honestly?

You believe that I blacked out and killed her? How could I possibly forget something like that?"

Hampton stood up, not breaking eye contact. He walked toward the door with a quickened pace. Rachael watched him approach the guard.

"I need a private word with my client. No one is to come through this door. Let me know when we have five minutes left."

He shut the door without waiting for a response and turned back toward Rachael. "I don't know what to believe, Rachael. From the time you met me you've hated me, pushed me away, even yelled at me. I'm trying to do my job. I'm doing it the best way I know how to but I need your help. I needed your help six months ago when we could've made a decent case instead of doing this all on my own. You wouldn't help me, you wouldn't give me anything to work with. Hell, you didn't even tell me about the accident. I had to find out on my own."

"You wrote me off as guilty the second you took this case. What good would it have been for me to talk to you?"

"Look, I get it. This sucks, but Rachael, this is happening. It's real. I'm sorry for that, but sorry doesn't fix it. Right now we need to deal with this because in about an hour, a decision will be made and it'll be too late, if it isn't already. I'm out of witnesses; I'm out of ideas. This is where I need you to suck it up and just talk to me. I'm going home either way after this, it's your choice what happens to you."

Rachael wiped the tears from her cheeks. "You're right."

"Thank you."

"No. You're right that you can't imagine what this is like. Before this, my life was good. Apparently, not as good as my husband's, but good. Before this, my biggest concern was making sure that my daughter finished her homework or that my dance class was ready for their recital. Then the accident happened. The moment I lost control I just started praying. I prayed and I prayed that God would protect my family. On the way to the hospital the EMT's couldn't tell me anything. I didn't even know if my family was alive. So, I started bargaining with God: if my husband lives, I won't fight with him anymore. If Brinley is okay, I won't yell at her about her messy room ever. If Davis survives, I'll never complain about watching Elmo again. My prayers were answered, Hampton. My family was remarkably well. After the accident I thought we would all get closer. I thought we'd all realize how important we were to each other. And do you know what changed? Nothing. We went back to normal almost instantaneously: late nights at work, dishes piling up, never ending laundry, the kids fighting. I was hurt by how quickly it all went back to usual."

She closed her eyes, her forehead wrinkling. "Do you know what I would give to go back to the normal I hated so much? On the morning I was arrested, I'd made up my mind to leave my husband. We were fighting when I noticed the first cop car pull into our driveway. All sorts of terrible scenarios played in my head. I thought maybe something had happened to his parents or our friends. My studio was broken into last spring, so I wondered if maybe it had happened again. I never once thought that they were there for me. *Not once.* I'm not a criminal. I pay my taxes on time, I don't run stop lights, and if I leave a store and realize I forgot to pay for something, I always go back. I never dreamed they could be there for anything but sympathy."

She looked away, her chin quivering. When she could speak again, she turned to him. "Caide knew though. He told me to hide, thought they were there for him. I thought he was joking. When something that off the wall happens your brain doesn't comprehend it. I can't explain it. He told me to hide, take the kids and hide. He didn't want them to see him being arrested. I went and woke Brinley up, throwing our son over my shoulder and toting them to my bedroom. I held them in my arms and we waited. When my bedroom door opened, I expected Caide. Instead an officer walked in. He told me to stand up, said that he was there to arrest me."

She wiped a stray tear away, her voice shaking. "It all seems like a dream now. I remember how hard the cuffs were, slamming into my wrists. I tried to smile at my children—I try to teach them cops are nothing to be afraid of, but I was terrified. I didn't know Blaire. She was always just a girl at Caide's office. Until this trial, I didn't even know her last name. Then you came in. That was when I realized how very real this all was. Caide hates you. You're his biggest competition and I knew he'd never hire you, unless it was serious." His eyes locked on hers as she spoke, his thumb rubbing her hand. "But you never even thought I might be innocent. In the movies, the lawyers always believe their clients, but you never believed in me."

"I was trying to help you, Rachael. I opened up to you about my wife because for the first time, I understand the person I'm representing. I understand the crime. I've never worked this hard for a case. Never. I usually wouldn't have even taken a case with this much against us. I *want you* to win. I do not want to see you go down for this."

She shook her head. "I still don't understand it. In jail, I just kept quiet. I didn't talk to anyone, I didn't eat much. I became a shell of myself. I thought if I was still long enough I'd finally wake up and this would all just be a terrible dream. Even in court I kept waiting for the big reveal—for someone to jump out and yell 'got ya.' I want to believe someone is setting me up, but when I saw that video...that was *me* standing there. It was me talking to Blaire. I wasn't sure at first, but I was even wearing a shirt that Caide got me last year for my birthday. As I sat there, watching myself doing things I can't remember, I kept waiting for some big flashback moment to sneak up and smack me in the face, but it never did. I know it was me, but I don't remember any of it, I swear."

He nodded. "Okay. What do you remember?"

"I went to sleep in Brinley's bed. I read her a story and we were asleep by eight. Caide still wasn't home. When I woke up, I was still in her bed, still wearing the nightgown from the night before."

"Do you have a history of sleep walking?"

"No. Not that I know of."

He knelt down, eye level with her once again. "I believe you, Rachael. Even if that makes me crazy, I do believe you. That's not going to be enough though. I just need more time than we've got. If I'd been able to research sleep disorders, maybe head injury induced, maybe I could've found something. You have to believe me when I say I'd literally do anything to save you. We've just run out of time."

She sucked in a deep breath, trying to pull it together. "Put me on the stand. Let me say what I've told you."

Argus shook his head. "No. You're far from okay. You've gotten sick too much, you're pale and shaky. Avery would chew you up and spit you out up there. The doctor, I'm afraid, was our last hope." He glanced at his watch. "Rachael, I need you to listen to me, okay?"

She looked at him, his eyes filled with despair. He was silent for far too long and Rachael feared she knew what was coming.

"They're going to convict you."

The words were like knives, destroying what little resolve she had left. Rachael's heart began to pound, her skin growing cold. Argus leaned into her, his face only inches from hers.

"I'm going to keep digging, okay? I'm not giving up on

BECOMING MRS. ABBOTT

you. I'm going to fight their decision until you're home. I will get you home, do you hear me? Until that time, I need you to be brave, okay? It's not going to be easy. Keep your nose down, keep to yourself, and stay strong."

Rachael nodded, though she felt as if she was going to faint. He placed his hand on her cheek, brushing away a stray tear with his thumb. His hand was rough against her cheek, but nice. She sighed, and internally yelled at herself not to cry and not to faint, though either was definitely a possibility.

CHAPTER FORTY-SEVEN

HAMPTON

Hampton looked into Rachael's doe-like eyes and felt more useless than ever. There had to be something—something he was overlooking. He reminded himself that he'd known what to expect when he'd taken the case on, but that didn't make this any easier.

Just then, there was a scuffle outside of the doorway. The door opened cautiously and Hampton glanced at his watch. "We still have twenty minutes. I specifically told you no one was to come in this room." He stood up to face the intruder.

The young guard stuck his head in. "I know, sir. I'm sorry. She insisted."

Audrey Hagen entered the room, looking persistent as ever. Her long black hair stood in every direction, giving Hampton the notion that she'd been running.

"Audrey?" Rachael asked, genuine concern on her face.

"What is it?" Hampton asked.

"I've got an idea." She smiled brightly.

"What is it?" Rachael stood from her chair.

Hampton's attention was drawn from Audrey to the door, which was now opening again. Hampton watched as a middle-aged woman dressed in a bright white suit entered the room. He didn't recognize her and he could tell by Rachael's expression she didn't either. Without waiting for an introduction, the woman tossed her brown curls off of her shoulder and reached for Rachael's hand.

"You must be Rachael."

Rachael nodded, shaking her hand in return.

"I'm sorry, but who are you? My client and I are on a very tight schedule and we don't have time to chat."

The woman flashed Hampton a dazzling smile. "Forgive me, but you'll want to hear what I have to say, trust me." She held out her hand for his. "I'm Shayna Steele."

Shayna Steele. Where had he heard that name before? Before he could place it, Rachael answered his question.

"I've heard of you. You're that psychiatrist that's always featured in the Hanover Tribune, right?"

Shayna's eyes lit up. "I've had a few exclusives on my work done, yes. When Audrey called me, I rushed down. I think I can help you." She glanced from Rachael to Hampton and back.

"What do you mean?" Rachael asked.

"I specialize in patients with late onset dissociative identity disorder, though you probably know it as multiple personality disorder. In general, patients experience symptoms of DID very young, but rarely it appears later in life. I'm trying to find out why, particularly as it relates to trauma. If I'm right, if Rachael has it and if the symptoms only started recently, we may be able to get you acquitted of all charges."

"I'm sorry, what? Multiple personalities? You think I'm crazy?" Rachael asked, her voice soft.

"I don't think you're crazy at all, Rachael. I don't think any of this is your fault and I'd like to help prove it. DID is a pretty common disorder. Typically with therapy and proper medication, you can live a very normal life. I'm hoping that if it's a trauma that has caused this, once you're fully healed the symptoms may disappear."

"And you're saying you are willing to testify in court that my client has this disorder?" Hampton asked.

She shook her head. "Of course not. Not yet, anyway. Why, I only met her five minutes ago. I'd like to run some tests—give her a thorough work up."

"How long will that take? Because unless you can be finished in," he paused, glancing at his watch, "twelve minutes, then it does us no good at the moment."

Shayna looked at Hampton, a small smile on her face. "I was actually hoping you could get the judge to postpone the remainder of the trial. I'd need a few sessions with her."

"You've got to be kidding. How do you expect me to pull that off?"

Her lips curled into a sly smile, her voice like honey. "Come on now, Hampton. I've heard all about you, you're practically famous, and I don't mean those dreadful billboards hanging over West End. You can't tell me you don't have a few tricks up your sleeve." She winked at him.

Hampton swallowed, feeling annoyed. "There's no way the judge will grant a continuance. What's your evidence? What exactly should I pitch to him?"

"My evidence? I don't have anything but what I've told you. Your doctor claimed to believe she'd suffered a blackout, right? What he lacked was proof. If my theory is correct, I can get you proof, an actual medical diagnosis. Doesn't it make more sense this way? Rather than asking the jury to believe something as farfetched and, frankly, unproven as a blackout let them believe it's something they've heard of. If we can prove that Rachael does in fact suffer from DID, it is very likely that another, more aggressive personality took over for a while. Personalities feed on each other's fears and angers. If this personality detected resentment toward Miss

Underwood, for any reason, it's likely it could've lashed out. It would not be Rachael's fault. Audrey tells me she was with you on the evening before the murder, is that correct?" She looked to Rachael.

"Yes," Rachael answered.

Hampton hadn't known that. "What time was that?"

Audrey looked at Rachael. "It was nearly two, I believe. I'm not sure exactly."

"What time did you leave?"

"Around five? Five-ish."

"Did Rachael seem like herself, Audrey? Was she acting peculiar at all?" Shayna asked.

"I don't think so. She wasn't doing anything weird. She used the same voice, talked to me and the kids, even talked to Caide. Would another personality know who we were?"

"It's hard to say, each case is different. Typically, though, personalities don't know each other."

"Wait," Hampton thought out loud, "you said she talked to Caide? Caide wasn't home at that time. That's impossible."

"He called me." Rachael spoke up. "He called to tell me he was working late." She scoffed, but Hampton noticed the pain in her voice.

"How did that make you feel, Rachael?" Shayna asked, her eyes drilling into Rachael's.

"I was upset, of course, but I'm used to it. I've come to expect it after all these...hang on. I didn't tell you it was Caide who called, how could you have known that?" Rachael looked at her best friend in confusion.

"You weren't exactly whispering, Rach. I heard you on the phone, sounding angry. When you came back you were doing that fake, tense smile like you do when something upsets you, particularly Caide. Plus, you fixed supper for the three of you, plus me. I did some educated guesswork."

Rachael looked uneasy but Shayna was not fazed. "Anger

can be a trigger, in a lot of cases. Look, if you can just buy me some time, I'll take anything I can get but as much as possible, I'll agree to testify the results, no matter what they are."

Hampton sighed, running his hands through his hair. "I can try, if you really believe you've got something. I'll go talk to the judge now, but I don't want anyone to get their hopes up. He's turned me down for a lot less before."

Rachael nodded at him, offering up a small smile. The hope in her eyes was going to kill him. He couldn't stand the idea of letting her down. He looked away, leading Audrey and Shayna out the doors and toward the judge's chambers without another word.

CHAPTER FORTY-EIGHT

JUDGE CRAFTON

On fine days like today, the judge would've rather been outdoors, enjoying the cool, crisp weather of fall. He remembered the days before Beth had left, before his son had moved away to college and forgot how to call, when they'd spend days like this at the beach, once all the tourists had left for the season. Nowadays, he just had Cedric to keep him company, his trusty Doberman.

When Cedric had been small, Daniel used to bring him to work and let him sleep on a small pallet in the corner of his office. As time had passed and his friend grew larger and crankier though, even that pleasantry had been abandoned. His thoughts were interrupted by a knock on his door.

"Come in," he called. His door swung open. Hampton entered, leading a woman with a tanned complexion and razor-like jaw line that told Crafton she must have a strong Native American lineage.

"Hampton, what can I do for you?"

"I'd like to introduce you to Ms. Shayna Steele."

Ms. Steele stepped up, holding out her hand for Crafton

to shake. "Ms. Steele, it's a pleasure to meet you. What can I do for you today?"

Hampton spoke up. "We'd like to request a continuance, sir."

Somehow, he'd known Hampton would have something like this up his sleeve. The man didn't like to lose. "A continuance? On what grounds?"

"Ms. Steele is a psychiatrist who believes my client to be innocent. She thinks, *we think*, my client may be suffering from a condition called dissociative identity disorder, possibly brought on after her accident. She'd like to prove it, sir, but we've run out of time. We only found each other a few minutes ago."

"And what makes you believe Rachael Abbott may have dissociative—what was it again?"

"Dissociative identity disorder, better known as multiple personality disorder, has been the disorder that I have devoted the past five years of my life studying, Your Honor. It interests me extensively. I plan to make it my life's work to know everything there is to know about it: how it works, how it's treated, but most of all how it's brought on. If I can run a few tests, possibly try hypnosis, I'd be able to know for sure whether Mrs. Abbott is a sufferer of DID and if so, be able to treat her. I don't need long, and I'm willing to report my findings in trial, no matter whose side they help."

"Why should I do this? Just so you can research? There must be hundreds of other patients out there."

"Of course it's not just for research," Hampton interjected. "If Ms. Steele can prove my client is suffering from multiple personalities, then it proves she is innocent, legally. We'd agree to make an arrangement for her to attend therapy and take medication in exchange for her acquittal." He paused, studying the judge's face. "Look, if we don't run these tests and my client is suffering from this, then we've just sent an innocent woman to prison. If we're wrong and my client is perfectly healthy, the jury can convict her and you won't hear another word from me."

Crafton rolled his eyes. "Somehow I doubt that. You've never followed the rules, Hampton, and I don't expect that you'll start following them anytime soon."

"Your Honor, I know you don't have to do this, but I'd consider it a personal favor. I know I'm right about this, we just need a little more time to prove it," Hampton begged.

Crafton sat back in his chair, glancing back and forth from Hampton to Steele. Two sets of hopeful eyes met his.

"You let my client's husband testify against her today. If that's not bending the rules, I don't know what is. Sir, please, we rushed the trial because it seemed like such a simple case, but I don't believe it is. There are too many questions left unanswered, too many improbable circumstances. If we are right, this could help us clear up several issues and fill in a few blanks. This woman is a mother. Let's not lock her up unless we're sure."

Crafton mumbled, rubbing his thinning scalp. "Even if I agree to this, *and I'm not saying I will*, I have a full docket for the next six weeks."

"That's perfect, actually." Ms. Steele spoke up. "Six weeks is the perfect amount of time. We'll have Rachael come to my office four times a week for all of the six weeks. That's twenty-four sessions."

"I will personally escort her to and from her home to each session."

Crafton sat forward in his chair, wagging a finger. "Now, wait just a damn minute, you're not actually expecting me to release her?"

Hampton looked at Ms. Steele who shrugged her shoulders. "Well, we think it would be best for Mrs. Abbott's mental state if she were somewhere comfortable. Being out of her comfort zone, it's likely to trigger other identities. We need to limit the stress she is under as much as possible in order for our sessions to be their most effective."

"And if you're wrong? Then we're just allowing a killer a chance to run or kill again." He rubbed his temple.

"Place her on house arrest, then. If she steps one toe out of the house, except to go to her sessions, you can place her back in jail and we'll end all of our sessions," Hampton offered.

"No," Crafton said, then again more firmly, "*No*. Here's what we'll do. I'll agree to a six week continuance, but Mrs. Abbott stays in jail. She will wear a house arrest bracelet at all times. It will be activated whenever she goes to and from her sessions. Four sessions a week, six weeks. Not one more, not one less. I want each of your sessions, notes, tests, and findings on my desk forty-eight hours before trial. Don't leave a page out. I'll have a doctor look over each of them and verify everything you've said. If there are discrepancies, if you guys try to blur the truth or cover up anything, I'll pull both of your licenses so fast you won't know what happened. Six weeks from today we'll have a trial. You will both show up and I won't listen to any objections or crazy ideas. You'll show your evidence, await the jury's decision, and then we will all move on with our lives. Do I make myself clear?"

"Yes, sir," they echoed, grins spreading to their faces.

"Good. Now, Hampton, you'd better find Avery. This ought to be fun."

CHAPTER FORTY-NINE

AVERY

Avery couldn't help but smile as she was escorted to the judge's chambers. Her trial was nearly over and it had been painless. She might even make it home in time to cook an actual meal for herself tonight. Gosh, did she even remember how to use the stove? Did stoves quit working after years of being ignored? She felt a twinge in her heart as she recalled the last time she'd made a meal—the night of her last anniversary—right before Lyle's death. Before she could dwell on it too much, she was in front of Crafton's door. She knocked anxiously.

"Come in," he called.

She pushed the door open and was immediately met by Hampton and a tall, unfamiliar woman. This had bad written all over it.

"Hampton." She nodded politely. "You wanted to see me, Your Honor?"

"Yes, Avery. Have a seat please." Crafton responded dully.

"What's this about?" She approached a chair but didn't dare sit.

"Avery," Crafton said, "the defense has asked for a continuance based on newly discovered evidence. We'll reconvene in six weeks to finish the trial."

"A continuance? Is this a joke? What evidence? What could you possibly have?" She turned to face Hampton in disbelief.

"Something that may clear Mrs. Abbott of all charges," the giant of a woman said, her face smug and unkind.

"And who are you?" Avery asked through gritted teeth.

"I'm Shayna Steele, Mrs. Abbott's psychiatrist."

"Mrs. Abbott's *what*? What are you playing at Hampton?"

"It's already been decided. That's all there is to it. Their case was enough to convince me and that's all you need to know," Crafton answered stiffly. Then, he added, "We'll see you all in six weeks."

Avery turned to Hampton once more, a fiery look in her eyes. "I don't know what you're up to Hampton, but I don't buy it. Not one bit. I'll see you in six weeks." She nodded politely at the judge once more, backing calmly out of the room, trying to ignore that pungent look on Hampton's face. She tried to tell herself, whatever Hampton was up to, it had to be just an effort to buy time. He couldn't actually have something to help his case. Avery had looked at it from every angle and there was no way she was going to lose to Argus Hampton, she'd make sure of it.

CHAPTER FIFTY

JUDGE CRAFTON

Crafton entered the court room, trying to uphold his firm face. This was the part of his day he hated the very most. Issuing a continuance, especially in a case like this, usually led to an uproar, a media frenzy, and an aggravated jury—none of which Daniel felt like dealing with today.

He took his seat, meeting worried and anxious eyes all around. "You may be seated," he addressed the room. They sat.

As the commotion died down, he cleared his throat. "In light of recent evidence, the defense has requested a continuance." He paused, waiting for an outcry. When he heard nothing, he continued. "Which I have granted. Mrs. Abbott will be held in the county jail for the next six weeks while the new evidence is being evaluated. We will reconvene in six weeks, at which point a decision will be made. Jurors, I ask that you all meet a bailiff in the conference room after we dismiss to be briefed on the protocol for continuances. Any scheduling conflicts are to be rescheduled. Until then, I'll see you in six weeks. We're adjourned." He pounded his gavel, standing before anyone else could speak.

He didn't dare meet Avery or Hampton's eyes, for fear they'd try to speak to him again, though he couldn't help but notice Shayna Steele sitting behind Hampton. Her dark eyes locked firmly with his.

She was noticeable. She smiled up at him. He hurried to his chambers, slamming the door behind him, and slipping off his robe. He needed a drink. He pulled out a glass and poured Scotch into it, the smell hitting his nose quickly. He glanced at the time, two thirty p.m. He sighed. He was long past the years of worry that he'd started drinking too early in the day. He gulped the drink down, welcoming the warm, familiar burn.

CHAPTER FIFTY-ONE

RACHAEL

Argus hadn't had time to tell Rachael the judge's decision before she was hauled into the courtroom, so hearing that she wasn't being sent to prison yet filled her heart with relief. She could've leapt with joy, throwing her arms around Argus's neck and—*no!* She shook her head, forcing the daydream to end.

Instead, she stood quietly, batting back tears and keeping her face solemn just as she'd been instructed to do. As the judge dismissed them, she turned to Argus, unsure of what to say. "Thank you. Whatever you did, thank you so much."

He patted her arm, like a child, and shook his head slightly. "Not here," he whispered, his eyes looking around the room. "Take care of yourself, nose down. I'll be in touch."

"But—" she protested.

He put his fingers to her lips, silencing her. Her lips burned from his touch. "Don't argue, they're going to take you back to your cell now. I'm not coming this time. I'll be back next week, maybe sooner. If you need something, call."

She nodded, fear filling her chest at the thought of going back to the cell she'd never wanted to see again. "I meant what I said, Rachael." He placed a hand on her shoulder, looking at her with worry. "I need you to promise me you'll take care of yourself in there. Don't cause trouble, don't react to other inmates, just fade into the background, okay? If I spend all my time worrying about you, I can't focus my energy on the case. I need your word. I need your word that you won't fall apart, like before. You have to eat, you have to sleep. Don't cry and, whatever you do, don't talk to anyone about your case without me—not the cops, not your cell mate, not your family. No one but me and Shayna, okay?"

Rachael nodded. "No one is going to look out for you in there. No one is going to let you cry on their shoulder or force you to eat. It's a different world. I need you to be okay for six weeks. I need that."

Rachael nodded again, though his words stung her. She'd been trying to hold it together, she honestly had. She was doing her very best not to crumble. She was terrified of her own mind and whoever else might be in it with her. She missed her children more than she could comprehend, and on top of it all, her heart was just broken. Everything she'd thought she'd known had been shattered before her eyes and she'd long since run out of the glue to put it all back together.

Before she had a chance to say anything else, she felt a hand grab her arm. She turned to see the younger of the two bailiffs.

"Come on, lady, back to your cell." He grinned wickedly at her, pulling on the chain between her handcuffs so they dug into her already bruised wrists. She tried not to let Argus see her grimace, for fear he'd accuse her of being weak. Instead, she stepped back, meeting his eyes one last time with the bravest face she could muster.

She was going to be okay. What choice did she have?

CHAPTER FIFTY-TWO

CAIDE

The Monday after Rachael's trial, as Caide pulled into his driveway, his phone began buzzing in his jacket pocket. He turned down the radio, pulling his phone out of his pocket and glancing at the screen. *Hampton.*

He flipped it open. "Hampton? What the hell? I've been calling you all weekend. How could you just request a continuance without even talking to me?"

Hampton didn't bother to hide his indignation. "Excuse me? Don't you mean, 'thank you, Hampton, for buying my wife more time?' Because, if so, then you're welcome."

"No, that's not what I mean. You bought her more time for what? What evidence could you possibly have at this point that could help? You and I both know this trial is going nowhere fast. It would take a miracle at this point to help her and you don't have it. I'm not paying you to have a pissing contest with Avery. You're only dragging out the inevitable at this point."

"Do you have so little faith in your wife that you've already written her off?"

"C'mon, Hampton. You saw the tapes, same as me. You

fought hard, man, but Avery all but wiped the floor with you. I did what I could to help but even I can't argue with the facts."

"Wait. You *tried to help*?" He let out a sarcastic laugh. "You ruined what little stability my case had. You did absolutely nothing to help your wife, despite your intentions. On top of it all, did you really just tell me you believe she's guilty?"

"I'm telling you that I've seen the case against her. I don't, for one second, want to believe my wife is capable of this. I meant every word I said on that stand. I love Rachael. I screwed up, and maybe she caught me. Maybe she suspected it for a while, maybe not. Either way, people do crazy things when they're hurt. Good people. That's why sweet, straight-A teens are always getting into trouble for keying their ex's car. Hell, we once defended a preacher who shot his wife when he caught her cheating and then set his house on fire with their kids in it. Everyone said the same thing: he was sweet, always helped out, so friendly. It's the same old story, Hampton. It's a crazy, awful world and we never truly know what someone is capable of. I don't want to believe my wife did this, more than anything I want to know they're wrong but facts are facts."

"You listen to me, Abbott. You did screw up. I'd like to see you burn for what you did to your family but Rachael did not do this. I don't ever want to hear those words come out of your mouth again. Not to me and damn sure not to anyone else. I will get Rachael off, and she may forgive you for what you did, but if she finds out you gave up on her, there's no pain worse than that. She needs your support right now, more than ever. Yours. Not anyone else's. The judge has allowed her visitors, it would be good for her to see her family."

"If you think I'm going to bring my children to that hell-hole, you're nuts. I won't do it. I won't put them through seeing their mother behind bars."

"Where do they think she is?" he demanded.

"I've told them she went away for a while, to help her Aunt and Uncle we never see. Once she's sentenced, I'll tell them there was an accident. I'll tell them that she's never coming home. It's better for them to deal with her death than to deal with anything as embarrassing as a murder charge."

"And you don't think they will eventually learn the truth? It's a small town. People talk."

"I'll deal with that when it comes."

"I can't believe you are making this about your ego. Those kids care more about their mother than about how embarrassing it'd be to visit her. What happened to the devoted husband who came to my office six months ago? I want that guy back. This one's an ass."

"That guy left the second he watched his wife kill the woman he loved," Caide said through gritted teeth. He hadn't been able to stop picturing it since he'd left the courtroom—the image of Rachael on those security tapes was permanently burned into his memory.

"You're pathetic. What am I supposed to tell your wife?"

"You don't have to tell her anything. I officially release you from our agreement. Resign and let them appoint someone else. Save yourself the embarrassment of losing like this. I'll have a check sent to your office tomorrow morning for the last of my bill."

Hampton was silent for a moment. When he spoke, his voice was softer. "Can you really be that heartless? *She's your wife.* You're willing to just throw her to the wolves in order to save face?"

"I work at a law office, Hampton. My parents own the biggest diamond distributor on the East Coast. Image is all that I have. You can't possibly understand what this is like for me."

"Oh, you're right. This must be terrible for you." His words were lined with venom.

"Look, growing up in my family was like growing up on the red carpet. Except it didn't end behind closed doors. All my parents cared about was making sure that I kept my image clean: no parties, no drinking, and no girlfriends who weren't from prestigious families. No time for anything. If I had an ounce of spare time between school, private tutoring, piano lessons, student class presidency, and golf, my parents would fill in with press conferences and dinner parties. My whole life, all I was allowed to think about was what others thought of me. My future was set before I was even born. I went to Duke with every expectation of taking over the family business. That's when I met Rachael. We went out a few times but it was never anything serious. She was just fun. Somehow, a picture of us ended up in a magazine and got back to my parents. Of course there was a big uproar. She wasn't wealthy. She wasn't *anything* like what my parents wanted for me. I told them it was just a fling and they about lost it. They told me Abbott's date to marry and that I was to break up with her." He stared at the steering wheel, sweat beading on his forehead as his anger grew. "The first time I ever rebelled against my parents was when I asked Rachael to be my girlfriend. A month later, her dad passed away. At that point, I was over my rebellion and ready to leave her. I just couldn't bring myself to do it when she was already hurting so bad. I stayed with her then, but in my mind, we were already over. Another month went by and I decided that she was stable enough to handle the breakup. The morning I planned to do it, she called me. She was pregnant." The night came back to him like a bad hangover. "So I did the right thing. We were married the next month. My parents disowned me. I haven't talked to them since. I've never regretted my decision. I've never held it against her."

"Why are you telling me all of this, Abbott?"

"I'm telling you this so that you understand. There have only been two times in my life that I've stood up for myself, against how I was raised. Both times were for Rachael. So now, for the first time, I'm doing what I believe is right for me and my children. You seem to be forgetting that I was having an affair with the woman whose murderer you're defending. It may have been a mistake, but I *was* in love with her. I was falling in love with her, more than I realized, and now she's dead and I'll never get to tell her that. So, I'd like to be left alone with my decision. I need time to grieve."

Hampton sighed. "I won't quit. I'm not going to give up on her, you can quit paying me if that's what you decide to do, but I'm fighting for her. You're a coward, Caide Abbott, a cheater and a coward and taking away your support will not help you now."

"Why do you care so much, Hampton?"

The line filled with silence as Caide finally asked the question he desperately needed to know.

Finally, Hampton answered, barely more than a whisper. "Someone has to."

There was a swift click on the end as Hampton snapped his phone shut, leaving Caide alone to deal with his decisions and the silence that enveloped him.

CHAPTER FIFTY-THREE

SHAYNA

"Today's date is November twentieth. It is nine fifteen a.m. and this is the first session in the six week course of the Rachael Abbott trial."

Shayna lowered the tape recorder from her lips and placed it on the glass table in front of her. She smiled at Rachael. "Could you please state your first and last name for the recording?"

"My name is Rachael Abbott." Her voice was shaky and gruff, as though she'd just woken up from a long nap.

"And Rachael, you understand that these tapes are for research only, correct? No one but you and I will ever hear them unless you give me permission."

"Yes, I understand."

"You also understand that I will be subpoenaed to appear at your trial. While I will not be able to repeat anything you've disclosed to me, I will be asked to give my opinion about your condition. Does that make sense?"

"Yes."

"Okay, great. Let's get started. Rachael, tell me why you are here."

Rachael paused, her eyes drifting toward the ceiling to her right. *Memory recall.* "I was, well, I am, being accused of murder. Of murdering my husband's mistress."

Shayna spied her hands ball into tight fists as she said the phrase. "Tell me about the past few months of your life," she coaxed.

Rachael looked at her with an expressionless face and began to speak. "The past six months have been the worst of my entire life." She shook her head. "Gosh, that doesn't even begin to cover it. One sentence can't begin to describe what I've been through. Six months ago, my biggest worry was whether I remembered to pack a spoon in my daughter's lunchbox or forgetting to pay the electric bill. That seems like a whole other life now. I guess it all started with the accident. Or, that's what we're hoping, right? I mean, it doesn't really feel that significant. We were on our way to the park, it was a Sunday morning. Caide and I were arguing. I don't even remember what it was about honest. Something silly, probably."

"Do you feel like you fight with your husband a lot?"

"Sometimes. Arguments more than fights. Six months ago, I'd have said they were all small and silly, meaningless arguments. That's all they were for me." She looked down at her hands, picking at a piece of skin beside her nails. "We fought about work. Caide picked at my job a lot. I always thought it was all in fun, but now I see I was probably wrong. He hated having a wife with such a frivolous career like dancing, even though my studio brings in an equal part of our income. We also fought about the kids, him working too much, just normal marriage stuff: whose job it was to do what around the house, who didn't hang up their wet towel, whose turn it was to get up with Davis at night. It was never enough to make me think my marriage was truly in trouble."

Her voice was shaky, but firm, making Shayna wonder if

she's rehearsed this. "Tell me, Rachael, during these fights, did it ever get physical between the two of you?"

"No." Rachael looked genuinely shocked, even defensive. "Of course not. My husband has never physically hurt me, never. Caide isn't a physical person. Even in college, he was never angry or aggressive—" She stopped as if she'd realized something and blushed. "Oh. You were asking about me, weren't you? You wanted to know if I'd ever hurt my husband? I just assumed you meant him…" She looked up at the ceiling and Shayna noticed small tears in her eyes. "I'm sorry. This is all so new to me. I've never hurt my husband. Our fights weren't like that."

"Okay," Shayna said simply, an encouraging smile on her face. "So you were telling me about the accident."

"Right. We were taking the kids to the park that morning. We drove around a curve on Waterford and I guess I took it a little too sharp. When I hit my brakes, nothing happened. I pushed them harder. Caide realized what was going on, but there was nothing we could do. It all happened so fast. We went into a ditch and tipped over into a tree. It could've been a lot worse, that's what everyone keeps saying."

"What do you remember about the moment you left the road?"

"Everything. Nothing. It all happened so quickly that it's all a blur. We went into the ditch head on and then there was a loud crash. I was touching grass through broken glass that had been my window. I remember tasting blood, that's what brought me back to reality. I didn't hear my children crying and I couldn't turn to see them. Caide was awake and I remember hearing him say my name. He said it over and over but I couldn't answer him. I knew I should, but I couldn't form the words, no matter how hard I tried. I couldn't remember how to speak. I opened my eyes but there was blood coating my vision, so I just kept them shut. I remember hearing noises. Caide was talking." She closed her eyes. "I think he got out of the car, but I don't remember. The next thing I remember clearly was waking up in the ambulance. They'd wiped my eyes so I could see and there was no one I recognized there."

"How did that make you feel?"

"Terrified. I was trying to remember what had happened. No one would tell me where my children were, if they were even alive. The paramedics kept asking me questions, but all I could think about was my children. I tried to sit up but my head was so heavy. I realized then that they had me strapped down."

"Did that trigger any fears? Claustrophobia? Entrapment anxiety?"

"I don't think so. I don't remember being scared for myself at all."

"What about your pain scale? Do you remember what it felt like? Do you remember what hurt the most?"

"To be honest, I don't remember feeling pain. I mean, not in an 'I can't feel my legs' kind of way, I knew I was hurt and I felt it, sort of, like in the back of my mind. I just couldn't think of anything except my children—not until I knew they were safe. That's what I remember most of all, wanting to see their faces again."

"I see," Shayna said, mentally noting that Rachael had not once mentioned worry over Caide.

"Is that bad? Not remembering much?" she asked, her voice noticeably higher.

"Do you think it is?"

"I don't know. I can see it all so clearly but trying to explain it, it's all fuzzy. I'm just having trouble deciphering between what I need to worry over and what I don't."

"Don't overanalyze my questions or your answers. I just want to know what comes to your mind first."

Rachael nodded. "Once we got to the hospital, they brought me in on a stretcher. I remember feeling the cracks in the sidewalk as they rolled me over them. They shined a light in my eyes. There were so many doctors, so many hands all over me. They were stitching me up and covering me in bandages and before I knew it, I was in the machine for my MRI. I fell asleep in the machine and they had to stop it to wake me up. They didn't want me to sleep at all. I remember how much that worried me. I was in the hospital the rest of the day, exhausted but they wouldn't let me sleep. That night, once they released me, I was finally able to see my children. They were both fine. Brinley didn't have a scratch on her, just a bump on her head. Davis had a broken leg and was pretty beaten up, but all in all, they were fine."

"And Caide?" Shayna tapped her pen against her notepad.

"Caide had a dislocated shoulder and stitches on his knee. Minor injuries. Everyone told us how lucky we were."

"It sounds like you were pretty lucky."

Rachael nodded. "I just wanted to say thank you again for doing this for me. Lately, it seems like everything is working against me. It's nice to have some hope for a change."

"I know this has to be hard on you. From what I've seen, I'd say you're handling yourself quite well." Shayna smiled at Rachael, waiting for a smile back. The one Rachael offered looked foreign on her sallow, grief-stricken face.

"Thanks." She wiped her cheek instinctively, though Shayna hadn't noticed a tear. "I appreciate you saying that, but I don't feel like I'm handling anything well. I'm falling apart."

"Someone once said 'you never know how strong you are until being strong is the only choice you have.' I always thought that was beautiful."

"I like that." Rachael nodded, looking around the room. "Is this your daughter?" She pointed toward a framed portrait on a bookshelf near the window. Standing up, she walked toward it, rubbing her finger across the glass.

"That's Lydia, my baby sister."

"She's beautiful," Rachael mumbled.

"Thank you."

"We're not supposed to talk about you, are we?" she asked, looking back at Shayna.

Shayna smiled sadly. "We've got six weeks together, I'd say it's okay to take a break from the job occasionally."

Rachael nodded, setting the frame down carefully. "Do you think it will take six weeks to diagnose me?"

"Everything in its own time. It's possible I could diagnose you in one week. But I want to do more than diagnose you, Rachael. I want to help you. I want to find out what caused you to be this way. I want to help find a cure, not just a treatment."

"This is important to you."

It wasn't a question, but Shayna nodded. "It's very important to me."

"Can I ask why?"

"You can." Shayna glanced at her watch. "But that's a story for another day."

CHAPTER FIFTY-FOUR

RACHAEL

Rachael leaned back on the couch again. It had been so long since she'd felt comfortable. In jail, even her bed felt as if it were made of concrete. She rested her head on a pillow behind her. *I'll be back tomorrow*, she told herself.

She closed her eyes, knowing that these sessions would end too soon and she may never sit on a couch so comfortable for the rest of her life. The thought was terrifying.

She found herself imagining heaven: could hers be lined with couches upon couches like this one? She'd never have to leave a couch again. She could only imagine that's what heaven would be like after a lifetime in prison with cold rooms and rock hard mattresses. Then another, more troubling, thought struck her. Do murderers get to go to heaven? Even if they can't remember committing their crime? Surely she could reason with God, make him see that she'd suffered and paid for her crimes enough on Earth already.

Even sentenced to a life in paradise, a life without her children would be punishment enough.

She couldn't help but wonder if Blaire was in heaven now. Was she looking down, laughing because even in death she'd somehow won Caide? Or at least prevented Rachael from having him.

There was a small part of Rachael that hoped Blaire hadn't gone to heaven. She hated the idea of that homewrecker floating around on a cloud for eternity, while she was forced to rot in prison. I mean, adultery broke a commandment, right? Surely screwing someone else's husband at least landed you in purgatory.

Rachael got a certain amount of joy picturing Blaire being stopped at the pearly gates. Maybe heaven was like *The Scarlett Letter* and Blaire was allowed in but she had to wear a giant red 'A' on her chest. Or maybe her halo was an 'A' instead. Maybe all of the angels teased her and gave her the glass of milk with spit in it at suppertime. Maybe she'd be picked last for angel sports and have to sleep on rain clouds rather than regular ones. Rachael was amusing herself with this fantasy when her thoughts were interrupted.

"He's here, Rachael."

Rachael looked toward the doorway and saw Argus waiting for her. "Thanks again, Shayna." She stood, casting a longing glance toward the light pink couch once more before she sulked out the door.

"I'll see you tomorrow. Same time, same place." She patted Rachael's shoulder. Rachael was surprised to see that Argus was not in the suit he'd worn this morning, but instead in jeans and a button down shirt, his sleeves rolled up.

As they walked to his car she found herself staring at the little tuft of chest hair peeking out from above his shirt.

"So, how did that go?" he asked, sliding into the car.

Rachael blushed, looking away. "I don't know. This is the first time I've ever hoped I might actually be crazy."

"Right," Argus said, furrowing his brow. "Well, they say Shayna Steele is the very best there is. We're lucky to have gotten her on such short notice."

"I'll owe Audrey big time if she can help us out."

He patted her knee. "She'll help us. I have a good feeling about this one. Everything's going to work out."

She ignored the tingling sensation that shot through her leg at his touch. "Thanks, Argus." She looked out the window, watching the gray sky roll past. "So, while I'm being kept in jail, will it be the same as last time? I mean, no contact with anyone?"

"Well, this time you're being held for a slightly different reason, namely, to give the prosecution some satisfaction. You'll be allowed visitors and phone calls."

"Could you do me a favor, then?"

"What's that?" he asked.

"Could you let Caide know? I know we aren't on the best terms, but I'd really like to see my kids."

He hesitated. "I can let him know. He may like to hear it from you, though. You could always try to call him."

"I could, couldn't I?" Rachael smiled at the small amount of freedom. "Has he told you how they're doing?"

"We don't talk much. Your husband is a hard man to get in touch with."

"Yes. He is. Usually, he's at work. I hope he's taking time off to help the kids adjust. I can't imagine how hard this has been on them."

"I'm sure he's doing whatever he can for them."

"I just want to see them."

"They'll visit if they can, I'm sure."

"What do you mean, *if they can?*" she asked, trying to read his guarded expression.

"Well, I just mean I'm sure they've got a lot going on right now. Besides the usual stuff they're now having to do without your help, I'm sure the press is blowing up the phones. I've seen for myself that they're at your house constantly. I just don't want you to be upset if they don't visit or call as much as you'd like."

"Of course. They will visit though, they'll find a way." Rachael couldn't help but feel offended as he tossed her worries aside. What could be more important than seeing their mother?

"Of course they will, Rachael." He smiled at her. "And I'll see you as often as I can. Of course, with you being out four days a week for your sessions, that will leave little time for visits. Just know that whenever you need anything, you can always contact me. I'll try to keep you up to date with whatever I'm working on as well."

She smirked, flicking a piece of fuzz from her pant leg. "Do you put this much effort into all of your cases?"

"I don't have any other clients at the moment, so you're my sole focus. Well, your case is." He let out a small laugh. "But rest assured, when I have multiple cases, I'm just like every other scummy lawyer."

Rachael smiled. His laugh was nice: warm and deep, sort of welcoming. The lines around his eyes told her of a time when he'd once laughed more than the dignified look he now carried. "What?" he asked, noticing her staring.

"Nothing. It's just that I don't think I've ever seen you laugh."

"Well, there hasn't been much call for laughter in our time together. Once we win though, you'll see me laugh a whole lot more."

"Do you really think we'll win?" She raised a brow.

He was silent for a second, staring out the windshield. When he spoke, it was with a calmness that slowed Rachael's breathing. "I think the prosecution's case is very strong. I also believe that people want to feel sorry for you, after what Caide's done. With Ms. Steele's diagnosis I personally can't believe they'd sentence you."

Rachael swallowed. "And without her diagnosis? If I don't pass her tests? Then what?"

He sighed, gripping the steering wheel firmly. "Without her testimony, without her diagnosis—I don't know. I want to believe the good guys always win, Rachael, I've seen so much bad throughout my career. I have to believe in the justice system. Judge Crafton is a fair man; I believe he will do what is right. I wish I had something more solid to tell you, I do, but the one thing I'll tell you that is definite is that I'll never stop working your case. I won't give up until you're free."

Rachael stared out the window as he spoke, taking in his every word. When he paused, she sighed. "I appreciate you, Argus. I know I was a pain in the beginning and I know how hopeless this case seems. I just…I want you to know that I do appreciate you. You've been so supportive throughout everything." He smiled, though he didn't look at her. "I'm sorry, by the way, about your wife. I never told you but I'm sorry you went through that. No one deserves to feel this way."

Hampton nodded, turning up the radio. "This is a good song," he said simply. They rode the rest of the way in silence, both lost in their own troubled thoughts.

CHAPTER FIFTY-FIVE

CORIE

Corie was going to be late for class…again. This was beginning to be an everyday thing. Unlike the rest of her classmates, she wasn't late because she was hungover or because she overslept—no, her tardiness had one cause: Caide Abbott.

She pulled into the Abbotts' cul-de-sac and saw the news vans, packed with hungry reporters ready to sink their teeth into anyone who dared turn down the street.

Corie had always assumed there were laws protecting people from the sort of harassment she'd encountered the past few months, but if there were, they were not being enforced. Reporters hassled neighbors as they tried to unload their groceries, questioned early morning joggers, even probed parents waiting at the school bus stops. The Abbotts' street had become barren quickly.

Corie saw the reporters approaching her car before she was even able to pull into the driveway. She edged forward at a snail's pace and placed her car in park. She pulled her gray hood over her head and pushed her sunglasses up on her nose. *Here goes nothing.*

Flashing lights instantly met her, even with the morning sun glaring down.

"What business do you have with the Abbotts?"

"Did you know Rachael Abbott personally?"

"Did you ever suspect Mrs. Abbott of such rash behavior?"

"Did Mrs. Abbott conspire to kill anymore of Mr. Abbott's mistresses?"

"Are *you* one of Caide Abbott's mistresses?"

She was hounded by cameras, questions, and microphones as she approached the door, praying Caide had remembered to leave it unlocked.

"Get back, you vultures!" she yelled as she felt a reporter shove into her. She grasped the cool metal of the door handle and was relieved when it opened and allowed her to shuffle into the house. She was met by imminent silence.

"Hello?" she called. "Anyone home?"

The patter of tiny feet alerted her that the kids were there. She passed through the living room—its floor littered with toys and empty food containers—on her way to the kitchen.

When she saw Brinley and Davis, Corie gasped. Had it been any other morning, under any other circumstance, she would have laughed when she saw the children. Instead, her stomach knotted up. "Brinley?"

The little girl, dressed in a plaid shirt which had been buttoned all wrong and shorts even though it was barely over thirty degrees outside, had her hair pulled up into a food-caked ponytail that looked like it hadn't been taken down the day before.

Her face was covered in what looked like marker, spaghetti sauce, and smudged pink lipstick. When she saw Corie, she stepped back as if she were in trouble. That's when Corie got a good look at Davis. He was sitting on the floor with one leg in a pair of bright red pants that it looked like he'd outgrown years ago. His white t-shirt looked vaguely like the one Corie had dressed him in yesterday except that it was now more brown than white.

Brinley had two bowls on the floor, both filled with cereal. The empty milk jug lay on its side, wads of toilet paper floating through the river of liquid that encompassed the kitchen. Suddenly, Davis began crying. Corie bent down to pick him up, careful not to kneel in the milk or the waterlogged pieces of cereal that were painting the floor.

"Shhh. Davis, baby, it's okay. What's going on, Brin? Where's your dad?"

Brinley, realizing she wasn't in trouble, rushed forward, hugging Corie's leg. Corie was immediately glad she'd chosen to wear her darkest pair of jeans.

"Daddy's still asleep," Brinley whispered. "He said not to wake him, but Bubby got too hungry to wait. I tried to get him dressed, but he just kept crying. I got all ready for school, but I spilled a mess on the floor 'cause the milk was heavy and cereal was all I could reach. I'm not supposed to climb on the counters to reach the paper towels so I had to use our potty paper. And I couldn't pick up Davis very high because he's so heavy so we had to eat on the floor." She sighed, sounding exhausted.

"It's okay, Brin. You aren't in trouble. You were a very big girl today, okay?" She squatted down so she was eye level with the girl.

Brinley nodded. "Daddy says I have to be a big girl now that my momma's gone. He says I'm in charge now and that's why he let me wear my momma's lipstick."

Corie felt sick to her stomach. Why would he tell them Rachael was gone? And how could he expect Brinley to care for Davis properly? Seeing the usually beautiful children covered in filth made Corie ill. Rachael would've had a fit.

She glanced at her watch and sighed. She stood no chance of getting Brinley cleaned up and to preschool before they were both late and there was no way she would leave Davis alone.

She grabbed a handful of paper towels, pulling Davis' leg out of the too small pants, and tapped Brinley's nose. "You're lucky I love you so much, kiddo."

"I love you too, Corie." Brinley happily took a paper towel from her babysitter and helped to clean up her mess.

CHAPTER FIFTY-SIX

CAIDE

Caide Abbott dreamed with liquor-filled dreams. First he was in court, surrounded by Mason, Meachum, and all of their families. He was trying to win his case, but every time he would start to speak a hippie in a flowing dress would play her guitar. When he walked up to confront the hippie, she turned into Blaire's mom. She stood, crying and wearing a black veil like he pictured her wearing to the funeral. When he turned around he was surrounded by dozens of black-clad grievers who cried tears of blood. He looked down, seeing that he was standing over a coffin where Blaire lay—bloody and disfigured, her blonde hair soaked in red. He stepped back, disgusted by her rotting corpse only to bump into something else. He turned around, facing his wife. She was wearing a yellow sundress and a straw hat, just like the summer they'd gone to the beach after they'd found out about Davis. Caide remembered that as being the happiest year of their marriage. Her blonde hair had been bleached brighter by the sun and her skin radiated a tan that made her pregnancy glow even more beautiful.

Caide had fallen in love with her all over again that afternoon.

Suddenly, he was overcome with a yearning for their life before all of this. He gathered her in his arms, hugging her tightly and kissing her head. Then a wetness filled his front, like he'd been splashed with warm water. When they pulled apart his wife's yellow dress had been stained a dark red, thick blood splattered all over her. He stepped back. She reached her arms out to him. "Caide? What's wrong?"

"Get away from me!" Caide yelled, paralyzed in fear.

"Why? What's wrong? What are you looking at me like that?" bloody Rachael asked, walking calmly toward him.

"You're not my wife. My wife is no murderer. I don't know you!" he screamed, panic filling his body.

"Please don't do that, dear, you're hurting my feelings," she said. Caide trembled like a child, sobs rattling his body as his blood-soaked wife inched toward him. "You can't hide from me, darling. I'll always be here. I'll always find you."

Caide whimpered, still unable to move. His wife stopped in front of him, her face nearly touching his. She smiled sweetly, her teeth coated in sticky red blood. He reached in his pocket, looking for something to ward her off with.

He pulled out a phone, trying to dial a number. Instead, it began ringing.

Then, he was awake and the ringing hadn't stopped. He rolled over, blinking away the black spots that clouded his vision. He wiped his drool-covered chin on the pillow and rubbed his eyes. The empty bourbon bottle lay on Rachael's pillow, reminding him of the night before. He glanced at the clock on the nightstand. It was nearly eleven.

God, no, he thought, and even the voice in his head was loud enough to cause him to wince in pain. The bright yellow curtains that Rachael had insisted would brighten up the room were doing that and more. He grabbed an extra blanket off the bed and tossed it toward the window, trying to block out the bright sun that shone through. One corner caught, but it did little good. Caide rolled over, face down in his pillow, welcoming the darkness to his bloodshot, hungover eyes. Did hangovers hurt this much in his twenties? Surely not, or he'd actually remember those years.

Then, the phone began to ring again—a loud, bellowing, earth shattering, mind blowing, nails on a chalkboard, screeching ring—and he remembered what woke him in the first place. At first, he believed it must be Mason, wondering where he was, but as the sleep-coated thoughts wore off, he recalled his last conversation with Mason six months ago and knew that couldn't be it.

That day, he'd arrived to the office an hour late after fighting with the kids and eventually calling Corie to get them ready. Mason met him at the door, asking to see him in his office. Once in the office, Meachum was already seated, and Caide had known what was coming. They'd been waiting for him. They smiled at him. "Have a seat, Caide," Meachum had said, gesturing toward the seat next to him.

"What's going on, guys?" Caide had known this was sure to be coming, but it still felt like a slap in the face.

"We need to talk about what's best for the company's immediate future."

"And let me guess: I'm not a part of that anymore," he said, running his tongue over his teeth.

"Now, Caide, this isn't easy for any of us. You've become like a son to us, to both of us," Meachum said. "Why, we've known you since you were knee-high and still running around in diapers."

Caide doubted very much that his mother had ever let him run around in diapers.

"Now, we aren't talking about anything permanent, of course," Mason added lightly.

"So what? I'm being let go?"

"Just temporarily, until the trial is over. After that, we'll make a long term decision. Think of it more as an extended vacation. Take the kids away from here. You all can enjoy some time off, away from this mess."

"This mess," Caide said with disgust, "is my life. I'm handling it. You guys have to know this isn't going to interfere with my job. I'm committed to this company as much now as I ever have been. You know me. I've pulled forty-eight hour shifts just to make sure you were ready for court. Before we got this office and the staff we have now, I put in all the extra work, work that we now have split up between three people. I have put more effort into this company than anything else in my life. You have to know that none of that changes now. This trial changes nothing."

"It changes everything, son," Mason said. "I have no doubt your work ethic won't change. We may be old men, but we do realize you are a huge part of what makes this company tick. Believe me when I say this was not an easy decision. We wish it could be different, Caide. You haven't been around the past few days to notice but over half of our clients have dropped us since the murder. The other half are just barely hanging on. I'm sorry, Caide, but unfortunately, no matter how much you've done for us—no matter how much you mean to us—the fact remains that until your wife's name is cleared, any affiliation with you or lack of reprimand may well ruin our company."

"And if her name isn't cleared? If she's found guilty?"

Mason looked shocked by the question. Meachum patted Caide's shoulder. "We all love Rachael, son. We do, but surely you know we can't continue to employ the man whose wife murdered another employee. It's guilt by association. It's just bad business."

"Of course," Mason added, "we'll be glad to give you the

option to resign respectfully. But yes, if your wife is convicted, your job here at Mason and Meachum...well, I'm afraid you may have screwed yourself out of it. No pun intended."

Meachum's cheeks had grown red from attempting to conceal his laughter. The two hyenas probably laughed themselves silly over this joke once Caide had left.

Caide shook the memory from his brain, focusing on the shrill ring that was blaring for the third time. He pushed himself off the bed slowly, so as not to make the room spin. He stumbled across the room, trying desperately to shield his eyes, to where his phone lay charging. He checked the caller ID. The number was not one saved to his phone, but one he knew by heart.

Bile rose in his throat as he recognized it. He pressed the answer button after a brief hesitation. There was no point ignoring her, she'd only call back.

"Hello?" he said softly, so as not to erupt the hangover-fueled volcano in his head.

"Hello, Caide Matthew," she said, her voice cool and crisp —just like he'd remembered.

CHAPTER FIFTY-SEVEN

SHAYNA

"How are you feeling, Rachael?"

"Fine." Rachael smiled. "As fine as I can be I guess. I'm enjoying being out, getting fresh air. Even though I'm not really out at all." Rachael gestured toward her ankle, where the house arrest bracelet rested.

Shayna nodded. "Today, I'd like for you to talk to me about your childhood. Your parents, siblings, friends, whatever feels important."

"Okay. Well, I grew up here in La Rue. My dad worked at the port all my life. No siblings, although you've met Audrey, and she may as well be my sister. We've been best friends as far back as I can remember."

"And your mother?"

She looked up at the ceiling, tucking her hands underneath her legs. "I never knew my mother. She passed away giving birth to me. My dad talked about her all the time, though. You know how when one parent dies, sometimes the other parent shuts down and refuses to talk about them?"

Shayna nodded.

Rachael smiled, her face lighting up at the memory. "My

BECOMING MRS. ABBOTT

dad was the opposite. He never stopped talking about her. He told me everything I wanted to know. He showed me every picture he had of her. Whenever we'd go shopping he'd make me stop and smell the perfume she wore or look at a color or pattern she would've loved. It was like she never left, and he never stopped loving her. In some ways, it was like my mother lived through him. I never got to meet her, but I feel like I know her."

"Did your dad work a lot when you were growing up?"

"Not excessively, but yeah, he was a hard worker. He always tried to get home before I did, especially when I was young. As I got older, he started working longer shifts. He had to support us on his own, so I understood why he worked as much as he did. He never missed anything I needed him for though."

"How did you feel about his work? About how often he worked?"

"I missed him when he was gone, obviously, but it was never for too long. He'd come home on his lunches and call during the evening breaks. I was proud to have a father that worked so hard. We were far from wealthy but he made sure I never wanted for anything."

Shayna nodded. "And where is your dad now?"

"He passed away when I was in college."

"I'm sorry to hear that."

She tucked a piece of hair behind her ear. "Thank you, it was hard. My dad and I were close. When I got the call that there had been an accident—"

"A car accident?"

She shook her head, running her fingers along the glass table to distract herself. "An accident at work. He slipped on one of the ships and hit his head. Before anyone could get to him, he'd fallen overboard. They rushed him to the hospital but he'd been without oxygen for too long. By the time I got there it was too late. He'd always seemed invincible, it seemed impossible for him to really be gone."

"Who was with you? At the hospital?"

Rachael shook her head, unable to speak.

"No one?"

"There was no one to come. My grandparents were already gone. My dad was an only child and my mother's sister never came around enough for me to consider her family."

"So you were all alone? You were only a child."

"I was twenty-three—not really a child." She inhaled deeply. "I remember noticing all the wrinkles on his hand, like they'd appeared out of nowhere. All the hairs on his arms had turned gray. Somehow it had all managed to slip past me. Sometimes we don't realize how quickly time passes until it's right there in black and white. I just sat there with him. I cried and cried until I just couldn't cry anymore. The next morning, I let them take him. I went back to our house to start getting things in order."

"Just like that?" Shayna furrowed her brow, shocked by her words. She was trying to be strong, but Shayna could see the pain in her eyes.

"I knew there was no one else. Someone had to do it."

"No one should have to deal with that alone."

"I wouldn't have wanted anyone else there. It was the experience I needed to have closure. I went through everything of his, fully intending to box things up and give them away, but I never did. I just couldn't. It broke my heart to think of anyone else having his things. So, I packed them away in the attic. That's where they are now. I need them close to me."

"So, what happened when you went back to school?"

"I missed a lot at first. After a while, I found out I was pregnant. Caide and I were married a month later."

"So, how do you think your father's death affected you?"

Rachael frowned. "I mean, it made me see a lot more darkness in the world, I guess. Up until that point, I'd never lost anyone close to me. I'd never felt pain that immensely. It matured me, made me realize that no one is invincible. It was the first time I'd ever felt so alone in the world…the first time my heart had ever been broken…the first time I'd ever doubted my faith. Imagine every single person in your family—everyone you'd ever cared for—imagine they all died at once. That's how it felt. My dad was everything to me."

"Would you say it was the hardest thing you'd ever dealt with?"

"It was the only tragedy I'd ever experienced firsthand. When my grandma passed away, I was twelve and she'd been in a nursing home my whole life. It was hard on me, but I'd always known it was coming. My dad wasn't even fifty years old." She paused, wiping her tears away. "It was the hardest thing I've ever dealt with *to this day*. I wouldn't wish that pain on anyone."

Shayna nodded, waiting for the tears to stop falling before she pressed on. There was something about Rachael, something oddly comforting about her presence. Even as an accused felon, Shayna just felt at ease with her. Rachael was the kind of person you could become entranced with. "So who did you turn to when you were grieving? Was that Caide?"

"Sort of. Once I got back to school, it was hard to talk to him, hard to talk to anyone really. Caide was great though. He'd listen when I could talk. There were some days when he'd just hold me and let me cry until I fell asleep. He was comforting, like he'd been doing it all his life. He'd rub my head and rock me while I just fell apart. It was what I needed at the time." She smiled sadly. "Then something changed. He became distant. We stopped talking, stopped going out as much. I think maybe it was all just too much for him. I couldn't blame him, honestly."

"Did you feel the need to turn to any substances to help with the pain? Drugs or alcohol?"

"I was a twenty-three year old college kid. Half of my diet was already alcohol." She snorted loudly. "But yeah for a few months after he died, I drank a lot."

"Define a lot."

"Some days it was all day, every day. Between going through his things and dealing with his bills and accounts and cancelling his subscriptions—it was all just too much. Alcohol helped me. It wasn't an addiction or anything—I could never get used to the taste. It was Band-Aid, and at that point, I desperately needed one. When Audrey found out what was going on, she convinced me to stop."

"Audrey seems like a good friend. She really worries about you."

"We worry about each other." Rachael nodded. "Our families were close. Her dad worked with mine. Growing up together, we learned to take care of each other."

"Now, you mentioned that your relationship with Caide sort of fell flat after your father's death. What happened to fix it?" Rachael was silent, a hint of something on her face. Shayna studied her for a moment before recognizing it: *embarrassment*. "Rachael?"

She looked down. "Brinley happened. Our daughter. She was the duct tape on our relationship. It was never really fixed, just sort of held together. After my dad passed, even once I was back in school and sober, I wasn't responsible. I was thoughtless, basically a zombie. When Caide started pulling away, it brought me back to reality. By the time I realized I was nearly three months late, the morning sickness had already set in. I bought a million tests, but they all confirmed what I knew. I called Caide that night. We hadn't slept together in months, hadn't even seen each other in weeks, so when I told him I was pregnant I expected some shock. I figured he may even demand a paternity test. I honestly figured he'd bolt."

"But he didn't," Shayna confirmed.

"No. He freaked out a bit, I mean, we were young and he had a future mapped out that didn't involve me or our child. A baby was never in the plan for him. But instead of running, he just asked me to marry him. *Just like that*. Like he was asking me to dinner. I had to say yes. I was so scared and I had this whole new little life to worry about and take care of. It was terrifying. So we did the one thing that made sense. We got married the next month, moved home to La Rue, into my dad's house, and pretended it was all part of the plan. Brinley came a few months later and we got to play this happy couple down the street with a beautiful baby girl. We were a family and I thought maybe, just maybe, that would be enough. I thought saying it daily, playing the part, maybe it'd make it so."

"Did it?"

"At first, maybe. After we were married, Caide's parents disowned him. They wrote him out of their wills and never spoke to him again. They've never even met their own grandchildren. So, I think in the beginning he felt the loneliness that I'd been feeling since my dad passed. The selfish part of me was...somehow happy about that. I mean, I could see how much he was hurting, but selfishly, I just felt so relieved. Like now, we were all each other had. I was happy to see him suffer." Rachael stopped, staring at nothing in particular. Shayna sensed that maybe she was admitting that to herself for the first time. "Misery loves company, I guess." She sighed.

"So then what?"

"Then we found a routine, started going through the

motions. The first year was really rough. With Caide's plans to run Abbott Jewelers out the window, we were both freshly out of school with no jobs lined up. I took a job waitressing downtown. Luckily, my dad's house was already paid for, and even after buying my studio, I still had a little bit of money left over from the insurance. We survived on that."

"That must've been hard for Caide, coming from a wealthy family to barely scraping by. How did he handle it?"

"Caide's…prideful. He grew up in a family where image is everything. Waiting tables or bartending—to Caide that would've been like begging on the street. He would've rather starved than let the world see him taking a job like that. He wanted it to seem like we had it all together at all times. The insurance money lasted us a little while, but after Brinley was born it began to go a lot quicker. When Brinley was a few months old, after Caide had had dozens of bad interviews, we finally got a call. Two of Caide's family's closest friends wanted to hire him as an executive assistant for a law firm that they were starting. The salary was great. It meant I wouldn't have to go back to work and we could finally give our daughter a good life, a life I'd longed for and that Caide had taken for granted. After he'd been there for a while, I was finally able to really work on building up my studio. One or two classes a week started filling up, and within a few years I had a waiting list two pages long. Everything started falling into place. We just forgot about our past and pretended, even to ourselves, that we'd had some fairytale love rather than a marriage of convenience."

Shayna smiled, glancing at her watch. "I'm really glad you felt like you could share that with me. I finally feel like I understand a little more about you. Unfortunately, our time is up for today, so I have to cut you off. We'll pick up right here tomorrow, though."

Rachael looked at the clock on the wall, her mood visibly

depleting. "Oh. I didn't realize how quickly time had gone by."

"We've covered a lot of ground today. Most clients aren't so eager to dive right in. It really makes a difference in our progress."

"I just want this to be settled. I'll tell you anything you want to know, anything that will help me. Consider me an open book. I just want to go home. I just want to kiss my kids and complain about my laundry. I want this all to be over."

Shayna smiled, reaching for the arm of the couch where Rachael's hand rested. "We're going to do everything we possibly can for you, Hampton and I. We want to help you. We want you to walk out of that jail and never look back." She rubbed her thumb over the back of Rachael's hand, comforting her. "Let me go check and see if Hampton is here."

Shayna stood up, walking toward the door. The psychiatrist in her couldn't help but notice how Rachael's cheeks had flushed at the mention of Hampton's name. She'd be willing to bet, too, had her hand been still enough to catch her pulse, it would've been racing.

Rachael Abbott had a few secrets of her own, that was for sure.

CHAPTER FIFTY-EIGHT

HAMPTON

Hampton pulled up to Shayna Steele's office. He looked in his rearview mirror, adjusting a stray hair and got out of the car. As he walked into her lobby, the cheerful red headed secretary jolted up. "Good afternoon, Mr. Hampton."

Why was he so terrible with names? He glanced around quickly, finally laying his eyes on a black and white name plate at the corner of her desk.

"Good afternoon, Kortnee. I hope you're doing well."

"I am. Thank you, sir." She smiled at him genuinely.

"They nearly finished?" he asked, pointing toward the door.

She glanced at the clock. "Should be any minute now."

Hampton nodded and sat down on the large gray chair in the corner of the room. Shayna Steele's office was a teen girl's dream. In the center of the lobby, pink and gray couches surrounded a fuzzy white throw rug. Hampton supposed it could be comforting to some, but it just made his skin crawl.

The office door swung open and Shayna popped her head

out, meeting Hampton's eye. Her sly smile told him she had a secret to share. Standing up to face her, he smiled back.

"Hampton. Right on time. We nearly ran over today."

"Yes, well, I'm sure she wouldn't mind that." He smirked, trying to spy Rachael through the space between Shayna and the door. Shayna, noticing his actions, pulled the door shut and walked toward him.

"We've been making quite a bit of progress. She's very cooperative."

"What does that mean? Do you think you have something? Something to help?"

Shayna grinned, shaking her head. "Hampton, you give me too much credit. I'm good, but I'm not *that* good. It's only been a few sessions."

"Right, of course." He felt a tiny bit of hope deflate.

"Oh, don't look so upset. I know how important it is to you that we help Rachael. I just wanted you to know how hard she's working."

"That's great," he said sarcastically. "Lucky you. When I met her she was stubborn as hell. I warmed her up for you." He smirked, recalling their first encounter. "So, be glad."

Shayna's eyes twinkled in delight. What did she know that he didn't?

CHAPTER FIFTY-NINE

SHAYNA

She nodded. "I'll take your word for it. That's nothing like the girl in my session now." Shayna backed up a step, grabbing the door handle behind her and pushing it open.

"Rachael," she called, "we're ready for you."

Rachael stood up off of the pink couch, making her way toward the door. Shayna turned to Hampton. She knew the exact moment Rachael was in his eyesight before she could even hear her footsteps approaching.

Dilated pupils.

Hands adjusting his jacket.

Touching his neck. His hair.

Shayna took into account every move Hampton made until Rachael stood in front of him. She couldn't help but feel delight.

My, oh my, you two. Things just became a whole lot more interesting.

CHAPTER SIXTY

HAMPTON

Even in the faded gray sweatshirt and black sweat pants she'd worn from the jail, Rachael still looked better each day. The color was coming back to her cheeks. Her eyes —a dull, sallow green when he'd met her—were beginning to brighten up. As she approached him, he couldn't help but smile.

"Hey," he said, his heart pounding in his chest.

"Hey," she replied, her eyes locked on his.

"You ready?"

She gazed down. "Do I have a choice?"

"We'll be back tomorrow. Thanks again, Shayna." He nodded toward the therapist, whose ear-to-ear grin was beginning to alarm him.

He placed his arm on Rachael's back and led her outside to the car. As they walked across the parking lot, their feet crunching loudly on the gravel, he released his arm from her back.

"So, Shayna tells me it's going well. I'm glad to hear it."

"She told you that? What did she say?" she asked anxiously.

"That it's going well," he said slowly. "What do you mean?"

"What tone did she use?" she inquired, biting her lip.

"She was happy, I guess. I don't really know. She just said that you're being cooperative. Why?" He shook his head at how confusing women could be.

"I just can't tell how it's going. She doesn't tell me anything at all. She just asks me questions—questions that aren't even about the trial, just about me. About me and Caide, me and my dad, me and Audrey. She's making me dig up the darkest, most traumatic events of my life and talk about them. I'm doing whatever she asks, talking about things I never talk about, things I've never told anyone. All the while, she isn't telling me if I'm passing or failing this little test. I'm so sick of talking about everything without knowing how I'm doing."

Hampton didn't think Rachael could possibly have an issue with talking. Once you got her going, the woman never shut up. He, however, didn't think it'd be wise to point this out. "Well, look, she obviously knows what she's doing. Just give her some time to work. I'm sure whatever she's asking you about is relevant to her tests. Just keep talking."

Rachael smiled halfheartedly. He smirked at her. "She also said you weren't being stubborn. Is that something you only reserve for me?"

She crossed her arms. "I'm not stubborn."

He raised his eyebrows. "Right. Okay. I must be thinking of some other Rachael Abbott who yelled at me the day we met."

She shoved him playfully. "Hush. You come in all Mr. Hot Shot—'I'm a lawyer, bow down to me.' I had every right to be stubborn."

He opened her door for her, before climbing into the car himself. "You're right. I may have come in with an attitude problem. This job can give you a big head sometimes."

"Sometimes?" She laughed.

"It just makes you sort of indifferent to your clients. It wasn't anything to do with you. It was just a job. I didn't really care that much in the beginning," he said seriously.

"But you feel differently now?" she asked, sensing his tone.

He started up the engine. "Yes, now it's different."

"What changed?" she asked.

Hampton pressed his lips together, not entirely comfortable with where this conversation might end up. "I don't know. I guess, I never really looked at you in the beginning. I took this job because it paid well, and because frankly, it was an ego boost to be hired by my competition."

"That's still why you're working this job?" She looked hurt.

He waved at the driver trying to pull into the lot, turning onto the busy road carefully. "Not at all." When they made it to the stop light, he glanced at her. "Do you remember the day I told you about my wife? That was the first day I ever really saw you. I mean really, really saw you. I looked past the job and actually tried to understand how you could turn down what I believed to be a great option. I'll never forget how you looked that day. You were so broken. Your face, it just snapped me out of my trance. I'd become so numb to it all. The people I usually represent they're just angry, maybe scared, but always angry. I win those cases. That's what I'm used to. Your case, Rachael, your case is the hardest I've ever dealt with and instead of being angry, you just looked empty. It made me remember the days after Diedra left. Right then, I knew this wouldn't be just another case to me. I couldn't look at it, or you, the same way after that day."

"Why are you so nice to me?" she asked softly.

He swallowed, looking away as the light changed. "You deserve to have people being nice to you."

She pulled her feet up into the seat, crossing them underneath her like a child. "Do you want to know the hardest thing about being in jail? My whole life people have been kind to me, courteous. Growing up in the South, you just learn to expect it. But it's different in jail. No one treats you like a person. They say whatever they want, look at you however they want, and it's just accepted. That's been the hardest part for me: not the separation, not being a prisoner, but having people being completely and mercilessly rude to me. That's why I appreciate you so much. You're different. You treat me like a person."

Hampton patted her arm. "You are a person, Rachael. That's the only way I'll ever see you."

Rachael placed her opposite hand over his. She smiled at him, a smile so wide and genuine it was impossible to believe this woman had ever felt heartache. In that moment—that small, careless moment of pure honesty—Hampton realized he was breaking his one and only rule. It was then, staring at this woman dressed in a sweat suit at least two sizes too big, eyes dark from lack of sleep, and messy hair pinned back, that Hampton realized he was falling in love with his client.

It's a beautiful thing to love someone in their most unlovable moments, to hold them at their sickest, or to support them at their weakest; but to fall for someone because of a brutally honest, completely simple moment such as this was breathtaking. There is nothing more amazing than seeing someone in an imperfect moment: their houses unkempt, mascara-stained tears on their cheeks, laughing so hard they are no longer making sounds, so drunk they can only be unnecessarily truthful, so in love that nothing else matters, or so broken they stop knowing how to live. These moments are rare and fleeting. To love someone despite of them is a beautiful thing, but to love someone *because of* them...there's nothing so intense.

Hampton rubbed his thumb along the bones in Rachael's hand. He felt her eyes on him, taking him in. Heat rushed to his face as he stared ahead, hoping his feelings weren't written on his face.

It had been so long since he'd felt this way. He'd felt attraction since losing Deidra, but nothing like this—the pulse in his face as it grew hotter and hotter, the rush of giddiness in his chest as he tried desperately to look nonchalant.

Quickly, possibly even rudely, he pulled his hand back.

Rachael is married. Rachael is on trial for murder. Rachael is a client. Rachael is off limits. He repeated the mantra in his head.

"You okay?" Rachael asked, locking her fingers together in her lap.

"Yeah." He couldn't look her way.

"What are you thinking about?"

"The trial."

"Did you think of something else?" she asked hopefully.

"I'm working on it. I still believe we've missed something. I've got four and a half weeks to come up with something great."

Four and a half weeks left and so far all he had was *'Your Honor, you can't convict this woman. Why, you might ask? Well, simply because I can't bear to imagine life without her.'*

Something told him that probably wasn't going to cut it.

CHAPTER SIXTY-ONE

CAIDE

"Mother?" Caide said into the silent phone line.

"Yes, darling," she responded smugly.

"Uh, how are you?"

"Don't flatter me with small talk, Caide Matthew."

"Then what do you want? You called me, remember? I'm not in the entertaining mood. You haven't spoken to me in years so whatever it is you'd like to say, just say it."

"Caide Matthew." She gasped, he could picture her grasping her pearls in shock. "That's no way to speak to your mother. Like I didn't birth you. Like I didn't raise you and give you everything a boy could dream of, just to have it thrown back in my face for some floozy. I called to check on you, my boy. I heard about your wife." The word dripped with disdain from her tongue.

"Her name is Rachael, Mother. It won't burn your tongue to say it. So basically, you called to say 'I told you so?'"

"Oh, *that tone.* I did *not* call to rub it in your face that your wife is a no good, piece of garbage just like I warned you, or that she ruined your life like I knew she would." She paused, letting her words sink in. "I called to see if my son needed help."

Caide laughed. "Help? I asked you and Dad for help years ago when our daughter was born and we were both without jobs. You told me no then, what has changed now?"

"The wounds were still fresh back then, son. You'd just abandoned your father and I for some knocked up woman we'd never met. What did you expect?"

"I expected you to help me. I expected you to be a normal grandmother and want to meet my children, want to meet my wife," he told her. Martha scoffed. "Look, I know our marriage was less than ideal, but you wrote me out of your will, you told me never to contact you again. When I, against my better judgement, called you begging for help, begging for help that would've meant nothing to you, do you remember what you said to me?" Without waiting for an answer he continued. "You said 'you are not our son. Our son is dead.' Do you remember that, Mother? You said 'you are dead to us.'" Anger welled inside of Caide, remembering that day.

"I did not call to reopen old wounds. You were making a mockery of yourself and I was not going to help you to do it. No one is important enough to ruin a reputation for, not even you, son." She cleared her throat. "Actually, that's why I'm calling. I have a proposition for you."

"A proposition?"

"Bart Meachum has informed us that you were recently let go."

He rolled his eyes. "*Temporarily*."

"Temporarily, *if* that wife of yours is found not guilty, the way Bart tells it. Are you really willing to risk it all on those odds?"

"What choice do I have?"

"Your father and I are willing to wire you two hundred

and fifty thousand dollars today to help you sustain yourself over the next few weeks. After which, should your wife be found innocent, you can return to your old job at Mason and Meachum and keep the money. However, should your wife be sentenced and you are not allowed to return to your job, you could come to work for your father. We'd even grant you access to your old trust fund and consider meeting with the lawyers to have you added back into our will."

Caide's mouth watered at the thought of money like that. He and Rachael had never been very good at saving. What little they had put back would be gone soon, with no money coming in. Not in a month, no, but after the trial, if he couldn't return to work he'd made no plan for what would happen then.

The offer was too good to be true, though. Knowing his mother, it'd come with a steep price. "What's the catch?"

"I'm not trying to swindle you, son." She remained quiet for a moment before speaking again. "I would, however, need you to publicly drop your support from your wife's case. In the off chance that she is released, *obviously*, you would have to force a divorce."

"You want me to *what?*"

"Well, you can't stand the negative press that will undoubtedly come if you continue to play the poor, doting husband. If you announce that you no longer believe your wife to be innocent and you withdraw your support now, before the verdict, they are more likely to believe you."

"Or I'd just ruin her case."

"You shouldn't pay for her mistakes, Caide Matthew. You didn't kill that poor girl. You'll agree to work openly with the prosecutor for the remainder of the trial. Oh, and bring your children into it. Say you won't raise your children around a monster—the press will love it. You'll go from a lying, cheating husband, to a devoted father." She laughed loudly, obviously proud of her plan.

"My children are not pawns in this trial, Mother. A move like that will ruin Rachael's chances at being acquitted."

"She killed someone, Caide Matthew. Open your eyes," she said angrily.

"She *may have* killed someone. It hasn't been proven. She's still my wife, she's still a good mother. I agree that I don't want to support her. I've already told her lawyer that—"

"You did?" she asked, her voice filled with excitement.

Caide sighed. "I'm an Abbott at heart, Mother. After the trial I realized that's what I had to do. If this all ends badly, I'll be able to say I backed out."

"That's not going to be enough, don't you see? Any fool can say that once it's over with. You have to be one step ahead of the game. You have to make the statement now."

"She's still my wife. Our marriage may be falling apart, she may even be a murderer, but I have to know that I did this to her. If I hadn't cheated on her, none of this would be happening. I'm not blameless here."

"Nobody made her do this, Caide Matthew, least of all you. You mustn't blame yourself."

"I'm not blaming myself. I'm just admitting that I put her in the situation. Withdrawing support now will make me look even worse than I do. You can't honestly expect me to do this. She may have done something terrible—"

"Unspeakable," his mother added in a heated whisper.

"But I don't want to see her burn for it if she doesn't deserve to. To do what you're suggesting, it would tip the scales unfairly. Her lawyer believes she may truly be innocent—"

"That's what he's paid to do."

"Not anymore."

"Excuse me?"

"I sent in his final paycheck the day after the trial. Whatever it is they've got, it's good enough for him to continue without pay."

"You don't even know what he's planning?"

"I don't, Mother, and I don't care. Whatever it is, she deserves a fair chance without the jury being swayed. I won't do that to her. I still care about what happens to her."

"You still care about her, yet you're refusing to pay her lawyer?"

"What can I say, Mother? You raised me to be just like you. Image above all else, right? Isn't that the Abbott motto?" he asked grimly, running a palm over his face.

"So you've made up your mind then? You won't take our money?"

"I'd take your money if it were actually to help me, not just to spite my wife. My decision is made."

"Very well. Should you come to your senses and change your mind, you just let me know."

"Goodbye, Mother." Caide snapped his phone shut, his head pounding with anger. He glanced at the clock and realization overtook him. *The kids.* He'd overslept. Brinley missed school. *Way to go, Caide. Great freaking job.* The voice in his head sounded eerily like Rachael.

He grabbed a pair of gray pajama pants from the top of his closet and threw them over his boxers. He kicked the empty bourbon bottle underneath the bed and rushed from his bedroom toward Brinley's room. He flicked on her light and saw her white and purple canopy bed, unmade and empty.

"Brinley?" he called out, fear gripping his heart. He darted across the hall from her room to Davis'. The red race car bed that Rachael bought for his last birthday was rumpled with covers and pillows, but Davis was nowhere in sight.

Nightmares began to fill his mind: what if they'd tried to

walk to school? What if they were outside in an ocean of reporters? What if they'd tried to eat breakfast and choked? What if they'd been kidnapped? What if social services had taken them from their beds? Where were they?

If you've never lost a child, even briefly in a department store or because of a miscommunication about which parent was supposed to pick them up, you can't even imagine the feeling. Ice cold fear grips your organs, gruesome images of milk carton children fill your mind, and nothing at all seems like the right plan of action. The fear filled Caide, making his heart pound and his stomach churn. Everything began happening in slow motion. He turned to run out of Davis' room, checking the kitchen table, beneath the computer desk, in the refrigerator and cabinets he knew they couldn't possibly be in. He threw back curtains in the living room, overturned couch cushions, he checked the washer and dryer, the backdoor, the pantry. He hurried wildly throughout the house in the hopes that his children were playing a simple game of hide and seek. He stopped in the hallway, hearing a faint sound. Running toward the bathroom, he spied the light shining under the door.

Could it be? He burst through the door, his last hope, and let out a sigh of relief.

"Corie?"

Corie was seated on the bathroom floor. Davis sat in front of her, wrapped in a green bath towel, as Corie ran a comb through his dark brown curls. Brinley sat in the bathtub, pouring water from the faucet to her head with a cup. She pushed her soaking wet hair from her eyes when she saw him.

"Daddy's awake! Daddy, look who's here!" Brinley pointed to Corie happily.

Caide smiled at Corie, who politely nodded his way, before turning back toward Davis. "Brinley, sit back down and rinse, sweetie. You're going to get shampoo in your eyes," Corie instructed. Brinley sat back down obediently, gathering another cup of water.

"Corie, I'm so sorry. I don't know what happened. I just overslept. I can't thank you enough for being here. I'm just so embarrassed. I'll triple your pay this week. I can take it from here if you need to get to class," Caide offered, unsure of what to say.

Corie didn't bother to look his way. "It's okay. I'm already late for my last class. I'll just catch up tomorrow. I fixed the kids breakfast and they're almost done with their baths. You can bring me outfits to dress them in, if you'd like. If you need to go to work today, I can stay with them."

"Thanks. I don't plan on working today. You're free to go whenever. I'm going to call Brinley's school to let them know why she wasn't there."

"Already called them." A hint of annoyance rang in her voice.

"Oh, right. Well, thank you again. I'll go get those clothes for you." He backed out of the bathroom like a scolded child.

Upon entering Brinley's closet, Caide was struck with just how much he'd missed. Sometime or another, when he'd been at work, his daughter had apparently outgrown all the frilly dresses and jumpers he still pictured her closet being filled with. He realized he couldn't remember the last time he'd even actually been in her closet. He could've sworn the last time he was there it was pink. When did it get painted purple to match her bed? Surely Rachael didn't paint it herself.

He faced the white dresser in front of him, gambling at which drawer might hold what he needed. After several wrong guesses, he pulled open a drawer that held several folded t-shirts and pants. They all looked so big. When did Brinley start wearing size five?

He flipped through six or seven pairs of jeans before he finally reached a pair he recognized. They were bright red corduroy pants that Brinley had worn for her second Christmas. Rachael brought them home from some sale she'd seen on her way home from the studio one day. Caide remembered throwing a fit over the one hundred and sixty dollar Christmas outfit. It had a white shirt to match, decked out with Christmas trees along the hem. It was cute, sure, but just as Caide predicted it had been worn for only an hour or two before it came off for her to eat. Then, of course, she couldn't wear it out of season and she'd outgrown it by the next year. Caide thought she'd forgotten about the outfit, like he had. He should've known better. Rachael didn't forget.

The fight that year had been brought up in several arguments throughout the years—not the outfit or the waste of money, no, those had been Rachael's fault, so of course they were forgotten—it was Caide's mistake that night that had never been let go.

Rachael had come home from the mall toting Brinley on one hip and a shopping bag on the other. Their finances had sorted out since he'd taken the job with Mason and Meachum, but Christmas shopping had put a damper on the budget Caide had laid out. Rachael had insisted on buying each of her students' new tutus. Mason and Meachum had received new watches with golden plating. Caide had gotten Rachael a new diamond necklace and earring set, they'd sent Audrey and John a new wine cooler, and their tree was loaded up with gifts for Brinley. Still, Rachael had yet to find the right gift for Caide. She was supposed to have been out looking when she came home that day, grinning from ear to ear.

"You'll never guess what I found," she exclaimed, sitting the bag on the kitchen table.

"If you tell me, doesn't that ruin the surprise?"

She waved a hand at him. "Not for you, silly goose. It's for Brinley."

"I thought we'd agreed we were done shopping for Brinley?"

She smiled brightly. "This isn't a present. It's for her to wear on Christmas Day. Wait 'til you see it." Rachael dragged him into the kitchen. She grabbed the bag—Caide couldn't recall now what store it had even been from. She opened it and pulled out the red pants and matching shirt. "Isn't it cute? She's just going to love it," she squealed, holding it up to Brinley's chest.

"Seems kind of pointless to buy her a Christmas outfit, don't you think?" he asked, cocking his head to the side.

"Why would it be pointless?" she asked, her smile fading.

"It's an outfit for one day, Rach. She'll outgrow it before she can wear it again."

She pulled the outfit away from their daughter. "You don't know that she'll outgrow it. Besides, I want to get a good Christmas picture for her to see when she's older. It's her first real Christmas. Last year she was too young to understand."

"Fine. Whatever." Caide held his hands up in surrender. "I'm not arguing."

"Thank you," she said, sounding relieved. Caide nodded, turning to walk away. "Can you go hang this in her closet for me? I don't want it to wrinkle."

He took the outfit from her, knowing that whether or not it was wrinkled, Rachael would be sure to iron it incessantly the night before and probably the next morning as well. Somehow, as he'd spun around with the outfit, the tag managed to come loose, allowing him to see the price. One hundred and sixty-six dollars.

He turned back to face her, placing a fist on his temple.

BECOMING MRS. ABBOTT

"Please. Rachael, *please* tell me you did not spend two hundred dollars on this." He held the outfit in the air.

She wouldn't look at him. "Oh, practically one hundred and fifty. Don't exaggerate."

"Are you kidding me? I mean, you realize we aren't made of money, right?" he asked, swinging the outfit as his arms moved wildly.

"Caide, can you just…not?"

He tightened his jaw. "Not what?"

"Not make this a bigger deal than it is. It's one outfit." She walked past him to get Brinley a snack from the pantry.

He spun around, his gaze following her. "It *is* a big deal, Rachael. You can't just go blow that much money on an outfit that'll get worn for an hour and then hang in the closet for months before you eventually decide to throw it away."

She froze, staring at him with wide eyes. "I just wanted her to have a nice outfit like you did growing up."

"She isn't me, Rachael. We aren't my parents. You know you aren't going to take pictures and even if you do, they'll never end up developed. No one will see her but us."

Her chin began to quiver and he knew the tears were coming. "That's not true. Someone could stop in."

"No one will stop in, Rachael. No one ever stops in. We aren't the freaking Brady Bunch. I know you try to do up Christmas because you're insecure about our life—"

"I'm what?" Rachael's voice grew louder, her face red. "You think I'm insecure about our life?"

"You always do this. You buy presents for people who don't get you anything in return. You make us dress up just to change two hours later, you spend a month decorating every inch of this house and no one sees it but us, and you cook a meal large enough to feed us for a year and half of it goes bad before we even get to it." Seeing her tears falling, he lowered his voice. "I know you love holidays, Rachael. I get it.

I know your dad went all out for you as a child and I get that you want that for Brinley. That's fine, but sweetie, it's just not realistic. Our family is gone. You can't keep pretending we're something that we're not. I'm sorry, this is too much. You have to take it back."

She turned away from him, but spun back just as quickly. *"How dare you?* How dare you make this about the money?" she demanded. "It's about the feeling our daughter will get when she wakes up to a house full of presents, a pie baking in the oven, and our family—no matter how small—dressed up and ready to celebrate. I don't know what Christmas was like for you, Caide. I'm sure, like most of your childhood, it probably sucked. But our daughter won't grow up that way."

He let out a small laugh, trying to get her to calm down. "Our daughter is two years old. She barely understands any of it. She doesn't need a dress to make her feel special. She won't even remember it. What she *will* remember is living in the streets because her mother spent us out of house and home."

"We have the money! I get that you're used to a huge bank account, but ours has plenty in it. Caide, we have more now, after buying Christmas, than I ever had growing up."

He shook his head. "We do not have the money, Rachael. We're managing, yes. We're better off than this time last year, but we aren't *this* comfortable yet," he said, gesturing toward the outfit.

She crossed her arms, stepping toward him. "Then take back whatever you got me, if you're so worried about money."

"I have to be. You spend it as quickly as I can bring it in."

Rachael slapped him. "Don't you do that. Don't you act like you're the only one bringing in money here. I work hard."

"*When* you work. When you aren't cancelling class

because Audrey is fighting with John again. When you aren't taking in charity cases, doing lessons for free, or buying your students expensive gifts. At least six of your twenty students are coming for free and you're buying their little outfits," he waved his hand in the air, "and shoes and whatever the hell else they need."

"Lucy's mom has leukemia, Caide. She can't afford lessons anymore. And Amber's mom does pay when she can—she has two other kids she's supporting all on her own. And Chloe's mom, I've told you about her, there's always some new boyfriend picking her up from practice. I like knowing she has something stable in her life. Jasmine—"

He held his hand up. "I get it. They all deserve your help. I'm not saying you don't work. I don't even want to be on this subject."

"No, you'd much rather talk about how we don't have a family, right? How we're alone so we should just give up? That'll be a great lesson to teach our daughter, huh?" She bent down, scooping Brinley up off the floor and handing her a juice cup from the fridge.

"Just drop it, Rachael. Keep the damn outfit. Forget I said anything."

Tears were in her eyes once again, and Caide knew it wasn't over. "You want me to forget that you basically called our life a joke?"

"Don't be dramatic. I only meant that it'd be different if we were going somewhere to visit family, if we were leaving the house at all. But I said it's fine. Just don't worry about it."

"No, Caide, you know what? You're absolutely right. It's pointless to try to do anything special for the holidays. They should be reserved for families. See, I was under the impression that we *were* a family. Since you've made it so abundantly clear that we have no family, don't even bother coming to Christmas at all. I'm sure it'll be nothing special."

She stormed out of the room, taking Brinley with her. Minutes later, he'd heard her cries through the bedroom door.

Of course, he *did* come to Christmas and—like he predicted—the outfit was worn for less than an hour, no pictures were ever developed, and over half the dinner was tossed out a week later.

He hadn't seen the outfit since. Until now, he'd assumed she'd thrown it out years ago. Caide rubbed his hands over the rough corduroy, remembering that day.

His fingers felt a lump in the left pocket. He dug into the pocket until his fingers connected with something cool and smooth. He pulled it out and scrunched his brow, turning the small golden key over in his hand. There was no key chain or label, nothing at all to tell Caide what the key belonged to or to warn him of the secrets it would uncover.

He ran his hands through the drawer again and then through all the others, checking to be sure there wasn't a hidden lock somewhere. He hurriedly searched Brinley's closet, overturning totes and checking every pocket in sight, but found nothing to end his search.

Finally, Caide let out a disappointed sigh. He folded the pants back neatly and returned them to their hiding place before sliding the key into his pocket. He left the closet, carrying an outfit for Brinley back to the bathroom. He told himself he'd come back and search every inch of the house if necessary. He had to find out exactly what it was Rachael had to hide.

CHAPTER SIXTY-TWO

AVERY

Jeanna Avery sat in her office. It had been a slow day—slow enough that she'd opened up a bottle of wine and was starting on her third glass when a knock sounded on her door.

She shut the file that lay open on her desk, corked the bottle of wine, and cursed herself for sending her secretary home early. "Come in."

Her door crept open slowly and a stout woman with short, graying blonde curls walked in. She wore a black pant suit with a floral pink blouse underneath it. Her neck boasted a set of pearls to match her large earrings.

Avery stood, offering her hand. "I'm Jeanna Avery. I don't believe we've met."

"Good afternoon, Ms. Avery. My name is Martha Abbott."

"Martha Abbott? As in Abbott Jewelers? As in Caide Abbott's mother?"

"The very one." Martha smiled warmly.

Avery gestured toward the chair in front of her desk, letting her guest sit before she did. "It's a pleasure to meet you, Mrs. Abbott. What can I do for you?"

Martha set her purse on her lap, pressing her hands gently on top of it. "I'm here because I have some information for you. Information that may help you win your case."

She blinked. "I see. And what were you hoping to get in return?"

Martha laughed out loud. "I think you misunderstand. I don't want anything other than for you to win this case."

"Let me get this straight, you actually want me to win? You do realize that would mean your daughter-in-law would go to prison, right?"

"Of course," the woman said, her lips pressed into a thin line.

"Okay. So I'm assuming you have some evidence for me?"

She put a hand to her chest. "My son called me the other day and we discussed this dreadful case. The things he had to say about his wife were terrible. Something has to be done." She frowned.

"I see. Mrs. Abbott, Caide has already been on the stand. If he had something to say, that was his chance. I won't have another opportunity to call a witness. I'm sorry you wasted a trip down here."

"That's no problem, you see, my son won't agree to say what he's told me to anyone else. He's always been very loyal." *Loyal.* Avery had to force herself not to roll her eyes as she thought back to the security tapes. "He's just afraid of what it'll do to his wife," Martha continued.

"So what was your plan, then? I can't just take your word for it. That won't stand in court and, even if it did, I've told you I have no more chances to call a witness."

Mrs. Abbott smiled menacingly. "Actually, I was thinking of making this known to a larger audience. Much larger."

"You were going to go to the press? Mrs. Abbott, with all due respect, you said your son doesn't want to talk about it. How do you plan to get him to open up to the press?"

Martha leaned forward, her voice carrying throughout the room. "Two years ago, we had a bomb threat on one of our warehouses. Police evacuated the warehouse, investigated, and found it to be a prank. Six months later, it happened again. Once again, it was nothing, probably some insolent kid. Nevertheless, the police advised that we put in an automatic recorder to assist with investigations should we receive any other calls. That recorder has proven itself incredibly useful over the past year, including now."

"You're telling me you recorded your son and now you're going to use that against him?"

Martha's smile fell from her face. "Can I be frank, Ms. Avery?"

"Sure."

"You can't repeat anything I tell you, it's illegal. Of course, you know that." She paused, looking around the room. "I don't care one little bit about my son or his dreadful little wife. They're no family of mine. What I do care about, however, is my company. It's all I have, and my husband and I have worked too hard to let it get destroyed now. This is our best season. From October to February, our sales skyrocket. This year, however, after news of the trial, our sales have been dismal. Our mere association with my son and his wife, however unfortunate, is ruining our company. It is not acceptable. My company will not suffer due to a mistake we did not make. However, if our son is made out to be a worried father, scared of what his own wife is capable of, then he'd be called a hero. People will love him, pity him even, which will turn our sales back around. As a much added bonus, it will also turn the public opinion on Rachael from bad to worse. No one will listen to the defense, you'll be a shoo-in to win." She clapped her hands together, pure excitement filling her face.

Avery felt sick to her stomach. "I'd like to win this case,

Mrs. Abbott. I want to see Miss Underwood's killer behind bars just the same as everyone else, but I'd like to win fairly. Winning is only winning if it's done right."

"Oh, go knit that on a pillow. We're talking national success, Ms. Avery. We could make you famous, the prosecutor who locked the ruthless killer away and eased a community's worst fears."

She folded her hands together on top of the desk. "Fame doesn't interest me, Mrs. Abbott. Justice does. Why would you come to me?"

"I assumed you'd want to help me. I'm going to the press today."

"I'm afraid you thought wrong. I'm sorry, Mrs. Abbott, I can't help you." Avery stood, walking toward the door.

"Very well then. I took you for a very different type of lawyer. I assumed you'd, like any *good* lawyer, want to win at any cost."

Avery pressed her lips together in frustration. "You do realize that the jury most likely won't be swayed by gossip and rumors? It's against the rules for them to watch the news, read the papers, or discuss the case at all. There's a good chance the only person your betrayal will hurt is your son. There are rules in place to prevent this sort of thing."

Mrs. Abbott stood up, adjusting her jacket and walking out the door. Before she was completely past Avery she stopped, turning to look her in the eye, and smiled. "I understand the rules quite well, Ms. Avery. But, then again, husbands aren't supposed to cheat and wives aren't supposed to kill. If everyone followed the rules, we wouldn't be having this conversation. Good day." Her gray eyes bore into Avery like knives, the cruel grin on her face looked so comfortable it must have been worn quite often.

"Good day," Avery said firmly, shutting the door behind

her. She let out a breath she hadn't realized she'd been holding, reaching for her bottle of wine.

CHAPTER SIXTY-THREE

RACHAEL

Rachael awoke for the third time that morning to the sounds of her cellmate snoring. Abby Baker was a hard and deep sleeper who didn't seem the least bit fazed by the lumpy mattresses in their cell.

In the weeks since they'd met, Rachael hadn't spoken more than a few words to her new cellmate. She rolled over and slowly climbed out of bed, attempting to be quiet, though her century-old bed made that an impossible feat. She walked softly over toward the toilet, pulling her pants down and edging her bottom onto the icy seat.

Her toes ached from the cold concrete, despite the two pairs of socks they'd allowed her to wear.

"You cold or something?" Rachael glanced over at the bunk. Abby was awake, staring at her sleepily.

"Freezing." She slid her pants up, avoiding eye contact.

Abby, apparently oblivious to any awkwardness, stretched in her bed. "You get used to it after a while. Sucks that your first time's in the winter. But, then again, you'd hate summer too. You sweat a few pounds off a day here in July." She eyed Rachael. "Then again, maybe that wouldn't be a bad thing for you." Her gaze rested on the pudge around Rachael's gut.

Rachael looked down, tugging at her orange jumpsuit.

"So, what'd you do before this?" Abby asked.

"Huh?"

"Like for work. Did you have a job?"

"Oh, I taught dance. I own a studio downtown," she said, looking at the small window near the top of their cell.

"That's it?"

"Well, it takes up a fair share of my time. I'm a mother, too, so that takes up the rest."

"My mom stayed home with me when I was young, it was nice," Abby told her.

Rachael nodded, imagining what kind of home life this poor girl could've suffered from.

"What about your mom?"

"I never knew my mom," Rachael said. It never got easier to say that.

"Oh. What about your dad then?" Abby asked, not missing a beat.

"My dad worked for the port in La Rue. He passed away too though, a few years ago."

"That sucks." Abby looked truly sorry. Beneath her rugged exterior—the graying black hair, the scar that ran from her eyebrow to just below her nose, and her slightly wrinkled face—Rachael saw a softness in her eyes. She must've been no older than forty, but the woman had known sorrow.

She climbed down off of her bunk and crept toward the toilet. Rachael sat on the concrete floor despite the cold, and avoided looking her way.

"You don't have to look so uncomfortable. I have kids. I'm used to people watching me, don't worry."

Rachael nodded, turning her head slightly, but still avoiding looking in that direction. "So what do you do?"

Abby let out a loud belch. "Don't do much now. I was a teacher for over a decade, taught third grade." She grabbed a wad of toilet paper off the wall.

"You were a teacher?" Rachael couldn't hide the shock in her voice.

"Don't act so surprised. Both my parents were teachers. My dad taught high school chemistry, mom taught kindergarten. I guess you could call it our family business. Only my brother took a different path. He's a pharmacist."

Rachael's confusion welled inside of her. "Where are they now?"

"Still working. My dad's getting ready to retire. We try and tell Mom her class is too much, but she loves those kids so much. It just does no good. My brother lives in Tennessee; he has a wife and a little girl named Kaitie." Abby stood up from the toilet, pulling up her pants and walking over to sit back down on her bed. "You can sit up here, you know. I'm not going to bite."

"I'm okay."

Abby shrugged, stretching out once again. "Suit yourself."

"What about your kids?"

"I have two little boys, Malakye and Cody. Sweet boys. They're seven and eleven."

"I've got two also. Brinley's almost six and Davis is two."

Abby laughed. "Those two-year-olds, I tell you what, terrible twos? They sure got that right, didn't they?"

Rachael nodded. "I know it. I don't remember Brinley being as bad as Davis either."

"The first ones never are. I think it's because there's only one at that time. They say it gets worse with each one."

When Rachael pictured a hardened criminal, Abby might've had the physical appearance of one, but talking to her was as easy as talking to a friend. She hated herself for feeling so judgmental, but couldn't wrap her mind around the entire scenario.

"All right. Quit staring at me like I have three heads or something," Abby said firmly, a slight smile on her face.

"You're just different than I expected. I'm sorry. I mean how many times have you been in here?"

"Total? Oh gosh." She laughed. "I think this is my sixth time. I've nearly lost count."

"Wow," Rachael said. "You just act so casual about it."

"What? You think all criminals just sit around spitting and snorting and stabbing things? You think we only talk about drugs or robberies or our latest kill?" she asked angrily.

Rachael scooted back, her hands up in surrender. "No, of course not. This is all just new to me. I'm sorry, I don't mean to offend you."

"Girl, you need to chill." Abby slapped her knee from laughter. "I ain't mad. You first timers are all so nervous. It's cute. Look, just because I'm a criminal don't mean you can judge me any more than anyone else. I've seen thieves go back to pay for what the cashier missed, I've seen dealers playing board games with their kids, and I've seen murderers in the front pews on Sunday morning. What you need to realize is that what we've done, that's all it is. It's what we've *done*, not who we are. We do bad things, but so do all the rest of them out there. Everyone breaks the law sometime or another, we're just the ones who get caught. Bottom line, ain't a soul out there knows anyone's situation but their own. You don't even know your best friend. Things go wrong, situations go south. We all just deal with it the best we know how."

Rachael blushed. "I get it. Bad things happen to good people."

"Nah." Abby shook her head. "You don't get it. Bad things don't happen to good people and bad things don't happen to bad people. Bad things happen to people. Good things happen to people. Period. End of story. There are no good or bad people. There are just people. Just six billion people. And at the end of the day we're all just trying to get by. Things happen: horrible, disgusting things and beautiful, amazing things. No one's life is just one thing: good or bad. We all just take whatever happens and deal with it and then we go from there. That's it. You can't live your life looking at everything as good or bad, black or white. Nothing works like that, sure as hell not life."

Rachael nodded. "So what did you do, then?"

"That's a long story, for another time." She looked at her wrist, though it contained no watch. "Don't you have somewhere you need to be anyway?"

Rachael looked toward the window again, where sunlight had crept in without her really noticing.

She stood up, walking toward her cell door. It was almost time for Hampton to come for her. "I suppose you're right." She smiled at Abby, who leaned back against the concrete wall and closed her eyes.

CHAPTER SIXTY-FOUR

HAMPTON

Hampton walked into the county jail. Three officers sat around their desks, rubbing sleep from their eyes and shooting their morning coffee like it contained alcohol.

"Morning, Hampton."

"Morning, Dawson." Hampton waved casually. "She ready?"

Dawson Stanelle looked at his watch. "Dennis went to get her a few minutes ago. They should be out soon. Grab a cup of coffee while you wait."

"Thanks." He walked over to the coffee pot and filled a paper cup. Coffee was going to be his best friend this morning after a long night of going over evidence again. A loud buzzer announced that a prisoner was being escorted out. All eyes turned toward the door.

Hampton's phone chimed in his pocket, alerting him to a text message. Before he was able to see Rachael, he pulled his phone out and snuck a glance at the screen.

J. Avery. What could she want? He pressed the button and read the message quickly.

Have you watched the news today?

He hadn't watched the news, in fact, because he had spent the last twelve hours tirelessly flipping through every file he had on Rachael's case. He tapped the button to craft a reply.

What did you do?

His gut filled with dread as he awaited her response. Just then, the door to the hall opened and he shoved his phone into his jacket pocket. Rachael walked out of the hallway, a small smirk on her face directed toward him.

"Hi," she said softly.

"Hi." He smiled, hoping he'd wiped the worry from his face.

Stanelle grabbed Rachael's cuffs from Dennis, he gently nudged her forward. Hampton jumped in front of her, holding the door open. He walked quickly to his black BMW and opened her door again.

"Be safe." Stanelle nodded toward Hampton formally.

"Thanks," Hampton replied, sliding into his car.

He'd pulled out of the station before Rachael spoke up. "You okay?"

He nodded, cranking the heat in the cool car. "I'm fine. Why?"

"You seem different today."

The woman was good, he'd give her that. "I'm tired. I was up all night."

"Oh?" she asked, her voice hopeful.

"Nothing yet, but if there's something to be found I'll find it."

"I know. I trust you. I just feel like we're running out of time."

"Don't stress over it. I know that's impossible for you, but just relax and let us handle it. Seriously."

"Relaxing is not something I'm good at," she told him.

"I've noticed."

Rachael offered up a small smile. "Hey, have you talked to Caide or my kids? They haven't come by and they aren't taking my calls. I'm starting to get worried."

He attempted to smile at her. "What did I just tell you? Stop worrying. They're fine."

"So you've heard from them?" Her face lit up at the mere possibility.

"I talked to your husband after the trial. Just once."

"What did he say? Did you tell him the kids could come to see me?"

He nodded, choosing his words carefully. "I did. He's just been really busy. I'm sure it isn't easy without you."

Rachael nodded. "I just miss them."

"You'll see them again, Rachael," he assured her.

She nodded, though her mind was clearly already elsewhere.

CHAPTER SIXTY-FIVE

SHAYNA

Shayna's door crept open.

"Mrs. Steele," Kortnee said quietly. "Mrs. Abbott is here."

Shayna glanced at her watch. "Oh, of course. Send her in." Kortnee stepped back, allowing Rachael to walk through the door. "Rachael. Good morning, how are you?"

"I'm okay, thank you. How are you?"

"I'm well, thank you. Would you excuse me for just a second?" She set her mug down on the coffee table and rushed out of the office. "Hampton," she yelled, watching him walk out the door.

A startled Kortnee jumped at her outburst. Shayna smiled apologetically before hurrying out the door behind him. "Hey!"

He stopped, turning around to face her. "Yeah?"

She panted heavily, catching up to him. "Have you seen the news today?"

"Why does everyone keep asking me that?"

"You need to watch it. Before you pick her up." Her voice was firm, her eyes locked with his.

"Why?"

"Trust me," she said, turning to walk back toward the door.

"What station?" he asked.

"All of them," she called over her shoulder before walking in her lobby.

"Is everything all right?" Rachael asked as Shayna made her way back into the room.

"Everything's fine," she said, smoothing her hands over her pants as she sat down. She took a deep breath. "I just needed to speak with Hampton for a second. So, now, since our first two weeks are nearly over I'd like to get into a few more relevant topics. You've told me how you and Caide came to be married, tell me more about your marriage."

Rachael didn't look totally at ease. She tapped her fingers on the arm of the couch nervously. "Um, okay. Well, my husband is a great partner. He really is. Despite our imperfect beginning, I do love Caide and he does love me. Getting married young, it means we've been through it all together. We've been poor and well-off, we've had car wrecks, we've graduated, bought cars, built a home. I watched him become a father. We've struggled and celebrated and every moment of that has been together. I didn't plan for my life to go the way it has, but despite the obvious flaws, I wouldn't trade it. Caide gave me my two greatest blessings, so even if I go to jail, even if he cheats on me until I die, I'll always love him for that. Sure, we've fought. We've been young and headstrong and stubborn, but we've also been really, insanely happy."

Shayna rested her chin in her palm, her elbow balanced on her knee. "What is your favorite thing about your husband?"

"Seeing him with our kids. He really is such a good dad. Even though Caide misses a lot, when he's there he's really great. Our kids adore their father."

"Rachael, I notice when you talk about your parents love: how inspiring it was, how it influenced you, you talk about how they loved each other, how their love never died. It's interesting to me that when you mention their love, despite never knowing your mother, you talk about how they loved each other yet, when you discuss your marriage, your love, you only mention how good he is to your kids. How great of a dad he is. How happy he makes you when you're with the kids. Why do you think that is?"

She answered without hesitation. "My kids come first. My children are everything to me. I'm happiest when they're happy."

"So you don't have any expectations from your husband as far as simply being your husband?"

Rachael frowned. "I don't think I've ever really thought about it. We've always had the kids. They're always there. I don't think about Caide and I without them."

"Don't you ever have date nights?"

"We don't have family to watch the kids. We have a babysitter, but she's there so often as it is, I try not to use her unless it's necessary."

She nodded, sitting up straight and picking up her notepad from the side table. "Rachael, when is that last time you and your husband were intimate?"

Rachael blushed, pressing her fingers to her lips.

"Don't be embarrassed," Shayna assured her.

She touched her mouth. "No, it's not that."

"What is it?"

She was quiet, looking down. When she finally looked back up, she met Shayna's eyes with shame. "I can't even remember. We've only recently gotten Davis into his own bed at night and Caide usually comes home long after I'm asleep."

"A rough estimate will be fine," she said, making a note of

that and avoiding Rachael's eye with the hope that it would make her feel more at ease.

"Maybe when I was pregnant with Davis? Two years ago? I can't remember any time after that…" She trailed off.

Shayna steadied her face before she looked up. "I see."

Rachael covered her face. "I know that's bad. We stay so busy. Our kids have school and dance and doctors and Caide has work and I have recitals and school projects for Brinley. There's just no time. We forget."

Shayna would bet Caide didn't forget. "Rachael, I need you to be honest with me. I know you are a good mother. I see that. I trust that. I need to know if you're a good wife."

A nerve had been struck, it was written all over her face. She didn't speak at first, staring at her hands. Finally, she looked up. "I was there. I was there when no one else was. I was there when his family dropped him and he had no one else. When all of our savings had been spent and we were splitting cans of soup for supper. When he had the flu and I had two sick children on my hips while I ran a fever myself. When he leaves something at home that he needs for court and I have to drop whatever I'm doing and drive an hour away to bring it to him, I'm the one who's there. I'm the one who wakes up at four in the morning to bake him a birthday cake or iron his pants. A wife is supposed to be a partner. I may not have always had my legs waxed or my hair done or been awake at midnight when he drags in dog tired or drunk just waiting to be had; usually I'm passed out, covered in snot and wearing whatever I woke up in. I may not have been the greatest lover or the best housekeeper, but I was a damn good wife." Rachael breathed heavily as if merely talking about her life exhausted her.

"Okay."

She heard a sniffle and Rachael stared at her with a hopeless expression. "You know, I didn't deserve this. Not any of this. I've been good to him and faithful to him. I've taken care of our house and our kids. And what do I get for it? I get to be told that my husband is cheating on me in front of a crowd of people just waiting to judge me. I get to sit and watch him cheat *on tape*, and I don't get to act mad or yell at him like a normal wife. I have to hold my composure because people are watching, waiting for me to lash out. I had my heart ripped out and stomped on in front of fifty people, all of whom I've never met. I didn't even get to grieve because all I get to think about is the next question or next witness, the next piece of evidence. Do you have any idea how that feels?"

"Tell me how it feels," Shayna urged her.

"It feels *terrible*. I feel helpless and pitiful and alone and worried about my kids and scared to go to jail and pissed off at Caide and pissed off that no one believes me and *pissed off* because I have no idea what's going on inside my own head. It's like my own body is betraying me. I'm just so exhausted all the time." She placed her face in her palms, her sobbing preventing her from talking anymore.

Shayna was quiet, feeling unsure of where to go from here. Rachael's cries were so genuine she felt as if it were only logical to console her. She knew, however, it was ill-advised. Through great sorrow comes truth and Shayna knew this was as close to a breakthrough as she'd ever come with Rachael. Now was the time to push.

"Rachael, how do you feel about Blaire? Knowing what you know?"

Rachael wiped her eyes, grabbing a tissue and trying to catch her breath. "Up until now, Blaire was always just some girl at Caide's office. He never mentioned her and I never honestly gave her much thought. I always insisted he buy her a Christmas present like he did for the rest of his coworkers, but other than that, she never crossed my mind." She shook her head. "Now, if I'm being honest, I hate her dead as much as I would have alive. Audrey gave me too much credit. I wouldn't have forgiven her. I mean, don't get me wrong, I'm sorry about what happened to her, it's terrible and no one should die like that. She was young and she probably had a lot left to do with her life. But that'll never change what she did. I'll never be able to un-see my husband sliding up her skirt." She looked into Shayna's eyes, hurt filling her face. "She knew me, Shayna. She was nice to me. She wasn't some unsuspecting girl my husband pulled one over on. She *knew* he was married, and no matter what good she's done, no matter how horrible her death, there is a lump of hate in my heart for her and I don't know if that will ever go away."

Shayna pressed her lips together, studying her expression. "Rachael, did you know your husband was cheating on you? Or that he ever had?"

Rachael swallowed, her gaze sliding to the left for a split-second. "No," she said simply.

Shayna nodded.

That was the first lie.

CHAPTER SIXTY-SIX

HAMPTON

Argus Hampton pulled up to his ranch-style home at half past ten. His stomach was filled with a bubbling fear. He climbed out of his car, his giant sheepdog rushing toward him, tongue flopping.

"Hey there, Gus." He patted the dog's fluffy head as he walked across the porch to the side entrance of his kitchen. Laying his keys on the bar, he walked toward the living room, sinking into the couch. He grabbed the remote, took a deep, agonizing breath and pressed the power button.

He flipped through several channels of infomercials and cartoons before he finally landed on a photograph of Rachael. He recognized her instantly, though the picture must've been from years ago. She was around twenty pounds lighter with her blonde hair chopped short and highlighted red. Her arms wrapped around a younger Caide's neck with ease. She was smiling brightly, looking just past the camera, while he smiled at her.

Hampton found himself captivated by how happy she looked. His smile was wiped away instantly as he noticed the caption.

Frightened husband reveals that he no longer believes his wife could be innocent.
"I don't want my wife around my children."

Hampton cursed, turning up the volume just as a blonde reporter came on.

"Sources have confirmed that Caide Abbott, husband of accused murderer Rachael Abbott, is choosing to no longer stand behind his wife in her murder trial. Most of you have heard of this case by now. Mrs. Abbott, local owner of Tutu's dance studio on Market Street, is being accused of having viciously bludgeoned twenty-seven year old Blaire Underwood to death."

Rachael's picture disappeared, to be replaced by a picture of Blaire Underwood.

"To make matters worse, Miss Underwood is believed to have been having a long time affair with Caide Abbott. Now, just weeks before the final trial date, a tape has been released to us. Our source does wish to remain anonymous but tells us that Mr. Abbott admittedly withdrew payment from his wife's lawyer and no longer believes his wife may be innocent. He also reportedly said that he does not intend to support his wife's case any further. Mr. Abbott has asked for peace and respect as he mourns the sudden and untimely death of the woman he loved. He has requested that all questions and comments be kept quiet around himself and his children as they embark upon these next few months in what is sure to be a rocky road to a new normal. More on this tonight, I'm Jodie Hopkins with Channel Fourteen News. Thanks for watching."

Hampton flipped the channel as it went to a commercial and found that seven or eight other channels all bore pictures of Rachael and this ridiculous story. Hampton slammed the remote down on the coffee table, cursing.

He picked up his phone, unsure of who to call and found himself dialing Caide Abbott's number.

"Hello?" An annoyed sounding Caide answered the phone.

"What did you do, Abbott? What could you possibly have been thinking?"

"What do you want?"

"I want to know what could possibly possess you to do this to your wife. Do you really hate her that much? So much that you would damn her to a losing battle before she even has a chance?"

"Thought I'd made this clear. I am doing what is best for my family."

"She is your family, you son of a—"

"My children are my only concern now," he said stiffly.

"Your only concern is yourself and any mud that may sling on your perfect little name."

"You don't know me, Hampton. You don't know anything about this except what she's telling you. I don't know what it is you think you're going to get out of this whole thing but I want no part of it."

"When I get your wife acquitted, she will know what you've done. She will never forgive you and she will never forget."

He groaned. "You and I both know Rachael will never see freedom, not ever again."

Hampton was seething, his anger reaching a boiling point quickly. "She waits for you, did you know that? She asks about you. Even after what you did, she asks about you and wishes you'd come see her."

"I'm only going to say this once: I never want to see my wife again—not ever—and so help me, she will never see my children again. Now, I'm going to hang up. Do not contact me again, Hampton, unless you want harassment charges filed on you."

With that, the line went dead. Hampton slammed his phone shut. His face grew hot with fury as he tried to think of how to get Rachael out of this mess.

Suddenly it occurred to him…what if the answers he'd been searching for, the secrets he'd been trying to find—what if they'd been right under his nose the whole time? It was then that something struck Hampton: there was one option he hadn't weighed at all.

CHAPTER SIXTY-SEVEN

CAIDE

Caide sat at the white marble kitchen table, staring at the very man he'd never planned to see again.

Click, click.

He heard her heels approaching the dining room before he saw her. Her graying hair was piled high atop her head, her makeup layered pristinely. She wore a white pant suit with a green floral blouse. He stood as she entered the room, out of habit rather than respect.

"Hello, Caide Matthew."

"Mother." He nodded.

She gathered him in a cool, unwelcoming hug and pressed her cheek lightly on his—the only way she'd ever kissed him. "I suppose you've seen the news."

"Yes, I suppose so." He tapped the table, trying to remain calm. "I just want to know why."

"Why?" she asked, staring at him as she sat down. "Because it had to be done, that's why. You weren't man enough to take action, so I did. I was protecting you."

"Protecting me? Mother, you betrayed me. You turned me

BECOMING MRS. ABBOTT

into someone I never wanted to be. You spoke for me and twisted my words."

"I used a tape of exactly what you said," she said simply.

He bared his teeth in a grimace. "But you used it out of context and without permission. How could I ever forgive you for that?"

"Whether or not you forgive me, Caide Matthew, is no concern of mine. What *is* my concern, is the public opinion of you. People pity you, now. They see you as a fool who loved the right woman at the wrong time and now you are paying the ultimate price. People will revere you, articles will be written. Think of all the press you will bring to the family."

"I don't want press, Mother, don't you see that? I want peace. I want time to figure everything out. Your actions pretty much guaranteed that won't happen anytime soon."

"Son, I agreed to meet with you, but I am a very busy woman. You will not fight what I've done or you will be publicly humiliated. Life has dealt you a hand of cards and you have to deal with that. Stand up for yourself—for your children—build yourselves a new life. I won't waste my time arguing with you, it is of little importance to me anymore. In time, you'll see that what I've done for you was a favor and if you don't like it, well, I haven't talked to you in six years, another six won't kill me. So, stop your pity party and guilt trips, it won't work on me. You brought this on yourself when you married that girl. I will not have my business or my name run through the mud because you made a mockery of your life." Her face grew red as she spoke. "I will protect my family and my company above all else, and unfortunately as far as the public is concerned, that includes you."

Caide looked to his father, his wrinkled face unwavering behind the thick shadow of his mother. He sighed. "So when will I get the money, then?"

His mother folded her hands politely in front of her. She raised her eyebrows. "Money?"

"The money you promised me if I cooperated."

"You chose not to cooperate."

He spoke through gritted teeth. "You left me no choice. If I deny this now, I look like a liar. I have to play along. You got what you wanted, like you always do."

"The money was a one-time offer, son. That offer has expired. I suppose we could find a job for you in one of our warehouses somewhere." She glanced toward her silent husband, her face suddenly lighting up. "Why, we could make it a community event, can't you just imagine?" She held her hands up as if framing a headline. "Billionaire owners' son works his way up the company ladder from the bottom." She laughed with excitement.

His jaw dropped. It was a slap in the face. "You'd put me in a warehouse? I'm your son."

Her head jerked to look his direction. "I have no son, Caide Matthew. I've told you. The moment that you walked away from this family, you became just another mess I have to clean up after because you wear our name."

Caide stood, staring at her in disbelief. His mother remained calm. "Now, you just play along and when your wife is safely tucked away in prison, we'll find you a nice warehouse job somewhere close by. We'll give you benefits and fair pay. Of course, it'll be nowhere near what Mason is *undoubtedly* overpaying you, but it'll be enough. Keep your nose clean and we'll even give you a week of paid vacation after your first year."

Caide felt a lump growing in his throat. She stood with him, patting his head like a child. "That will be all, Caide Matthew. You may go."

Caide brushed his fingers through his hair, avoiding eye contact with his parents. His stomach churned with anger and embarrassment. He walked through the kitchen and toward the large oak doors. Before he could open it, he heard his mother's heels.

"Wait," she demanded.

Angry at the hope he felt in his heart, he turned around. She put her arms around his neck, pulling him into a loving embrace. His face filled with confusion until she pushed open the door and it dawned on him.

Flash. Flash. Click. Click. Flash.

Reporters. They were everywhere. She hugged him tighter, rubbing his back. The gesture felt foreign to him, though he couldn't help but wish this were a genuine act.

She held him in a hug for what seemed like an eternity before pulling away. His mother grasped his cheeks, forcing a smile he could only assume looked genuine from far away. Her eyes were distant. Caide knew she wasn't even seeing him. She placed her hand on his back again, ushering him out the door and waving ferociously as he left. She wiped away her nonexistent tears and blew him a kiss as the cameras continued to flash.

Playing along, though it sickened him, he waved back before climbing into his car. The reporters ate it up. Deep down, Caide hated himself for playing into her charade, but closer to the surface, joy bubbled as he saw the reporters' pity-filled faces.

He couldn't deny the happiness that pleasing a crowd brought him or the ease with which he could make people believe his lies. He was, after all, an Abbott. And when you're an Abbott, you're an Abbott through and through.

CHAPTER SIXTY-EIGHT

HAMPTON

Hampton pulled into Shayna's parking lot, his head still stirring with questions. He marched through the lobby and smiled at *oh, what was her name?*

She smiled back. Her name plate was turned so he couldn't see it.

"Running a little late today, Mr. Hampton?"

"Yes, I guess I am. I've had quite a bit going on today."

"Well, I figured you would with everything that's been going on. I'll just let Ms. Steele know you're here."

"Thank you." He smiled at her, racking his brain for where he had misplaced her name. He made his way over to the couch near the window and eased himself onto it, awkwardly pushing a throw pillow out from behind him.

He glanced at his watch, though he didn't read the time, his mind was entirely elsewhere. After hearing the news report this morning, he'd busied himself with a new lead. He'd gone over the police reports, testimonies, and records. He'd called old friends at colleges and a few of his witnesses.

His theory may just be the answer to the case, and though

it was a long shot, he only had one missing piece to make it plausible.

The door opened and Shayna and Rachael walked out.

"Hey." Hampton smiled at the both of them. "Shayna, could I talk to you for a second?"

"Of course. Rachael, would you excuse us?" Shayna headed back to her office.

"Actually, we can't leave her out here." He held up a hand to Rachael apologetically. "Not that I don't trust you, it's just against court order. Can you have her wait in the office? This will only take a second."

Shayna nodded, holding the door open for Rachael. Rachael sighed, walking back into the office slowly. Hampton knew he'd offended her.

Once the door was shut, Shayna began to talk. "So I'm guessing you watched the news?"

He nodded. "You can't turn on the TV without seeing it. It's on every channel."

Shayna's gaze fell behind Hampton. "Kortnee, would you please excuse us?"

"Oh, of course Ms. Steele. I'm sorry." Hampton heard clamoring behind him as Kortnee left the room.

"So, what's the plan?" Shayna asked once they were alone.

"Well, first of all, that man is an ass. I just want to throw that out there."

Shayna nodded. "Agreed. What on earth would make him do that?"

"I can only think of one reason that would make sense: he's trying to sway the jury."

Shayna nodded thoughtfully, crossing her arms. "I thought about that, but why?"

He frowned. "Well, I don't know for sure, but I have a pretty good idea. It's a little out there."

"Is there anything about this case that isn't?" Shayna asked, a curious smile on her face.

"I'm still working out all of the bugs, but I can only think of one reason he could possibly have for trying to make the jury believe his wife is guilty."

Shayna stared at him, realization setting in on her face. Her jaw dropped. "If the case is over, they stop looking. Caide Abbott has something to hide."

"Something big." Hampton nodded, a small smirk on his lips.

"Something like murder?" She narrowed her eyes at him.

Again, he nodded. "It all fits. Think about it."

"You think he set her up? He planned all of it?"

"It's all so laid out. What other reason is there? He was so mad when I asked for the continuance, I can't believe I didn't see this before."

"So now he's taking matters into his own hands."

"That's what I think, yes. I've still got some research to do. I want to have everything figured out before I tell her."

She sucked in a sharp breath. "So, you're going to tell her what Caide's done? With the press?"

"I don't see a point in upsetting her now, before we know everything. Eventually, though, she'll need to know the truth."

"What if there's nothing to find out? What if he genuinely does believe she's guilty?"

"Then she'll get her heart broken again. I'd like to spare her that, if possible."

"Her heart will break either way. If, God willing, we're right—that still means her husband, the man she vowed her life to, is willing to watch her go down for a crime he knows she's innocent of. There's no bigger betrayal." Shayna rubbed a finger over her lips.

"I realize that. I'd just like to have some form of good news for her when I give her all of the bad."

Shayna looked at him inquisitively. "You really care about her."

"Is that a question?" Heat rushed to his cheeks in the form of a blush.

She cocked her head to the side. "An observation. The question is why?"

"She's my client. If I can win this case, it'll be great for my career," he told her plainly.

She continued staring at him, doubt all over her face.

"What?" he asked.

"It's more than that, Hampton. Your cheeks flush when you see her, your pupils dilate; after you speak, you always look to see her response. You're going above and beyond the call of duty for her—don't think I didn't see that you aren't getting paid anymore. Others are calling this case doomed, but you just won't give up. Admit it."

"Admit what?" His pulse quickened.

"Hampton." She pressed her lips together.

He lowered his voice, suddenly aware that the only thing separating them from Rachael was a thin wooden door. "She is my client, Shayna. It would be unethical. I just know what it's like to be in that place. I know what she's going through and I know what it's like to feel like you have no one to turn to. No one should feel that way."

He met Shayna's understanding eyes again, silently begging her to let it go, and she nodded. Nothing else needed to be said.

"Has Rachael mentioned anything about Caide's computer skills?" he asked.

Shayna shook her head. "No, nothing."

"I know he had the motive and the means, I just can't figure out how he got her on tape. That's the most powerful thing they have on us. That's what we need to discredit. Can you try to find out if he was good with computers, and if she'd had any strange, unexplained cuts? We need to figure out the DNA too."

Shayna's expression was serious. "I'll do what I can."

"All right, let's go get her before she gets suspicious."

She turned around, walking back toward the door before stopping once more. She glanced at him over her shoulder. "You know, my second semester in grad school, a girl dropped out of my sociology class. We'd all heard that she was pregnant, but the rumor was that the baby was the professor's. No one could ever prove it and nothing was done, but after graduation, I heard they got married. I ran into her last year and guess what? They're still together. She showed me pictures of their three little girls. They're really happy together, Hampton."

"What's your point?" Hampton asked.

She smiled at him sadly. "My point is sometimes the heart isn't ethical. And sometimes that's okay."

CHAPTER SIXTY-NINE

RACHAEL

Rachael sat on the corner of Abby's bed, waiting for her cellmate to return. It was Saturday. Abby always called home to talk to her children on Saturday. Rachael knew that her fifteen minutes would be up soon, and she'd grown to look forward to hearing about the phone calls.

Sure enough, she heard the buzzer that meant someone was headed down her hallway. Shortly after, Abby appeared in the doorway, followed by Officer Eden. Her grin was contagious. As the officer opened the door, she ran and launched herself onto the bunk.

"So, how are they?" Rachael asked.

"They're great. Malakye is doing so well with his spelling words and Cody finally passed that science test." She touched her chest. "I miss them so much it's unfair."

Rachael nodded. "Why are you in here so much anyway? You never told me."

Abby sighed. "Basically, I just got involved with the wrong people. It started out as rebellious teenage stuff. I mean, I met this guy when I was in high school and just fell head over heels from him. His name is Simon, but everyone calls him Fig. We got married when I was nineteen and he moved us to Boston to help his friend start a record label. A year later, their little company tanked and we moved home to live with my parents while I finished my degree. Fig picked up odd jobs, but it was my career that ended up buying us a house. Another two years later, Fig started taking *business* trips back up to Boston."

She closed her eyes, shaking her head. "He started coming back with cash. He told me business was picking back up and I believed him. I don't know why. Maybe I just wanted so badly for him to be telling the truth. In the end, I found out he'd been selling drugs for months, maybe years. I wanted to tell, I swear I wanted to turn him in. I begged him to stop. We had this huge fight and he left. I didn't see him for two months."

She sighed, biting at a bit of skin by her pinky nail. "Eventually though, money got tight, bills were due and I had become accustomed to his extra, however illegitimate, income. I called him to come back. I wanted no part of the business, just for things to go back to normal. Once I knew, though, it could never go back to normal. After a while of being around it, it became our new normal, then it became acceptable, finally it seemed right. I started going with him to Boston, picking up shipments. I even helped him sell a few times. Like they always do, eventually our empire crumbled. We'd built a good life on our dirty money, but once he got caught, everything was seized. In court, they revealed he'd killed over debts. I never knew. Turns out, he'd killed a teenager."

She had tears in her eyes as she spoke of it, her lips quivering. "Some dumb kid who owed him money. A couple hundred bucks. They had nothing connecting me to the murders because Fig had never told me about them. He knew I would've called it off if I'd known. For me, it was just good money. I never got so deep into how it all worked like he did. So, they charged me as an accessory to the drug charges, I went away for four years. Fig got life. He never forgave me."

"But you got put back in? After you were released?"

Abby nodded. "A year after I was released, a guy knocked on my door and asked to use my phone. He said his car had broken down. The next day, the cops busted in my house with a search warrant. They found drugs in the drawer beneath our phone. Convenient, right? Of course, that violated my probation so I was back in jail. Three years later, I was out again. That's when I met Will, my husband. We got married. I was pregnant with Cody the next time the cops came to my house. There was a pound of marijuana taped to the bottom of my car. Fig has been sending his guys after me ever since. This is the first time in about five years."

"That's it? Why don't you just move away?"

She pursed her lips. "I wish it were that simple. Fig isn't stupid. His plans are clever, they always catch me off guard. We moved to Georgia once and he found me within six months. I refuse to keep uprooting my life, to keep uprooting my children's lives because of a stupid mistake. If he continues to come after me, I'll continue to fight him every step of the way. I'll spend the time that I'm not locked up enjoying it with my children." She looked at Rachael and chuckled. "I know I sound completely ridiculous."

Rachael remained silent, a sad smile on her face.

"You just become accustomed to things, you know? Anything can become normal to you. Honestly I was just tired of feeling helpless. I wanted to take charge of my life however I could."

"You shouldn't have to become accustomed to being arrested for a crime you didn't commit. That's ridiculous. There's nothing anyone can do?"

"You just don't get it. It all comes down to my past. I get these free attorneys who don't know or care about my side of the story, half the time they don't even know my name."

"That's what our legal system has been reduced to?" Rachael asked.

"Aren't you seeing that first hand? People decide if you are guilty long before you ever step foot in court."

Rachael thought back to her experience these past few weeks: the harsh treatment from the cops, the heartless stares from the jury. "You're right. Whatever happened to innocent until proven guilty?"

"It died. Along with chivalry and Pac Man." She laughed, laying her head back onto the wall.

"It's not fair," Rachael said.

"You going to try and call your family again today?"

Rachael shrugged, trying not to look as pathetic as she felt. "I've called them five times already. They never answer."

Abby shrugged. "So try again. That's all you can do."

Rachael sighed, standing up. She walked to her cell door. "Wish me luck."

CHAPTER SEVENTY

BRINLEY

Today is Saturday. Bubba and I are sitting on the floor watching Power Rangers. Daddy is somewhere in the kitchen, probably cooking us breakfast. If it's eggs it will probably be too runny, but anything else will be burned. Daddy's food never tastes like Momma's. She always puts ketchup in my eggs, which I love. Daddy doesn't remember.

Then, right before Ivan Ooze breaks out of his egg, I hear our phone ringing. The rules are I'm not supposed to answer the phone and I'm not supposed to talk to strangers. I know the rules, but the phone keeps on ringing and Daddy isn't coming to get it.

I walk toward the couch, by the phone. If it rings one more time I'll answer it. It does.

"Hello?" I say.

"Brinley?" Someone says my name. I think it's my momma.

"Momma?" I ask. I just know I'll get into trouble now.

Instead of being mad, she says, "Yes, baby. It's me. It's Momma. Oh, I miss you so much. It's so good to hear your voice."

I'm so happy to talk to her too, but I'm sad because Dad told me she's away helping my uncle and she never even told me bye.

"I miss you, Mommy. Come home please." I say to her, because I really wish she would.

"Soon baby. I will soon. What have you been doing? Have you been a good girl for Daddy? How is Davis?"

"I've been helping Corie with Bubba. We've been having fun, but I want you to come home."

"I know, love. Has Corie been there a lot? Where has your dad been?" she asks.

"In bed. He sleeps a lot now. He's here though. I think he's making us breakfast."

"Breakfast? Brin, it's almost noon."

"I told you he sleeps a lot." I giggle.

"Where is your brother now?" Mom sounds mad.

"We're watching TV."

"Have you been going to school?"

"Umm," I say, because I don't remember. I drop the phone on the couch and run back to ask Daddy. I see him coming out of the kitchen.

"Have I been going to school?" I ask.

He looks confused. "What?"

"Mom wants to know."

"What are you talking about, Brin?" he asks, looking around the room.

"She's on the phone," I tell him.

He looks at the table where the phone is supposed to be. "Who answered the phone?"

I look around, wondering if I can blame Davis. Before I can answer, my dad picks up the phone from the couch and puts it on his ear. "Rachael?"

Then, before he says anything else, he just puts the phone back on the holder and hangs up. "She was already gone."

I don't tell him I know he's telling a lie. I don't tell him I heard my mommy say his name back before he hung up. Instead, I go to the kitchen and sit down at my chair.

My tummy is growling.

Grownups are so weird.

CHAPTER SEVENTY-ONE

HAMPTON

Argus Hampton's body was filled with dread as he pulled up to Shayna Steele's office. He'd been quiet the whole drive over, rehearsing silently how they were going to have this dreadful conversation. Rachael had been quiet too, seeming to be lost in her own deep thoughts.

He absentmindedly pulled open her door and led her into the lobby.

"Well..." She turned to him, waving good morning to the redheaded secretary. *God, what was her name?* "I guess I'll see you at four."

"Actually," Hampton said softly, "I'll be joining you for your session today."

Surprise filled her eyes. "You will?"

"We have a few things we need to discuss. Shayna thought it'd be best if we all sat down together."

"Bad news?" Rachael looked defeated.

"Depends on how you look at it." Hampton shrugged his shoulders, looking toward the door as Shayna stepped out. Hampton recognized the same fear in her eyes he'd seen in his own mirror.

"Good morning, Rachael. Hampton." She smiled. "Come on in."

Hampton walked into the office, realizing then that he'd never gotten a good look inside before. He chose a pink couch to sit on and seated himself uncomfortably on the edge. He cleared his throat as Rachael took a seat diagonal from him, followed by Shayna who sat in the chair directly across from her.

"Now, Rachael, as you can see this session is going to be slightly different. We have a lot to go over in a very short amount of time so we need you to listen carefully." Shayna paused, glancing in Hampton's direction. He nodded, mentally willing her to go on. "Some of this is going to be hard for you to hear, some of it you won't want to believe, but all of it is important and it's important that you know what we've learned over the past few weeks."

Rachael nodded, her expression hard to read.

"First things first, Rachael, after the past four weeks of sessions, I'm sorry, but I was unable to successfully diagnose you with DID," Shayna stated.

When Rachael was silent, Shayna continued. "After listening to you and seeing you daily, it's obvious to me that you are clearly in your right mind. I've seen no signs that would lead me to believe you are not completely healthy and stable."

Rachael's forehead wrinkled with concern. "How can you say that? We still have two weeks left. You said you'd do everything you could for me." She covered her mouth, breathing heavily in shock.

"Rachael, I need you to stay calm. I'm not saying I've given up on you, quite the opposite, in fact. That's why we're here. Hampton and I have been working on a theory for a bit, and we finally think we are ready to tell you."

"What are you talking about?"

"We think we've found something to save you," Hampton said. He'd been waiting to use that line. Rachael's eyes lit up at him, though her face contained no smile.

"Look, in order for us to tell you, you'll have to be open-minded. We've sifted through this theory over and over again, making sure we've looked at it from every angle before we brought it to you. But, the problem is, we've hit a snag. We need your help with the rest, Rachael. It's time that we filled you in."

Rachael nodded. "If it's going to save me, it can't be that bad."

People who work retail know not to brag about how slow their store has been or else the entire town will stop in all at once. Brides know never to brag about how pretty the weather will be on their wedding day, or else it just may come a flood. Hampton was a firm believer in jinxes, and Rachael Abbott had just jinxed herself.

He grimaced at her hopeful face. It could be that bad. It could be worse.

CHAPTER SEVENTY-TWO

RACHAEL

Rachael watched anxiously as Argus flipped through a stack of papers in the manila folder on his lap.

Shayna spoke first. "Rachael, the other day I asked you about Caide's affair, if you'd known about it. Do you remember what you told me?"

Oh, God. Oh no. "I told you no." Rachael's heart pounded loudly in her chest.

"Is that true?"

"Of course it's true. Why would I lie?" Rachael asked, forcing a convincing smile.

Shayna looked at Hampton and then back again, her tone apologetic. "Maybe you think admitting you knew about the affair gives you a motive. Maybe you thought we'd stop believing you." When Rachael was silent, Shayna went on. "Rachael, one of the most important things you learn when studying psychology is how to detect a lie. We have to know how to determine when someone is consciously lying. It's one of the most, if not *the most*, important parts of my job. When you told me that you didn't know about the affair, your body language told me—very clearly—that you weren't being truthful."

Rachael pressed her lips together, holding in the one secret that had held her family together for so long.

"We can't help you if you won't tell us what's going on," Hampton said softly.

Rachael sighed, conscious of her betraying body language. "Well, I mean, what wife hasn't suspected her husband of cheating at some point, right? He works long hours, we aren't always happy, so of course it's crossed my mind. But there was never proof. It's always just been mindless worry that I knew would do nothing more than incriminate myself further. If there had been more, of course I would've told you. There was nothing to tell." She smiled, praying to be believed.

"That's what you want me to believe? That's all there is?" Shayna asked.

"That's the truth," she said firmly. That was her truth, anyway.

CHAPTER SEVENTY-THREE

HAMPTON

Hampton tapped his pen on his yellow legal pad, his heart flitting from fear.

"All right, Rachael, before we get into the research I've done, I need to tell you why we're looking into the lead that we are. I'm not going to lie to you, the first couple of weeks I've run into dead-end after dead-end. Nothing was adding up and there was nothing I could find to help you. Then, two weeks ago, I turned on the TV and saw Caide."

He ran his palm over his knuckles nervously. "There's really no easy way to tell you this, but he has withdrawn his support from your case. Publicly."

"What do you mean?" she asked.

"He's been telling the press that he no longer believes you're innocent. He no longer plans to back you in court and —" He paused, looking down at his paperwork.

"Hampton, go on," Shayna urged. "She needs to hear it."

"He doesn't want your kids to speak to or see you. Rachael, I know this must be hard for you to hear, but it's important that you have all of the facts. I've tried calling him, I've asked him to visit you, but he's refusing."

She began hyperventilating, her chest rising and falling rapidly. "You've known this all along? You didn't tell me anything? You've just let me keep calling, keep feeling like I was letting my family down by not calling when they're home, when you've known all along they're just ignoring me? My own husband doesn't believe me anymore? What happened to everything he said about me in court? How I'm a good person? How he loves me? He's just taking it all back? *Just...just kidding?* Why? How could he do this to me? What kind of a person does this to their wife?"

Hampton swallowed, the words leaving his mouth before he'd planned it. "The kind of person who frames his wife for murder."

CHAPTER SEVENTY-FOUR

CAIDE

Caide threw open the lid to the washing machine, ending the horrible screeching sound it was making. Just what he needed, one more thing to go wrong in his ever-crumbling life. He pulled the load of towels out, searching for the culprit. As he pulled the last towel from the machine—there it was.

He'd all but forgotten about the mysterious key since he found it weeks ago, but there it sat—stuck to the bottom of the washing machine, screeching and scratching as if begging him to find it. He reached to the bottom, tugging on it firmly. It remained tucked just under the agitator. The pile of wet clothing was now beginning to form a rather large puddle around itself, and Caide found himself clueless as to whether or not Rachael kept tools in the house.

He'd never been one for fixing things—growing up in a house where if it was broken, you just had it replaced—he was embarrassed to admit, even to himself, that he'd never learned how. He was sure Rachael kept some of her dad's old tools somewhere. He wandered to the garage, trying to remember a time when they'd ever had to fix anything. He vaguely remembered her complaining about a cabinet door not shutting right, and once, a few winters ago, a pipe in the kitchen had burst. The kids had knocked a hole in the wall last summer, one that he'd promised to fix. Caide hadn't fixed a thing, though, and he couldn't, for the life of him, remember how they'd actually gotten fixed. Sometime or another Rachael had stopped complaining, stopped asking for help, and Caide realized now, that all of those things had been taken care of.

The garage was empty except for their cars and a few old toys. Caide looked around briefly to no avail. He looked under the sink, but found only cleaning supplies. In the bathroom, he found old bath toys and a box of tampons. About to give up, he decided to check his closet, where Rachael sometimes hid Christmas presents, as if Caide wouldn't see them.

Would she have hidden the tools from him? Maybe to shield him from a reminder of his childhood which lacked that meaningful father and son bonding time where he'd learn how to hammer a nail? Maybe to keep her dad's things separate from the emptiness that had become their lives? Maybe just to keep Brinley and Davis out of danger? Either way, as Caide walked into the closet, his gaze fell upon a worn burlap bag in the far corner, nearly hidden behind the vacuum and an old suitcase.

He pushed the suitcase aside, pulling the bag out. It was filled with odds-and-ends tools, all worn and dirty from years of use. He recognized the metal hammer with wood banded around its handle. The initials R.C. were carved into the handle. Ross Cline. Caide put it down, digging further into the bag. He pulled out tools he didn't have a name for and couldn't venture a guess as to how they worked. As he neared what felt like the bottom, his fingers met a cool, smooth metal, unlike anything else he'd found in the bag. He pulled on it, its heaviness surprising him. It was a black metal box with a small silver handle on top. He was sure right away it was no tool, and by the relative new-ness, he was certain it hadn't belonged to Ross. Rachael had owned this. Rachael had hidden it from him. The silver metal keyhole did not match the golden key that was now stuck at the bottom of his washing machine, but he was curious to try it anyway.

He picked up the box, grabbing a blue-handled tool with an end that looked like tweezers. He ran back to the laundry room, filled with an odd sense of hope and worry.

As he entered the laundry room, he set the metal box on top of the dryer, careful not to make too much noise and draw the kids from the living room. He grasped the key firmly with the tool and pulled. Once, twice, and the third time, it was out with a loud groan.

Still ignoring the pile of sopping clothes, he turned his attention to the box, inserting the key. His heart leapt as it fit right away. His hands shook as he turned the key, wondering what he was about to uncover. With one swift motion, he threw the lid open and gasped.

Whatever he'd been expecting, this was worse.

CHAPTER SEVENTY-FIVE

RACHAEL

Rachael sat across from Argus and Shayna, staring at them strangely. "Excuse me? You think my husband set me up? That's ridiculous."

"Is it?" Hampton implored. "Rachael, look, he was sleeping with Blaire. He was the last one with her. He sent everyone else home that night. He was the police's first suspect. There's all of this mounting evidence that makes him look really bad, but then suddenly there's this random evidence against you."

"None of which makes any sense, by the way," Shayna added.

"Right. There are all of these questions—timing, DNA. You've got no cuts on yourself whatsoever, yet your blood was found on the murder weapon. For you to have committed this murder, you literally would've needed to be in two places at once. It's just impossible, but it's also easy. People want to believe what's easy. Even I missed it. Until Caide made his little statement, that is. It got me wondering what kind of a monster would do that. Even if he didn't believe you; even if he was grieving over Blaire's death, I just can't imagine a reason to do what he's doing *unless* he needed you to look guilty. Unless he somehow benefits from you being in prison." Hampton leaned forward, his eyes burning into hers. "Think about it, Rachael. Say he was struggling with trying to balance the affair and his marriage. Then he gets this idea. She's out of the way, you're out of the picture, he gets to play grieving, unsuspecting husband. He keeps the house, your cars. It all works out in his favor. Hell, maybe they even planned it together. Maybe she wasn't supposed to die, maybe she was going to say you attacked her, but something went wrong. He hit too hard."

Rachael's head grew fuzzy. She stood from her seat. "No. There's got to be some other explanation. Caide may be an awful, awful man but he's no murderer."

"If he's not, then who is? We have less than two weeks to figure something out or you are going to jail. We don't, for one second, believe you're guilty, Rachael, but someone is. If we don't find that someone--whoever they are—you are going down for this. The police were ready to lock Caide up until, suddenly, there was convenient, foolproof evidence against you."

"So what? What are you asking me to do?" she demanded.

"We're asking you to trust us," Hampton said.

"And be honest with us," Shayna added, her eyebrows darting up.

"So then what? Where did my blood come from? You said yourself I'm not cut anywhere. And what about the tape? How do we explain that? Caide is no computer expert. You expect to convince the jury he framed me with what—his extensive knowledge of Solitaire?"

Hampton shook his head. "It would've been way too easy for him to get your blood anytime and freeze it. Who knows how long he's had to plan this out. The tape is trickier and that's why we've been hesitant to come to you so far, until now. We've talked to old college professors, roommates, and friends. We've looked up records, grades, talked to Caide's bosses, even your students." He paused, and she could tell something bad was coming. He stood from his seat, taking a step toward her. "Rachael, we were at a dead end, until...do you remember a Professor Prather from your junior year of college?"

Rachael thought hard, recalling all of her professor's names, but drawing a blank. "No."

"We figured you wouldn't. See, she didn't teach you or Caide, but when she heard about your case, she reached out to us. Apparently she was really fond of you."

"But I don't know her," she insisted.

Hampton's gaze softened. "I think you do. You see, Professor Prather taught computer science, and though she never taught you, she seems to know you quite well. Apparently, you were always around with a person who she claims was her best student."

It hit Rachael then, like a ton of bricks. The weight of what they were suggesting caused her eyes to blur and fog to fill her thoughts.

No. No. No.

CHAPTER SEVENTY-SIX

CAIDE

Caide stared at the pile of money in front of him. The metal box was filled with rubber-banded stacks of cash. Counting it out, he'd come to a grand total of eighteen-thousand five-hundred and eighteen dollars. He had no idea where she could've come up with such a large amount of cash or what she would have needed it for.

The other items in the box gave few clues. In amongst one strap of cash, Caide had found a key to an old Honda—a car they'd never owned.

Attached to it was another, smaller key, probably to a padlock. The last item in the box was the one that had crushed Caide the most. At the bottom of the box sat another white box. It was marked with red writing: *At Home Paternity Test.* The packaging pictured a man holding a baby, a carefree smile on his face that Caide couldn't have mustered if his life depended on it.

A sickening feeling filled his stomach, like he may vomit and cry all at the same time. Questions raced through his mind. When had Rachael bought this? Why did she need it?

Why had she never used it? How much did he truly not know about his wife?

He wondered which of his children the test had been meant for or if maybe there'd been another child, one he'd never known about. Had Rachael been having an affair? Could he believe that?

Up until finding the box, the very thought might've made him laugh, but he now realized he may not have known his wife as well as he thought.

Caide knew one thing for certain, as he looked over the cash, keys, and test: his wife had been prepared to run, but why and to or from whom remained quite unclear.

CHAPTER SEVENTY-SEVEN

RACHAEL

She sank back into the couch. "You can't be serious. No way. *No way.* She's my best friend."

"Rachael, you have to look at the facts here. She is a computer science major. You didn't think you should've told me that?" he argued.

"Argus, Audrey is my *best friend.*" She smacked the back of her hand into her palm for emphasis. "Yes, she works with computers, but she hates Caide. She'd have no reason to help him. More than that, she'd have no reason to hurt me."

"You have to admit it's convenient. She just happens to work in computer technology. There's a serious issue with the timing of everything that happened that night, yet somehow the jury believes it. *Why?* Because of the tape." He wagged a finger in the air. "Because tapes don't lie. Unless, Rachael…unless they do. If we can prove that it's a fake tape, if we can give them a reason to believe someone framed you, that would be enough. You'd be free."

Hampton moved to where she sat, getting on his knees in front of her. He grasped her hands in his and stared into her eyes. His breath smelled of coffee and spearmint gum, and the whiskers on his chin had a few gray places Rachael hadn't noticed before.

"Rachael, if you tell me there's nothing to find, I'll believe you. But if you believe, even just a tiny bit, that it's possible, you need to tell me. I know she's your best friend, but I also know you didn't commit murder. I just don't want to see you in prison for it. Your children deserve to have their mother. They deserve days at the park and picnics. I want you to help your daughter pick out a dress for prom and dance with your son on his wedding day. I don't want to see Caide steal that away from you." He squeezed her hands gently. "Unless you allow us to help you, you're giving up. Unless you help us, you've already let him win."

He brushed a piece of hair from Rachael's face and she began to lose herself in his eyes.

She could no longer see any way around it. For years now, she'd kept the secret that could ruin the life she'd worked so hard for. But in that moment, his thumbs rubbing the backs of her hands in an attempt to ease her fears, she found herself remembering that night. The night everything changed.

She sat still, anchoring herself in his gaze—afraid that if she were to blink, she'd drown in a sea of lies she'd created. And then, before she knew what was really happening, she began to speak.

"I don't know when it started. Probably in college, but I never suspected it back then. I mean, they hated each other. I always thought maybe they were just jealous of the time I spend with the other, I don't know. After we got married and moved home, Audrey stayed in Durham. We kept in touch. Not like we used to, but still a phone call every week or two. She told me she'd met John and that she was falling in love with him. A few months after their wedding, Caide's job started with Mason and Meachum and he, almost immediately, started having long business trips that would take him out of town."

She frowned, squeezing his hands for comfort and making sure they were still there. "On Brinley's first birthday, Audrey told me they were moving home. My brilliant, free-spirited, 'never coming back to that dump of a town' best friend was moving home of her own free will." She rolled her eyes. "I should've seen it. But I didn't. I was just excited to have her home. A few months later, she told me they were trying for a baby. They'd been trying for a little while and she was beginning to worry. A few months after that, she called me in hysterics. She told me that John was sterile. They started having a lot of problems after that. We didn't realize how serious the problems were until she showed up alone to Thanksgiving. We never even talked about it. I was so scared to say the wrong thing or to hurt her worse somehow. That night, after dinner, I sent her home with half of our leftovers. Caide walked her outside while I stayed in with Brinley. I was going to get her ready for bed when I noticed Audrey had forgotten her part of the apple pie. I picked it up to bring it outside to her and that's when I saw them."

She swallowed hard, looking away from him for the first time. "Her arms were thrown around his neck. I thought they were hugging at first. But when I saw him pull away, he held onto her face like they were teenagers. I watched her run her hands through my husband's hair and I watched him biting her lip like it was nothing. Like they'd been doing it for years. Like they weren't standing on our front porch, just feet away from me catching them."

She paused, remembering that night. She recalled the pain like a slap in the face. "It all made sense then—how his business trips had stopped occurring after she'd moved home, how their playful banter could turn cool and hateful with no notice at all, how I'd come home from the studio and find them there together, watching TV or cooking supper. John was never there. It was right in front of me the whole time." She wiped away a tear as she felt it run down her cheek. "I should've done something. I should've screamed, should've thrown something, kicked her out, or hell, even kicked him out. Instead, I snuck quietly back into the house, like I was the one doing something wrong. I put Brinley to bed and cleaned up the kitchen. He came back in a few minutes later, offering no excuse as to why he'd been outside for so long. When he kissed the side of my head, I remember holding my breath. I was so afraid I'd smell her perfume and that would break me."

Hampton rubbed her arms gently, inching closer to her. "I never saw them together again. That spring, she told me she was pregnant. I pretended to be happy for her, but I knew what it meant. I'd started stashing money away after I caught them. I told myself if I caught them again, I would leave. I don't know if I actually would have, but it made me feel better to believe it at the time. What kind of a weak woman stays after that?" She looked at Argus, back to the present for just a moment.

He placed his hand on her shoulder, merely inches from her face now. Shayna's presence was nearly forgotten. "Go on."

She sucked in a breath. "So, I used cash to buy a car from out of town. I put a suitcase and a car seat in it. It was our little getaway plan, just me and Brin. I bought a paternity test. I was going to make her take it. If the baby was Caide's, we'd leave. I would take my daughter and we'd sneak off into the night, never to be heard from again."

She smiled sadly. "Caide cares what people think of him, that's what he cares about more than anything, I think maybe that's why he never left me. He'd be terrified to be the man who left his wife and child. Anyway, I kept saving, kept planning for the baby to be born, for my question to be answered. Then, when she was eighteen weeks along, Audrey miscarried. I went to the hospital with her; I cried with my best friend and held her because she needed me to. I hated myself for being glad it was over, but that didn't stop the relief I felt knowing I'd never have to look at that awful paternity test ever, ever again."

She dropped Hampton's hand then, rubbing another tear from her eyes. He backed up slightly. "That night, I slept with my husband for the first time in nearly a year. He was so full of hatred and passion, I was sure he was going to admit to everything. I wasn't sure if I should tell them what I knew, after waiting so long, so I continued to put it off. Six weeks later, the morning sickness hit me. It was so much worse than it had been with Brinley. When I broke the news to Caide, I think it was what he needed at the time. Those nine months were the happiest we'd ever been, the happiest we'd ever *be*. I locked up the money and the test and I hid it away where he'll never find it. Once our pregnancy was announced, Audrey and John moved back to Durham. As much as it hurt, as pissed as I was, I could never bring myself to tell them. Audrey is still my best friend. She's the only person who's always been there for me. She would never do what you're accusing her of."

Argus rubbed her hands once more before moving back to his seat. "Rachael, when did Audrey come home?"

"Recently." She thought back to the day Audrey had shown up and gasped. "The day of the murder, actually."

Shayna pressed her lips into a fine line, a worried look filling her face.

Rachael shook her head, trying to piece everything together. "No. She wouldn't. You don't think…I mean, *no*.

You don't think they planned this, do you? They couldn't have." Rachael shook her head in disbelief.

"We know this doesn't make sense to you, but you have to look at the fact that it *does* make sense. Audrey comes back into town the day Blaire's murdered. Caide is the prime suspect until suddenly, they have a tape proving you were there, even though this tape goes against any logical time frame. Caide supports you in court, hires me, and plays a doting husband while he thinks you are just a prison time-bomb, but then when we suddenly have something that could vindicate you, he gets mad. He refuses to pay me and then, when I continue to work your case, he publicly says he thinks you're guilty. If one thing's been made clear here, it's that even if Caide doesn't believe you're guilty, he certainly wants everyone else to."

Rachael felt fury in the far corners of her body. If Argus was right, she'd been betrayed and this was not going to be an easy fix. "So how do we find out for sure?"

Argus looked to Shayna before speaking. "Well, first of all, we have to hear it from you. Is Audrey capable of altering a tape like this?"

Rachael mustered a deep breath. "If you're asking me if I believe *my best friend*—the girl who helped me get ready for my first date and pick out my prom dress, the girl who cried with me when I found out I was pregnant, who held me at my dad's funeral and made me soup when I got mono—if you're asking me whether I believe she could've framed me for murder, whether she could sleep at night knowing I'm rotting in a cell for something I didn't do, just so she could have my husband, I can't answer that. Not now, not like this." She paused, hating herself for what she was about to admit. "But...if you're asking me if Audrey is talented enough to alter a tape, or to even *create* a tape, given the right amount of time, the answer is yes."

Argus nodded. "Then you need to know, we don't have the time or resources to investigate this tape or have it sent off for analysis before your trial. The judge won't allow it and, frankly, the police may not hand it over. That being said, we have no other choice but to have it be our word against theirs."

"Just like that?"

"Your husband is a horrible human being, Rachael. And you are a caring wife. The jury wants to side with you. The world *wants* to side with you. If we give them our evidence, it's my hope that they'll take it and run with it. We just have to give them enough reason to believe us," Hampton told her.

Shayna spoke up. "Rachael, you know what this means, right? You'll have to go up on the stand. You'll have to testify against them. You'll have to admit you knew about their affair."

Rachael's jaw dropped. "Based on what? A theory? We have no more on them than they have on us. You want me to ruin their lives, even if they're innocent, just to save mine? How can you ask me to do this? After all I've been through? You want me to do it to someone else?"

"Not if you don't believe it. Notice I said *don't* believe it, not *don't want to*. We won't ask you to lie on the stand," Argus said.

Rachael was silent once more, thoughts and emotions rattling through her.

Shayna sighed. "Rachael, either way, I'm going to have to testify that you aren't suffering from DID. I have to tell the judge I don't believe you dissociated during Blaire's murder. If you're convicted, which you likely will be, you'll be sent to prison. Federal prison. For life. We believe you're innocent, if you believe in yourself like we do, then you know that someone out there did this. And someone out there is about to get away with it if we don't stop them."

"Theory or not," Hampton added, "we have a damn good case against them—one that stands a chance in any court. And Shayna's right. Now, we can either let them take you off to jail with our tails tucked or we can fight like hell to get your life and your freedom back. The choice is yours."

Rachael sulked. "This is just a lot. I need some time to process."

"Of course," Shayna said.

Argus nodded, almost grumpily, but agreed. "We need to know though. Sooner rather than later, so we can prepare."

Rachael nodded, resting her head on a pink pillow beside her. With Shayna and Argus both staring at her, she closed her eyes, hearing the clock on the wall tick as she, for once, counted down the minutes until she could go back to jail.

CHAPTER SEVENTY-EIGHT

PAM UNDERWOOD

Out of her entire fifty-two years of living, Pam Underwood had very few memories that weren't blurred by alcohol or drugs.

She remembered her first day of fifth grade—how the new pants her mother had gotten her from Goodwill had someone else's name written on the pocket, and how no matter how hard she tried, she couldn't convince her classmates that Jessica Stewart was a famous designer, rather than the previous owner. She remembered her seventeenth birthday—her first "real" date and how he'd tried to feel her up before they even got through dinner. She remembered how on the way home he'd told her that she shouldn't dress like a slut if she wasn't going to put out.

She remembered the day she went into labor—fourteen hours of excruciating pain, all for a little pink ball of skin who kept her up all night for the next two years. She remembered the first time she'd held her daughter—how the nurses had *ooh*-ed and *ahh*-ed over the little bundle of joy. She remembered looking into Blaire's little, round face and wondering what the fuss was all about.

To say Pam had been a bad mother was a bit of an exaggeration, mostly because she was never much of a mother at all. She'd worked two jobs most of Blaire's childhood. She'd never been one for crafts or bake sales and she wasn't the type of parent that the school asked to chaperone school functions. Though it'd been rough, and she'd never really cared much for her daughter, she'd always tried to do the best she could for her with what little they had. Of course, as Blaire grew older and more headstrong, Pam saw Blaire's actions as less of a good thing and more of an insult to Pam's simple way of life.

She hadn't spoken to her daughter in over three years and hadn't seen her in four, yet somewhere in the back of her mind she'd always figured her daughter would eventually come to realize that the city wasn't the place to live and she'd come home. She'd always imagined that one day they'd build a relationship.

Of all her memories, even the clear ones, none was more clear than the night Pam got the phone call telling her that her chance for a relationship with her daughter would never come. She'd been on the couch after a twelve-hour shift at Ralph's Pub, when her phone started to ring.

She'd picked it up with dread, instantly fearing she'd be called back into work.

"Hello?"

"Is this Mrs. Pamela Underwood?" a man with a gruff voice asked.

"Who's asking?" *Damn bill collector.*

"This is Sheriff Al Markowitz with the Farthington County Police Department. I need to speak with Ms. Underwood immediately, please."

If Pam hadn't been trying to figure out if she'd recently committed any crimes, she might've noticed the sadness in his voice. Instead she said, "I ain't ever heard of no Farthington County. You got the wrong number, mister."

Before she could hang up, she heard his voice again. "Are you Blaire Underwood's mother?"

She was silent for a second, wondering whether she should lie. "Yeah, why?"

"Ma'am, I'm so sorry to do this over the phone, I really am. Your daughter, Blaire, was found dead this morning."

Losing a child, even if you didn't think you really liked them that much, is a pain unlike any other. The icy cold fills up your soul, leaking out your eyes in the form of tears. Pain grips your insides; physical pain that makes you unable to move or talk or do anything that would make it seem real.

Pam was unable to hear the officer's voice, though she was sure he was talking again. She was sure she'd dropped the phone at some point, yet she could still feel the hard plastic there in her hand. She let her brain float away, swimming somewhere far from herself, refusing to believe any of this was anything but a sick, sick dream.

Finally, when words found her, punching her stomach like an air bag, she let out a noise somewhere between a sob and a scream.

"Where is she?" she tried to ask.

"Ma'am?"

"Where is she? Where is my daughter?"

"We're transporting her body to the morgue now, ma'am. You're welcome to come say your goodbyes there. Is there anyone else I can call? Someone to bring you here? Someone close to your daughter?" He spoke with the quiet professionalism of someone who'd been doing this job a long, long time. This was just another case to him—another body.

"There's no one else," she said angrily. "Where is she?"

"Ma'am, I know this is a lot to take in, especially over the phone. Whenever you get into town, you just come on over to the station and I'll take you to the morgue myself. I sure wish you'd get someone to bring you. You really shouldn't be driving by yourself right now."

"No, I mean, *where* is she? What city are you in?"

"Oh, um." He paused, obviously thrown off by the question. "Well, we're in La Rue, ma'am."

"La Rue, right…"

"*North Carolina*," he answered the question she refused to ask.

"I knew that," Pam said, wondering if detectives could detect lies over the phone, while she searched for a pen and paper.

"Right. Well, again, I'm so sorry for your loss. If there's anything else we can do for you, you just let me know."

"Right, okay." Pam wondered why she could never find a pen when she needed one. Before she'd realized the conversation was over, she heard a sharp click on the other line.

She gave up looking for a pen and headed for her bedroom to pack, wondering how long she'd be expected to stay after the funeral.

As she packed, she silently cursed her daughter, scolding her even in the grave.

CHAPTER SEVENTY-NINE

CAIDE

Caide heard a knock on his door, interrupting his thoughts about the contents of Rachael's secret box.

He rushed toward the door, passing his children who were playing quietly. He made no move to acknowledge them. As he got to the door, the sinking feeling in his stomach that he'd become so accustomed to was back.

"Audrey," he said, walking out and closing the door behind him. "What could you possibly be thinking showing up here?"

"I had to see you. How are you?"

He looked at her in disbelief. "That's a bit of a stupid question, don't you think?"

Audrey shook her head. "Probably. I don't know what to say to you. After everything we've done, how do we even move forward? Where do we go from here?"

"I can't have this conversation here. Can't you just wait a little while? This is the last thing I need right now."

"Caide, please don't push me away. I need you. I waited for you. I waited for the reporters to all move on, so they wouldn't catch us. Just like I waited until Davis was older.

Just like I waited until Rachael was out or asleep. Just like I waited for her to get over her dad's death. For the last six years, Caide, all I've done is wait. I thought now we could finally have our chance. You told me to come back. *This was all your idea.* So, don't you dare tell me you don't need this right now. I did everything you asked. I'm here."

"It's more complicated than that and you know it. People are watching my every move." He stopped, noticing the anger on her face. "Look, we just have to be careful a little while longer. Once the trial is over, it'll just be the two of us, I promise."

She nodded, though it didn't seem to pacify her entirely. "We have to talk more about Blaire, though, you know that, right? I mean, I know I'm the other woman and I have no right to be jealous, especially now, but you have to know that I am."

"I don't owe you an explanation for her, Aud. Look, I'm sorry but I don't. You were gone for two years. Two whole years and I never heard from you. Even when you were here, I was never sure what we were. We never said. You'd just flake out for months at a time. Nothing was ever certain."

Audrey threw her hands up in exasperation. "Do you even understand that Rachael is my best friend? Do you realize how hard this has been on me? I don't take what we're doing lightly, Caide. Nothing is more important than my friendship to that girl. I love you so much but it's breaking my heart. It breaks my heart every day. She is my best friend. What we've done, what we have, that doesn't change how I feel about her."

He glared at her. "You think I don't get that? *She's my wife.*"

She rolled her eyes. "Yeah, and we all see how much that means to you."

"Don't do that. Don't you try and make it look like I don't love her, too. She's the mother of my children."

"*You screwed me on the morning of your wedding, Caide*," she whispered heatedly, trying to keep her voice low.

"I'd just lost everything: my parents, my money, my future. It felt like Rachael was to blame. I hated her then, and I can't believe you'd throw that in my face right now." He looked around, expecting to see reporters. "Look, I don't have time to argue. Just give me until the trial's over, let everything cool down, and then we'll go from there."

She froze, her demeanor changing. "Go from there? Are you having second thoughts about us?"

"What? No." He kissed her quickly on the mouth, surprised to find that spark he was used to was now dim. "I just need time to process. It's been a long couple of months."

"Okay." Audrey pouted, all the fight gone from her voice. "You'll call me, right?"

"Of course."

She leaned in to kiss him, her mouth tender on his. He pulled away, probably too quickly. "You should go."

She nodded, a hurt look filling her face. As she walked away, Caide remembered the paternity test. "Hey, Aud?"

"Yeah?" she called over her shoulder, turning around.

"Did Rachael ever mention having an affair to you?"

"Rachael having an affair?" Her brow furrowed.

"Yes."

She stared at him intently. "No, never. Why?"

"Just curious," he said, grabbing hold of the door handle.

"Okay." She turned to walk away again.

"Would she have?" he asked.

She turned again. "Have what?"

"Would she have told you? If she were having an affair?"

Audrey offered him a small, sad smile. "She's my best friend, Caide. She tells me everything."

CHAPTER EIGHTY

PAM

Pam stumbled into the bar at half past eleven. "Give me a beer," she yelled to the bartender.

"Sure thing, lady," the kid with glasses shouted back.

"Hey, lady, ain't I seen you somewhere?" grunted the other bartender—the short, round one with bad acne.

"Nah, I'm just passing through."

"You look awful familiar. Maybe I've passed you somewhere else. I've been all over. Where you from?" he demanded.

"Where you been?" Pam took a swig of her beer.

"Where you from? I'll tell ya if I've been there," he said, leaning against the bar.

"Where you been? I'll tell you if I'm from there," she said with a wink.

He leaned further into her, smiling. "I asked you first."

"Buy me a drink and maybe I'll tell you."

"Dude, stop flirting with the customers," the kid with glasses mumbled.

"Shut up, Sammy," Porky teased. "I'm just being friendly with the lady."

"The *lady* is trying to have a drink and you are supposed to be working, remember?"

Porky rolled his eyes, but remained seated. "I ain't bothering yeh none, am I?"

Pam shook her head ferociously. "Oh, no. Not at all."

"See there." He smirked at Glasses.

Glasses looked annoyed, frowning impatiently, but said nothing else. After a few minutes of chatting, it became increasingly obvious to Pam that she was going to have to work quickly. Her buzz was growing more strong by the second and she was beginning to feel tired. More tired than usual, anyway.

Without thinking, she leaned over in her chair, bumping into a blonde-haired young girl who barely looked old enough to be in a bar, let alone sitting in the lap of some ponytailed biker who was at least twice her age.

"Whoopsie," she muttered, laughing so hard she spit her beer all over Blondie.

"Ewwww," the girl screamed, flailing her arms around. "I can't believe you just did that."

Pam smiled again, offering up a beer in a drunken salute. "Ahhh, it'll dry. Here, you want the rest?"

"You are disgusting," the girl screamed irately. "Get out of here!" She stormed away to a corner booth. Her boyfriend, who looked too drunk to care, followed suit.

Pam hastened after her. "You get out!" she said, slurring her words.

"You can't tell me what to do. Why are you bothering me?" the girl demanded.

Pam slid down in the seat beside of her. "I ain't bothering you. I'm just hanging out."

"Just leave me the hell alone." She tried to push Pam away so she could get out of the booth, but Pam had thirty years and fifty pounds on the girl. She wasn't moving.

Suddenly, her oblivious biker boyfriend on the opposite side of the booth spoke up. "Look lady, you got a problem with us or something?"

"No problem here, baby. Just having a chat with your girlfriend."

Then, an idea struck her. She stood up, without giving the man time to process her actions and threw her arms around his neck. Her lips met his prickly, graying mustache with a bang. She tasted beer and blood, realizing she'd busted her lip on his teeth.

He froze for a moment before throwing her off of him. "Someone call the police! This psycho is drunk off her ass."

Murmurs of agreement could be heard around the bar.

It was ironic that it was Sheriff Markowitz who walked into the bar a few minutes later, as if he'd been waiting for her. As if, somehow, he knew what she was up to.

His hands in his pockets, he smiled politely at Glasses and asked where the problem was.

Glasses pointed across the bar where Pam still sat, attempting to stop her ever-bleeding lip. Markowitz started his walk toward her. As he neared, his expression softened. "Miss Underwood?"

"What do you want?" she asked, though it sounded more like *whaaddooant.*

"Ma'am, I'm afraid you've caused quite a stir here tonight. Let me get you home. I know how hard these past few weeks have been on you, but I'm glad to see you stuck around. You should be glad it's me who found you tonight. Some of my guys are cuff-happy." He chuckled, obviously trying to cheer her up.

"Go away," Pam muttered, scooting further back into her booth.

"Now, there's no need for all of that. I just want to get you home safe. You'll sleep this off and feel better in the morning."

"No. You can't take me home, you old *pervert*," Pam shouted, drawing all eyes to them.

The sheriff's face grew bright red, even in the dim bar lights. "Ma'am, look, please don't do this. I just wouldn't feel right arresting a grieving woman. Now, quit acting crazy. Let's just get you home. I'll call you a cab if you'd prefer."

Pam picked up her bottle, still half full of beer and sloshed it in his face. "I said go away." She set the bottle back down angrily, a menacing smile on her face.

Markowitz wiped his eyes slowly, blowing foam off his lips. He searched for his cuffs and Pam knew what would come next.

"Pamela Underwood, you are under arrest for public intoxication and assault on an officer. You have the right to remain silent..."

Pam didn't listen to the rest of her rights being read to her, there was only one right she cared about now: the right to justice. Without even knowing it, Sheriff Al Markowitz had just made sure she'd get it.

CHAPTER EIGHTY-ONE

RACHAEL

Abby waved her hand in front of Rachael's face.

"Hello? Rachael? Anybody home? Earth to Rachael."

Rachael shook her head. "I'm sorry, Abby. I was trying to listen, but…do you recognize that woman over there?"

Abby looked over her shoulder to the table on her left.

"Who? Lena?"

"No, the older lady beside her. Has she ever been here before?"

"Oh, no. That must be the new one they brought in last night. I heard she attacked some cop."

"What?" Rachael gasped.

She popped a carrot in her mouth, chewing it loudly. "Yeah, some of the girls were talking about her this morning. I figured she was a repeater, but I've never seen her before."

"She just looks so familiar to me. I can't figure it out." She continued to stare at the woman, trying to determine where she knew her from.

"She doesn't look familiar to me. You've probably seen her around town or something. Why does it matter?"

"I guess it doesn't. It'd just be nice to see someone I knew from the outside for once."

"Right. Well, I'm done eating. Speaking of outside—want to go out for a while? They say it's not too cold today."

"Sure." Rachael picked up her tray absentmindedly and dumped the remnants in the trashcan. As they walked out the double doors to the fenced yard, she was surprised to see a small amount of snow on the ground. It wasn't even enough to cover all of the grass, small sprigs still poked through, but it took Rachael's breath away, nonetheless.

Abby bent down, picking up a small handful of snow and touching it to her lips. "My grandma used to make snow cream for me. Every winter, she'd freeze bags of it and it'd be there…even in the summer. When she died, they found six bags in her freezer, just waiting for us."

"My best friend's mom used to make some for us, too. On snow days, I'd go over to her house and we'd fill up bowls of it and pretend we were cooking." Rachael bit her lip, feeling slightly bitter that even her best memories were now dulled by the possibility of Audrey's betrayal.

Suddenly, she felt an ice cold glob of snow slither its way down her back. She laughed, fanning her sweatshirt so it would fall out. "I can't believe you did that."

Abby let out a loud belly laugh. "Think there's enough snow for a snowball fight?"

Rachael looked around to the white ground beneath her, some of it already melting. She bent over and scooped up a handful. "When there isn't enough snow to make snowballs, my kids call it a snow-throw fight." She squealed, tossing the snow at Abby, but missing her completely. They both laughed, grabbing handfuls of snow and running in opposite directions. As she ran through the snow, Rachael forgot all about the problems that surrounded her, even if just for the moment.

CHAPTER EIGHTY-TWO

PAM

Pam threw her lunch away, placing her tray on the stainless steel counter. Her heart pounded as she felt the metal fork sliding around in the baggy sleeve of her sweater.

She watched as the cafeteria worker picked up her tray, waiting for her to ask about the missing utensil. Instead, she began spraying it off, oblivious to anything suspicious.

Pam turned to walk out of the cafeteria, careful to make sure no one was behind her. Rachael and her friend had just left, so they couldn't have gotten too far. Her pulse raced as she walked out the double doors to the fenced yard.

Just ahead was another building. She tried to remember the way back to the gathering room where Lena had shown her she could watch TV or read magazines, figuring Rachael must've gone that way. She was trying to decide whether the hall was to her left or right when she heard laughter. She looked around the small yard, trying to determine where it had come from. There was no one in sight until Rachael popped out from behind a picnic table, throwing a snowball at her friend.

The girls didn't see Pam at first, so she was free to watch them romp in the snow like children, not a care in the world—as if they were actually happy. How dare she play in the snow when Blaire would never see or touch or play in the snow again?

Pam thought back to when Blaire was younger, trying to recall a single time they'd played in the snow together, rolled snowballs to make a snowman maybe, but she couldn't. A combination of anger and nervousness built up in her throat as she ran her fingers over the fork, gently poking her fingers with the ends and wondering if they'd be enough to do the job.

Quieting her thoughts she stepped forward onto the grass, clutching the fork in her large sleeve tightly. "Can I play?"

CHAPTER EIGHTY-THREE

RACHAEL

"Can I play?" the cigarette-scarred voice asked from behind her.

Rachael spun on her heels to face the woman who'd looked so familiar in the cafeteria. She was a squat, blonde woman who might've been pretty once, but now just looked wrinkled and exhausted. Her dark eyes were eerie, her gaze haunting.

"I'm...I'm sorry, what?"

"I asked if I could play."

"Oh, this?" Rachael looked at the snow melting in her palm. "We were just goofing off, not really playing. You're new, right? I'm Rachael."

"Pam," the woman said stiffly, her lips hardly moving.

"It's nice to meet you. That's Abby." She pointed to Abby as she jogged across the yard toward them.

Pam seemed agitated by everything Rachael said.

"Everything okay?" Abby asked, still breathing hard from laughter.

Pam looked out at the snow, shielding her eyes from its bright reflection. "Oh, it's fine. I just don't understand how you girls are out here having fun. I mean, you are in jail, after all."

"Oh." Rachael couldn't help the sickly feeling that washed over her. Something was not right. "Well, it gets better. I mean, it's jail so it's never good but we all just take it one day at a time. After a few days here, you'll settle in and it won't seem so bad."

Pam smiled, though her smile gave Rachael a repulsive feeling in the pit of her stomach. "I see. I'm glad you're all *settled in* then. It's just…I can't help but think that the woman you murdered is far from settled in, wouldn't you say?"

Her sentence was so far off subject, it took Rachael a second to realize what had been said. "Excuse me?"

"You *are* Rachael Abbott, aren't you? The woman who murdered Blaire Underwood?"

"I—" Rachael started to defend herself before trailing off. It was then that she realized just where she knew the woman from—then that she realized where she'd seen those haunting brown eyes before, once filled with oceans of tears, now only with white hot rage. "You…you were in the courtroom, the day of my trial. Did you know Blaire?" She stepped back out of pure instinct.

"She was my daughter," Pam replied simply.

"Oh." Rachael let silence fill the space between them, unsure of what to say or how to react. Her throat grew tight with tension as she stared at the woman for too long.

Abby touched her shoulder. "Rach, we should go. We're both sorry for your loss, but we need to get back inside." She filled the silence, though no one acknowledged that she'd spoken.

With more force, Abby pulled her arm, turning Rachael away from Pam and forcing her to walk the opposite direction, practically dragging her.

Rachael was merely a few steps from the door when pain

shot through her back. Hot and sharp, it was unlike anything she'd ever felt before. She staggered, letting out an animal-like cry.

She was vaguely aware of Pam running away, of Abby's worried hands trying to prevent her from falling, asking what was wrong.

She felt her knees smack the concrete walkway though she felt no pain. She heard Abby's bloodcurdling screams as she laid her down slowly. She smelled blood, though how she knew it was blood she was unsure.

She was unsure of a lot of things, once she thought about it. What was this pain? How could anything hurt so badly? What was so warm, dripping thickly into her mouth? Why were tears falling from her eyes? Where was she? Why was everything getting dark?

CHAPTER EIGHTY-FOUR

SHAYNA

Shayna Steele did not like hospitals. After her sister's death, she'd prayed never to step foot back into one.

She rushed through the first set of double doors, her curls flying behind her. "Hampton!" she shouted frantically as she spied him pacing the hallway.

"He won't even bring her kids to see their mother," he said, as if they'd already been having a conversation.

"Huh?" she asked, desperately trying to catch her breath.

"*Caide.* His wife is dying and he won't even come to see her. Won't even bring their kids to see her. Who does that? What kind of a person—" He exhaled, gripping his knees, and meeting Shayna's patient eyes.

"How is she?" Shayna asked, not mentioning the stray tear that fell down his cheeks.

"They said we could go in, as long as we're calm. It nicked an artery in her neck. Half an inch over and—" He stopped, covering his mouth with a closed fist. "I just can't go in there and tell her that her kids aren't coming. I can't do it."

Shayna put her hands on his shoulders. "Hampton, listen to me. She needs you. She needs to see you. You keep her calm, I've seen you do it. You can do this…for her." She slid one hand onto the back of his arm and let him lead her to Rachael's room.

With shaking hands, they pushed their way into the room and Shayna felt a lump rise in her throat, suddenly understanding why Hampton was so upset. This was bad.

Rachael's blonde hair was splayed across the white pillow, her neck covered in gauze. A small tube drained out of her wound into a bag draped beside the bed. Her skin looked nearly translucent under the bright white lights.

Her eyes fluttered open at the sound of them shuffling into the room and Shayna found herself wondering if she might cry as she spied the handcuffs restraining Rachael's wrists to the hospital bed.

She smiled at Rachael, trying not to glance at the pitiful look she knew Hampton would be wearing.

"Hey," Shayna said softly.

Rachael blinked her eyes lazily, still mostly asleep. When she spoke, her words came out slow. "Shayna…I can't believe you came. Is it that bad?"

Hampton spoke up, his voice stiff. "No. No, of course not. Everything looks good. You're stable. They're just saying they want to keep you here tonight to make sure you stay that way."

"I wish I could say I was looking forward to getting out." She gazed around the room as much as she could without moving her neck. "But this place sure beats the alternative."

Shayna tried to smile at the halfhearted joke. "Rachael, do you remember what happened?"

Rachael closed her eyes for a second and Shayna wondered if she might be falling back to sleep.

"I remember Blaire's mom was there. She was at the jail."

Shayna looked at Hampton and then back to Rachael,

trying to decide if the pain medicine had her hallucinating. "She visited you?"

Rachael attempted to shake her head, but stopped, wincing. "She was…in jail. A prisoner, like me. She came up to me. I didn't know who she was, at first. She was so angry."

"What did she say?" Shayna asked.

"Nothing, really. It wasn't what she said, it was how she stared at me. She hates me so, so much. I could see it. The doctors don't really talk to me, they just sort of talk *around* me, so I know she stabbed me, but I don't remember it. I remember walking away. She must've done it then." She moved her free hand to her neck, rubbing the bandage.

"It's okay, Rach. You don't have to talk anymore if it's bothering you."

"It just feels weird…sort of numb."

"Well, I don't want you to worry. We will get this taken care of. Ms. Underwood will pay for what she's done to you," Hampton said authoritatively, clearing his throat.

Rachael nodded, her fingers still rubbing the gauze. She looked as though she may be getting sleepy again.

As silence filled the room, the door opened and an older nurse with pixie-cut gray hair entered. "Visiting hours are up. Only one visitor in the room overnight. I'm going to have to ask the other to leave." She smiled politely at the three of them before ducking back out of the room.

Shayna looked at Hampton, who was staring at Rachael sadly. "You should stay," she told him.

"No, it's all right, you stay with her," Hampton said.

She pressed her lips together. "Hampton, really. You should be the one here."

"Thank you," he said, walking to touch Rachael's hand. "But I have work to do. I need to find out exactly how this happened and make sure it never happens again." He leaned down and pressed his lips to her pale fingers. "I'll be back in the morning."

Shayna nodded. He turned back to walk out of the room but met Shayna's eyes once more. "You'll take care of her?" he asked.

"She'll be fine," she promised, touched by Hampton's obvious compassion for Rachael. He left the room quietly, leaving Shayna to listen to the buzzing of the machines. She walked to the chair beside the bed, sitting down.

Rachael's sea green eyes opened sleepily. "You don't have to stay, you know. I'll be fine."

"I know you will." Shayna rubbed Rachael's fingers as she'd seen Hampton do. "But I'd like to stay. Since you managed to get out of our sessions, I'll be needing the company." She crossed one leg over the other, looking around the room.

"You don't like hospitals," Rachael said intuitively.

She looked back at her patient. "No, I don't."

"Have you spent a lot of time in them? With your patients?"

Shayna swallowed, running her free hand over her pants. "With my sister."

"Your sister? The one in the picture?"

Shayna nodded, a sad smile on her face. "Lydia was in a pretty bad skiing accident when she was fourteen. She spent eight months in and out of hospitals. When she was finally released, she began acting odd. There were days when she'd just stay in her bed and refuse to speak to anyone. A few months later, she was diagnosed with DID."

Rachel's eyes widened. "Oh, Shayna. That's why this means so much to you. You research to save her?"

"At first, yes. My sister was perfectly healthy before her accident. But after…it's like we never got her back completely." She looked up at the ceiling, trying to keep the tears at bay. "They, um, they gave her some medicine to ease her symptoms. Some days she was Lydia and she'd wake up and take her medicine and be just fine. Then sometimes, she'd claim she wasn't Lydia, she wasn't sick, and she'd refuse to take her medicine. The personality she'd dissociate into didn't take care of herself. She wouldn't eat, she wouldn't drink. She'd just sleep constantly. We tried every kind of medicine they had, but in the end it wasn't enough. She passed away when she was seventeen." She couldn't bear to look at Rachael as she wiped away the first tear. "We watched her die right in front of us and there was nothing we could do. Some part of her just…didn't care enough to keep living."

"I'm so…so sorry." She scoffed. "That seems so insignificant to say."

"No, it's okay. Thank you," Shayna said, finally meeting her eye.

"It's not, though. It's terrible. Please, please don't stay because of me. I'd feel awful making you stay here."

Shayna smiled at her. "It's true I don't like hospitals—they freak me out—but I'd like to stay with you anyway. Who knows? Maybe some of your bravery has rubbed off on me."

Rachael's eyes narrowed at her. "You think I'm *brave*?"

Shayna nodded. "You know in my field of work, I see a lot of things. Some are crazy, some are tragic. It's very rare that a client comes in and earns my respect like you have. You've been so brave and so strong through something I wouldn't wish on the foulest person I could think of. And you…are not the foulest person I could think of, I assure you." She winked, tears still brimming her eyes. "I'm just so sorry that this is happening to you."

"Thank you. Most days I don't feel strong at all. I just hope Hampton can pull this off. I just want to get back to normal."

She was quiet for a while and Shayna stayed still, listening to her breathing. After a moment, she said, "Will it?"

"Will it what?" Rachael asked.

"Will it go back to normal for you? After all you've been through? What does life look like for you…after all of this?"

"I guess it'll never go back to how it was before. The four of us. I pray that Caide isn't guilty of this, but I'll never forgive him for what he's done. I don't know if I'll be able to stay here. I don't want to face this town every day. We may just have to create a new normal, somewhere else. Just me and the kids. We don't get enough snow here, I think. The kids love snow," she said thoughtfully.

"You're going to leave La Rue?"

"I don't know. I think it'd be for the best."

"I know one person who'd disagree." Shayna frowned.

"You?" Rachael asked with a laugh.

"Well, I'd love it if you stayed, but I was thinking of someone else."

"You can't mean Argus." She rolled her eyes. Shayna smiled, raising her eyebrows, but not saying anything. "Argus is a great lawyer. He's done more for me than I'll ever be able to thank him for, but Shayna, this is just a case to him. Once it's over, that'll be it."

Shayna patted the rail of her bed. "Well, if you believe that, bravery has done nothing for your intelligence."

Rachael blushed. "What do you mean?"

"Rachael…" she said, trying to get her to admit what they both knew.

"What?"

"All right. We can play that game. All I'm saying is that he cares for you. You aren't *just* a case to him. Don't forget his feelings before you go disappearing into the Alaskan tundra."

"You really care about him."

"I care about him because he cares for my client."

"You really think he cares about me?"

She gave her an odd look. "If I couldn't figure that out, the degrees on my walls would be useless."

Rachael's cheeks grew red. "He's never said anything."

Shayna pursed her lips. "You're married—to a jerk, by the way—and Hampton's a nice guy. Plus, he's your lawyer. No one gets the treatment you get from him, trust me, least of all his clients."

Rachael blushed again. "What about you?"

"What about me?"

"Are you married?"

Shayna laughed. "No."

"Why's that funny?"

"I don't have time to date. I stay so completely busy and absorbed in my work. My mom used to say I have a one-track mind and it's always on the same track. I guess I've only ever wanted success."

"That can't be true. You haven't ever been in love?"

She clicked her tongue. "Nope. I mean, I've dated, I'm just not really into the whole dating scene. It's overrated. Getting all dressed up, going out, and being uncomfortable? No, thank you. I just don't like leaving my comfort zone and I see no reason to change that."

"But what do you do for fun? When you aren't working."

"I'm *always* working."

Rachael stared at her. "You don't have hobbies? Or friends?"

"Not really, no. I mean, there are a few people I keep in touch with from school and colleagues I have brunch with occasionally, but my hobby is my career. I'm one of those crazy people who actually, genuinely loves her job. I want to learn all I can about every aspect of it. Don't you feel that passionately about anything?"

Rachael thought for a second. "My kids. I mean, I love

dance. I love my job, but my kids are my passion. I want to learn everything about them and spend every second I can with them."

"You seem like such a good mom."

"There are days where I don't know if I'll make it to the evening, but they're the best things that have ever happened to me."

Just then the nurse was back, she walked into the room with a ring of keys, jingling them into the air. "You've got a good lawyer, kid."

Rachael looked confused. The nurse turned to Shayna. "You're staying with her all night?"

Shayna nodded. "I am."

"She's on your watch, then." She fumbled with the keys, finally pulling one out and unhooking Rachael's handcuffs. Rachael rubbed her wrists cautiously. The nurse smiled, nodded farewell, and left.

Silence filled the room and Shayna watched as Rachael's eyes began to flutter. "Go on to sleep if you need to. I'll be here," she told her.

Without needing to be told twice, Rachael was out. She watched her sleep soundly for hours on end, though Shayna couldn't make herself sleep in the hospital chair, no matter what position she maneuvered into.

Instead, she sat quietly as Rachael slept, careful not to make too much noise as she aimlessly flipped through the TV channels.

Around one a.m., Rachael awoke and watched the end of a cheesy soap opera with her. "Audrey and I used to spend our summers watching shows like this."

"It must be really hard for you to question your friendship."

She bit her lip. "It is. She's my only friend, you know? I hate myself for even considering it. I wish there was another possibility. Why couldn't it be the mailman? I have no personal attachments to our mailman."

Shayna chuckled.

"When I found out about their affair, I should have left."

"You can't blame yourself," she assured her.

"I know…but I do. I'm not that woman. The woman who stays while he cheats. If it'd been anyone else, if I'd known about Blaire too, I would've left. It's just that admitting what I knew—leaving Caide—it meant I'd lose Audrey too. I just couldn't do that. She's all I have."

"That's not true." Shayna placed her hand on Rachael's. "Not anymore. You have me, Rachael. You have me and Hampton. Even once all of this is over, you'll still have us."

Rachael wiped a tear from her eyes. "To change the subject, this is pretty embarrassing, but do you think you could help me to the restroom?"

"Will they let you up?"

"They did before. I should be fine, but I'm still a bit dizzy. As long as you help me get to the door, I'll be okay."

"We should really call a nurse."

"It's just peeing," Rachael said. "I mean, my legs aren't hurt. I…I want to be able to do this on my own." She laughed. "With your help."

Shayna thought for a moment, before hesitantly agreeing. She stood and Rachael pulled back the covers. Rachael's hospital gown was pulled up to her belly button, revealing a large brown spot on her left upper thigh, near her hip.

They both blushed. Shayna averted her gaze quickly, trying to give her some privacy. Once Rachael had adjusted her gown, Shayna turned back to her.

"What happened?"

"Huh?"

"The bruise on your hip. Was that from the attack?"

"Oh, that? No, that's just a birthmark." She dismissed

Shayna's concerns. As she hoisted herself from the bed, Rachael threw her arm around Shayna's shoulders.

They stood still for a moment, letting Rachael steady herself.

"Oh, good. It caught me off guard. I was worried you really had hurt your legs."

They made their way across the room slowly, Shayna lifting most of Rachael's weight as she swayed with each step.

"Nope, just a birthmark. It's been there my whole life. It sort of looks like a tree, doesn't it?" she asked.

Shayna looked at her from underneath her arm. "A tree? Yeah, I guess it does. I hadn't even realized it."

"You were looking at it upside down. From my angle, it looks like a tree. I always thought it was neat. Like a giant oak tree or something."

Shayna paused. "Did you say an oak tree? Have you told me about that before?"

"No, why?" Rachael asked, wincing as she took the next step. "I'm dizzier than I thought."

An oak tree birthmark. Why did that sound so familiar? "I feel like I've heard about someone having an oak tree birthmark. Maybe not."

"I don't think I've told you about it. It doesn't usually come up in casual conversation," Rachael joked, swinging the bathroom door open. She gripped onto the sink, shifting her weight to lean on the toilet. Shayna pushed her IV cart gently behind her and turned around.

She was still searching her brain for the memory when it hit her moments later: a realization so completely unexpected she gasped aloud.

Oh no. Oh no, oh no.

CHAPTER EIGHTY-FIVE

AUDREY

Audrey's head swam with emotions as she pulled into her driveway. John's car hadn't been home in the weeks since she'd told him about the affair. Her devoted husband had finally had enough.

Being alone didn't bother Audrey—it was being without Caide that hurt her the worst. Since the day, so long ago, when the affair had begun, she'd kept him in the back of her mind constantly.

She was always counting down until the next phone call or night together. Now, for the first time in years, Audrey was unsure of where she stood with him and that had her nervous.

She got out of her car, her feet noisily crunching on the snow-covered grass. Her thoughts halted as she noticed there was another set of footprints leading up to her doorstep. Had John come back?

She walked quietly toward the door and stopped when she noticed a small, white envelope on her brown welcome mat. She bent to pick it up with shaking hands, opening it carefully. Inside, she found a photograph. Her heart pounded in her chest, so loud she was sure she could hear it. She stared at the photo of herself, arms wrapped around Caide's neck, lips locked together.

It was from earlier that day, her visit with Caide. Someone had worked quickly. She couldn't help but fear the sort of warning this must be.

Her blood ran cold as someone cleared their throat behind her. She gulped, shoving the picture into her pocket quickly. She spun around and was surprised to see a very familiar face.

"It's *you*. What are you doing here?"

CHAPTER EIGHTY-SIX

PHOEBE MOORE

Phoebe Moore loved three things in life: warm fires, hot tea, and chilling mystery novels. Her fire had long since burned out and her tea had grown cold when she put down her book and realized it was past three a.m. already.

She remembered the days when four o'clock meant heading to work, but her days now were filled with quiet evenings and books she couldn't put down.

Realizing it was so late caused her worry when her phone began to ring. Phoebe's husband had passed away years ago and they'd never had any children. She had no relatives or neighbors close enough to be calling so she was left with confusion as she picked up the receiver.

"Hello?"

"Is this Phoebe Moore?" a woman's voice asked.

"Yes it is. Do you have any idea what time it is?"

"Of course. I'm sorry to be calling so late, Phoebe. This is Shayna Steele. Do you remember me?"

"Of course, Ms. Steele, what can I do for you?"

"I think it'd be easier to explain in person. I know it's a lot to ask. I know it's the middle of the night, but it's important that I see you soon."

"Of course. When?"

"The sooner the better." Shayna's voice sounded urgent.

"Should I come now?" she asked, fear gripping her belly.

"Would that be a problem? I wouldn't ask if it wasn't important."

"It's no bother. Are you still in the same office? I wasn't planning to sleep tonight anyway," she joked.

"Yes. The same office. I'll be waiting for you, just come on by."

"Sure thing. Let me get dressed and I'll be right over."

"Thanks."

Phoebe hung up the phone, catching her breath. She hadn't spoken to Shayna in nearly twenty years. What in the world could she possibly need now, after all this time?

CHAPTER EIGHTY-SEVEN

SHAYNA

Shayna paced circles around her office, watching impatiently for headlights in her window.

She'd played Phoebe's tape over and over again since she'd found it in her file. She couldn't believe it. She couldn't believe the answer had been so close all this time. She just had to see Phoebe to hear it all from her one last time.

Finally, headlights shone through the blinds, alerting her that Phoebe had arrived. She paused the tape and closed her file, walking calmly toward the door to let her in.

Phoebe had aged terribly—her face weighed down by wrinkles, her once brown hair now gray. Despite the changes, Shayna recognized her warm smile immediately.

"Phoebe." She pulled open the door, wrapping her old client into a friendly hug. "How are you?"

"I'm okay, thanks. Hope you are?"

"Thank you for coming on such short notice." Shayna nodded.

"So, what's going on?"

"Well, I think we'd better sit down. I'm afraid I may have

some bad news." She led Phoebe through the lobby and into the office.

"What kind of bad news? You're scaring me." She sat obligingly.

Shayna sat across from her, attempting to steady her hands. She ran her fingers along her file. "Phoebe, I want you to know, first of all, that I've never told anyone what you told me. The details about that night have never left this room. But…I have to ask you to help me now. Someone I care about very much is in trouble and I think you can help her."

Phoebe looked hesitant. "What can I do?"

Shayna flipped open the folder in her lap. "Well, first things first, I need you to tell me everything there is to know about the baby with the oak tree birthmark."

CHAPTER EIGHTY-EIGHT

AUDREY

Rachael stood in front of Audrey, her face radiating fury. Audrey remained frozen in fear.

"Rach? What are you doing here? How did you…how did you even get out?"

Rachael stayed still, not responding.

"Look, I can explain this." She held up the photo, guilt filling her chest. "Well, I mean, not really. I just, I'm sorry, Rachael. I'm so sorry. You have to know I never meant for this to happen. Never. You're my best friend. This doesn't change that. I'm so sorry." Emotions flooded her brain, tears rolling down her cheeks. She'd never felt so stupid as she did in that moment.

She wanted Rachael to hug her, to let her cry it out, to tell her everything would be okay.

She didn't.

Audrey knew she didn't deserve it, but it was still hard to watch her best friend stand, completely unmoving, at the sight of her tears. She sniffled a few more times, attempting to stop the tears from falling, but they were relentless.

"Look, *this* means nothing," she said, turning the picture over so she wouldn't have to look at it anymore. "It means nothing compared to our friendship. It was a mistake. A huge mistake. You have to believe me. I'm *so* sorry."

She realized, in that moment, nothing had ever been truer. She *was* sorry. She wished, more than anything, that she could take it all back. She approached Rachael, her eyes swimming with tears.

"I can't believe what I've done. I don't know why I did it. I know you'll never forgive me but—"

Audrey never got to finish her sentence. At that exact moment, something cold ripped through her stomach. The pain took her breath away and she staggered backward, away from her friend. A kitchen knife stuck out from just under her rib cage.

"Rachael—" She gurgled, her lungs burning as they filled with blood. She fell down to the ground as her legs gave out under her.

The pain was so intense, it consumed her thoughts and left her with nothing to do but wait for it to end. It hurt to move, it hurt to breathe, and it hurt to cry.

She laid down in the snow, noticing the cold felt surprisingly good. Rachael stood above her, not smiling, not crying —just watching. She bent down and, for a brief second, Audrey hoped for help.

Instead, Rachael pulled the knife out with a sharp tug. Audrey let out a horrific cry, trying to maneuver her snow-covered fingers onto the wound to stop some of the bleeding. It was no use. As her friend walked away into the night, not bothering to even look back, Audrey watched her blood dye a crimson ring around her.

Her body grew cold, though it hurt to shiver, and she knew her end would come soon. Her life didn't flash before her eyes; she didn't see a bright white light. Audrey Hagen died—cold and alone—feeling as deserted, scorned, and helpless as she'd ever felt in her very short life.

CHAPTER EIGHTY-NINE

CAIDE

A sharp rapping at the window woke Caide from a deep sleep. He jumped out of bed, wondering why he'd chosen not to own a gun. He hurried to the closet and grabbed his bat.

"What the hell?" he asked as he whipped the curtain back.

Rachael smiled at him. "Let me in. It's freezing out here."

"Rachael? What are you doing here? How are you out of jail?"

"I wanted to see you. Now, let me in."

He opened the window slowly, allowing his wife to crawl inside. "What's happening?"

"I had to escape. Oh, Caide, I couldn't stand another minute in that awful place. I missed you so much." She threw her arms around his neck. Prison had slimmed her, his arms now fit loosely around her waist and as she pressed up against him, he could distinctly feel her rib cage.

Her breath smelled of cigarette smoke. When had she started smoking? Her mouth met his without warning—her kisses sweet at first, but quickly growing passionate. Her hands explored every inch of him with a determination she hadn't had in years.

"Rachael," he mumbled, pushing her back, "we can't do this. You have to leave."

"Why?" she asked, kissing and nipping at his neck.

"Because they're going to come looking for you as soon as they realize you are missing."

"We have time. Just kiss me." She pulled her shirt over her head and then his, kissing his chest.

Just like that, he forgot about their fight, forgot how angry he'd been with her, and gave in. He pulled her mouth up to meet his and kissed her feverishly, like they hadn't kissed since long before the wedding.

He lifted her up, shocked by the ease with which he now could, and pushed her up against the wall.

"I love you. I love you," she whispered.

He pulled away, shocked to see tears in her eyes. "Do you?"

"I do." She nodded. "I really, really do. I've missed you so much."

"What about our fight? You said that you were going to leave me."

She let out a breath. "You *cheated* on me, Caide. I think that makes us even."

"I did, but you're a murderer, Rach. Do you realize that? You actually *killed* someone. How could you?"

She narrowed her eyes at him. "Don't blame me for cleaning up your mess. She shouldn't have taken what wasn't hers."

Caide loathed the hardness in his pants. He'd never been so completely disgusted and turned on all at once. There was something about this side of Rachael, a side he'd never seen before, that had him wanting to taste her again.

He couldn't help but to be turned on by the wildness in

her eyes. He bit her lip, pulling her jeans down to her ankles. She smiled at him crookedly and he knew right then it was over.

He pushed her onto the bed with no time for foreplay. He needed her—right then. He took what was his for the first time in so long, listening to her moan his name.

He ran his hands through her hair, tugging at the blonde strands he'd missed so much. He felt tears in his eyes as he realized just how much he had missed her.

As he pulsed inside of her, he whispered over and over again how much he loved her and how sorry he was. And, for the first time in years, he found himself meaning every word he said.

CHAPTER NINETY

HAMPTON

Hampton burst into Rachael's room the next morning, a large smile on his face. He glanced around. A tired-looking Rachael smiled back at him. Shayna was nowhere to be found.

"Where is Shayna?"

"Oh." Rachael rubbed her eyes. "She left."

"She *left*?" Hampton asked. "What the hell do you mean she left? She swore she'd stay."

"It's okay, Argus. She said she had something to do. I don't need a babysitter. It's no big deal."

He put a palm to his forehead. "Yes, actually, it's a very big deal, Rachael. I got them to un-cuff you with the understanding that you'd be supervised all night. This could be so bad." He pulled out his cell phone and dialed furiously.

"Nothing happened. Nothing's wrong," Rachael insisted.

"What time did she leave?"

"I really don't remember. Maybe around two?"

"Damn. That's like six hours unsupervised. I swear—"

"Hello?"

"*Shayna, where the hell are you?* Do you realize what you've done?"

She took a deep breath. "Hampton, I'm sorry. I know you're angry. I need to see Rachael today. In my office."

"Do *what*? What are you talking about?"

Her voice was clipped and cold. "I need you to bring her here. As soon as you can."

"Are you serious? She's just been in the ICU all night. You can't honestly expect me to get her released."

"It's important. It's so important that you do."

"Stop being cryptic. What's going on?"

"I can't explain now. Just get her here," she said.

"Okay. Fine. I'll see what I can do." He slammed his phone shut, his face pale.

"What's going on?" Rachael asked, attempting to sit up.

"We've got to get you out of here. I'll be right back." Argus hurried out the door before she could say anything else.

HAMPTON WAITED IMPATIENTLY BY THE NURSES' station for someone to return with Rachael's doctor. He sighed, staring at his watch. It had been nearly an hour and a half since Shayna had called and his fears were growing larger by the minute.

Finally, a middle aged man in a white coat rounded the corner, carrying a clipboard. "Are you here for Rachael Abbott?"

"Yes. Yes, are you her doctor?"

"Yes. Rachael's vitals look good, they stayed strong overnight. Her fluid intake and output are right where we want them to be. She'll need to take it easy for the next few days. Don't let her get the stitches wet and don't let her scratch them. We've called in an antibiotic to ward off infection, so they'll be sent to the jail. No heavy lifting of any kind, no strenuous activity."

"You're saying you'll release her?"

"I need to see her back in four weeks to remove the stitches. I want her to get plenty of rest. If they start bleeding, if she has any pain, or if it gets infected, I need her back here immediately. I've relayed all of this to the physician on call at the jail, but I wanted you to be aware as well. They said you are in charge of her transport to therapy, so it's best to keep an eye on things."

"But she's released?"

"There's no reason she should have to stay. She's doing great. It was a clean cut and we were able to repair it nicely. I think she's going to be just fine."

"Great. Thank you so much."

"You'll need to sign for her release."

Hampton took the clipboard from him, scribbling his name where he was told. He handed it back to the doctor and rushed toward Rachael's room, zigzagging through the crowded hallway.

CHAPTER NINETY-ONE

RACHAEL

Rachael tapped her feet anxiously, sitting in the passenger seat of Argus' car as he made phone call after angry phone call.

The current call seemed to be to the judge. Rachael's neck ached a bit, and try as she might, she just couldn't get comfortable. God, she missed morphine.

She sat quietly, resting her face against the cool window. She watched as they passed fields and trees, car after car. It seemed like it had been so long since she'd been out of the hospital, though it had only been a day. The pain in her neck was beginning to give her a headache.

He hung up the phone. "So the woman who attacked you has been charged with attempted murder. Our case is solid and your friend has agreed to testify as a witness. She's in isolation until her court date, but I'm sure we'll win."

Rachael nodded.

"Did you know who she was?"

"Not at first, no. She looked so familiar but I didn't know why. She was at the trial. I didn't realize it until she mentioned Blaire."

"Rachael, I'm afraid people are going to want to hurt you now. You have to take care of yourself. This shouldn't have ever happened. I'll make sure she pays for what she's done."

"It was her daughter, Argus." She reached for his hand. "I can't say I wouldn't have done the same thing. I don't want to imagine how she was feeling. No one should have to bury their child."

Argus touched her cheek with the back of his hand. "Hey, you didn't do this. You don't have to feel guilty."

They were silent for a moment, each lost in their own thoughts. When Argus spoke again, Rachael pretended not to hear his voice crack. "Rachael, if something had happened to you…I don't know what I would've done."

She squeezed his hand gently. "I know."

He sighed. "Anyway, I…um, I talked to Judge Crafton. He's agreed to release you for eight hours today instead of four to make up for yesterday. Shayna said we'll need some extra time."

"Do you have any idea what she's got planned? I thought we were done with the tests now that she knows I don't have DID?"

"I don't know what she's planning, but it'd better be good. If she left you for no reason last night, it could ruin this case. She'd better know what she's doing."

"She does," Rachael said with confidence. As they pulled into Shayna's parking lot, Rachael's pulse picked up. She hadn't realized how nervous she was until just then. Argus climbed out of the car and walked around to meet Rachael.

He held his hand out to help her and she took it gratefully, more to hold his hand than because she needed help.

"Here we go," he whispered.

"Knock, knock," Rachael called as she opened the door to the lobby, noticing Kortnee was not at her desk. The building was surprisingly quiet, allowing them to hear the approaching footsteps. Shayna pulled the office door open, a grim look on her face. Behind her was a plump, older woman. She smiled at Rachael.

"Rachael," Shayna said softly, "I apologize for leaving you last night. How are you feeling?"

"I've been better," Rachael said. "But I'll be okay. I'm glad to be out of that hospital. Of course, it was better than where I'll be going next."

"Actually…" Shayna grinned. "If everything works out, you may not be going back to jail after all."

"I bought us eight hours, but you'll have to work fast," Argus told Shayna pointedly.

"Right. Well, let's all go into the office and sit down. We've got a lot to talk about and very little time to do so." Shayna held the door open, leading them through. They each picked couches awkwardly. Rachael sat on a gray one with Hampton beside her. Shayna across from them. Her friend sat carefully in a pink chair, obviously uncomfortable.

"Okay, so what is going on?" Rachael asked, feeling frustrated by her growing headache and lack of answers.

"First things first, Rachael, I'd like you to meet Ms. Phoebe Moore. She's an old client of mine."

"It's nice to meet you, Ms. Moore." Rachael smiled politely but cast a confused look back at Shayna. Phoebe nodded but said nothing.

Shayna cleared her throat. "Well, I guess we'll just jump right into why we're here. Last night, Rachael, when I saw your birthmark, do you remember me telling you I'd heard about it before?"

"Yes."

"Well, it turns out I was right, I just hadn't heard about it from *you*. I came back to my office, replaying old tapes and trying to jog my memory. That's when I found Phoebe's folder and it hit me. She was kind enough to meet with us.

She's a little nervous but she has a story she needs to tell you." She grimaced slightly. "It's not going to be easy for you to hear, but you need to know the truth about what's been going on and, as luck would have it, there's no one better to tell you than Phoebe."

Phoebe scooted forward in her chair, wringing her hands nervously together. "Okay, well, like she told you…I'm Phoebe. I've lived in La Rue all my life. I was a nurse at La Rue Baptist Hospital for twenty-two years."

"That's where I was born," Rachael said.

Phoebe nodded. "That's right. I was there the night you were born. In fact, I was the nurse who delivered you." Rachael was taken back by this news, feeling strangely violated. "Now, first of all, you have to understand that the year you were born was one of the toughest of my life. I lost my father to a heart attack, and I had three miscarriages before finding out I'd never be able to carry a child full term. I lost my third and final child the night before you were born."

"I'm so sorry," Rachael said instinctually.

"Thank you," Phoebe said. "I had been sixteen weeks along, the furthest my husband and I had ever made it. We'd done everything right. We read all the books, ate the right foods, I stayed off my feet, but in the end, the good Lord called my child home anyway. Afterward, they told me I'd need a hysterectomy. They told me another miscarriage would kill me. I don't know if they were right, *physically*, but mentally there was no question. So, we decided to quit trying. I felt like my body was betraying me. The doctor told me to take a week off, but I needed much more. I didn't just lose a child that night, I lost the future I'd always hoped for. Unfortunately, when working at a hospital, sometimes the time you need off is not what they're able to give you."

She paused to wipe her eyes before continuing. "Back in

those days we didn't have a labor board or an HR hotline, when they told you to come to work, you came to work. So, when the attending called me that night, he said it was bad. There was a full moon and a horrible storm. Accidents were coming in left and right—a lot of pregnant women, too. The other attending on call had gotten stuck in traffic and so we had forty pregnant women, one doctor, and five nurses. I'll never forget walking into the maternity ward that night—it was pure chaos. People were running around; there were patient beds in the hallways, charts lying about. They were sending patients to nearby hospitals, but for some of the women it was too late or other cases took precedent over theirs. The storm really messed up travel. We were told to keep the mothers calm and healthy while we waited for other doctors to arrive."

She paused, staring off into space, "Come to think of it, I don't think they ever did. *Anyway,* we had a car crash come in. A woman, husband, and their son had hydroplaned on some water. They went off in a ditch, flipped six or seven times. The husband was declared dead on arrival. There was a little boy, Ben. He was only six. He died later that night. The mother, Marianne, was eight months pregnant and in rough shape. She was unconscious and bleeding. They were able to get her stable, but the baby was in distress. He had to be delivered right away. That gave us forty-one moms and counting. The doctor told us to grab an aide and start delivering. The nurses, myself included, were divided up. They gave us each four or five moms to take care of, while the doctor delivered the higher risk babies."

"They let nurses deliver babies? *Alone?*" Argus asked, obviously appalled.

"This was a different time. Not so many rules back then. Besides, delivering babies isn't rocket science. Women had been having babies in fields long before hospitals came along. Anyhow, I was assigned to the car accident. I was also assigned to your mother," she told Rachael. "She was my first to be fully dilated. I remember she was so ready to meet you."

She shifted uncomfortably in her seat. "She'd woken up in the middle of the night when her water broke. By the time she got to the hospital, you were already starting to crown. We rushed her into the only delivery room we had available, which also happened to be Marianne's. Your mom was chattering away. She was so happy that night, even in the middle of her labor, she was *so* ready to be a mom. She told me all about your father, all of the toys they'd bought for you, and how they'd decorated your nursery. She was...enchanting, your mother. We delivered you within the hour—an easy delivery. I remember seeing your birthmark. The oak tree birthmark. Most babies take months for them to show up, but yours was right there from the beginning. Your mom cried when she saw you. She told me your name was Rachael. I gave you to my aide and had her take you to the nursery. After you were out of the room, I went to check on Marianne. Her vitals were crashing again, so I had to leave your mom..." She stopped talking, biting her lip.

"Go on," Shayna encouraged her.

"God, I shouldn't have been there that night. I was just too emotional. When I got to Marianne, I just couldn't find the baby's heartbeat. I had to do a cesarean. I called for the doctor, but he was in the middle of a delivery. He told me to go ahead. I couldn't wait for my aide any longer. We didn't have any operating rooms open. I had to do the surgery right there. I was...I was so nervous. When I cut her open, I remember how badly my hands were shaking. I got to the baby, but...there was...there was just so much blood. She'd been bleeding internally and we'd missed it. When I pulled the baby out, he was so stiff. Cool. He didn't move. I laid him down, my aide should've been back but she wasn't. I tried everything I could to save that little baby. He was so beautiful."

Phoebe's haunted face was ghastly as she spoke, giving Rachael cold chills. "He just wouldn't start breathing. I had to leave him. I started sewing Marianne back up. Once I finished with her, I hurried back to your mom. She was asking for you. I told her I'd get her all cleaned up and then we'd go get you. She joked that if you were anything like your father you'd be starving and ready to eat. When I lifted up the sheet to sew her up—" Her voice caught as her fingers touched her mouth in horror. When she spoke again, it was a whisper. "There was another little head poking out. I thought maybe I'd gone crazy, she wasn't even pushing or in any pain but…there it was. Another baby. I bent down, ready to pull the baby out. I told your mom to push. When she did…blood just started pouring out of her. *Pouring.* The baby was so covered in blood, I nearly dropped her. She was alert and screaming. I wrapped her up and set her on the bed, underneath a lamp to keep her warm. I began working on your mother right after that. I tried so hard to stop the bleeding, but she'd already lost so much. I…I wasn't trained for that. The bed was soaked. I did all that I knew to do…but in the end, it wasn't enough. I spent thirty minutes with her, before she was gone. The doctor came in and we tried to resuscitate, but she was just *gone*. It was the most heartbreaking night of my career. Other nurses came in to help clean up your mother and Marianne, and the babies, of course. You have to understand…the stress I was under after my miscarriage…I know it's no excuse but it had taken a toll on me. Everything hurt so bad."

Tears began to fall steadily from her eyes and she clutched her chest. "So, when the nurse asked me which baby belonged to which mother—I saw your mother lying there, she'd left your father a beautiful baby girl. He had a baby he could raise and love; and then I looked at Marianne, who'd lost her son and her husband all at once. I just couldn't stand to take one more thing from her. So, I lied. I let them switch the babies, let them tell Marianne that she'd delivered a healthy baby girl and both families went home with a baby. I know what I did was wrong and there's no way to make it right. I would've done anything to save your mother. It was all my fault. I was a wreck and my head wasn't clear. It should never have happened. It's the biggest mistake I've ever made. It's haunted me every day since then. Night and day. I left the hospital shortly after, took to drinking. That's when I found Shayna. She was a life saver. She helped me to accept what I'd done and move forward. Then, last night she called me and told me your story. I knew it was time to come forward, to accept the consequences of my actions. I won't let anyone else be affected by my thoughtless misjudgment. Please, dear girl, please let me help you. Please know that you can never hate me the way I hate myself." She stopped talking, tears streaming down her wrinkled cheeks.

Rachael sat in pure disbelief, unable to think about or process what was being said. The room was silent, all eyes on her. "So you're telling me…what exactly? My mother had another baby? I have a sibling?" she asked, half expecting someone to laugh.

"I'm saying that you have a sister, honey."

"A twin sister, Rachael. An *identical* twin sister," Shayna added, begging her to catch on.

"No one ever knew? Her dad wasn't shocked when they only gave him one baby?" Argus asked, his voice filled with surprise.

"We didn't do ultrasounds back then. The ones we did have were considered luxury. With a stethoscope, it's pretty common for one baby to hide behind another. Neither of your parents knew they were having twins, not even their doctor."

"How ironic." Argus scoffed, looking at Rachael.

Rachael pressed her lips together, trying to comprehend what she was being told. "So, you're saying you believe that my *twin sister*, who I've never met and who I have no reason to believe even knows I exist, killed my husband's girlfriend and then left me to take the blame?"

Phoebe and Shayna looked at each other before Shayna answered. She leaned forward, speaking slowly. "It's farfetched, we know, but it *would* make sense."

"*Make sense*? Are you kidding me? This makes even less sense than believing Caide did this." She stood, walking toward the window as she tried to remain calm.

Shayna stood to face her. "Rachael, honey, I know this is tough. Nothing about this is easy, but it's happening. The story matches your mother's death, the birthmark testimony is on tape from twenty years ago—way before this case, before I met you. It explains why you don't remember being on that security tape—not because you were suffering from some mental disorder—but because it wasn't you. Don't you see?"

Rachael's head swam with confusion. "But why? Why would she—what reason could there possibly be? You believe it's just a coincidence?"

"Well." Shayna bit her lip. "We don't know. That's what we still need to find out. Unfortunately, we have no records of the other baby, no way to know where she ended up or where she is now. We don't even know if she knows about you."

"And if she does?" Argus asked.

"What?" Rachael looked at him.

"What if her plan was to frame you, Rachael? I mean, she didn't bother covering her face at all and she killed your husband's girlfriend. That makes you the obvious suspect and it becomes extremely easy to lock you up. Maybe that's what she wanted all along."

"But why?" Rachael whined.

"I don't know. Your dad never mentioned another baby, did he? You never met any little girls who looked like you? Never had anyone strange ever contact you?"

"No." Rachael sank back onto the couch. The room grew silent, each of them trying to figure out the answer to their dilemma. When Argus' ringtone tore through the silence, they all jumped. He looked at the screen, a weird look on his face, before stepping out of the room.

"Rachael, I need you to think hard, okay? Phoebe has agreed to testify, at great personal risk, but her testimony alone won't be enough. There's no medical proof of you having a twin. We need something solid for court. We need to know if she is trying to frame you, and we need to know why. We need to find out what she wants. Without something solid I'm afraid the evidence will be tossed out. *Think*. Why would she be after you?"

Before Rachael could respond, the door opened again and Argus reentered, a ghastly look on his face. He still held his phone in his hand, not making eye contact with anyone. Rachael felt a lump in her throat once again, knowing a look like that could only bring bad news. "Argus?"

"I don't think it's her." He was staring at the floor, his eyes wide.

"Huh?" Rachael asked.

"I don't think it's you the twin is after," he told her, looking her way finally.

"What do you mean?" Rachael stood.

"News of the affair between Caide and Audrey just got out."

Shayna gasped. "What?"

Rachael's head began to spin. "What are you talking about?"

He swallowed, glancing at his phone. "Audrey Hagen was found dead this morning. I don't think this woman is out to get you. I think she's getting rid of anyone close to Caide."

"*No!*" Rachael screamed, her legs beginning to shake. *The kids.*

CHAPTER NINETY-TWO

ELISE MOSS

Elise Moss was three years old the first time her mother told her she hated her.

Elise had always known that she'd had a father and a brother once, long ago, before she'd come along. Her mother didn't like to talk about them and whenever Elise would ask, she'd just turn the TV up and ignore her altogether. Elise knew there was a time, before she existed, when her mother had been happy, when her father led a church youth group, and her brother played on the school's soccer team.

Sometimes, when her mom's drinking got too bad, Elise would hide in her closet and try to imagine that time. She pictured her mother singing, her father rocking her on his lap, even her brother teaching her to play one of the board games that now sat in the back of his closet gathering dust.

When Elise was eight years old, her mother moved her out of the nursery, out of the crib she hadn't fit in in years, and into Ben's old room. It was blue and green—a boy's room—with monster trucks and soccer balls on the wall. Elise taught herself to play soccer in the small bedroom where she was expected to spend her days, not making too much noise and staying out of her mother's way.

By the time she was ten years old, Elise knew how to fix every meal for herself and her mother. She knew how to make a dirty martini just the way her mother liked it, and she knew how to layer all of her clothing so that it looked like it may fit and she didn't have to ask her mom for anything new.

By the age of twelve, she learned that she could take exactly three dollars a week from her mom's purse without her noticing and if she saved long enough, it was enough for her to replace something she'd outgrown. Sometimes, she could even get her hair trimmed if she found clearance shoes.

At age fourteen, she learned to keep her bedroom door locked at night whenever her mom had a boyfriend over.

When she was fifteen, she got her first period. Her mother's advice was simple: "Better be careful now or else you'll wind up with a baby. Babies ruin everything."

When she was seventeen, her mother's drinking hit an all-time high. She got fired from her job, and she punched Elise for the first time. Thinking back now, Elise couldn't even remember what she'd done to piss her off, only the indignant look on her face after. Elise missed a week of school before the swelling finally went away.

She never learned to ride a bike, never had a birthday cake, never decorated a Christmas tree, or waited anxiously for Santa. She spent more of her childhood taking care of her mother than she was ever taken care of herself. She never had a pet, never got to have a sleepover, never went out to eat at a restaurant, never went on vacation, and never had a hug or a kiss goodnight. Elise was never told that she was good or worthy or wanted. She led a quiet life, the little girl in the back of the classroom who never raised her hand and always looked like she needed a bath. The summer after she graduated high school she came home to find her mother on her bed, crying and cradling a bottle of vodka.

"Mom? What's wrong?"

Marianne had a box of pictures that Elise had never seen laying open on the bed. Pictures of Marianne, Isaac, and Ben. Pictures from before the accident, before Elise.

Elise picked up a picture, one where Isaac and Marianne were smiling at each other with Ben standing in between them. Her mother was almost unrecognizable, so healthy and happy. She flipped through the pictures: Ben's birthday parties, first days of school, soccer trophies, Isaac and Marianne on their wedding day, Isaac with his arms wrapped around Marianne's pregnant belly. The three of them at the beach, at the zoo, at the park. Ben kissing Isaac's nose. Elise felt her heart breaking, knowing that she would never be a part of this family: a family that was happy, a family that loved.

"It's okay, Momma," she said, trying to keep the pictures safe as Marianne spilled her drink on the bed.

"I should've died." Marianne sobbed loudly.

"What?" She tried to take the bottle away, but her mother moved it hastily, taking another swig.

"I should've died that night. They all died, it's not fair. I'm the only one who lived but I should've died too. They left me here alone."

"You aren't alone."

"I'm alone. Everyone died that night. *Except me*," she cried, snot and tears soaking her face.

Elise grabbed a washcloth from the hall closet and wet it. She attempted to wipe her mother's face, her frizzy red curls getting in the way. "You aren't alone, Momma. Do you hear me? I'm here. I love you so much." Elise wiped her mother's tears softly.

"You should've died too. You never should've been born. You were never my daughter."

Elise was used to drunken insults, but this one stung particularly badly. "What? Of course I am."

"No. No. No. After the accident, you quit kicking. You'd been kicking all day, but you stopped. You just stopped." She took another swig. "When I woke up in the hospital, everything hurt so much. I wanted to scream, but I couldn't do it. I couldn't do anything. I couldn't open my eyes but I could feel everything. I felt that doctor pull you out of me. Oh God, it hurt."

Elise grabbed a trashcan in time for her mother to spew vodka-infused vomit. She wiped her mouth, then took another sip and continued. "You didn't cry. I sat there counting—waiting for you to cry—but you never did. Not once. So, I let myself sleep. It hurt so bad." She pointed to her stomach.

"Then, when I woke up again, they brought you to me. You were alive. You were crying."

"So, they saved me," Elise insisted.

"*No.* They shouldn't have. You were dead. You weren't supposed to live. I wasn't supposed to live. I've always known it. I fought to get better for you, but I shouldn't have. I should've died with them and I hate you for making me fight."

Elise helped her mother lie down on the bed, slipping the bottle from her hand. She swiped the rag across her forehead and left the room.

That night, Elise packed a bag and left town. She drove to a small town miles down the road and got a job waiting tables at a local bar. She dyed her hair black, ashamed of the blonde hair her mother had always hated so much.

She would never know whether her mother even noticed she was missing. A few months later, she received word that she had passed away. Elise would never go back to that town or that house.

She started attending a community college where she made the first friends she'd ever had.

There, Elise fell in love. For the first time in her life, someone told her she was wanted—that she was worthy of being wanted.

He was a professor who taught communications. They dated for most of Elise's college career. He was several years older than her and just so happened to be married. He made it clear to Elise that he loved her and that he would leave his wife soon. Elise, never having been loved before, believed him.

In the middle of her last year of college Elise's period came late, and then the next month, it didn't come at all. An over-the-counter pregnancy test confirmed what Elise's mother had warned her about: a baby was on its way.

At hearing that his student was carrying his child, Dave Hartley finally told Elise the truth: he'd never planned to leave his wife and a child didn't change that plan. He asked Elise to drop his class and keep their secret. He told her it would be best if she aborted the child and that he wanted nothing else to do with her or the baby. So, Elise Moss was, once again, completely alone in the world.

On the night that Elise's roommate was dumped by her longtime boyfriend, the girls decided to get a drink at a small bar somewhere away from home. Elise was three months pregnant and still trying to keep her secret. The girls found a bar on the outskirts of a town nearby that was filled with bikers and older men ready to give the girls all the attention they craved.

The place was called Carlton's. Elise was on her third cosmopolitan when she spotted a guy staring at her from across the bar. His confidence was obvious and her pregnancy hormones got the best of her.

By the end of the night, Caide Abbott had charmed the pants right off of Elise. He was funny, incredibly sexy, and kissed like a champ. They'd gone back to a hotel room at Elise's suggestion, and after a few more drinks from the mini bar, they'd found their way into the bed.

When Elise had awoken, Caide was standing over her. She cracked her eyelids, waiting for him to sneak out like Dave always had. Instead, he stared at her for a moment, he brushed a piece of hair from her eyes, and he whispered the three words Elise needed to hear more than anything else: *I love you.*

The next day, the events of the past night swam through Elise's brain, muddled by an alcoholic fog. Elise felt elated by the memory that remained clear, this man loved her.

He'd felt the same, amazing spark that she had. He'd known, just as Elise had, that it was love at first sight. Elise had to let him know she felt the same way. She went back to Carlton's Bar and asked about Caide. She discovered he lived nearby, though no one was quite sure where.

For the next month, she spent every night at the bar waiting for Caide, but he never came. Elise knew he must be looking for her too. She wouldn't give up. She dropped out of college and spent her days aimlessly searching for the man who loved her so. She eventually took a job as a bartender at Carlton's, waiting for the day when her love would walk in the door.

In June, Elise awoke to a puddle of blood soaking her sheets. At only five months along, she was losing the baby. Elise knew this would only leave room for a new baby inside of her: Caide's.

When she finally saw Caide again, three years had gone

by. She was jogging through the park one day when she heard his voice. His magical voice.

"Hey!" he called.

She turned to see him, instantly remembering his voice. Tears formed in her eyes when she realized that it was, in fact, her true love.

She opened her mouth to call out to him, but stopped when she saw the little girl on his shoulders, her blonde ringlets flowing in the wind. Her white sundress flapped around his neck as she giggled.

"Faster, Daddy!" she yelled.

Daddy. The word stabbed Elise's heart like a thousand knives. Before she had time to wonder who he had betrayed her with, she saw him approaching a group of three other people. There was a young, attractive couple, both with icy black hair, and a blonde woman whose face Elise couldn't quite see. They all sat down at a picnic table, the blonde laying out food for everyone and the brunette woman pouring them each a glass of wine.

Elise watched as Caide set the young girl between the blonde and himself, kissing them both atop the head. She sat for hours watching the couples talking and laughing before the lunch was finally over. The blonde hugged the brunette woman while the men shook hands.

Elise jogged from her hiding place to her car, keeping her eyes on them. She followed them home, to a town three hours away. They had a small house in the country with a swing set in the front yard, the kind of home Elise would've killed for.

Elise watched them get out of their car. She tried to get a good look at the woman. When she finally turned her head, Elise gasped. It was *her.* Elise was staring at herself.

The woman had blonde hair, the color Elise's had been before she'd dyed it. She was shorter and a bit rounder than

Elise, probably from carrying the child, but it was obvious, nonetheless, that this woman was the spitting image of Elise.

For the next several months, Elise followed the family around. She followed Caide to a law office and his wife to a dance studio in the downtown square. She rented a house nearby and got a job working from home. By stealing their mail, she learned that the woman's name was Rachael Abbott, by doing her research she learned all about Rachael.

She watched the Abbotts day in and day out, occasionally breaking into their home and learning her way around. It wasn't until she watched Rachael begin to swell with Caide's second child that she formed her plan.

Elise was going to become Rachael Abbott.

A year after their second child was born, Elise lightened her hair back to her original blonde. She stopped her morning jogs and packed on a few extra pounds. She began to test her theory on Rachael's students and Caide's bosses. It was obvious that she could fool almost anyone into believing she was Rachael.

The real test, of course, would be Caide. Watching him, Elise learned that sex was Caide's vice. He was sleeping with the same brunette woman from the park years ago, and he had something going on with his perky bimbo of a secretary. They'd have to go.

Of course, nothing could happen until she figured out how to get rid of Rachael once and for all.

First, Elise tried cutting Rachael's brake lines. There'd been an accident, but everyone survived. Lucky thing, since Caide was also in the car.

The secretary wasn't supposed to go first, but when Elise had caught them kissing it was clear she couldn't wait any longer. That's when the plan became evident. Rather than kill Rachael, she'd let Rachael kill the others. It would be her, of course, not actually Rachael, but no one would ever know. Elise was as invisible now as she'd ever been.

Then, once everyone was safely out of the way, she could escape far away with Caide thinking Rachael had escaped to run away with him.

Putting her plan into action, Elise had slashed the office bimbo's tires, hoping to catch her alone and stranded one night when she left with Caide. When they never returned, however, Elise used a copy of Caide's office key that she'd made months ago to sneak into the attic of his office.

She'd dressed in clothing stolen from Rachael's closet and learned where all the cameras were. Then, the next night, she'd watched them together. When it all became too much, she'd stomped around upstairs. They needed to stop.

After Caide left, Elise had crept down, making sure she was on camera, and bashed that sweet little head in. Then, last night, she'd killed the brunette tramp just for the fun of it.

It was all falling into place. Now, here she was, cuddled up with the man she loved. Finally, her life was going to be good.

"Honey," she whispered, twirling her fingers in his chest hair.

He looked down at her, his eyes still sleepy. "Yeah?"

"The police will be looking for me, you know?"

He rubbed his eyes, sitting up to rest his face in his palm. "You're right. What are you going to do?"

"Well, I thought about going to Mexico. Somewhere by the beach. I think the kids would like that, don't you?"

"Mexico? The kids? You're wanting us to run away with you?"

"Well, yeah. I thought that after last night…?"

"Rach, look, last night was great, but you can't expect us to just uproot our lives. We have things here. The house…

work…the kids have school. Life on the road is no life for kids. You can't possibly want that for them."

"What I want is for our family to be together, that's all I want. Wherever that's possible. Don't you want that too?"

"Of course I do." He rubbed his head. "I want it to go back to normal, but imagine how awful their lives would be on the run. They need stability."

She furrowed her brow. "Imagine how awful their lives would be without a mother, Caide. There's nothing left for us in this town. We have to leave, don't you see? It's the only way."

CHAPTER NINETY-THREE

RACHAEL

"She'll go after my kids. That's how she'll get him alone. She's going to kill my kids. We have to go now." She rushed past Hampton, hurrying toward the door.

He grabbed her arm, spinning around. "Hold on a second, Rachael. You can't just rush out of here without a plan."

"I don't need a plan. I need to save my kids."

"You're only putting them in more danger if we don't think this through. We have about six hours, that's it. If we can catch her with your family, we'll call the police. They don't monitor you while you're here but once the time goes up, they'll know you aren't where you're supposed to be and they'll come after us. That means Shayna and I could lose our licenses. We could go to jail. We need to find out if she's even at your house. Listen to me, Rachael, if she is not there, we have to come back. And, if she is there, we are not confronting her." He held her face in his palms. "We know she's dangerous. As long as Caide is there, we have to believe your kids are safe." He turned to Shayna. "We should disguise her, in case she's seen."

Shayna took off her jacket, throwing it over Rachael's

shoulders and pulling up the hood. She ran to her desk and pulled out a pair of large sunglasses, pushing them up onto Rachael's nose.

"You be careful," she said firmly.

"I'll follow you. I'll stay a few cars behind, but don't do anything stupid, okay?" Argus asked her.

Rachael nodded. Then, before she could stop herself, she pressed her lips to his, just briefly. His mouth was soft and warm. He smiled at her when she pulled away, his eyes saying what he couldn't. She turned to the door, rushing outside.

"Rachael, take my car," Shayna called after her. Rachael took the keys to Shayna's little blue car and jumped in. It had been months since she'd driven a car and every ounce of adrenaline pulsed through her veins as she started the engine. She pulled out of the parking lot with ease and turned left.

Please hold on babies, Mommy's coming for you.

CHAPTER NINETY-FOUR

HAMPTON

Hampton pulled into the Abbotts' driveway minutes after Rachael. Shayna's car was parked, but Rachael was nowhere in sight. The house looked dark from outside. Argus cautiously made his way toward the house, cursing Rachael for not following the plan.

"You looking for someone?" A voice from next door made Hampton jump.

Embarrassed, he turned to see an elderly lady in a pink snow suit. She held her mail in one gloved hand. "I'm looking for the people who live here. Have you seen them?"

"The Abbotts? Isn't it awful what they're saying about Mrs. Abbott? I don't believe it for a second and I'll tell that to any reporter who'll listen. I tell you, I couldn't ask for a better neighbor. She's been in my prayers every night since I heard. Say, what business have you got with the Abbotts, anyway?"

"I'm her lawyer. She asked me to relay a message to her husband. Do you know where he is? It's important."

"Well, I think she beat you to it." The woman smirked.

"What makes you say that?" He tilted his head to the side.

"Well, I guess she got released or something. She was here this morning with him. They loaded a bunch of suitcases into the car and they left."

"Rachael was with them? You're sure?"

"Yes. Him, her, and the two children. Looked like they'd be gone for a while, too. Sure was a lot of suitcases."

He cursed under his breath. "What time was this?"

She twisted her mouth in thought. "Oh, I don't know. It was early. I'd say about six or seven."

"You didn't happen to hear where they were going, did you?"

"No. No, I sure didn't." She paused, looking troubled. "You're her lawyer, you say?"

"Yes. I'm Argus Hampton, Rachael's lawyer. I just want to help her."

"Well…I did hear Mrs. Abbott tell the little girl that wherever they were going, it'd be warm."

"Thanks," Hampton yelled, rushing into the house in a panic.

Rachael jumped up, swinging a baseball bat at him. "Rachael!" He narrowly ducked out of the way.

"Argus? *Oh, God.* I could've killed you. *Don't do that!*"

"I'm sorry." He pulled her into a hug. "Listen, they're already gone. I talked to your neighbor. She said they left this morning with their bags packed. All four of them."

Her eyes went wide and she slapped a palm to her forehead. "She's with them? What are we going to do? She can't hurt them. Where were they going?"

"I don't know. She said they were going someplace warm. Do you guys have a vacation house? Somewhere Caide may take you to hide?"

"No, we don't take vacations. Caide could never get the time off." She sat down on the couch, her head in her hands. "How can this be happening? We barely missed them." Tears welled in her eyes and she allowed herself to sob. Hampton placed his arms around her shoulders, rocking her back and forth.

Suddenly an idea struck him. "Rachael, I think I have a plan."

CHAPTER NINETY-FIVE

CAIDE

Caide listened to his children sing along with the radio. They seemed so happy for the first time in months. Rachael sat beside him, her feet on the dash. She seemed strangely carefree for a fugitive on the run.

Suddenly his phone rang. *What the hell?* The screen read: **Home.**

"Who is it?" Rachael asked.

"I don't know." Caide feared the worst: that the police had infiltrated the house and they were on their tail now. He had to keep up appearances if they were looking for Rachael, at least until they were safely out of the country.

"Hello?"

"Repeat after me: Yes, Brinley did have her last shots done. I must've forgotten to bring an updated record down."

"Huh?" The voice was familiar. He could've sworn it was Rachael. "Who is this?"

"*Caide*. Repeat it. Then I'll explain. Please."

"Um, yes. She did get her shots. I guess I forgot to bring an updated record in."

"Good, now listen to me. The woman you are with is not

BECOMING MRS. ABBOTT

who you think she is. This is Rachael. This is your wife." It was strange how much the whispered voice *did* sound like Rachael. But…it couldn't be.

"Is this some kind of joke?" He glanced at the screen again.

"Oh my god, shut up! Listen to me, your worst fear is drowning because you never learned to swim. We named Davis after Dave Coulier, who you'll never admit is your favorite actor to anyone but me. You like green tea more than coffee. You've never watched sports of any kind. Your favorite flavor of ice cream is vanilla." She took a deep breath. "It's me, okay? It's really me. I don't have time to explain—just know that the woman you are with right now is dangerous. Very dangerous. Where are you? And find some way to tell me without letting her know anything is up."

Caide looked to the Rachael, who may not actually be Rachael, sitting beside him. This felt crazy. How was he supposed to answer that in code? Was this some sort of trap? Why were there two Rachaels?

"Um, well, I couldn't bring you a copy today. We're on a family trip to Valdosta, Georgia. I'd be happy to bring it in later this week."

He heard Rachael on the phone, who also might not be Rachael, heave a sigh of relief. "Thank you. Please stop there. What exit will you be at?"

"Um, I believe she had those on," he said, looking desperately for an exit sign. "On the four-hundred twenty-seventh." He could've slapped himself as the words came out of his mouth. "I mean, April twenty-seventh." He laughed nervously. The Rachael in the car with him, who may or may not be Rachael, didn't seem to notice or care about his blunder.

"Oh, thank you," the Rachael on the phone said. "Please

stop there. Go to a hotel. Keep the kids safe and don't upset her. I'll drive that way. Ask her questions, you'll see that I'm telling the truth. Then, if you believe me, call me and tell me where you're staying."

"Thanks." Caide hung up his phone, looking over at Rachael-Who-May-Not-Be-Rachael.

She smiled at him. "Everything okay?"

"Yeah, that was Brinley's teacher. She needs her updated vaccination records."

"Oh, okay." She twirled her hair around her finger, biting a piece of skin around her nail.

Thinking quickly, he looked at her. "What was her name again? I can never remember."

Rachael-Maybe-Not-Rachael frowned. "You know I'm bad with names, Caide. I can't think of it either."

He swallowed, his heart beginning to race. "Right. Hey, let's stop here for the night."

"What? It's still early." Probably-Not-Rachael scooted forward in her seat.

"We're two states away from home and the kids are sleepy. It's time for us to stop and eat. They need their rest."

"Whatever. But we've got to make better time tomorrow," she said, annoyance in her voice.

"Of course. Besides, we can all go swimming in the hotel pool. Just like we did last summer. You know how I love to swim." Caide smiled nervously at her.

"Oh, of course. Yeah, that was fun. My little fish." She patted his cheek lovingly.

Everything in Caide's body turned ice cold. Chills crept down his spine. He grinned at Rachael, who was definitely not Rachael. She smiled back, blissfully unaware that she'd been found out. This felt like some crazy movie, rather than real life.

He wished he'd brought a weapon: the bat, a gun, anything to protect his family. Of course, he hadn't. Desperation filled his head as he veered off onto the exit, trying to act casual. His heart felt as though it were sure to explode in his chest at any moment.

CHAPTER NINETY-SIX

RACHAEL

Rachael pulled into the motel parking lot Caide had told her about. It was nearly six, which meant the police would notice she was gone shortly, if they hadn't already. She had merely minutes and no real plan at all.

In her rearview mirror, she saw Argus' truck pull in behind her. The cool metal of her father's gun poked into her hip. It felt out of place on her.

She climbed out of the car as Argus approached her. The rundown motel had blue doors and rusting white handrails.

"Let's go," Argus told her.

"Argus, I need you to wait out here." She held her hand up.

"What?" He shook his head. "No. You aren't going in there alone."

"My family is in there. I need you to be out here in case she makes a run for it. I know you want to protect me, but this is something I've got to face on my own. Besides that, I'd never forgive myself if something happened to you."

"Rachael, no. I don't like it."

"I'm the one with a gun. You'd be of no use except as a

weakness to me. I can't let you get hurt because of me. I'll be okay. We don't have time to argue."

He opened his mouth, but closed it again. "Nothing crazy." He made her swear.

"Nothing crazy," she said with a quick nod.

"Don't try to play hero. Get your kids, get Caide, and get out. The police will be here soon."

"Right." She nodded.

"Remember what I said: don't shoot her. Whatever you do, do not shoot her. The gun is to scare her. Get her locked in a bathroom or something if you can. Knock her out if you have to. Safety is the first concern, but we need her here and we need her alive when the police get here. That's the only way we'll clear your name," he said firmly, emphasizing his words.

"Okay." She turned to walk away.

"And, Rachael?"

"Yeah?" She spun back to him.

"Please be careful. We know what she's capable of."

"I'll be fine, Argus. I promise."

"If things go bad in there, if you are in danger, you get out. You've got the element of surprise. You've got the upper hand here."

Rachael nodded. He kissed her cheek, resting his lips there for a short time. Rachael listened to the erratic way he breathed. "Thank you for everything."

He smiled at her sadly and then nodded toward the motel. She turned, walking quietly up the rusty metal stairs and across the balcony until she reached room one hundred and four. She pressed her palm to the doorknob, feeling the cold metal beneath her hand, and turned. *Click.*

It was locked. So much for the element of surprise. She pounded on the door. Silence. No one spoke to announce that they were coming. She heard no footsteps. She waited a few more moments, ready to knock again, but stopped as she heard a soft click from the other side of the door.

It opened slightly, enough for her to squeeze in. She pushed it open further. It took a second for her eyes to adjust to the dimly lit room, but when she did she recognized the two figures on the bed.

"*Brin? Davis?*" she cried, losing sight of the moment and running toward her children. The door slammed shut behind her and she whirled around to see her twin, nearly a mirror image of herself, standing behind the door. She held a knife, long and sharp, against Caide's neck.

"Caide!" She gasped.

"Ah, ah, ah, not too loud, Rach," the twin hissed. Rachael froze, aware of the gun's weight on her side. Upon getting a closer look at Rachael, the twin's jaw dropped. "Holy shit, you really do look just like me."

"I know." Rachael backed up toward the bed, feeling her children tugging on her shirt. "You're my sister."

"Mommy, what's going on?"

"It's okay, Brin. It's okay," she soothed, putting her hands out to her sides to shield them as much as possible.

"Why are there two Mommies?"

"Shh, Davis." Rachael whispered, feeling his little fingers in hers.

"Shut up!" the twin screeched. Rachael snapped her attention back to her. "Sister? What the hell are you talking about? I don't have any sisters."

Did she loosen the knife on Caide's neck or was that Rachael's imagination? "You're wrong. I am your sister—your twin sister. We were separated at birth." Rachael eased forward half a step.

"You're a liar." The twin twisted the tip of the knife further into Caide's neck. "You just don't want me to hurt your precious little husband."

"No." Rachael held her hand up. "I was born on June twenty-first, 1972, at La Rue Baptist Hospital, same as you. The nurse separated us."

"How do you know?" the twin asked, looking genuinely interested, though the knife remained steady.

"Look, I can explain it all, just please let him go. Let Caide go and we can talk. This doesn't have to end badly."

"Let him go so you can call the cops?" the twin asked.

Rachael's hands went into the air. "I don't even have a phone. No cops. Just let my family go. This is between me and you."

"No! No one leaves this room. No one."

"You don't want to hurt him. You like him, don't you? That's why you did this? For Caide?" Rachael asked, her voice quivering.

The twin's face fell.

"That's why you killed Blaire, right? And...Audrey?" The name hung in her throat. She ignored the distraught look on Caide's face, telling her he hadn't known. "That's why you wanted me out of the way, right? You like him. You can't honestly want to kill him." Rachael's heart pounded as she prayed she was right.

She watched the twin push the knife into Caide's neck until the skin surrounding it was pure white, then she released him.

"You wearing a wire or something?" she asked, walking away from Caide and toward Rachael, her knife drawn.

"No," Rachael said, her hands up in surrender again.

"Go to the bathroom, kids. Don't come out," Caide yelled, rubbing his neck.

Rachael was relieved to hear their tiny footsteps run away and the door shut. The twin placed the knife on Rachael's chest. She ran it down her stomach, cutting her shirt open to reveal a bare, unwired chest. Rachael winced in pain, but refused to scream as warm blood trickled down her chest, toward her navel.

The twin lowered her knife. Rachael attempted to cover herself back up. Her twin walked to the counter, facing them, her knife still grasped firmly in her hand. "So, why are you here, Rachael? To avenge your friend? To save your family? Did you think you'd just march in here and save the day?"

"I came for my family. That's all I want. I just want them safe."

"And you? You'll just go on back to jail?"

Rachael felt tears gathering in her eyes. "I'm not out to get you. I haven't told anyone about you. Take me. Kill me. It'll look like I escaped. Just please let them go."

"Rach—" Caide choked out.

"You really just want them safe?" the twin demanded.

"Yes."

"Even though your family didn't realize they were with a complete stranger all day?" She took a step back toward Rachael.

"Even though," Rachael said with a firm nod.

"Even though he hasn't done anything but disrespect you and whore around on you since the day you were married?"

It stung. Rachael held back her tears, keeping her face still. "Even though."

"Oh, oh, wait a second. I'm wrong. It was before you were married, wasn't it?" The twin cackled.

"Excuse me?"

"The spring of ninety-four, were you married then?"

Rachael shook her head, unable to speak.

"Really? 'Cause that's when I met Caide. *That's* why I'm here." The twin looked at Caide, a smile growing on her face. "That's why we're all here."

"What are you talking about?" Caide demanded.

"Don't act like you don't remember our night together.

The next time I saw you, you had a bouncing, baby brat. She had to have been about three. If my math is correct that means you were together on the night we met, right?"

"I have no idea what you're talking about."

"Oh, gosh." She smiled, touching her lips. "It's the blonde hair. You see, I've never been much of a fan of it, but Rachael does seem to pull it off nicely." She circled Rachael like a shark waiting to strike and tugged at a piece of her hair. "Picture me, if you will, with *very* dark hair. A red dress. Cosmo in my hand." She winked at Caide. He continued to stare at her in confusion. "Staring across the bar at you in a little dive bar called…Carter's? No, what was that bar? It started with a C…" She waited for him to answer the question.

Caide's eyes filled with sorrow as he finally seemed to catch on. "Carlton's."

"Carlton's, that's it." She pointed at him with delight.

"Rachael, I—" Caide's jaw dropped, his eyes darted toward her.

Rachael's voice was filled with fury when she spoke. "You *slept* with her? Are you kidding me? My twin sister?"

"I didn't know she was your sister. She was just a girl in a bar. It meant nothing. God, please don't—"

"I told you I was pregnant that spring, Caide," Rachael said, her head growing hot with rage.

"I'm so, so sorry. It was so long ago." He tried to approach Rachael, his arms outstretched.

The twin stepped between them. "Not long enough for you to forget that you loved me, right?"

Caide's forehead wrinkled. "What are you talking about?"

"You told me you loved me. That night. After we slept together. Don't you remember?" the twin asked innocently.

"I didn't love you. I didn't even know you." His face wrinkled in disgust.

The twin pulled her knife to Caide's chin. "Take it back. You told me you loved me."

"You're crazy. If I said I loved you it was only because I was drunk."

"Caide!" Rachael yelled, but it was too late. The twin dug her knife into his cheek. Rachael watched the blood pour from his wound, saw his teeth from outside of his mouth. The children's cries grew louder from the bathroom.

"Oh God." Rachael covered her mouth, her hand shaking as she reached for the gun. She pulled it out, surprised by the weight of it in her hands. "Let him go," she shouted, her voice shaky and unconvincing.

The twin turned around. Her eyes widened at seeing the gun, but she laughed loudly. "You're going to shoot me?"

"Not if you just leave. Now."

The knife stayed unwavering next to Caide's neck. "See, here's the problem with that Rach: you shoot me...I kill him. Then you've got four bodies on your hands." She covered her mouth in feigned surprise. "What on earth would you do then?"

Rachael's hands shook. "Take him then."

"What?" Caide and the twin said together.

"Take him. You said he loves you. He's probably just lying to me. He's really good at that."

She cast an angry glance toward Caide. "Just take him. You guys go on to wherever you were planning to go. I'll take my kids. They'll just get in your way anyway."

"You'd just let me take your husband? Just like that?"

Rachael lowered her gun. "He hasn't been a husband to me in a long time. All I want is for my kids to be safe. You guys need to get far away." She lifted her pant leg to reveal the house arrest bracelet. "The police will be here soon and that won't be good for either of us. You go now and that'll be the last of it. I don't ever want to hear from either of you again."

"How will you get that off?" The twin glared at her suspiciously.

"Does it matter? You're wasting time," Rachael said. The twin looked at Caide and then back at Rachael, her eyes wild with desperation. "Go," Rachael insisted.

The twin held her knife up. "Go. Now." She led Caide out the door, seeming not to notice that his blood was now soaking her shoulder.

Rachael shut the door behind them, latching all three locks and resting her back against it. She looked at the cut on her chest. It wasn't deep, just painful. She tied her shirt together, trying to cover what she could. She allowed herself ten seconds to panic before standing up. She ran to the bathroom, pounding on the door. "Babies, it's Mommy. Open up please. It's safe now."

"Real Mommy or Mean Mommy?"

"Real Mommy." The door opened slowly and two little faces poked out. She kissed their heads, gathering them into her arms and whispering into their ears. "I love you. I love you. I love you." She picked them up, surprised by their growth in such a short time and headed for the door.

She watched as the SUV pulled out of the parking lot, turning right, before she ran down the metal steps to Argus' truck.

"Thank God. What happened?" He pulled them into his arms. "I was so worried. Shayna called me. The police are on their way."

"No time to talk. Get them out of here, someplace safe. She took Caide."

"Rachael, don't go after her. Let the police handle it. Please just come with me."

She handed the kids to him. "I can't. If she kills him, I'll never forgive myself. Keep them safe."

He nodded, placing the children in his truck. "Please be careful, Rachael. If anything happens to you, I'll be the one not forgiving myself."

She kissed his cheek, grabbing her keys and hopping into Shayna's car. She pulled out of the parking lot, turning right. She prayed they weren't too far ahead of her already. The road was twisted and dark. There were no other cars to be seen, just miles and miles of trees.

Rachael sped up, careening around the curves with ease. She drove faster and faster, nearly giving up when she finally laid eyes on the taillights up ahead. She hit the gas once more, her hands clutching the wheel until her fingers were stiff. As she approached the car, she could see it swerving. What in the world was she doing to him?

CHAPTER NINETY-SEVEN

CAIDE

Caide held his aching jaw. It was unlike any pain he'd ever felt, even dull and nearly numb.

"Well, well…looks like wifey lied. She's coming up behind us now."

"You don't have to do this, you know," Caide said, trying to hold his cheek together. In an attempt to talk, he kept biting pieces of his face.

"Do you know my name?"

"Huh?"

"Do you even remember my name?"

"Did you tell it to me?"

"That night, I told you that night. I remembered yours. I even went looking for you. I never gave up on you and you don't even remember my name." She pressed down on the gas. Caide heard the car accelerate.

"Look, it was a long time ago. I'm sorry, okay? I'm sorry I don't remember. I drank way too much that night. I wasn't thinking clearly."

"You said you loved me. How can you not remember my name?"

"That night was the night Rachael told me she was pregnant. It was traumatic and so, whatever I said or did, it was just out of confusion. There's no need to do this because of me. Trust me, I'm not worth it."

"This is not just about you anymore," she said through gritted teeth. "We're way past that. This is about every stupid boy who's allowed to get drunk, sleep with a girl, and then forget her. Every man who can leave someone alone with a problem he created, every bully who's allowed to tease or degrade people just to make themselves feel bigger. For every fucked up person out there who has to make the world twice as fucked up just because they can."

"What do you call what you're doing, then?"

"Evening the score." Her smile grew wicked.

"No. You don't get to do that. You don't get to have this noble cause and carry it out by doing something just as awful."

"You don't get to tell me what to do. You have no idea what I've been through."

"Everyone goes through bad things. Everyone. Whatever you've been through, someone has it worse."

"Probably so, but not you. And not Rachael. Do you know how it feels to know that I could have—no—*should* have lived a good life? I was supposed to be happy. I could've had pancakes for breakfast and birthday parties and maybe even been read a bedtime story. I could've had a life if some idiot doctor would've just picked the other twin, or if…I don't know…someone who didn't switch babies for kicks had been in the delivery room that night. Do you know what it's like to know that everything in my life could have been different? I just happened to be the unlucky one." She shook her head, glancing at him with a horrified expression. "My whole life, my mother hated me. She despised me, and now I find out that that wasn't how it was supposed to be. I was supposed to have a real family. How am I supposed to take that? You'll never know how that feels."

"You're right. Though, I'd imagine it's about the same as knowing that I'm responsible for two innocent womens' deaths. I'd say it's similar to watching my wife watching me screw up my marriage, to physically watching her heart shatter in a courtroom and having it become a spectator sport. I'd say it's pretty close to realizing that she's the only woman I've ever really loved and I was too stupid to realize it. Like knowing my life is over, my damn good life, and it's no one's fault but mine. I screwed ever—"

Elise interrupted him. "My mom used to drink. A lot. By the time I was five years old, I knew my way around the liquor store better than my own house. She'd lock me in my room for days at a time while she went on a bender. I had to eat anything I could find: crumbs of old food, bugs, dirt, sometimes nothing at all. I'd just sit in my bedroom for days, listening to her cry, and throw up, and cry again. She'd lock me up just because she could. I didn't have to do anything wrong. She just wanted me to be as miserable as she was. Do you want to know how many times my mother told me she wished I were dead? Twenty-two times. Do you want to know how many times she said she loved me? Or that she was proud of me? Never. Not one single time. I've been hated by every single person in my life for my entire life. Today, I found out that the one person who I believed loved me, he never actually did. You can tell me all about your terrible life all you want, but you brought it on yourself. I was just a baby when it started for me. I didn't deserve any of it." She was crying now, her voice slurring from sobs.

"Look, bad things happen. I'm sorry that happened to you —I am, but this won't make it better. This won't help you."

"Nothing will help me."

As she said the words, Caide was struck with a clear

understanding of his situation. His jaw had gone numb from losing way too much blood. He was beginning to grow tired and dizzy. He wouldn't make it much longer and his only chance to help Rachael was to get this car to stop. He unbuckled his seatbelt, gripping the door handle firmly. He slowly pulled it, dragging it backward. The inside light came on.

"*Shut that door!*" the woman screamed, lunging toward Caide and nearly driving the car off the road.

She leaned all the way over, her hand holding his door shut.

"Watch what you're doing," he yelled, trying to grab the steering wheel from her. They were a tangled mess of hands and arms, all tied together with no hope of untangling when she let go of his door. It was almost slow motion, she kissed his bleeding cheek and then stepped on the accelerator, shoving his hand away. Tears streamed down her face as Caide began to scream.

CHAPTER NINETY-EIGHT

RACHAEL

The car sped up, trying to get away from Rachael, but she remained close.

She wiped the tears clouding her vision, trying to remain focused. She saw them swerve once, then twice, then speed up again. Rachael knew what was going to happen.

She watched helplessly as the silver SUV sped around a curve. The brake lights never came on and the wheels never turned.

Rachael watched the car plow through the forest of trees before crashing into one. Her screams were drowned out by the sickening, metallic crunch of metal on wood. It was so sudden, so definite. Smoke rolled out of the engine.

Maybe they're dead. That was her first thought. Did that make her a bad person? To wonder, even hope for a brief second, that they were dead? That all of the madness was finally over? She climbed out of her own car before it was even at a full stop. She fell to the ground, feeling the icy grass chill her fingers. She crawled toward the car. Her cries sounded as if they were coming from so far away.

She smelled the burnt rubber. The headlights blinded her

as she made her way around to the front of the vehicle. Caide was on the hood of the SUV, halfway through the windshield. In the dark, she could only make out dark shadows on his face, which she knew would be blood in the daylight. The twin's head rested on the steering wheel.

Rachael didn't approach the car any closer. She held her queasy stomach together and breathed. She wasn't sure how long she'd been standing there, frozen in place, when she finally saw the police lights. They came for her, like she knew they would.

She remained still as a young cop got out of his cruiser, followed by more, their guns raised.

She was silent as they slapped the cuffs on her, leading her to the squad car. She watched as they called for backup, staring at the bodies. She rested her head on the cool window as they drove her away.

She couldn't cry anymore. She was done. All cried out.

CHAPTER NINETY-NINE

HAMPTON

Hampton walked to the table in the center of an almost empty room where Rachael was waiting.

She didn't make eye contact with him, her eyes hollow and glazed over. She was pale. Empty.

"Rachael?" He sat down slowly. She looked at him, though it was like she was staring straight through him. "How are you?"

She remained silent, her face emotionless.

"I talked to Brinley and Davis. They're doing fine. They really like the family they're staying with. We were very lucky that they managed to stay together."

Nothing.

"I hope you know how hard I tried to find someone to keep them. A relative, a friend." He faked a small laugh. "I even asked about me keeping them for a while. They wouldn't allow it. We're not on the best terms with the government right now."

Silence. More staring at nothing at all.

"And Shayna, well, we're working on getting her charges dropped. She's not in jail though, so that's good."

Stares.

"She doesn't blame you. None of us do."

Nada.

"Caide's doing better, too. They've been able to keep him awake for longer lately. He's still got a ways to go, but he's getting there."

She began picking at a piece of skin on the side of her finger.

"Look, I know you're mad, okay? I get it. But your trial is today. We've got to prepare. You have to talk to me. We're talking about two murder charges now, Rachael. With the charges for Audrey against you now too, things look bad. But you have to talk to me."

"There's nothing to say. Nothing to prepare," she said finally, her voice emotionless. "She's dead. My twin sister, my only hope, is gone. She dies and I go to jail—you said it yourself. Our case is over. Shayna has to testify that I don't have anything wrong with me, you have to testify that I escaped your custody. Even with Phoebe's testimony, we're still screwed. Just give up."

"I'm not giving up on you," he swore. "I will find something to fix this."

"I've been in isolation for a week, Argus. My children are in foster care, my husband is barely hanging on, and everyone I've ever loved is dead. So don't come in here with your false hope crap. I don't want to hear it and I don't care."

"People need to know the truth," he told her.

"The only truth people care about is the one that lands me behind bars." She stood, kicking her chair out of the way.

"Rachael," he called as she walked away.

She didn't turn to face him and she said nothing else. Hampton pounded his fists on the table, mad at her for saying what he already knew.

CHAPTER ONE HUNDRED

SHAYNA

Shayna was on the stand. This was her first time seeing Rachael since the night of the accident. She couldn't believe how sick she looked, like she'd gone on some miracle diet that sucked fifteen pounds of life right out of her. She seemed weak. Hollow. Empty.

"Ms. Steele." Jeanna Avery stood in front of her. "Six weeks ago, you convinced the court to grant a continuance. Can you tell us why?"

"I wanted to examine Mrs. Abbott. I believed she may have been suffering from dissociate identity disorder."

"How often did you see her?"

"Four days a week for the past six weeks."

"And what did you discover?"

She sighed, wishing Rachael would just look up at her. "Mrs. Abbott does not seem to be suffering from any mental disorder."

"You're sure?"

"Well, it's just one doctor's opinion, but yes."

"So, you believe Mrs. Abbott was of sound mind the night of Miss Underwood's murder?"

"I do, yes."

"I see. Now, Ms. Steele, during the time you were meeting with Mrs. Abbott were you always in your office?"

"Yes, we were."

"So you didn't accompany her to the hospital on the evening of December eighteenth?"

"Yes, I did." She could read Hampton's angry thoughts from across the room.

"But you just said—"

"I was under the impression you were asking if, while under my care, we were always in the office. The answer is yes. On that particular night, I was not on duty. I was simply visiting an injured patient."

"Okay, and did you or did you not tell the nurse that you'd stay with her in order to get Mrs. Abbott's handcuffs removed?"

"Well, some variation of that, I guess."

"Yes or no, Ms. Steele."

She sighed. "Yes. I did."

"And did you stay with her?"

"I got called away."

"Did you stay with Mrs. Abbott all night?"

"I didn't, but—"

"And are you aware that on that night, Mrs. Audrey Hagen was stabbed to death outside of her home?"

"Yes, I am."

"The night that you were supposed to chaperone Mrs. Abbott, but failed to do so?"

"Yes."

"The first night she'd been left unsupervised in over six months."

"Is there a question here, Your Honor?" Hampton asked.

"Ms. Steele, were you aware of a picture that was found on Ms. Hagen's body when it was discovered?"

"No."

Avery smiled. She held up a bag containing a photograph and laid it on the witness stand. It still contained bloody smears that made Shayna feel ill. "Do you recognize the people in this picture?"

Chills ran down her spine. "I do."

"Can you tell the jury who it is?"

"It's Caide Abbott kissing Audrey Hagen."

She passed the picture to the jury. "Does it strike you as odd, Ms. Steele, that on the one night Mrs. Abbott was unsupervised, another of her husband's mistresses turned up dead?"

"I'd hardly call Mrs. Abbott unsupervised. She was in a hospital full of doctors and nurses—"

"Answer the question, Ms. Steele."

She folded her hands together in her lap. "It's convenient, yes."

CHAPTER ONE HUNDRED ONE

HAMPTON

Hampton watched Rachael's hands shaking as Phoebe finished telling her story. She'd been flawless—every detail of her story lining up, all as heartbreaking as ever. The nervousness she'd displayed before was not evident once she hit the stand.

"So you're telling us that Mrs. Abbott has a twin sister?"

"Yes, that's correct."

Hampton smiled at her. "And Ms. Moore, you realize what you are testifying to here today is a serious offense?"

"Of course."

"You've gotten off free all these years. You could've continued to keep your secret. You'd most likely be just fine the rest of your life. Why come forward now?"

Phoebe looked down. When she looked back up, her expression was fierce. "Because people need to know the truth. I can't watch an innocent woman go to jail, leave her children motherless, for a crime she's innocent of. Not if it's my crime that caused it."

"So, you're willing to face whatever consequences come of this for a complete stranger? Why?"

"I'm guilty. I did what I did and I'm willing to face my crime in order to save an *innocent* stranger."

He patted the witness stand. "No more questions, Your Honor."

Avery approached the stand, rolling her eyes pettily at Hampton. "Ms. Moore, is there any proof at all of what you're telling us? Any medical record of Mrs. Abbott having a twin?"

"Well, obviously not."

"So, we're just supposed to believe you? A woman who, by her own admission, is a criminal and a liar."

"Objection, Your Honor." Hampton chuckled. "If Mrs. Abbott doesn't have a twin sister and this story is made up, Ms. Moore is not a criminal. One relies on the other. Ms. Avery's question is moot."

"I'll rephrase," Avery said quickly. "Ms. Moore, how do we know? How can we be sure Mrs. Abbott has a twin? Are we only to rely on your word?"

"Well, you can obviously see the resemblance between the two. And it's not like it can't be medically proven. Their DNA would be identical."

"And if it is? Who's to say Rachael Abbott didn't escape jail and kill her twin to place the blame on someone else?"

"Your Honor, the circumstances of Elise Moss' death were ruled accidental. Rachael Abbott was not in the car the night her twin sister was killed and cannot be blamed for her death."

"I'll rephrase, Your Honor. How do we know it was Elise Moss who killed these people and not Rachael Abbott? Isn't it possible that Mrs. Abbott has just found someone else to take the blame for her crime?" Phoebe was silent. "Answer the question, Ms. Moore."

"It's possible." Phoebe sighed.

"Ms. Moore, what possible reason could Ms. Moss have for killing her twin sister's husband's girlfriends?"

"I don't know."

"Can you think of any reason Ms. Moss would've wanted to kill two innocent women who we have no reason to believe she'd ever even met?"

"Your Honor, my witness is not an expert on Ms. Moss' life. She couldn't possibly answer that question."

"Sustained, move on Avery." Crafton sighed.

Avery nodded. "Ms. Moore, can you think of any motivation Mrs. Abbott may have had to kill the women her husband was having affairs with?"

Phoebe looked to Hampton, her eyes screaming for help. "Possibly."

"Possibly?"

"Yes, Ms. Avery, I guess she'd have a reason."

"Can you agree, with what you already know, that she would have more reason than Ms. Moss to commit the murders?"

"Yes."

"Thank you. No further questions."

Hampton balled his hands into a fist. The judge looked at Hampton. "You may call your next witness."

Hampton looked to Rachael, who remained pale and uninterested. She hadn't spoken a word to him since earlier and he was pretty sure she wasn't even listening to the testimonies. He stood, his suit suddenly feeling too tight. "Your Honor, the defense rests."

"Very well. Does the prosecution have anything to add in rebuttal?"

"No, Your Honor. We are prepared to present closing arguments now."

"Very well."

Jeanna Avery walked to the center of the courtroom,

facing the jury. She wore a grim expression on her face. "On the morning of May eleventh, Blaire Underwood, a beautiful and hard-working young woman, woke up and went to work, like any ordinary day. She didn't know that she'd never come home again. On the evening of December eighteenth, Audrey Hagen's life ended suddenly and tragically. These young women will never again smell the roses growing in their gardens, never laugh at a sitcom on TV, never speak to their loved ones, never eat a delicious piece of chocolate. They were robbed of their lives before their lives had even truly begun. Their families are grieving and there is nothing that can heal a wound so deep. I, however, believe we can ease their suffering by making sure that the monster who killed their loved ones is locked up—making sure she can never put another family through this, never again end a life that isn't hers to end. You've heard Mrs. Abbott's psychologist admit that she is mentally sound. You've seen the tapes where Mrs. Abbott accompanied Miss Underwood into the room where her murder took place just moments before it did. Mrs. Abbott had motive. What is that old saying? Hell hath no fury like a woman scorned. Rachael Abbott was a scorned woman. You've seen the evidence, you've heard the testimonies, and now it's up to you." She glared at the jury. "It's up to you to make sure the right decision is made and the killer is behind bars. After the trial today, we'll all go home. We'll listen to music, we'll eat a warm meal, watch a good movie, and kiss the ones we love goodnight. Two innocent young women will never get that chance again. It's our job to make sure their killer never does either." She pressed her lips together firmly. Hampton could see her inner glow from his seat. She walked swiftly back to her chair, not bothering to look his way.

"Counselor." The judge nodded at him. Hampton stood up, refusing to look at Rachael's empty face.

"When the trial began, I told you all that as a defense attorney we work with a lot of gray, right? Well, it seems to me, it's the prosecution who is dabbling in gray this time. She wants you to believe that Rachael Abbott was caught on camera just minutes before the murder, yet somehow managed to beat her husband home, even though he'd left nearly an hour before she could have. She wants you to believe that she snuck out of a fully staffed hospital in order to murder Audrey Hagen and managed to get back inside without being caught by a member of the hospital staff or on camera, less than twenty-four hours after suffering a serious stab wound. You've heard our witness testify, risking her own freedom to tell you how she kidnapped and split up twin babies at birth. A twin would explain why Mrs. Abbott was caught on camera somewhere she couldn't have logically have been. It would explain why her DNA was found at the crime scene, why she was so willing to be seen on security cameras. A twin answers all of the questions this trial has left unanswered. No one here could possibly know what motive Ms. Moss had in murdering these young women, but we have all seen that she was here. She was with Mr. Abbott at the time of her death. For whatever reason, Ms. Moss found herself involved in Mrs. Abbott's life, and very possibly in the lives of the women we've lost. In my opening statement, I asked you to look at the gray, to *believe* in the gray. But in this case, I think I'll ask you not to. This one is pretty black and white, if you ask me. What makes sense and what doesn't? So I ask you only this, instead of believing that my client is capable of the magic acts it would've taken to pull off these crimes, look at the logical alternative. Look past what seems like a complex case, look past the gray. Look at what's reasonable. See the black and white."

CHAPTER ONE HUNDRED TWO

JUDGE CRAFTON

"What seems to be the problem?" Crafton asked as he walked into the room.

"We can't decide, Your Honor. We can't come to a unanimous decision."

"Why not?"

Doug Potter rubbed his bald head. "She's the deciding vote. She doesn't think she did it." He gestured toward an elderly woman at the end of the table. Her name tag showed her name was April.

"April? If you don't mind me asking, what's stopping you from deciding?"

"I just don't think we have enough evidence, Your Honor," she said bravely.

"A security tape isn't enough for you?" Bianca asked.

"She has a twin. We can't possibly know who was on the tape," April argued.

"The woman's husband is a dog. When my husband cheated on me, I could've done the same thing. Trust me, I know what people are capable of in that situation. The girl did it," Chantelle said.

"The twin had no motive," Doug argued.

"Then why was she with the husband when she died?" April asked.

The room buzzed with arguments. Finally, Doug spoke up above the crowd. "Look, we have DNA, we have the tape, we have motive, and we have opportunity. Why can't we just convict her and call it a day?"

April crossed her arms. "This is her *life* at stake. She has children. I won't just agree with you so we can all go home. I need to believe I voted for the right reasons."

Judge Crafton nodded. "April needs more time. Look over everything again, re-read testimonies, do what you must. I don't want you to make a decision that you aren't comfortable with. If you still can't decide, we'll call a mistrial and set a new court date. I ask you all to open your minds and make an educated decision. I'd like to see this settled today if possible."

He frowned, sliding the folders of evidence toward April. She let out a sigh of relief, opening up a manila folder and beginning to read again.

CHAPTER ONE HUNDRED THREE

RACHAEL

Rachael was led back into the courtroom. Argus stood beside her as the jury, and then the judge, were let back in.

They wouldn't look at her. Not a single one of them. A month ago, it would've hurt her. Today, however, she was a stone. She'd listened to everyone telling the jury how she was evil, a heartless murderer. She's seen Argus' sideway glances, willing her to trust him, but she couldn't. She couldn't trust and she couldn't hope. Not anymore. Everything she'd ever known was a lie.

She was alone. Her thoughts had a sunken quality to them, like she was floating underwater or maybe drowning. She stared at her hands. She really needed to cut her nails.

"Chin up," Argus whispered. She was vaguely aware of a paper traveling from the jury to the judge, of the judge nodding. Argus was holding his breath. How long had he been doing that?

As Judge Crafton began to speak, she tried to focus on his words. "In the case of the State vs. Rachael Abbott on the charge of first degree murder of Ms. Audrey Hagen, how do you find the defendant?"

A man near forty, wearing glasses and a button down shirt over his round belly stood. He pushed his glasses up onto his nose. "We find the defendant not guilty, Your Honor."

Argus heaved a sigh of relief, but Rachael didn't feel it yet. "And on the charge of first degree murder of Ms. Blaire Underwood, how do you find?"

"Guilty, Your Honor."

There was a sigh heard throughout the courtroom. Argus gasped, gripping the table so tightly Rachael was sure it would break. Meanwhile, her head was empty. No thoughts, no feelings. Just meaningless observations. Argus smelled of coffee today. The judge's robe had a white stain near the collar.

"Thank you. Rachael Abbott, you will be detained in county lockup while you await sentencing. Jury, you are dismissed. Bailiff, take Mrs. Abbott away." He banged his gavel.

Argus grabbed Rachael's arm. "Rachael?" She didn't look at him, she couldn't. Instead, she backed up, allowing the bailiff to place the handcuffs back on her wrists.

"Come on," he whispered, his breath hot on her neck. Somewhere in the distance, Argus was yelling for her. She looked away, embarrassed and angry, as she was led once again through the door to her now certain new home.

CHAPTER ONE HUNDRED FOUR

HAMPTON

They say that eighteen hours without sleep makes you mentally equivalent to someone with a blood alcohol level of .05 percent. Twenty-four hours without sleep and you're basically legally drunk.

Argus Hampton hadn't slept in nearly five days, but he'd never been more awake. He'd flipped though his notes, played the coroner's report from Blaire's autopsy, and talked to Shayna. He'd done it so many times, it had grown old. He'd managed to get Shayna's charges dropped with ease, yet he couldn't manage to save Rachael.

It was destroying him. He couldn't rest. He couldn't let his mind lay dormant or his thoughts would destroy him. He missed her. He knew in his heart that he'd allowed an innocent woman to go to jail and he had to fix it somehow.

Somehow, he had to save her.

CHAPTER ONE HUNDRED FIVE

RACHAEL

When you're in prison, it doesn't matter if you're guilty or not...because you are. If you ask, no one's guilty. But no one asks.

The women there were more terrifying than most men. Rachael was on a first name basis with every nurse in the place. She'd been stitched up twice already, but she knew there'd be more.

She got weekly reports on Caide, so she knew he was recovering. *Freaking good for him.* She couldn't help but feel bitter.

Argus hadn't been to visit her since the trial, not that she blamed him. Everyone was better off without her, it seemed.

She'd talked to her children once before she was sent to prison—they seemed happy living with Chad and Sophia, happy for the first time in so long. They deserved that. They had a house on the beach and they were making new friends.

Rachael felt as if she were fading from their lives and honestly, maybe that was the best thing for them. Maybe it was all for the best.

Rachael would never make it out of this prison alive, but she was getting out, and it helped to know her children were safe and loved. Rachael had made up her mind that morning: she wouldn't spend another night here. She wouldn't spend another night alive.

CHAPTER ONE HUNDRED SIX

CALVIN MCMILLAN

Calvin McMillan's phone rang. *Again.*

If it was Hampton, he swore he'd scream.

"Hello?"

"McMillan, it's me." *Of course it is.*

"Hampton, I'm on my lunch break."

"Good, so you have time to talk. It's really important."

"It was important the last eighteen times you've called me, man. Listen, if there was anything I could do for you, I would. I've examined Elise Moss' body over and over. There is nothing pinning her to the crimes. No DNA from the victims, no wounds that couldn't be attributed back to the car crash. Your best bet is going to be to wait until the husband is able to talk, ask for a retrial, and let him testify."

Hampton scoffed. "A head wound victim, who's already slandered his wife, will have no credibility in court and you know it. Even if I could get a retrial, it'll be months, maybe years. There has to be something you missed."

"No. Hampton, I don't think there is. I know you want to help your client, and I admit, the twin does make things interesting, but she was caught red-handed on that tape.

You had to know how this would end. I wish I had better news."

"Yeah, she was caught red-handed, all right. They just weren't her hands." Hampton cursed under his breath. "Why couldn't her birthmark be on her arm, rather than her leg?"

Suddenly, it hit him. "Wait a second, you're right."

"Huh?"

"Well, I mean, *if* you're right—you could still be wrong, but *if* you're right, it wasn't her hands that committed the crime. They were the twin's hands. Elise's hands. You could be right and we may be able to prove it."

"Okay, I haven't slept in way too long, so I may not be at my sharpest, but you've lost me."

"They're identical twins, Hamp. *Identical.* Everything's the same: DNA, hair, eyes, and everything."

"Right."

"*Wrong.*" The grin spread wider on his face. Why hadn't he thought of this before?

"What are you talking about?"

"Everything is the same except their birthmarks and their hands."

"Their hands?"

McMillan tossed his sandwich into the trash and grabbed his lab coat. He rushed out of the break room. "That's right. More specifically, their fingerprints. Rachael Abbott's fingerprints weren't found on the murder weapon for the Underwood murder, right?"

"Right."

"So, I'll bet you anything Elise Moss' are."

Hampton took a deep breath. "You're saying we could prove she's innocent?"

"If the twin's fingerprints are on the murder weapon, then yes."

"How long will it take?"

"Well, I'll have to fingerprint the body and run it against all the prints on the murder weapon. Depending on how many prints there were..." He trailed off, trying to think.

"How long?" Hampton demanded.

"A few hours, maybe? Possibly a day. I'm not promising anything. If we're wrong, or if she wore gloves, we're back to square one."

Hampton, always the charmer, growled. "Just run the damn prints. I'm going to see the judge."

CHAPTER ONE HUNDRED SEVEN

JUDGE CRAFTON

"Hampton, this is the last time I'll tell you to drop it," Crafton announced as Hampton made his way into his chambers. He didn't have to guess what the visit was about. "Jesus, man, you're a mess. When is the last time you slept? Or showered, for that matter?"

"I don't remember," Hampton answered quickly, walking closer to the desk. "There's something you should know."

"Hampton." The judge sighed, taking off his reading glasses. "I didn't give her the death penalty. I could have, but I didn't. She's alive. I don't know what else you want from me. I've got other cases now. I'm sorry it didn't go how you had hoped, but there's nothing else we need to discuss."

"No, I know that. I've found something else. Something we overlooked before."

The judge stood up. "Hampton, let it go. The trial is over. I don't want to hear any more evidence. You're all out of chances. Just let it go, let the families grieve."

"What about Rachael? What about her family? Her children are without a mother. What if we were wrong, Daniel?

What if we were really, really wrong and an innocent woman is paying the price?"

Crafton's eyes grew soft. "I'm sorry. I know you grew to care for her. I've been there, but facts are facts, Hampton. You agreed you'd drop it if I granted the continuance, which I did. Please just stick to your word and excuse yourself."

"That was before we found out about her twin. Daniel, you have to know—"

"I said *enough*," Crafton bellowed. "You need to leave."

Hampton bowed his head, squeezing his eyes shut. "Twins don't share fingerprints," he blurted out.

"What?" Crafton did a double take.

"I said twins don't share fingerprints. Rachael's fingerprints weren't on Blaire Underwood's murder weapon. What if Elise Moss' were?"

The judge sat back down in his chair, twirling his glasses.

"If Ms. Moss' fingerprints are on the murder weapon, it will prove that she, *not Rachael*, was the one who killed Blaire Underwood, most likely Audrey Hagen too. If I can get you that proof, then will you listen? Will you hear me out?"

"Do you have someone testing your theory now?"

"The medical examiner should be calling me back any minute with the results." Hampton tapped his phone in his jacket pocket.

The judge laughed. "Hampton, you sure are one bull-headed man."

"So, you'll listen to me?"

He nodded, scooting closer to his desk. "Have the results sent over. If you can show me that Elise Moss' fingerprints were on the murder weapon, I'll have Rachael Abbott released."

"Okay. Yes. Thank you, sir." Hampton turned to walk away.

"Oh, and Hampton?" Crafton called.

"Yes, sir?" He spun around.

"I'd suggest getting some sleep and a shower before you see her. You're kind of disgusting."

CHAPTER ONE HUNDRED EIGHT

RACHAEL

Elise.
Her name was Elise.

Rachael's sister's name was Elise.

Saying it over and over again didn't help to make it feel more real. People talk. Someone told someone who told Rachael that her name was Elise.

Her body was being turned over to the state for cremation, since no one had come to claim it. Should she feel bad about that? That no one loved her sister enough to claim her body? That she'd never have a funeral? Maybe. Maybe, deep down, she did feel bad. Way deep down. On the surface, she felt only hate. Hatred for the woman who killed the only person who'd ever felt like a true sister to her.

Rachael held eight little white pills in her hand.

"Don't take more than two," Wanda had warned her. She hadn't said what would happen, but Rachael didn't care. Tonight, she had waited long enough. No more unanswered questions, no more regrets, no more hate, no more pain.

Tonight, Rachael Abbott would take eight pills. She'd pray

that her children would be taken care of, and that someday, Argus' pain would ease. Then, she'd drift off to sleep and leave this awful world behind.

CHAPTER ONE HUNDRED NINE

CAIDE

Caide awoke from a morphine-coated slumber to a nurse standing above him.

"Mr. Abbott, can you hear me? It'll hurt to move so, if you can hear me, just blink once for yes, twice for no."

Blink.

"Good, I'm Kyleigh, one of the doctors on your case. You had a few head injuries, but we believe you're going to be just fine. You've probably noticed your jaw is wired shut. We had to put stitches in your left cheek and we wired you shut so you wouldn't rip the stitches trying to talk. We're going to have to keep it that way until you're completely healed. Do you understand?"

Blink.

"Is there anything you need?"

Blink.

She handed him a piece of paper and a pen. "Can you write it down for me?"

Wife. Kids.

She looked at the paper. "Mr. Abbott, I'm sorry to tell you

this but your wife was convicted of Blaire Underwood's murder. She's in prison."

No. No. He shook his head frantically, pulling wires and IV's out.

"Mr. Abbott, please calm down. Calm down or we'll have to sedate you again." She reached across him, reattaching wires. He tapped the word 'kids' sharply. "Your kids are staying with a very nice family, just until you're better."

No. No. None of this was right. Caide jerked, pulling himself up from the bed, despite the immediate pain he felt. His head was heavy.

"Mr. Abbott." The doctor tried to restrain him as he flailed and shook, trying to get up. Suddenly, a nurse came in, rushing to her side. She held a syringe in her hand. He wasn't able to see where she stuck it before everything went fuzzy.

CHAPTER ONE HUNDRED TEN

RACHAEL

Rachael prayed in between pills. Her pillow was now soaked from tears as she continued to gag on each pill. She had nothing to help them go down. Her cellmate was snoring above her.

Please help my children. Let their new family love them more than anyone else. Let them be smart. Let them be kind.

A loud buzzing interrupted her prayer. The lights in the dark hallway flickered on.

"You can't just barge in here. It's after hours," someone yelled.

"Rachael? Rachael Abbott?" someone else yelled.

She recognized that voice. Argus? Could it be Argus? She stood from her bed, letting the pills fall from her hand.

"Argus?" she shouted, rushing toward the door. She squeezed the bars, tears rolling down her face.

"*Stop*," the first voice called. "I said stop. You can't be here."

"Rachael?" Argus' voice grew closer.

"Argus, I'm here," she yelled, her heart pounding.

And then, there he was, standing in front of her, his hair

disheveled and his clothing rumpled. There were tears in his usually stone-cold eyes.

The guard finally caught up to him, grabbing his arm. "Sir, you can't be here. Visiting hours are over."

"I'm not visiting," Argus said, not taking his eyes off Rachael. He thrust a paper into the man's hand. "Read it. You should've gotten a call."

The buzzer sounded again. Another officer approached the group. "Simmons, he's fine. They called earlier, I was on the phone when I let him in."

The officer released Argus' arm, his eyes examining the paper.

"What is going on?" Rachael asked.

Simmons looked up at her from the paper. "Rachael Abbott, you are no longer in the custody of the State of North Carolina. Your conviction has been overturned due to new evidence." He slid the cell door open. "You are free to go."

Rachael stood in disbelief, staring at the open doorway. Argus scooped her up into his arms, kissing her firmly. Their tear-soaked faces rubbed together as he held her hair. They pulled apart finally. She felt dizzy from a combination of the pills and his kiss.

The second officer spoke up, talking to Argus. "The county was arranging transport for her, by the way. She would've been sent home in the morning."

Hampton shook his head, still holding her close. His eyes never left hers. "She didn't deserve a single moment here. I wasn't going to let her spend another second, let alone another night. Let's go home." He held her hand, their fingers intertwined. She felt safer than she had felt in months.

Home. She felt at home.

CHAPTER ONE HUNDRED ELEVEN

RACHAEL

THREE MONTHS LATER

Rachael stood in the doorway of Caide's hospital room. He was being released today. She stepped forward into the room. He sat on the edge of his bed. "Rach." He held his arms out, seeing her. She hugged him.

"You didn't bring the kids with you?"

"They're with Corie. We needed to talk."

Caide grabbed her hand. "I agree. Over dinner?"

"No, Caide. Now."

"Okay." He patted the bed beside him.

She shook her head. She just needed to say it. "I'll stand. These past few months, I've been here daily. I've watched you heal and I've taken care of you. I've been your wife. Today, that ends. I allowed you to heal in peace, a courtesy that was never extended to me."

His gaze darted back and forth between her eyes. "Rach, please don't. I know where you're going with this. I cheated on you. I hurt you. I can't imagine what you've gone through because of me. But, we can move past this. I can be better. When I was in that car, I thought I was going to die and all I could think of was you: how much I love you, how sorry I am, how if I ever got the chance to make it better, I'd never stop trying." He rubbed her cheek, pulling her to him.

She pushed his hand away. "No. You don't get another chance. You *cheated* on me. So many times. I hate that word—cheated—like we were playing a board game. It was a marriage, Caide. A life. *My* life. Our children's lives. You're right you have no idea what I went through because of you. And you never will. I was the one on trial for murder, but as far as I'm concerned, it's you who's the killer. You killed this family. You killed this marriage. Everything we've worked for, everything we've built is gone and that's on you."

"Rachael, please—"

"No." She pointed a finger to her chest. "It's my turn to talk. When my best friend was being murdered, I was somewhere believing she may have been the one who killed Blaire. I believed she framed me. I was somewhere hating her, while she needed me. I was so angry with her, while she was dying just for knowing me. For knowing you. I have to live with that. Every day for the rest of my life, I have to wake up and know that. I sat in jail for so long wondering what went wrong, wondering how you could've done what you did. I grieved for our marriage publicly. I was humiliated by that tape. I watched you defile our marriage in front of a crowded room and had to maintain my composure when all I wanted to do was *rip your head off*. I know I'm not perfect in this. It takes two and maybe I quit giving us my all, but I could never do what you did, Caide. And then to go on TV and say what you said…" She trailed off.

"Rachael." Tears streamed down his cheeks.

"No, let me finish." She wiped a single tear from her face.

"See, I've spent so much time hating you and being mad at you, but it's exhausting." She exhaled exuberantly. "I'm exhausted. So, I'm done with it. That's what I came here to tell you. I'm done arguing. I'm done fighting. I am done hurting. We have two beautiful little kids who depend on us and who look up to us. They need us. You know, I always swore that I would never let my kids be from a broken home, but I'm starting to realize that we are *far* more broken together than we could ever be apart." She handed him the yellow envelope.

"Divorce papers?" he asked, his jaw dropping.

"I love you, Caide. You gave me the two best gifts I've ever gotten. Now, I'm giving you one."

"This is not what I want. I want you. I want us. I want our family." He stood, towering above her, his chin quivering.

She shifted her mouth to one side. "Maybe this isn't what you want right now, but once the dust settles, you'll realize it is. It's what you've always wanted. I think we stayed together for the wrong reasons: because it was easy, because it seemed right, because the kids deserved a whole family. But the truth is that sometimes marriage brings out the worst in people. Our marriage brought out the very worst in us and we deserve better."

He sat back down, his face devastated. She wiped a tear from his cheek and he wrapped his arms around her stomach, pressing his head to her chest. "How can this be right if I love you so much?"

"Maybe it's right *because* we love each other so much. I want us to end on good terms. I want us to move on and live the lives we deserve. That doesn't mean that I'll ever stop loving you, or that I'll ever stop wanting you to be happy."

"Rachael, I'm so sorry. Please don't do this. Please. You're so good. You didn't deserve what I did to you. You are a good person. I don't know what's wrong with me. I don't know why I did it. I'm just…I'm not like you. I'm not good. I'm just so sorry."

She pulled his head from her chest, looking into his eyes. She thought of Abby then, her words of wisdom that Rachael had held onto. "No. I'm not a good person. I'm not a bad person, either. Neither are you. There aren't good or bad things happening to good or bad people. We're just people, Caide. We're just people and we have this one life and things happen. You deal with it and you move on and life goes on and the world keeps turning. You just keep living because…because not everyone gets to do that. Not everyone keeps living."

Caide sighed, wiping his eyes. She kissed the top of his head and stepped back. "I have to go." She left the room without looking back. She had more living to do.

THEY PULLED up to the cemetery. Rachael held the flowers in one hand and the urn in the other. The urn was plastic—generic. It was the kind of urn that the state gives to people who don't matter too much.

She set it down and walked to the freshly dug grave where her best friend lay. She laid the flowers on Audrey's headstone and sat down on the dirt mound.

"Hey, Aud." Tears filled her eyes before she could even speak. She hugged her knees to her chest. "It's spring. I picked you some tulips from my garden. The yellow ones didn't bloom this year, but I brought you some of the pink." She sighed, choking back tears. "I just want you to know that…I forgive you. For everything. Of course, I forgive you. I wish you were here so I could tell you that. And I'd tell you that I miss you. God, I miss you so much. You're my best friend, Audrey Marie, a little bit of death doesn't change that." She tried to laugh. "I'll bring the kids by to see you soon, they don't really understand any of it yet. Oh, and John visited me yesterday. He's doing well…considering. I thought you'd want to know that." She kissed her hand, placing it on the stone that bore her best friend's name. "I love you, Aud. I love you so much. I'll miss you every single day." She laid her head down on the dirt, feeling a tear run down the side of her nose.

She heard approaching footsteps. She didn't have to look back to know it was Argus' hand who rubbed her back until the tears stopped falling.

She stood, walking to pick up the urn. They walked back to the tree line, away from any of the other graves.

"Should we say something?" Argus asked, filling the silence. Rachael thought for a second, twisting the top off of the urn. She took a few steps forward.

"I'm sorry, Elise. I'm sorry I never got to know you. I'm sorry we never got to fight over who was the oldest or the prettiest. I'm sorry that you ended up where you did and that your life was as awful as you thought it was. I'm sorry I never got to hear you laugh or braid your hair or be your friend. I'm sorry I never got to hold you when you were sad or protect you when you were scared. I'm sorry you never got to meet our dad—" Her voice caught. "He was amazing. He would've loved you…that's just who he was. I'm sorry you never got to learn that life is worth living. Because it really, *really* is." She held the urn out, letting the ashes blow into the woods. They were silent until the last bit of her sister had blown away. "I hope you find your peace, little sis."

She sat the urn down, feeling the wind blow through her hair. She laced her fingers through Argus' and they walked to the car. He smiled at her, making her heart jump in a way Caide never had.

Rachael would bring her children here one day when they

were older, when they'd understand, and she'd tell them all about the aunt they'd never gotten to know.

She didn't know if she'd ever truly forgive Elise, but there was one thing she was absolutely certain of: Rachael had found her place, her family, her happiness, and her home and she had a series of very bad things to thank for that.

EPILOGUE

Hampton rushed toward the door, feeling a gust of wind hit him as he swung it open.

Outside the door, a man in a dark blue suit stared at him from behind thick-rimmed glasses.

The man frowned. "I'm looking for a Rachael Abbott." He stared down at a box in his hands that Hampton hadn't noticed before.

Hampton shook his head. "She's in bed. I'm her husband. What do you need with Rachael?"

"I have a package here for her. From the New Hanover County Clerk's office," he said firmly.

"I'll take it." Hampton held his arms out.

The man eyed him. "Okay, I guess."

Hampton read the label, **Property of Elise Moss, C/O Rachael Abbott**.

"What is this?" he asked, holding it out as if it were contaminated. "Is this some sort of joke?" Anger bubbled in his stomach, thinking of his wife, who was finally finding her way again.

The man held his hands up. "Your wife is the last living

relative of Ms. Moss. Her property legally belongs to Rachael now."

"What are we supposed to do with it? She never even knew Elise," Hampton insisted.

"I can't tell you what to do with it, but it's yours. Or your wife's rather." He waved over his shoulder and disappeared off the porch.

Hampton shut the door, cursing the package. He couldn't imagine how this would hurt her. He jumped as Brinley strolled into the room rubbing her eyes.

"What are you doing?" she asked.

"Nothing. How are you feeling?" he asked, placing the package on his hip.

She nodded. "Better. Hungry."

"I'll cook us some breakfast in just a minute, okay?"

She agreed, sitting down on the couch. "Can I help?"

"You've got it," he promised. He turned as the bedroom door creaked open. Rachael walked out, her hair standing up in every direction.

"Hey," she mumbled, sleep coating her voice.

"Hey, sweetheart."

"What have you got there?"

He didn't answer straight away.

"Argus, what is that?"

He sighed, handing over the package. "It was just delivered for you. Elise's stuff." He told her softly, trying to judge her expression.

Her eyes widened. "What?"

"We don't have to open if you don't want to. We can throw it out. Whatever you want."

She wrapped her arms around his waist. "I love you for trying to protect me." He kissed the top of her head. "But I have to open it."

He nodded, knowing her answer before she said it. They

walked, hand in hand, into the bedroom and sank onto the bed. She stared at the box.

"This is everything? Everything she owned fit in this box." She shook it lightly, listening to the contents rumble around. With a swift motion, she pulled open the box, looking inside. She turned it over, gently pouring out the contents.

She gasped at pictures of her family: Caide, herself, and the children. Candid, unexpected shots that Elise must have collected over the years. Hampton watched as her jaw twitched and her face grew pale.

"I don't know if I can do this," she said quietly.

Hampton pulled the pictures from her hand. "It's okay." A hairbrush, three shirts, and an envelope were all that remained on the comforter. Rachael placed the hairbrush and shirts back into the box, her eyes looking over them dismissively. She picked up the envelope with cautious hands.

"Should I open it?" she asked. "Is it to me?"

He shrugged. "Only one way to find out." Anticipation loomed in the room as she placed her finger under the seal and eased the envelope open.

She began reading, tears filling her eyes as they danced back and forth over the page. She stopped a few times, hand over her mouth, trying to catch her breath. When she finished, she handed it to him and he began to read.

Momma,

There is a little girl sitting somewhere in a closet, singing 'Happy Birthday' to herself. She's probably hungry and probably dirty. She hasn't seen sunshine in a few days. She's spent every birthday in that closet, in that room...wishing more than anything that she could run away, or better yet that she'd never existed at all.

That little girl is me, Mom. Do you know that? Did you ever even notice me? Where I was? How I lived? Did you even care? It's my birthday today and I treated myself to a cake...a whole cake.

Chocolate. I never knew if I liked chocolate, because I never had it. You never bought me a cake. Tomorrow, I'll try a different flavor. Strawberry, maybe. Vanilla. I can try any flavor I want now...now that you're gone.

I found out that you died last week. You never tried to contact me when I left. I don't know if you even noticed I was gone. I don't actually know if you ever really noticed I was there to begin with.

Knowing you're gone brings me a strange sense of peace. I feel free knowing that your ugly soul isn't in the world anymore and I hate myself for feeling this way.

This letter is to tell you that I forgive you. I forgive you for every horrible thing you've ever done to me, and we both know there was a lot.

I have a life now, Mom. A real life and I can do whatever I want with it. I can be whoever I want. I'm not that little girl in a closet anymore. I'll never be her again.

So, wherever you are...know that I forgive you, though I doubt that you care. And more importantly, that I think you forgive me. You forgive me for making you fight to live the night Dad and Ben died. You forgive me for surviving. You forgive me for doing what I had to do, for buying those pills...for making sure they ended up in your drink. I only wanted you to be free.

So, rest in peace, Mom. You're with Ben and Dad now. Forgive me.

Elise

DON'T MISS THE NEXT PSYCHOLOGICAL THRILLER FROM KIERSTEN MODGLIN!

Every six months, a new list appears.
Six months later, everyone on the list is dead.

Purchase *The List* today:
www.kierstenmodglinauthor.com/thelist

ENJOYED BECOMING MRS. ABBOTT?

If you enjoyed *Becoming Mrs. Abbott*, I humbly ask that you consider leaving me a quick review.

It doesn't have to be long, just a few sentences to let other readers know how this book made you feel. Who knows? Maybe your kind words will be the thing that makes a new reader take a chance on my books! As someone who works so hard to put out the best books I can and support my family with my words, your review will mean more to me than I can tell you.

If you'd like to leave a review, please visit:
kierstenmodglinauthor.com/becomingmrsabbott

Thank you so much in advance!

ACKNOWLEDGMENTS

First and foremost, to my husband and daughter, who put up with all the craziness this author life brings, thank you! I love you both so much.

To my family, thank you for believing in me from the very beginning. Your words of encouragement have kept me going.

To the many amazing teachers who believed in my work long before it was good, thank you for encouraging a kid with crazy dreams that I could make them happen.

To my Twisted Readers, my Street Team, and my Review Team, thank you for always pushing me to keep going. I love you guys and am so thankful for the unending support you show me and my work.

To Brittany, my PA and, most importantly, friend, for always being there to bounce around ideas. Thank you for being in my corner from the beginning!

And, of course, to you. If you read this book and enjoyed my story. Thank you for helping me to follow my dreams and for supporting art.

I wished for this.

I wished for you.

ABOUT THE AUTHOR

KIERSTEN MODGLIN is an Amazon Top 10 bestselling author of psychological thrillers. Her books have sold over a million copies and been translated into multiple languages. Kiersten is a member of International Thriller Writers, Novelists, Inc., and the Alliance of Independent Authors. She is a KDP Select All-Star and a recipient of *ThrillerFix's* Best Psychological Thriller Award, *Suspense Magazine's* Best Book of 2021 Award, a 2022 Silver Falchion for Best Suspense, and a 2022 Silver Falchion for Best Overall Book of 2021. Kiersten grew up in rural western Kentucky and later relocated to Nashville, Tennessee, where she now lives with her family. Kiersten's readers across the world lovingly refer to her as "KMod." A binge-watching expert, psychology fanatic, and *indoor* enthusiast, Kiersten enjoys rainy days spent with her favorite people and evenings with her nose in a book.

Sign up for Kiersten's newsletter here:
kierstenmodglinauthor.com/nlsignup

Sign up for text alerts from Kiersten here:
kierstenmodglinauthor.com/textalerts

kierstenmodglinauthor.com
www.facebook.com/kierstenmodglinauthor
www.facebook.com/groups/kmodsquad
www.twitter.com/kmodglinauthor
www.instagram.com/kierstenmodglinauthor
www.tiktok.com/@kierstenmodglinauthor
www.goodreads.com/kierstenmodglinauthor
www.bookbub.com/authors/kiersten-modglin

ALSO BY KIERSTEN MODGLIN

<u>STANDALONE NOVELS</u>
Becoming Mrs. Abbott
The List
The Missing Piece
Playing Jenna
The Beginning After
The Better Choice
The Good Neighbors
The Lucky Ones
I Said Yes
The Mother-in-Law
The Dream Job
The Nanny's Secret
The Liar's Wife
My Husband's Secret
The Perfect Getaway
The Roommate
The Missing
Just Married
Our Little Secret
Widow Falls
Missing Daughter
The Reunion
Tell Me the Truth

The Dinner Guests

If You're Reading This…

A Quiet Retreat

The Family Secret

Don't Go Down There

Wait for Dark

You Can Trust Me

Hemlock

ARRANGEMENT TRILOGY

The Arrangement (Book 1)

The Amendment (Book 2)

The Atonement (Book 3)

THE MESSES SERIES

The Cleaner (Book 1)

The Healer (Book 2)

The Liar (Book 3)

The Prisoner (Book 4)

NOVELLAS

The Long Route: A Lover's Landing Novella

The Stranger in the Woods: A Crimson Falls Novella

Made in United States
North Haven, CT
05 June 2025